The Complete Cabalistic Cases of

SEMI DUAL

The Occult Detector, Volume 1: 1912

THE COMPLETE CABALISTIC CASES OF

SEMI DUAL

THE OCCULT DETECTOR, VOLUME 1: 1912

BY

J.U. GIESY
JUNIUS B. SMITH

INTRODUCTION BY
GARYN ROBERTS, PH.D.

BOSTON : 2013

© 2013 Altus Press • First Edition—2013

EDITED AND DESIGNED BY
Matthew Moring

PUBLISHING HISTORY

"Introduction" appears here for the first time. Copyright © 2013 Garyn Roberts. All Rights Reserved.

"The Occult Detector" originally appeared in the February 17, 24, and March 2, 1912 issues of *The Cavalier Magazine*. Copyright © 1912 by The Frank A. Munsey Company.

"The Significance of the High 'D'" originally appeared in the March 9, 16, and 23, 1912 issues of *The Cavalier Magazine*. Copyright © 1912 by The Frank A. Munsey Company.

"The Wistaria Scarf" originally appeared in the June 1, 8, and 15, 1912 issues of *The Cavalier Magazine*. Copyright © 1912 by The Frank A. Munsey Company.

THANKS TO
Glenn Goggin, Everard P. Digges LaTouch, Rick Ollerman & Garyn Roberts

ALL RIGHTS RESERVED

No part of this book may be reproduced or utilized in any form or by any means, electronic or mechanical, without permission in writing from the publisher.

This edition has been marked via subtle changes, so anyone who reprints from this collection is committing a violation of copyright.

Visit altuspress.com for more books like this.

Printed in the United States of America.

TABLE OF CONTENTS

Introduction i
The Occult Detector 1
The Significance of the High "D" 83
The Wistaria Scarf 161

INTRODUCTION
GARYN ROBERTS, PH.D.

ALMOST AS if he was beckoning from the great beyond, that oft amazingly almost forgotten yet archetypal psychic detective of the pulps, Semi Dual, is about to be resurrected like Lazarus. Though not Biblical, this is a very good renewal of life.

On Laurie Powers' website, Walker Martin writes,

> For decades, lovers of the bizarre and unusual have wondered why the popular Semi Dual stories were never published in hardcover or paperback. [J.U.] Giesy and [Junius B.] Smith were often paid 2 cents a word and received hundreds of dollars for each story, most of which were serials and complete short novels. This was back when $25 a week was a good salary.
>
> Semi Dual was more popular than any other occult detective, appearing in over 30 stories. Giesy is best remembered however for his Palos Trilogy.
>
> Prince Omar of Persia got the name Semi Dual by solving problems with two solutions, one material and one occult. When Altus Press publishes this series it will be a major pulp reprinting project.
>
> And the mystery of why the Semi Dual series was never collected in book form will finally be of no concern for mystery readers.

A LITTLE CULTURAL CONTEXT FOR, AND SOME PULP HISTORY FROM, 1912

Semi Dual first appeared in the real-life and fictional pyrotechnics of early 1912. Just weeks after his premiere, White Star Lines' *Titanic* sank in the North Atlantic in the most famous maritime disaster of human history (April 15).

By this time, Sigmund Freud, "the father of modern psychoanalysis" (1856-1939) had at this time achieved worldwide acclaim for his theories and practices. Freud's colleague, understudy and dissonant, Carl Jung (1875-1961) was studying the connections between medicine and spirituality, and advanced some pretty attractive and credible theories regarding the "collective unconscious" which endure to this day.

Jules Verne (1828-1905), the father of scientific romance and prolific writer of Adventure fiction, and H(erbert) G(eorge) Wells (1866-1946), internationally acclaimed social historian and science fiction writer, were household names in 1912.

In 1912, Edgar Rice Burroughs (1875-1950) introduced two fictional legends of science fiction romance and adventure fiction. Burroughs' John Carter of Mars debuted in a serial entitled *Under the Moons of Mars* in the February through July issues of *The All-Story Magazine*. The author's "Tarzan of the Apes" first appeared in a full-length pulp novel in the pages of the October 1912 issue of *All-Story*.

Popular print fiction was in the midst of a major format and delivery change in 1912. And Burroughs' initial tales of John Carter and Tarzan captured the allure of the old medium and helped usher in the new. "Dime novels," or popular story papers, had been around sporadically between about 1830 and the start of the Civil War (1860); from 1860 into the 1920s, dime novels sold millions and millions of copies. They flourished from the 1870s into the teens as America's most popular media entertainment form. Their history is fascinating and important in the understanding of the place of Semi Dual in popular fiction. Charles Bragin, Everett Bleiler, Edward T. LeBlanc, J. Randolph Cox and others have documented the history of the dime novel in a range of books and articles that are definitive.

Yet, more was happening in 1912—that almost apocalyptic real-life and fictional year when Semi Dual began his run. The United States Postal Service underwent some major changes at this time. Parcel Post was introduced that year, and this helped retailers of bulk goods in terms of wholesale distribution and related logistics. However, some other rule changes for U.S. Postal shipping combined with worn out, overly conventional dime novel formulas signaled a change in the landscape of popular fiction. The dime novel was on its way out; the pulpwood magazine (with its new format, usually credited to publishing mogul Frank Andrew Munsey (1854-1925) in his mid 1890s publications of *The Argosy*) was designed to be less dependent on the United States mail system and became increasingly sold through newsstands. Again, the history—particularly of the United States Postal Service—at this time is fascinating, though not the focus here. So, among its many strengths and facets, Edgar Rice Burroughs' fiction of 1912 is even better appreciated in the context of that transitional time between the dime novel and pulp eras. Burroughs' fiction at this time was a really effective synthesis of dime novel and pulp magazine traditions.

J.U. Giesy and Junius B. Smith's Semi Dual reflects this same literary and cultural history.

Sax Rohmer (pseudonym for Arthur Henry Sarsfield Ward, 1883-1959) serialized the first adventures of his "yellow peril" super villain in 1912/13's *The Mystery of Dr. Fu Manchu*. Tales of Fu Manchu were sort of reverse Sherlock Holmes stories. In these mysteries, the villain replaced the hero—Fu Manchu replaced Holmes—in order of importance. Nayland Smith and Dr. Petrie, the detectives of the Fu Manchu mysteries, were weak imitations of Holmes and Dr. Watson. The insidious Dr. Fu Manchu was not above all kinds of deviltry and explorations and exploitations of the physical and metaphysical. More importantly, Sax Rohmer would become increasingly fascinated by the occult and supernatural. His book-length study of magic, mysticism, Egyptology and the supernatural, *The Romance of Sorcery*, appeared in 1914.

Arthur Conan Doyle (1859-1930), physician and historian best known as the creator and perpetuator of the archetypal Sherlock Holmes stories, began publishing his tales of Professor Challenger—a scientific adventurer—at this time. These included three novels: *The Lost World* (1912), *The Poison Belt* (1913) and *The Land of Mist* (1926), and two short stories: "When the World Screamed" (1928) and "The Disintegration Machine" (1929). Deeply invested in the study of spiritualism and the mystic later in his life, Doyle published his minor treatise on the subject, *The Edge of the Unknown*, in 1930.

Algernon Blackwood's (1869-1951) physician and occult detective, John Silence, appeared in a collection of adventures entitled *John Silence* in 1908.

Nineteen-twelve saw the publication of William Hope Hodgson's (1877-1918) epic novel of gothic fantasy and the supernatural, *The Night Land*. This was preceded by the author's *The Boats of the Glen Carrig* (1907), *The House on the Borderland* (1908), and *The Ghost Pirates* (1909). In 1912, Hodgson also introduced us to Carnacki the Ghost Finder, one of the most famous psychic detectives of popular fiction ever.

Giesy and Smith's Semi Dual was in good company.

Seabury Quinn (pseudonym for Jerome Burke, 1889-1969) introduced readers to psychic detective Jules de Grandin and his Watson-like sidekick, Dr. Trowbridge, in 1925. Toward the end of the long, literary career of Semi Dual, in 1928, August W(illiam) Derleth (1909-1971) introduced readers to Solar Pons.

Ed(ward D.) Hoch (1930-2008), a kind, talented man and Guest of Honor at PulpCon a few summers back, was a prolific and very talented author of detective fiction, science fiction, and science fiction based detective fiction. Many of his stories from about 1971 to the time of his passing in 2008 feature detective heroes whose family tree included Semi Dual.

THE AUTHORS

J(ohn) U(lrich) Giesy (1877–1947) was born near Chillicothe, Ohio. He was a medical doctor and prolific author, and spent a good part of his life in Salt Lake City, Utah. His most famous series is the Jason Croft series, a group of interconnected scientific romances that ran between 1918 and 1921. Though an accomplished scientist of medicine, Giesy relied much more heavily on theoretic, intangible "sciences" such as astrology as subject matter and plotting devices for his pulp stories.

Junius Bailey Smith (1883–1945) was born in Salt Lake City; his grandfather was a brother of Joseph Smith, the founder of the Mormon Church. Junius Smith was an attorney who supplemented his income with pulp writing. Often, he wrote in collaboration with John Giesy, but he also wrote and published as a single author.

Both Giesy and Smith were devoted students of astrology, and both were "Fellows of the American Academy of Astrologicans, which possibly explains the depth of Dual's technical explanations." (Sampson, 84)

THE SERIES

Over the course of their long run, exploits of Giesy and Smith's detective hero were first published by pulp magazine mogul Frank A. Munsey, then by Munsey's rival, Street and Smith, and then again by Munsey.

The prose style in Giesy and Smith's Semi Dual stories is downright fun. It is a window into the world of the early twentieth century. Consider just a few of the words the authors employ—"dog house," "motor patrol," "the blotter," "roundsmen," "pen," "turnkey" and so on. Then, consider the larger contexts of the individual sentences and paragraphs in which these words are found. Especially in the early stories from 1912 reprinted here—the United States was still a few years from entrance into "The Great War" (what would later be called "World War I"), and we were not yet in the era of Prohibition, "flappers" and the roaring twenties—we see indications of what is to come in terms of character types, storylines, settings, types of crimes, popular mindsets and paradigms, rituals and iconography in pulp magazine adventure, detective and science fiction.

Period pulp story conventions are in place. What would become motion picture staples are predicted. For example, in adventures of Semi Dual we find cosmopolitan crimes and corruption, newspaper settings and reporters, and first person narration.

Here's the "neat" thing. While Semi Dual's adventures are period pieces and can be really appreciated in their original cultural and social contexts, they have a timeless quality and appeal. They are still, 100 years later, great fun.

The three stories showcased in this volume, the first three complete serials, begin with "The Occult Detector," *The Cavalier* (February 17 and 24, and March 2, 1912). *The Cavalier* was one of the Munsey company's properties. A more than satisfactory, professionally crafted adventure, this is the origin story for the series. Generally, most often but not always, origin stories are some of the most boring stories in any ongoing series. Often, the origin story gets mired in character development and the complex idiosyncrasies of characters, justification of the hero's/es' cause(s), and extensive discussions of settings and situations. All of this is somewhat necessary but often laborious and delineated to painful extents. Consider the movie adaptation of Alan Moore's *The League of Extraordinary Gentlemen* (2003). The origin story delineated in this motion picture is so cumbersome, and populated by too many complex characters, that there is really no realistic possibility of a successful sequel.

One of the single best—if not the best—pulp origin stories was crafted by Walter B. Gibson (1897-1985) in "The Living Shadow" (Street and Smith's *The Shadow Magazine,* April 1931). The good news here is that Giesy and Smith's "The Occult Detector" works both as captivating tale and effective origin story.

Robert Sampson (1927 to 1992) was one of the all-time top scholars of pulp magazine history. His six-volume *Yesterday's Faces* series (1983–1993) and other volumes, including *The Night Master* (1980), *Spider!* (1987), and *Deadly Excitements* (1989), are cornerstones of this cultural history. In regard to the beginnings of Semi Dual, Sampson provides the following:

"The manuscript that arrived on the Editor's desk, one day in 1911, was evidently titled by amateurs." "Semi Dual" it was headed, a collaboration between J. U. Giesy and J. B. Smith. As the editor later remarked: "The contents and their nature had never greeted editorial eyes before. Here was a different story...." (Editorial introduction to "The Opposing Venus," *Argosy,* October 13, 1923, 1. This is found in *Yesterday's Faces: Volume 2,* 81.)

That manuscript became the three-part serial, "The Occult Detector."

Semi Dual practiced his skills as an astrologer, mystic, telepathist, philosopher and practical psychologist. Sampson writes that the detective's moniker was designed to reflect the hero's ability to solve criminal problems with "dual solutions": one material for material minds, and one occult for those who preferred something deeper behind the philosophic explanations. Throughout their prose the authors variably referenced their detector as "Semi Dual," "Semi" and "Dual." (Consult Robert Sampson's *Yesterday's Faces: A Study of Series Characters in the Early Pulp Magazines, Volume 2: Strange Days.* Bowling Green, OH: Bowling Green University Popular Press, 1984 for further commentary on the literary landscape of Semi Dual and his peers in the early days of the Twentieth Century.)

"The Significance of the High 'D'" (*The Cavalier,* March 9, 16 and 23), the second chronicled adventure of Semi Dual, picks up the pace of "The Occult Detector" and moves forward at classic pulp magazine pace. Giesy, in particular, was known for an incredible personal drive and work ethic, and perhaps we begin to see this almost fanatic behavior reflected in his occult investigator. "The Wistaria Scarf (*The Cavalier,* June 1, 8 and 15) is heavily invested in fast-moving dialogue and....

For now, we will leave specifics of plot and characters and settings and solutions of these three tales for discussion later.

A fourth three-part serial appeared in the October 5, 12 and 19 issues of *The Cavalier.* It was entitled "The Purple Light."

Giesy and Smith's adventures of Semi Dual continued the next year (1913) in the pages of *The Cavalier*. These were the one-shot "The Master Mind" (January 25), the two-part "Rubies of Doom" (July 5 and 12), the three-part serial, "The House of the Ego" (September 20, 27 and October 4), and the one-shot "The Ghost of the Name" (December 20).

In 1914, the exploits and investigations of Semi Dual moved to *All-Story Magazine,* another Munsey pulpwood. The one-shot novelette, "The Curse of Quetzal," appeared in the November 28 issue. Semi Dual remained in *All-Story* until 1917. (*All-Story* became a weekly in 1916.) A two-part serial entitled "The Web of Destiny" (March 20 and 27) and a three-parter entitled "Snared" (December 11, 18 and 25) appeared in 1915; 1916 saw the publication of the three-part serial, "Box 991" (June 3, 10 and 17); and in 1917, the four-part serial, "The Killer" (April 7, 14, 21 and 28) debuted.

By May 1917, Giesy and Smith's master detective moved to the pages of a Street and Smith fiction magazine. That year, "The Compass in the Sky," a one-shot, appeared in *The People's Magazine* (May).

A strange publication schedule from two rival publishers ensued.

That same year—1917—Semi Dual returned as a Munsey property in "The Unknown Quantity," a three-part serial in *All-Story Weekly* (August 25, September 1 and 8), and "Solomon's Decision," *All-Story Weekly* (December 1, 8 and 15), another three-parter.

In 1918, "The Storehouse of Past Events" and "The Moving Shadow" graced the pages of Street and Smith's *People's Favorite Magazine* (February 10 and June 10, respectively). These were two one-shot stories. A third Semi Dual one-shot, "The Stars Were Looking," appeared in the July 1 issue of Street and Smith's *Top-Notch* magazine.

In 1918 also, Munsey published the three-part serial "The Black Butterfly" in *All-Story Weekly* (September 14, 21, 28). Semi Dual completed his investigations for that year in the one-shot "The Trial in the Dust," published in Street and Smith's *People's Favorite Magazine* (October 25).

For the next sixteen years until 1934, J.U. Giesy and Junius B. Smith's Semi Dual remained the property of Munsey. Two three-part Semi Dual serials appeared in the pages of *All-Story Weekly* in 1919. These were "Star of Evil" (January 25, and February 1 and 8), and "The Ivory Pipe" (September 20, 27 and October 4).

Nineteen-twenty saw the publication of the four-part serial, "House of the Hundred Lights," *All-Story Weekly* (May 22 and 29, June 5 and 12). Soon after, Munsey merged *All-Story Weekly* with *Argosy*. "Black and White," another four-part serial, appeared in the new *Argosy All-Story Weekly* (October 2, 9, 16, and 23).

The four-part "Wolf of Erlik" (*Argosy All-Story Weekly,* October 22 and 29, November 5 and 12) appeared in 1921. After "Wolf of Erlik," the publication schedule for adventures of Semi Dual became a little more sporadic.

Two years later in 1923, *Argosy All-Story Weekly* featured the ongoing tale of "The Opposing Venus" (October 13, 20 and 27, November 3). In 1924, "Poor Little Pigeon" appeared in the same magazine's August 9, 16, 23 and 30, and September 6 issues.

Yet another two years later in 1926, the serial, "The House of Invisible Bondage," haunted the pulpwood pages of *Argosy All-Story Weekly* (September 18 and 25, October 2 and 9). "The Woolly Dog" followed in 1929 (*Argosy All-Story Weekly,* March 23 and 30, April 6 and 13).

Then in 1931, the six-part book-length serial, "The Green Goddess," appeared in Munsey's *Argosy* (January 31, February 7, 14, 21 and 28, and March 7). The "All-Story Weekly" part of the magazine's title was now dropped.

J.U. Giesy and Junius B. Smith's last recounting of Semi Dual adventures appeared in 1934. It was "The Ledger of Life" (*Argosy,* June 30, July 7, 14 and 21).

Wow. You are already holding this book, and maybe you have made a shrewd investment and bought the same. Think about this: If you could even find each and every one of the installments of J.U. Giesy and Junius B. Smith's Semi Dual adventures in readable condition—you probably never could, and if you did it would take years and lots of money to acquire these—where else can you find these stories in such a readable, clean, archival package?

Why were the Semi Dual cases never collected before? Clearly they have wonderful merit as entertainment, and cultural and literary history. The answer is probably very obvious. The sheer length of the complete stories will require nine volumes from Altus Press. In the past, this length would have been prohibitive for just about any other publisher, short of my dear friend, Dr. George Vanderburgh. And, despite their tremendous popularity and circulation, even a few decades after their publication—and the World War II paper drives that consumed a great deal of what was considered by many as ephemeral print entertainment—a complete run was probably pretty difficult to assemble. Even in his extensive, legendary pulp magazine library, Bob Sampson was missing some pieces of the saga.

Thank you, Matt Moring at Altus Press; thank you, old friend and never gone-from-our-hearts Bob Sampson; thank you, Walker Martin, Robert Weinberg and other pulp scholars; for sharing with us Giesy and Smith's massive tome which began more than 100 years ago: *The Complete Cabalistic Cases of Semi Dual, The Occult Detector*.

There is more to tell! Look for volume two of the Semi Dual adventures coming soon.

THE OCCULT DETECTOR

CHAPTER I.

A STRANGE ASSIGNMENT.

THE CLOCK in the tower of the *Record* struck two. Although I didn't know it then, the clock of my destiny struck at the same time.

Hard on the throb of the chime Smithson stuck his head out of the door of his den, and swept his eyes over the local-room. He found nobody but me. Every one else was absent. As for me, I was having a smoke after a light lunch, and waiting for something to do.

"Nobody here but you, eh?" said Smithson. "Well, c'm'ere."

Smithson was city editor of the *Record;* therefore, I cast aside my cigarette and complied with his request.

He bobbed back into his room, withdrawing his head from the door very much like a turtle drawing into its shell. I followed him and stood waiting his next remark. When it came I didn't know just what to make of it after all.

Said Smithson: "Know anything about Semi Dual?"

You couldn't bluff with Smithson. I shook my head and told him the truth. "Nothing," I said shortly. "Is it a newspaper or a race-horse, or what?"

Smithson grunted and rummaged among the papers on his desk for a moment, found some sort of memorandum and finally deigned to reply. "It's a man," said he.

"Funny name," I remarked, for lack of anything else to say.

"From all accounts he's a funny man," Smithson came back. "Now see here. Some two months ago this fellow came here and takes quarters in the Urania. I understand he has a full floor up there. He lives there, and beyond that I can't find out anything about the chap.

"Nobody seems to know what he does for a living, or if he does anything at all. Yet it seems from the reports of the elevator operators that quite a few folks call to see him every day. Well, that's about all. Shove some copy-paper into your pocket and go up and get an interview. There may be a story in the thing. Maybe we can make a Sunday feature out of it if it's any good."

"From his name he might be an Oriental fakir," I remarked. "Dual is suggestive at least."

"How?" said Smithson.

"Why, Dual—Do All."

"Maybe he does," said Smithson, not even grinning. "Find one."

He began to rummage among his papers again, and I went out and down to the street.

It was a hot day, and I felt no particular interest in my assignment. "Semi Dual," I muttered as I turned toward the Urania, a couple of blocks away, and I confess I managed to put no small contempt into my speaking of the words.

Thoroughly convinced that Smithson had started me out on the trail of some successful charlatan, who would reap a lot of free advertising from my story, I trudged grudgingly toward my task.

The Urania was the last word in modern office buildings, and had been open for something like six months. Twenty stories it reared its walls above the pavements, not to speak of the tower which surmounted the immense pile.

The first thing of interest that struck me as I walked toward it was that this particular individual I was going to see should be allowed to dwell as well as office there. I had understood that there was an iron-clad rule against anything of the sort.

I began to wonder if the Semi chap might not prove of some interest after all. Surely he must be possessed of some unusual influence to gain such a concession from the owners, as he evidently had.

I passed into the magnificent foyer of the Urania, and stopped for a moment to gaze at its chief adornment, a magnificent portrait-bust of Urania Marsden, deceased wife of the principal owner, who had given her name to the great building which he had reared. And then I started for a cage which would take me up to Dual's floor.

It occurred to me that I might as well find out any little thing about my prospective interviewee which I could pick up, and with that in mind I turned to the cage-starter and inquired the location of the man I sought.

"Semi Dual?" repeated the starter, as he clicked a cage away. "Dat's de ginny who lives on de roof."

I guess I showed my surprise, for the starter grinned.

"Dat's right," he continued. "He's got a three-year cinch on de whole tower an' de roof. He owns all of dis shack from de roof up."

"How do I get there?" I inquired.

"Take de cage to de twentieth, an' den walk," said my informant, and waved me to a car which had just come down.

I entered and leaned against the grill at the back of the car. More and more my errand began to assume the unusual…. I had never interviewed a man who lived on a roof. I began to think that I might enjoy this experience after all.

The car I was in was express, and made only four stops on the way up, so that I was still lost in a somewhat puzzled expectation when we stopped at the top floor, and the operator in response to my interrogation, waved his hand to a flight of stairs. I walked over, and stopped to examine these more closely before going up. They were a most surprising pair of stairs.

In most large structures like the Urania, the steps leading to the roof are for the use of occasional employees only, and are apt to consist of mere concrete or steel, or both, but there was an exception here. These steps were faced with marble, inlaid on their treads with beautiful tile arabesques, and railed in carved and twisted bronze.

They looked more like the grand staircase of an entrance-hall than a flight of steps leading to a roof. In front of them stretched the skin of an immense lioness, perfectly mounted and preserved, and each massive newel was surmounted by a life-size figure in bronze, holding an opalescent globe of glass, evidently a light.

All my former grouch over my assignment vanished, and I placed my foot on the first step of the stairs with much the same feeling of pleasant anticipation which must assail any one who finds the unexpected among the commonplace, and realizes that there is a promise of more to come. So with growing interest I mounted the stairs, and paused at the top with arrested stride.

I had stepped into a garden such as I had never seen or dreamed of before.

Straight before me ran a broad approach to the door of the tower, flanked on each side by shallow beds of flowers, set out in broad boxes of earth, and interspersed with small trees and shrubs. Other narrower passages led off in different directions, toward the high parapets of the buildings which were covered with climbing vines.

I smelled the breath of roses, and half forgot for the time that I was twenty stories above the busy streets. I seemed rather to be in a semitropical garden than on any roof of any building in the world. I stood for a moment and started to go on, only to pause again, before an immense inlaid plate in the floor. It was apparently of metal, inlaid with variously colored glass, set in the form of letters, which I stopped to read:

> Pause and consider, oh, stranger. For he who cometh against me with evil intent, shall live to rue it, until the uttermost part of his debt shall have been paid; yet he who cometh in peace, and with a pure heart, shall surely find that which he shall seek.

I read and looked about me, almost as one dazed. The thought flashed across me that I was in the abode of some crazy fanatic. Pleasant anticipation gave place to a feeling almost of foreboding. Then I laughed, and set my hat more firmly upon my head. After all, I was in the twentieth century and it was broad daylight.

The sentence inlaid in the plate might be rather creepy, but going back empty-handed to Smithson would be far worse. I knew what I'd get from Smithson. I resolved to explore the mystery of Mr. Semi Dual.

Wherefore, I stepped out across the plate, planting my feet upon its prismatic surface, and at once a low, sweet chime, as of distant church-bells, broke on the afternoon silence of the roof. Rather hastily, I got across, and went on up the passage to meet a very conventional gentleman's man, who had opened the door of the tower and stood awaiting my approach.

This party silently conducted me into what was palpably a reception-room, took my card, and disappeared through an inner door, returning shortly with a silver tray upon which was a long glass of purest crystal, containing a liquid in which floated some tinkling bits of ice. This he deposited upon a small table which he wheeled to my side. "The day is hot, sir," he suggested. "You will find this very refreshing, I think." He withdrew with a bow.

When I came to think of it I was both thirsty and hot. The glass on the tray looked very inviting. I stretched out my hand and lifted it, smiling at this most unusual manner of receiving a representative of the press.

I touched my lips to the iced fluid, and experienced a heretofore unknown delight. To my palate, it seemed that the very essense of all the flavors of the fruits of all known varieties was slowly passing over my heated tongue. I didn't even try to imagine what the stuff was, but took first one swallow after another until the drink was half done. Then I set the glass down, and sighed, and looked about the room.

There was nothing unusual there, unless its very simplicity might have been so called. It was just a plain reception-room, such as one might have found in the suite of many a professional man.

The rug on the floor was a monotone, of a hue between orange and brown, but of a quality which I had seldom seen. My feet sank into its pile as into a soft, shallow drift of snow. The chairs and tables while plain in every line, were of fine woods; the few engravings on the walls were undoubtedly genuine.

Severe simplicity was the key-note on the whole, but a simplicity combined with the nth degree of fineness in the materials used in bringing the effect about.

I drained the rest of my drink, and set the glass down. On the instant, as though my act had been a signal, the silent servant reentered the room. "If you have quite finished," said he, "Mr. Dual will see you now." He opened a door and stood aside for me to enter.

CHAPTER II.

THE MAN IN THE TOWER.

I ENTERED that room with a preformed wrong conception.

Just what I expected to see, or what sort of individual I expected to meet, I hardly knew. Now, in looking back, I fancy I half anticipated a sort of semioriental setting at least. The man's name had been largely responsible for that.

Whether I expected an atmosphere of incense, an individual in cap and gown and Turkish slippers, or what, I can hardly make up my mind even now.

At any rate, the reality came upon me almost as a disappointment, at the very first, for the room might have been the private consulting-room of any successful lawyer or physician for all the furnishings showed, and surely the splendidly formed man who rose as I entered and greeted me with a delightfully reserved courtesy might have been none other than the doctor or lawyer himself.

Six feet he was, if an inch, yet so perfectly proportioned that he gave an impression of being merely large, rather than tall. His brown hair was carefully trimmed and brushed up from a broad brow, and even his perfectly kept imperial could not disguise the strength of the lower jaw.

But it was his eyes which arrested me in that first moment of meeting, and have held me ever since. Everything else was nothing save what any one might encounter anywhere in his daily walk. There are hundreds of well-proportioned large men in every large city, hundreds of men with strong jaws and faces, hundreds of men even with a peculiar warm olive tint to their skin, but never have I seen such eyes, save in some famous picture of a world's hero or saint.

They were gray and deep. Deep? Oh, utterly, unfathomably deep; hundreds and thousands of years deep, yet Mr. Dual was certainly not an old man; and withal they were open eyes and frank. On the instant I felt subtly attracted to the man, and, hardly realizing the action, I put out my hand.

He took it in his and gave it a sturdy clasp, then released it, and waved me to a chair facing his own. "Sit down, Mr. Glace," said Semi Dual. "We shall have an interesting chat."

I took the indicated chair, and confess I felt a trifle confused. "Of course you know, Mr. Dual—" I began, when he took the words out of my mouth.

"That you are from the press?" he said, smiling. "Oh, yes; your card told me that. No doubt you were sent here to interview me. I have heard that the papers had interested themselves in the fact that I mind my own business. However, I was thinking of the man, rather than his occupation, when I spoke to you just now."

I laughed. "Frankly, I must admit that my reception has been out of the ordinary line of my experience. I half expected that the drink was doped when your man brought it out."

"Did you like it?" Dual inquired.

"I never tasted anything like it," I responded with enthusiasm. "If any bar or café could mix a concoction like that glass of ambrosia they would have to 'turn 'em away.'"

"It is a discovery of my own," Dual smiled back at me. "It cools, refreshes, and nourishes—all at the same time; also, it is a potent agent against the chief cause of human decay."

Here was an opening. "Are you, then, a chemist?" said I.

"Oh, dear, no!" my host objected. "What you drank was merely the natural juices of a variety of fruits, preserved after a method of my own. I have merely availed myself of a thing which every one could know if they would.

"But enough of that. No doubt you have some questions which you desire to ask me. Let us get that unpleasant part over, and then we can enjoy our chat. What shall it be? I believe the age and occupation generally preface most inquiries, do they not?"

I assented. "That, of course, Mr. Dual."

"Very well," said my most obliging acquaintance; "let us take up those first. As for my age, it is a thing I never think about, because it is of no importance to me; therefore, I do not see how it can reasonably concern any one else. As for my occupation, I may say that I am a psychological physician, I think."

I drew my note-book from my pocket. "A doctor of psychology?" I inquired.

Again Dual favored me with his smile. "You do not exactly comprehend my meaning," he replied, "though I admit a somewhat ambiguous nature in my remark. Let me explain.

"I live to help others in order that I may help myself. What a man soweth that shall he reap. If a man can distribute sympathy, comfort, happiness, he may receive the same if he shall ask it in return. If he gives health, he may be healthy. Do you see?

"It is my life-work to straighten some of the crooked turns of the life-paths of others. If I can but right one wrong and not create another, I have not lived in vain. If my course marks pleasant memories along life's path, I and those whom I have met upon the journey are the better for it.

"Therefore, I live in order that I may do good; that I may unravel some of the tangled skeins; that I may smooth out the way that some one's weary feet must tread."

While he spoke I sat and listened, even forgetting to make a note in my book. There was something compelling my complete attention in the soft rise and fall of the cadences of the man's voice, in the poise of his body, the expression of his face, in his entire personality, in fact.

As he ceased speaking I sighed, and came sharply back to the realization that I had drunk in every word. Knowing that I should make some comment, I yet sat silent, because I knew nothing fitting to say—until Semi Dual came to my relief. "Do you not see the difference?" said he.

"Faintly," I confessed; "but tell me, Mr. Dual, if your mission is to help others, why do you remove yourself so completely from their midst?"

"Meaning?" said Dual.

"This manner of dwelling which you possess—this taking of a roof for a home. I admit it is charming; the garden alone is wonderful.

"When I saw the staircase I almost fancied that I had accidentally rubbed a genii's lamp and got myself wafted to some enchanted palace, like the heroes in my 'Arabian Nights,' back home; and when I saw the garden I was sure. But all this is out of the way, more or less hard to reach. Thousands must pass by you who need help, but never know that it is in reach."

Dual nodded his head. "I see your point," he said; "but those who are worthy will receive. I do not care to meddle with the affairs of the idly curious. Only the sincerely interested appeal to me, or deserve my time. Those who are deserving shall seek, and to such a one what is a flight of stairs?

"That which is worth having is worth an effort to attain. One must climb to find peace. Besides, I have a seclusion here which I might not find on a floor of a crowded business structure such as this. Here I can be alone to pursue my studies as I will. The very air is pure. The first ray of sunshine, and the last, are mine. One who seeks to interfere in the destinies of souls must be able to meditate much alone."

"There is another thing which I would ask you," I said; "only that I fear to seem rather impertinent."

"Do not hesitate," urged Dual.

"Well, then, that warning, or caution, or whatever it is at the head of the stairs," I burst out. "When I saw it, I very nearly turned round and ran home. I don't just figure it out. If I hadn't known that Smithson was at the office, I really believe I would have turned back."

"Is Editor Smithson the master of your destiny?" said Dual.

"He's the master of my pay-check, which amounts to pretty much the same thing," said I.

Dual laughed. "And so you felt pretty much as one who was about to enter Pluto's realm, as described in the legends of old. Poor chap. Yet, why should you, my friend?"

"I didn't know whether my visit would be taken as friendly or not."

"Oh," said Dual, "I see. You are not always greeted cordially, I suppose. However, the motto on the plate need cause you no alarm."

He waved his hand toward one wall of the room. "You see, I have another of them here."

I followed his gesture, and my eyes fell upon a framed card upon the wall. I rose and went over to examine it more closely, for from where I sat I could read only the largest top line: "Noli Me Tangere," which I knew was Latin for "touch me not." Below this was written, in smaller type, a different version of the message of the plate by the stairs.

> Beware all ye who would do me wrong, for the curse of an Almighty God shall rest upon ye. Misfortune will be thine, through all thy life, until the uttermost farthing of thy indebtedness shall be paid. Take heed and curb thy greed, lest it destroy thee.

It surely was a "touch me not." I turned toward Dual, and this time I did not hesitate to express my surprise. What meaning lay beneath those peculiar words, to which he had called my attention by the wave of his hand.

Nothing certain, nothing tangible, yet so full of a subtly veiled meaning that even I, hardened reporter of sensational doings, felt strangely shaken, and shuddered as I read. For somehow I seemed to feel that it was every word true.

Something of my horror and sudden repugnance appeared in my next words, as I resumed my seat. "You mean, then, that you always revenge yourself upon any one who harms you in any way? Is that compatible with the doctrine of help and kindness which you uttered a moment ago?"

"Merciful Heavens, no!" cried Dual, spreading his hands in a gesture of negation. "That warning there is a warning; it is no threat. I revenge myself? It is the last thing I would ever think of trying to do.

"But, Glace, even I cannot change the law. Therefore I seek merely to warn others who might bring about their own destruction by seeking mine. Me they cannot harm, for I will not permit it, my friend.

"To an enemy I present passive resistance, which is the strongest in the world; because, while ever retreating, it is ever present, yet can never be reached. I merely refuse to be wronged, and the evil desire, which would harm me, finding no place to rest, merely returns to the source which sent it forth, and destroys. It is not I who revenge. It is the law."

"What law?" I said vaguely, seeking to prevent myself from falling under the strange influence which his words seemed to possess.

"The law of retributive justice," said Dual. "Of impersonal justice, if you prefer; which measures to a man exactly according to his acts.

"The law which rules the entire universe, which grows the grass, which rears the birds; the law which everything obeys save only man, and which he, for all his vaunted superiority, is too blind to see. 'Whatsoever a man sows that shall he reap.' That is the law. In all your career, young man, don't ever try to beat the law, for so surely as you do that same law will beat you."

"It sounds like Mosaical doctrine," said I.

"Moses was a wise man, and knew much truth," said Dual. "He was destroyed by his own greed. Man grows overconfident with a little truth. A little knowledge is a dangerous thing.

"I once knew two men, and the greed of one caused him to wrong the other. They both lost all they had. The one of greed suffered, but the other did not. Once a man wronged another who was ill. Shortly the well man fell ill and died. Once a man sought to take from another, and a thief took all he had."

"You speak in parables," I said.

Dual smiled. "The abstract doesn't appeal to you yet," said he. "Let me be more concrete. In the first instance, two men went into partnership. One had a certain number of animals, which were bound, in all natural ratio, to increase. He needed help.

"He offered another a partnership with a half-interest in the increase, in payment for his time and work. The increase exceeded what he had expected, and he sought to hold all over the stated number for his own. The entire herd sickened and died. The law was broken, and the law was avenged."

"Then," said I, strangely shaken, "you are a man so terrible that all who seek to injure you must suffer for the act."

"They suffer—not for, but by their act," said Dual in level tones. "It is cause and effect."

"From which I would gather," I resumed as he ceased speaking, "that any one may exercise this power which you possess."

"I possess?" Dual repeated. "I possess no power. I merely live in accord with universal law. Any one who does that need never fear. He may protect himself from all harm without lifting a hand.

"Not every one knows this; therefore I have sought to warn—to frighten, if need be—by appealing to the superstitious awe of the unknown which lurks in every uneducated mind, because I do not wish any one to suffer anything because of me."

His words surprised me, and I looked upon the man with a new interest. With no trouble he had apparently explained the paradox, as it seemed, to me, of what I had seen and heard. Instinctively I felt that he was sincere.

"I beg your pardon for the misunderstanding," I said as I rose.

Dual smiled. "Granted," said he. "One of my missions is to replace misunderstanding by knowledge. If I succeed in sowing one grain of understanding I am repaid."

"And," said I, "you make your living by giving advice?"

"I accept sometimes," said Dual. "I never ask. I am always willing to give to those whom I believe deserve."

"But you have to live," I insisted. "How then do you—"

"I take what I need," said Dual. "I care not for wealth. To me money is a servant; it is no master of mine. Should I lose what I have I should feel no remorse, for the wealth of the universe is at my disposal at need. Greed destroys—it can never build up."

I nodded. I confess I didn't believe. I thought of Saturday night and my paycheck. I knew what its loss would mean to Gordon Glace.

"Mr. Dual," I said, extending my hand, "these are queer theories to me, and interest me, I am free to confess. I shall see that they are fairly dealt with in the article which will appear in the *Sunday Record*—" And I stopped.

For the life of me I could get no further. A peculiar sensation started in the back of my brain, and, in spite of all my own volition, I found myself looking deep into the calm eyes of this most peculiar of men. Strangest of all, I found that I couldn't look anywhere else.

Presently I became conscious that he was speaking to me in a new manner: "You will do nothing of the sort, Mr. Glace. You will merely return to your editor, and tell him that you saw me, and that I forbade the interview's being put into print," Mr. Dual said.

"But I cannot do that," I cried in alarm. "Why, it would mean my job." I was strangely flustered—not at all myself. Under ordinary circumstances I would have given a gracious assent, gone my way, and—the interview would have appeared just the same.

But, somehow, Dual's words were not a request. They were a statement of fact, and for some reason in Dual's case I admit I feared to disobey.

At the same time I was filled with a sudden feeling, almost of anger, that any one could so control any act of mine. I opened my mouth for further protest, only to again feel the power of the man's eyes upon me.

"You will do nothing of the kind," he repeated, "and this interview, so far as your paper is concerned, will be as though it never was. If your editor should insist upon it, tell him that I said he should come here and read what is written at the entrance, and—meditate." He smiled full in my face.

My intellectual fog blew away before that smile. I felt relieved, and did not dread meeting Smithson at all. Contrary to my lifelong custom, I now resolved that I would not write an account of this interview; and yet, for the first time in my life, I was really afraid.

Almost in response as it seemed to my thought, Dual spoke again: "Thank you." And a moment after: "Fear not."

I rose. "I must be getting back," I said, and I seemed to speak in a dream. Again Dual smiled.

"Quite right," said he. "Even now Smithson is cursing because you are not there to go out on that murder case."

I started. "What's that?" I cried.

"Smithson wants you," said Dual. "It is important, so make haste." He touched a bell.

Once more the servant appeared. "Good day, Mr. Glace," said Dual, rising. "You will come to see me again shortly." He offered me his hand.

I took it, and followed the servant out. Once more I crossed the inlaid plate and heard the chime of bells.

Once more I traversed the staircase and found myself at the elevator-shaft. I hastened into the cage, and fretted and fumed at the slowness of the descent. Smithson wanted me; I wanted to reach the office, quick.

It never occurred to me to doubt the truth of the fact. It was only afterward that I wondered how Dual knew.

At the time I accepted the statement as fact, which shows how fully the personality of the man had impressed itself upon me.

I fairly ran out of the foyer of the Urania, and on up the street.

I entered the local room with a rush. Smithson popped out of his den like a jack out of a box, and greeted me with a howl. "Oh, there you are! Think I sent you on a vacation? Where you been?"

I started to explain, but Smithson cut me short. "Can that," he bawled. "Get up to 49 Jason Street just as quick as the Lord'll let you. There's a dead girl in a room up there. I caught a crossed-wire message fifteen minutes ago, and notified the police myself. Get out of here now, and for the love of Mike don't get lost!"

I started for the door on a run; but, even as I took the stairs three at a jump, my mind was busy with a thought, which, when it was fully developed, amounted simply to one short phrase: "Dual was right. He knew."

CHAPTER III.

A CARBON COPY.

I FOUND 49 Jason Street to be one of those warrens of human dwelling, commonly known as "family hotels." In it you could rent anything from a single room to a complete suite and keep your servants, if you could still afford any, in special quarters next the roof.

It had a handsome entrance, a showy foyer picked out with much gilding and studded with numerous electric-lights, though these were not turned on when I entered the place.

I told the hallman my errand, and he showed me to an elevator and ordered the boy to take me up to the room where the dead girl lay. The boy slammed shut the door and started the car, then turned to me with a grin.

"It's funny," said he, "how folks kin make a noise after dey're croaked. Dis here kid what's got hers never did nuthin' that I know of till now, an' now look at the fuss. I've took two bulls, three fly cops, and about six of you reporter fellows up to her room in de last fifteen minutes. Well, here you are."

He stopped the car and slid back the iron door. "Room ten," he directed; "straight down de hall to yer left. You kin hear de row when yer git there, I guess."

I made a note of the boy. He was loquacious and inclined to tell all he knew. I made up my mind that I would question him more presently; then turned and went quickly down the hall to room ten.

The door was closed, and I rapped lightly.

Jimmy Dean, of the *Dispatch,* opened the door and let me in. "Hallo!" said he. "We were beginning to wonder if the *Record* was asleep."

"What is it?" I asked.

"Murder, I guess," said Dean; "at least, that's what the bulls seem to think. Anyway, it's a cinch the girl never choked herself to death."

I turned toward the group of officers and plain-clothes men beside the patent, disappearing bed on which the woman's body lay, and drew in as close as I could.

The victim of the apparent tragedy was a girl of perhaps twenty-three or four, to judge by her looks, which were striking even in death.

Her hair was brown, as were also her eyes, and her face was that peculiar reverse oval which one sometimes sees, with a rather narrow forehead and a general fulness of the cheeks and lower mandible, so that the face really appears broader below than above.

Just now her body lay upon its back, with the feet projecting over the edge of the bed; the eyes open and staring, the lips slightly gaping, and with some flecks of blood dried on the lower lip and the chin.

About the throat, where the neck of her dress was partly torn away, were the purple marks of fingers. There was no possible doubt that she had met death by strangulation; probably, from her expression, fighting to the very last.

Yet she had not been strangled upon the bed, for its coverings were totally undisturbed; nor was the room to any extent disarranged. Save for the collar of her dress, her clothing even was in perfect condition; evidently death had come upon her with the suddenness of an overwhelming force.

She wore a black silk waist and a brown serge skirt with a belt. Her stockings were of black gauze, and she still had a pair of low pump-shoes upon her feet.

The apartment showed evidence of a good, if somewhat fussy, taste. It consisted of a living-room, kitchenet, and bath. Later, examination of the latter showed nothing of interest, though the remnants of a meal on a small table in the kitchen showed that the girl had dined before she died.

In one corner of the living-room was a small writing-desk with the leaf of its top open, and while I was still looking at the body on the bed Dean went over and began to inspect this in an idle sort of way. Watching him out of a corner of my eye, I saw his half interest suddenly give place to hardly controlled excitement.

With his eyes on the group of officers gathered about the bed, he put out a hand and picked up a piece of paper, to which he gave a hurried scrutiny before thrusting it into a side-pocket of his coat. I made a mental note of his action, and in a moment slipped over to his side. "What did you find?" I said quickly, speaking too low to be heard by the others in the room.

Dean shot me a sharp glance, then shrugged. "Darn you, Glace!" said he, half laughing. "Did you see me pick that up?"

"I can tell you which pocket it's in," I replied.

"All right," Dean surrendered. "Go out in the kitchen and get a drink. When I hear the water running I'll get thirsty, too, and we'll have a look at the thing."

I nodded, turned, and walked out of the room, and presently turned on the water-tap in the kitchenet. A moment later Dean sauntered in, pulled the bit of paper out of his pocket, and we bent our heads over what was evidently a half-completed note:

> Dear Reg:
> Am expecting—you know whom to-night. He seems to be inclined to cut up a bit rusty, but I am almost done with him, I think. You see, I can do as I please, while things make it necessary for him to be careful what he does. When I get that five hundred thousand—be still, my heart, so much money makes me faint—well, when I get it, and it's got to come soon, why, we'll hike out for a nice little place I know of across the blue sea, and have our very own honeymoon—just you, boy dear, and I.
> I hear the elevator stopping. I wonder if it is the old man. Hope it is. I expect to finish things with him for all time to-night. Gee, I will be glad when you and I can go away and be happy. Some one is rapping. More later.

But there was no more. There never would be any more from the hand which had penned those lines.

Dean and I glanced at each other, and he folded up the paper and put it away before either of us spoke.

"Dean," said I, "that is important; it's got to go to the police."

Dean stood for a moment, scowling; then nodded, and got the paper out. "Here," said he, "let's make a transcript of the thing. Then I'll pass it on: to the bulls. It may prove a clue for all we know. But—

Oh, Lord, don't I wish we could keep it for ourselves!"

We took a copy of the half-completed message, and then sauntered back into the other room, where Dean approached the precinct sergeant and tendered the note.

Robinson grabbed it and glanced through it, then called the detectives to his side. "Where'd you get this?" he inquired of Dean.

"It was lying on the leaf of the writing-desk," said the *Dispatch* reporter, smiling. "I thought it might interest you, so I copied it, and then passed it along."

"Copied it, did you?" grunted Sergeant Robinson. "Yep; I bet on that."

"Yes," said Dean, smiling. "I thought it best. I could have kept it, you know."

Robinson nodded, without apparently paying any attention to what Dean said; then turned to his men with a grin. "I rather guess this here settles the thing," he said.

"This kid here was playin' fast and loose with a money guy, and has a lover on the string at the same time. Well, one or the other of the two men got wise and put her away. Just a plain, old-fashioned killin' outer jealousy it looks to me.

"What we got to do is to try and find out who the two fellers was that come here the most, and then watch 'em a bit. When th' coroner comes he kin take th' body. Johnson kin stay here an' watch the room. Th' rest of us kin git out now."

While he had been speaking I had gone over to look at the body more closely, and in the course of my examination I picked up the dead girl's hand. What made me do it were some stains of blood which I noticed on the fingers.

I raised it to scrutinize the spots more closely, and then I kept it for a reason which interested me far more. The woman had worn her nails long, and as I raised and turned the hand I distinctly saw something caught under the index nail.

At first it looked to me like a little roll of thin paper; but, as I gazed upon it, it suddenly came over me what it was. It was a small rolled-up bit of human skin.

I laid down the hand and examined the woman's throat for any sign of scratches. There were none. I looked at the other hand. It was intact. Then I picked up the right hand again.

I looked at the fingers severally in turn, and under the nails of the first three I found those funny little rolls of dirty white substance. A great elation woke inside of me. I saw as in a dream what had happened. I saw the struggle as it had been; the man choking the life slowly from the woman's body; the girl fighting in desperation, digging those long nails into his hand, seeking to break his grip, succeeding only in tearing those little bits of skin from the crushing hand. I laid the hand down gently, and got up and walked about the room. I was sure no one else had noticed it. I had a beat on the rest, in so far at least.

The others were preparing to leave; that is, the officers and all the detectives save that one to whom the case had been assigned, and the reporters who would hang about to see what the coroner might say. It was then that I had a flash of intuition which changed my entire fate.

In one corner of the room there stood a typewriter, and as my eye fell upon it I went over and, drawing out the drawer of the table upon which it stood, I rummaged about until I found a sheet of carbon paper such as is used by all operators of writing-machines in making duplicate copies of their work.

With this in hand I approached Robinson and preferred my request.

"One moment, sergeant," I said as he was lighting a cigar before going back to make his report. "That note now. Would you mind letting me make a carbon copy of it before you go?"

"What for?" snapped the officer. "Hain't you fellers all got a copy of it?"

"But I want to run a photograph of the original," I explained.

Robinson favored me with a grin. "My, but the *Record* is gettin' yellow these days," he said.

But he gave me the note, and after smoothing it out I laid it on the carbon paper, slipped a sheet of plain paper—also taken from the typewriter-drawer—beneath it, and, taking a blunt pencil, traced over the lines of the writing, while my fellow reporters stood and watched me; each, I suppose, kicking himself mentally that he hadn't thought of the thing.

When I was done I had a fair copy of the note and handed it back to the grinning Robinson, who stowed it away and went stamping out.

Dean alone of those who remained seemed to sense that there was more in the thing than appeared. Catching me at a moment when we were sitting a little apart from the rest, he leaned over and asked me what I had up my sleeve.

I shook my head. "I don't really know," I told him. "Some way I've got an idea this will be a pretty hard case for us to crack. Something told me to get a copy of the note. I'll run it in the paper, of course, but it may be handy in other ways. Just now I don't know how."

Dean sighed. "If only you and I were famous detecs, now," said he, "we could deduce this girl's whole character from that note. Some people claim that you can do that from the handwriting, you know."

I did know it, but it had slipped my mind. Now I began to wonder if it might not be true. I made up my mind that I'd be very careful with my copy of the note.

My meditations were interrupted by the sound of footsteps outside, and a moment later the coroner entered the room. At his request, we described the appearance of the room and body when we entered, and after viewing the body himself he sent for the manager and put some questions to him.

From the manager's answers it appeared that the girl was known as Miss Madeline More. She had lived in the hotel for upward of a year.

She had always seemed a very quiet and reserved sort of a young woman, and seldom had any visitors, save a young man of apparently twenty-eight or thirty, of above medium height, and light complexion, who sometimes came and took her out in the evenings; and a prominent attorney, who was in the habit of coming to her with special legal work, which she did for him. She had made her living, so far as the manager knew, by doing general stenographic work.

He professed ignorance of the young man's name, but stated promptly that the attorney was Ex-Judge Barstow—a man known prominently in legal circles all over the State.

"Come to think of it, the judge called to see her last night," said the manager; "so she must have been all right then."

"What time was that?" the coroner asked.

"I don't just know," said Manager Jepson. "I can call up the office; perhaps they would."

Inquiry developed that the judge had come in about eight, and left some time after, stopping at the stand in the foyer to purchase a cigar.

Further inquiry from the various tenants and the operative force elicited nothing. No one had heard any disturbance at any time during the previous night or during the day which was now rapidly deepening into dusk.

The floor chambermaid had gone to Miss More's room several times during the day, finding the door, which had a spring-lock, fastened each time. Finally, growing surprised, she had gone so far as to climb up and look over the door through the transom, whereupon she had seen the girl's body lying fully clothed upon the bed, and had given the alarm.

When the door was broken open things were as they now remained, with the exception of an open window which gave upon a fire-escape.

This the chambermaid distinctly asserted was open when she looked over the transom, because she had noticed the curtains blowing into the room.

So much we could learn, and no more. Even the elevator-boy couldn't say what time during the day before or the evening the woman had come to her room, because there had been a break in the mechanism of the cage, and from three until six every one entering the different apartments had to walk.

After six he was positive that she had not come in, so that she must have entered her room between three and six in the afternoon of the day before.

With such meager gleanings the coroner had needs to be satisfied, though he did not appear so at all. However, he finally ordered the body taken to the morgue, and called an inquest for two days later, in the afternoon.

With his permission, the detectives and several reporters then proceeded to ransack the flat, but we found little for our pains. Beyond some purely personal notes and some legal papers on the typewriter or in its drawers, there was nothing to indicate anything about the girl's manner of life. As for myself, I watched Bryson, the plain-clothes man, closely. I wanted to see if he would discover what lay beneath the fingernails of the girl's right hand. Apparently he did not.

The coroner then ordered us all from the room, the door into the hall stood open, and one and all we stepped into the passage, and it was then that I quite inadvertently dropped my fountain pen in the darkest corner I could find.

I got down on my hands and knees and began to grope after it, while the others walked slowly down the hall. In spite of my most persistent endeavors, I didn't find the thing until I saw them enter the cage. I was just picking it up, when Dean yelled back to know if I wasn't coming.

Actually he made me drop the thing again, and I told him to get along, and I'd be down when I found my pen.

All of which leads up to the fact that I wanted to see my elevator-boy alone. I got him, and told him to run up to the top and then come down again slow. What he saw in my hand made him anxious to comply.

"See here," I began, as soon as we had started, "do you know Judge Barstow by sight?"

"Sure," said the kid, grinning. "He used to come up to ten a lot."

"What for?"

"Huh!" said the boy slyly. "Say, what yer tryin' to get at?"

"I just want to know," I replied.

"You're a reporter, ain't you?" said the boy.

I nodded.

"If I told yer, would yer write me up in de paper?"

Here was vanity, if I ever saw it. Again I nodded my head.

"Well, then," said the boy. "He used to come up an' bring papers an' things for her to write. She punched a writin'-machine, yer know."

"Yes."

"Well, he comes here last night, a little after eight, an' after while he come back an' got inter the cage, sorter whistlin' to hisself. Just when we was stoppin' down below he gimme a quarter, an' told me to tell Miss More when she come in that he'd been here an' lef some papers under the door."

"Done what?" I yelled.

"Pin stick yer?" quizzed my impudent informant, starting the cage down.

"What did he say he had done?"

"Lef some papers, I said," replied the youngster, "an' he wanted me to tell her to be sure an' get them done for to-night, 'cause he would be back for 'em sure."

"Did you tell her?" I asked.

"That's de funny t'ing," said the boy. "Up to then I didn't know she'd gone out, an' I don't know when she come in. She muster walked, but sometimes she did do that."

"Were the papers found—the ones the judge left?"

"I dunno, mister— Hully gee! Thanks!" He stopped the car, and I got out.

"Say," I said, "don't tell this to any one else for at least a day."

"All right, I'm hep," said the kid, grinning.

I turned and walked away.

I didn't go far. What the boy had told me had excited all my sense of curiosity. I wanted to know what the papers were. The room was guarded by a policeman, however, and would be until the body was removed. After that, no doubt, it would be kept locked.

I scratched my head and thought. After a bit the answer seemed to be the fire-escape. That meant waiting till night; but first I walked around to the side of the building and made sure of just where the fire-escape came down.

Then I went back to the office and wrote my story of the affair, as far as I could go.

Smithson read it and grunted approval. He never mentioned the story about Semi Dual. To tell the truth, I had forgotten all about it myself at the time.

A grunt of approval from Smithson was the same as a laurel-wreath in times of old. It fired me with an intense desire to make good on the later phases of the case. That and my natural desire to get into the heart of the mystery both made me decide to get into the room that night.

I knew that it was but one chance in a thousand that the papers were there. We had all of us looked over the room. Even if they were there, they might not amount to anything at all. Still, I had thought of a possibility, which I wanted to prove or disprove.

I decided to get Dean. He and I frequently hunted in couples, and he was a fellow who would run fair. I called him up, and was lucky enough to find him still punching out copy. I invited him to a sandwich and something to drink, and met him half an hour later at a little rathskeller down the street.

There I unfolded to him my scheme for getting into the room and finding out if the papers were there. At first he was not at all enthusiastic, but after another drink he agreed to help me "make a fool of myself," as he predicted, and we got our hats and set out.

On the whole, the thing was easier than I had expected. Jimmy gave me a back up, and I managed to catch the lower round of the iron ladder on the fire-escape and hold on till I pulled myself up.

Then I took off my coat and let it down to him, and he managed to make it after a try or two. We sneaked up the ladder like a couple of thieves, and presently arrived at the window of what I knew ought to be the girl's room.

There we paused while I examined the sash and found that, though closed, it was not locked. It yielded easily to my efforts, and I soon had a way into the room.

"If there are any papers here—if Barstow really left any, he probably shoved them under the door," I explained again to Dean. "Maybe in shoving them under he got them under an edge of the carpet as well. Stay here; I'm going to find out."

"Go ahead," said Dean, seating himself on a rail of the escape. "Only, I'm in on what you get."

I slipped into the room. By the light which filtered through the transom of the hall-door I could see the lay of the place, and also that the body had been removed from the bed.

Walking on tiptoe, I hurried over to the door which gave into the hall, and got down upon my knees on the floor. And now I confess my heart beat fast.

It all depended upon whether the edge of the carpet in front of the door was loose or not.

My groping fingers found the edge and tried it in a tentative pull.

It gave!

I turned it back and thrust an eager hand beneath. My fingers touched a folded document, and, trembling now in every fiber with my eagerness, I drew out the paper, and, still searching beneath the turned-back carpet, convinced myself that I had found all which was there.

When I rose and swiftly regained the window, where I found Dean, for all his assumed skepticism, crouched, peering within. I shook the paper under his nose.

"There, you old skeptic," I whispered in jubilation, "for once you see you were a little bit off."

Dean whistled softly.

"Jumping fleas!" he exclaimed, helping me over the sill by the expedient of half pulling my arm off. "Did you find it, Glace?"

"It rather looks like it, doesn't it?" I chuckled. "Come on. Let's get back to the rathskeller, where we can see what the paper is."

We went down the fire-escape hand over hand, and dropped to

the ground. Then we beat it up the street toward the rathskeller, where we had had our sandwiches and drinks some time before, and managed to get a table far back in a secluded corner of the room.

Then, and not till then, I drew the papers from the pocket of my coat and laid them on the table before Dean and myself. To all appearances they were merely some copies of depositions, but thrust under the rubber band which held them was a bit of paper containing a few lines written in a penciled scrawl:

> Miss More:
> Came up to see you, but was so unfortunate as to find you out. Hope to find you at home tomorrow. Will call for the papers. Please make four copies of each.

"What do you make of it?" said Dean.

"It appears to bear out the elevator-boy's story," I answered slowly. "What gets me is why a man of Barstow's position should take his work around to the girl himself."

"Uh-uh," agreed Dean. "Funny the papers weren't seen this afternoon."

"Well, as to that," I said, "I fancy that when Barstow shoved them under the door they went under the rug. When the body was discovered nobody thought of anything else for a time. Probably some one, coming through the door, struck them with a heel, and sent them clear under, out of sight."

"That might explain it," admitted Jimmy. "I wonder if Barstow's known the girl long? Tell you, Gordon, we ought to try and look up that girl's past. We might find something there. Let's go see Barstow, if you don't mind."

I nodded. We drained our glasses and left the café for the street.

CHAPTER IV.

CONFUSED TRAILS.

JUDGE WILLIAM BARSTOW, ex-judge of the criminal bench, lived in a handsome residence, in the most fashionable part of the city.

There must have been at least four acres in the grounds, besides what was occupied by the house and garage. This was beautifully parked, and upon the whole was one of the show places of the town.

I confess I was rather loath, after we got started to call upon the judge at that hour of the night, but Dean urged me on. "Sometimes," said he, "a cold trail leads to a hot scent. He can't do more than have the butler buttle us out the door."

"All right," I assented. "All I ask is that you go first and take the first buttle for your own."

We dropped from the car at the corner and went up the winding walk to the front door. "Servants and solicitors at the rear," I reminded Jimmy. But he shrugged in high disdain. "Shut up," he told me, "and try to remember that you represent the majesty of the press."

Jimmy punched the bell rather viciously.

Then we stood and waited until the door was opened, and a very imposing functionary demanded the cause of our call. We gave him our cards and requested a few moments of the judge's time. After showing us into a reception room the servant departed to see whether we got it or not, and Jimmy heaved a sigh.

"He didn't seem impressed a bit," he complained. "I wish I'd worn my other tie."

"The one you have on will be enough to hang all our chances," I told him.

He was just about to make some sort of an answer when the butler returned and informed us that the judge would be down in a moment, and desired us to wait.

Although it was ten o'clock when the judge came down, he was dressed for the street, even to a top hat, light evening coat, and gloves. He came across toward where we had risen, with an extended hand, and greeted us smiling.

"You will pardon me, gentlemen," he said, "but I have just been called to a client of mine, and can give you but a few moments tonight. Still, as I am going to cross the business section, you can ride along in the motor, and we can talk on the way."

"What we want to learn will take but a moment, Judge Barstow," said Dean. "You no doubt saw the account of the death of a Miss More in the evening papers. It would be in the late editions, I suppose, though I didn't see one myself.

"We want to know just what you knew about the girl. So far we have been unable to find out anything about her at all, save that she was a professional stenographer."

"Yes, yes," said the judge. "I didn't see the papers, but I had heard of the affair. You see, a reporter was here earlier in the evening. I can, however, tell you but little of interest, I fear.

"She was at one time employed in my office, but later left it because she thought she could do better by doing piece-work. She was a very efficient typist indeed. Although she was no longer with me, I sometimes took or sent work to her when I wanted it done with particular care. But no doubt my car is waiting. May I give you a lift down-town?"

We accepted the invitation, and after we had taken seats in the judge's limousine Dean again renewed his search for facts.

"Did you call to see her last night, Judge Barstow?" he asked.

"I did," said Barstow. "Come to think of it, I left some papers under the door, with a note asking her to get them ready to-night. I meant to call for them, but was out of town all day, and the thing had slipped my mind. She was out at the time I called, and I asked the elevator operator to call her attention to the fact that they were thrust under the door."

"Did you often leave important papers lying around like that?" said Dean. "Are you in the habit of doing so?"

In the light of the street lamps we could see Barstow silently laugh. "No, Mr. Dean," he chuckled, "I am not. But it was safe to do so with Miss More. Her training in my office, together with her natural intelligence, made her sure to comprehend what I needed. Your point was well taken, however, I must admit."

"What do you know about the girl's antecedents?" I inquired.

"Not a thing," said Judge Barstow. "She always seemed quiet and well-behaved. If I remember rightly, she once told me that she was an orphan."

"Did you know that she expected to fall heir to some money?" I hazarded, thinking it likely that he would be asked to look after her affairs if she really expected to get such a sum as she had mentioned in the note Dean had found.

"I did not," said Barstow, and I fancied he frowned.

"Well, she was engaged, wasn't she?" said Dean.

"She had a young man," said the judge, as he offered us each a cigar from a case and lit one himself. "He was a chap of about twenty-eight, I should say. Whether they expected to marry or not Miss More never said."

"Did she ever tell you his name?" said Dean.

Barstow nodded. "I met him once or twice," he replied. "Watson, I think the name was."

The auto swerved and slid in toward the curb in front of the office of the *Dispatch*. Dean and I got out, and Barstow shook us each by the hand.

"Sorry," said he, "that I couldn't help you boys more at this time, but if there is anything I can do in the future, don't hesitate to call upon me." The door of the limousine closed on the last word and the machine got under way.

I turned to Dean. "Your cold trail is pretty well frozen up," I said. "I'm going to the office, and then to bed."

"I don't know. At least we got the fellow's name," said Jimmy. "Come and walk down the block. Barstow's office is in the Kernan Building, and while you have been babbling an auto stopped down there. It may be his car, and it may not—I'm for finding out."

We walked along slowly, and stopped just short of the office building, before which stood a motor with its engine throttled down. Jimmy pointed to the number and grinned. "It's he, all right," he announced. "I thought he said he had a client to see."

"Maybe he had to get some papers," I suggested.

Dean merely nodded and stepped back into the shadow of the building wall. "Anyway, I'm going to wait till he comes out," he announced.

Of course I stayed along.

Five and ten minutes passed, and then Judge Barstow hurried from the Kernan entrance, entered the car, and rode off. But as he entered the machine he spoke to the driver, and both Jimmy and I distinctly caught the one word "Home!"

I looked at Dean, and he upon his part looked at me. Finally: "Was the alleged client a plant?" he muttered. "Did he really just want to give us the shake?" Then he grinned. "Oh, I don't know about this trail being so cold, after all, Glace, old chap."

I confess I was puzzled. It had been a trying day. I shook a sadly topsyturvy head at my friend Dean. "Suppose we try the police station and see what they have done. The more I see of this thing, the more muddled and interested I get."

Dean locked his arm in mine and we set out, walking for the most part in silence, each busy with his own thoughts, until such time as the green lights of the station threw a ghastly light across the sidewalk, and we turned into its door.

It was a night of surprises; first the papers under the rug, then Judge Barstow's peculiar conduct, and now another which awaited us in the precincts of constituted law. At out first inquiry the sergeant laughed. "H'ain't you heard?" he asked.

"Heard what?" we chorused in reply.

"Why, they've pinched the girl's sweetheart. Looks like they've got him with the goods on, too."

Here was news indeed. Dean reached into his pocket and drew out a couple of cigars, which he solemnly laid on the sergeant's desk.

"Here," said he. "I was going to smoke them myself, but I guess they belong to you. We've been taking a Rip Van Winkle, Glace and I. Suppose you wind us up and give us the right time."

"Nothin' to it," said the sergeant, biting on one of the brown rolls. "This afternoon after everybody had left the hotel, a young feller answerin' to the description of the girl's man comes into the hotel and gets on the elevator and gets off at five. The elevator kid is wise to him, havin' took him to the girl's rooms more than once, an' he beats it down an' puts the office wise.

"In the mean time th' feller goes to the girl's room an' runs into our man, who was still waitin' for the dead-wagon from the morgue. He seems surprised an' asks what's wrong. Of course Johnson laughs in his face, an' the guy gets kinder fresh. Just then th' manager comes up an' tips Johnson off, an' he starts to make a pinch.

"Well, the feller tried to put up a fight, an' Johnson had to club him 'fore he'd be good. They brings him in, and when we searches him we finds a lady's watch, with the girl's name engraved in it, in the fob pocket of his pants, an' also a swell diamond ring that fit the third finger of her left hand. It sure looked good to us, so we sent him back. Pretty quick work that, eh?"

"If you've got the right man, it's chain lightning," said Dean.

"If?" said the sergeant. "Say, what yer want to talk like that for, Dean?"

"Well, what did the fellow say?" Jimmy asked.

"'Bout the usual thing," the officer growled. "Told a fairy story 'bout havin' broke his watch, an' the girl's lettin' him have hers to wear. Said the ring was one that had been his mother's what he was goin' to give the girl for a engagement ring. Claimed he didn't know she was dead."

"Well, if he did, why did he go up there?" I asked.

"He didn't say," said the sergeant with a grin.

"Had the ring been altered in size?"

"I don't know that either. I didn't look to see."

"If it had been we could probably trace the job and verify his statement if true?"

The sergeant nodded and got up. "I put 'em away in the safe, after we tuk 'em offen' the guy," he explained as he crossed the railed-in space back of which he sat. "Suppose we have a look at 'em now."

For a moment he busied himself with the safe, running methodically through the combination, with counting and pauses between each turn.

Presently, when the door swung open, he found the property taken from the recently arrested individual, and returned to his desk with the watch and the ring.

It was the latter which claimed our first attention. Dean and I went over and stood beside the desk, and together the three of us examined the thing. Nowhere in all its circumference was there any sign of a cut or a mend, in fact of any sort of work at all. To all appearances it was now as it was when originally made.

"It looks bad," said Dean. "Of course it is possible that the girl wore the same size ring as his mother, but it seems hardly likely to me." He picked up the watch.

It was a lady's ordinary chatelaine case of gold, contained a Waltham movement, and was engraved on the inner side of the case with the girl's name, and a date. Apparently it might have been a present to her at some time.

"What do you think?" said Dean as he laid it down.

"It looks like a real pinch," I was forced to admit.

The sergeant cocked Jimmy's cigar in a corner of his mouth and hooked his thumbs into his vest. Presently he blew out a great cloud of smoke, rose and gathered up the trinkets, preparatory to putting them away. Then he began to chuckle. "It's a sure enough pinch," he said.

"What was the chap's name?" I bethought me to ask.

"Wasson," said the now smiling sergeant. "Reginald Wasson for short."

I glanced at the clock. It was almost twelve. I rose and rolled a cigarette. "Come On, Jimmy," I said, "we've got a lot of writing to do. Good night, sergeant, there was sure some class to that work."

"Wasson—Watson," muttered Dean when we were outside. "Well, I guess Barstow meant to give it to us straight. The names sure are something alike. I wonder if they've really got the right man. What do you think?"

"I think I'm going down and write some sort of a story and get to bed," said I. "Only you can bet yourself a dinner I'd hate to be in Reggie Wasson's shoes."

Well, I did go to bed when my work was finished, but I didn't go to sleep. The events of the day kept buzzing like pinwheels in my brain.

It had been a most unusual day. First was my visit to the peculiar individual who dwelt on the Urania's roof, with all its unexpected circumstances, climaxing in the character of the man himself. That had been like a page torn bodily from some old romance. If written, half those who read it would hardly believe.

Men didn't build grand staircases to a roof-garden, unless for profit, nor inlay plates of mystical warnings, set over a mechanism for ringing soft-toned bells, from purely altruistic motives nowadays. Almost I began to wonder if I had seen it myself.

Then my mind switched to the later events, which Dual had partly foretold. How did he know? The girl had been handsome in her way. Who had killed her, and why? Where was she going to get so much money?

Wasson was arrested. Was he guilty? If not, how had he got hold of the watch and ring? Might his explanation be true?

I tossed, and fretted, and turned. It was hot. I had a vision of a long crystal glass with ice floating in it, full of a peculiar, limpid liquid, and all at once I was consumed with thirst. What was it Dual had said to me? "I will see you soon," or something like that. Well, why not. I wanted to see him. I wanted to drink again of that beverage which he alone possessed. I wanted to talk over this case with the peculiar man who had first told me that there was a case.

I rolled over and berated myself for an imbecile, but the idea wouldn't down. It was too hot to sleep.

I made up my mind I would walk down to the Urania and look up at the tower. I even thought that if there was a light I might go up and see if Dual was awake. Somehow I felt that he was the sort of person who might at times turn night into day.

I kicked off the hot sheet and began to dress, actually hurrying into my clothes, like one in a great haste. After a bit I went out and stole softly down-stairs. 'Way over in the east there was a faintly grayer line in the darkness, and the air felt cooler outside.

I took a great breath of it into my lungs and started away toward where the Urania raised itself toward the still dark central sky. An early milk-cart rattled by. A newspaper-wagon trundled toward a morning train. Night owls were slinking home.

It was that peculiar hour between darkness and dawn, when the night is dead and the day is not yet awake, and things take on an almost mysterious air. I remember that some sparrows twittered in a tree as I passed, and I thought whimsically of how cold they were going to be six months from now.

After a while I came to the darkened entrance of the Urania, and though I had not seen any light from below as I approached, I turned in as though led by some compiling force, and groaning in very spirit, began to mount the stairs. Up, and up, and up. After a bit I lost count and simply kept on until I should see the great staircase. Then I would know I was at the top.

After an hour of seeming climbing it appeared, and I went up it, and across the glass inlay of the plate. Far off I heard the mellow bells, and as I reached the door of the tower it swung inward silently, before I could lift a hand to knock or even look for a bell. The servant of the afternoon stood before me rubbing a sleepy eye. Without waiting for me to speak, he led me to an adjoining apartment, and pointed to a stair.

"The master awaits you," he said.

I began climbing again, and after a time I came out into a broad room, which seemingly took in the entire top of the tower. Its sides seemed to be mainly of glass, so that one could look directly out into the night, giving one a temporary sensation as of floating in space.

A dim light burned at the head of the stairs, and by its feeble rays and the beginning dawn outside, I could see various instruments of an apparently scientific nature, arranged about the room.

At first I did not see Dual, but as I advanced a step he turned from a telescope, which was pointed out of an opened portion of the glass casings, and addressed me by name. "Mr. Gordon Glace," said he, "you are a fairly hard individual to call."

CHAPTER V.

THE MAN IN THE STARS.

"**I AM** hard—to call?" I stammered.

"Certainly," said Semi Dual. "I desired to see you, so I sent for you. Why else have you come?"

"I couldn't sleep, and I was thirsty. I wanted a drink of that stuff of this afternoon. If you sent for me, I must have missed your messenger, Mr. Dual."

Again Semi Dual smiled dryly. "I hardly fancy you would evade, miss, or escape from my messenger," he said. "But you say you are thirsty: then let us go below."

"But I am disturbing you," I began. Now that I was here I felt like a fool. What sort of boy's trick had I been guilty of to thus break in on a man at peep of day?

"Not at all," protested Dual. "It is growing too light for me to work to the best advantage; besides, you are the next on the program. That was why I sent for you. I rather think I have found what I sought."

"Of course, you were studying the stars," I said. "One might think you a wise man of old, finding you like this."

"I was looking for a bad man of today, however," replied Dual.

"Looking for a man? In the stars? I thought the only man in the heavens was in the moon, and it's in the dark now."

"And yet," said Dual, smiling, "I found my man in the stars."

"Good Heavens!" I cried on the instant, as an idea burst in my brain. "Are you, then, an astrologer? I didn't suppose any one believed in that now."

"I believe in anything which is capable of a scientific demonstration, Mr. Glace," Dual said, as I thought somewhat coldly. "Suppose we go below."

He motioned me toward the stairway, and immediately followed me down.

We went directly into the chamber in which Semi Dual had entertained me that afternoon. He offered me a chair, then, excusing himself, passed through a door on the farther side of the apartment, saying he would return in a moment or two.

Left alone, I looked about the room, with a new interest in its furnishings, as the abode of the man who had met my morning intrusion with the air of something expected, and had even alleged that he had called me to him, at an hour when most persons might have been well in bed.

It was plainly, yet well furnished, carrying on the quality of quiet richness which I had noticed in the anteroom the afternoon before. Among other things I noticed what seemed to be a modified form of wireless receiving and sending apparatus. Also, there were several immense charts, seemingly of an astronomical nature, affixed to the wall.

A beautiful bronze female figure of life size stood at the side of his desk, holding an immense golden globe in her hand, from which poured forth a soft, mellow light. Casting back into my mythological education, I sensed it for a representation of Venus and her famous prize apple. As a work of art, it was superb.

Another thing which riveted my attention was a tall clock with a peculiar dial, showing the changes of seasons and months, the phases of the moon, days of the week, and months, and all sorts of things, as it appeared to me, besides the hours themselves. Truly, I began to feel that I was in the house of a most remarkable man; and then the door opened and the man himself appeared.

He was carrying a tray containing a couple of glasses and a small plate of cakes. These he deposited upon the desk, handed me a glass and a cake, and took the other glass himself.

"I will join you," he said, smiling. "After my night's work, I feel that it will do me good."

I lifted my glass and drank.

Again I experienced all the delight of the previous afternoon. I nibbled my cake; and I bethought me to apologize for my impulsive remark.

"Mr. Dual," I said, "I did not mean anything offensive when I questioned astrology a few moments ago; but I have always been led to think it a part of the superstitions of the Middle Ages. If I am wrong, I hope you will accept the statement as explaining my attitude."

Dual nodded, and set down an empty glass, wiping his lips.

"There were wise men in the Middle Ages, Mr. Glace," he began. "In fact, every age has had its percentage of those who knew the truth, and—the common mass. Sometimes they persecuted them, sometimes they crucified them, sometimes they burned them, sometimes—the exception, they listened to them—or at least a few did.

"I remember one instance, though it wasn't in the Middle Ages, when, had a noted man taken the warnings of an astrologer, he might have gone down to history as a benefactor, instead of a monster in human form."

"Then," said I, "am I right in supposing that astrology is an exact science, Mr. Dual?"

"One of the most exact in existence," my host replied. "It is in reality the earliest form of astronomy. If it were not a scientific fact, I would not care to waste time upon it. But I have proven it true; and right here let me give you some advice. Never accept anything for the truth unless it can be proven true, Mr. Glace; half the wars and sufferings of this world have come from unreasoning belief in fallacious facts."

"I wish you'd explain," I said.

Dual smiled. "An immediate application of my advice, eh?" he quizzed. "Very well, though I must be brief, as you have much more important things to attend to to-day. See here."

He rose and went over to one of the charts, picked up a long-bladed paper-cutter from the desk as he left his chair, and used it as a pointer for the chart. "Let me first ask you an elementary question of the common schools, Mr. Glace: 'What causes the rise, and fall of the tides?'" I felt his eyes upon me, and answered on the instant: "The moon."

"Quite right," said Dual. "Now, the moon is but an insignificant satellite of the earth, yet her magnetic influence affects the surface of the earth.

"The earth, in turn, is but one of a given number of planets revolving in the solar system of their sun. Each planet has a certain magnetic quality, which it radiates and which may be learned by observation. All these magnetic influences affect the earth, and are affected by the earth's own quality in turn.

"Now, if the moon admittedly affects the rise and fall of our tides—there was a foundation, in fact, for the superstition about planting seeds in certain phases of the moon, you see—why should we deny the effect of the other magnetic influences of the other planets equally upon the earth? There is no logical reason at all.

"Therefore, the fact of that influence remains. Given a certain part of the earth's surface, and a certain time, and a knowledge of the positions of the other planets, and what their individual quality is, and we can predicate the mean total of planetary magnetism operating on that point at that time."

His words impressed me, though against all my former training.

"It sounds plausible," I conceded as he paused.

"It is more than that; it is fact," smiled Dual. "Some day I shall prove it to you, Glace, but not now." He threw down the paper-knife and resumed his chair.

But I continued yet a moment with my questions.

"Then, with a given knowledge of the orbits of the planets, you could go farther, and predicate the influence at a certain point for a future time?" I inquired.

"Exactly," said Dual.

"Does the influence apply to human beings as well?"

"It does."

"Hence the soothsayers, Mr. Dual?"

"Rather the mathematical prognosticators, at whom ignorance scoffs," Dual replied.

"A rather nasty slap on the knuckles," I laughed. "What did you mean by saying you had sent for me?"

"The literal fact," Dual answered. "I did."

"Why?"

"I wanted to verify my own information by finding out what you had learned of the death of the woman in the Jason Street hotel."

Again I inquired: "Why?"

"Because," said Dual seriously, "I desire to see justice done. Not but what it would be in time, of course, but at times we may even rule Fate. Because I wanted to know if the suspicions of the authorities rests upon the right man; also, to prevent an injustice from being done."

"You talk as though you knew the guilty man!" I exclaimed.

"I know his general description," Dual responded. "I learned that to-night before you came. I need your assistance in finding him out; therefore, I called you, and you are here; now tell me what you know."

That was what I had come for. True, I had been distracted by the things which had occurred; but now, on the man's word, I was consumed with an eagerness to unburden my perplexed mind, and see if he could find any way out of the tangle of facts.

I began at the beginning, and went over all that had occurred. Now and then he interrupted with a terse question. For the most part, he sat with eyes closed, lying back in his chair, so that, save for an occasional slight quivering of his drooping lids, I might have fancied that he slept.

I ran over the finding of the body, the later conversation with the elevator operator at the hotel, the return to the room, and the finding of the papers and the note, the visit to Judge Barstow and his apparent attempt at evasion of any lengthy interview on the subject, what he had told us of the woman's history, the arrest of Wasson, and finally even my own peculiar sensations which terminated in my present visit to his rooms.

When I had quite finished, Semi Dual opened his eyes and sat forward in his chair. "Have you those notes with you?" he asked in a suddenly eager way.

"I have the genuine note which was on the papers under the carpet," I responded. "Of the girl's note I have only the carbon which I made."

"May I see them?" said Dual, extending his hand.

I got them out and passed them across to him, and turning his chair to the desk he quickly smoothed them out upon his blotter and began to pore over them intently, with an ever-growing interest.

"Dean said one might gain an idea of the writer's character from a sample of the handwriting—" I began speaking; but paused as I saw that my host was oblivious not only to my words but to my presence as well.

He had taken up a powerful lens and was going over the written lines word by word. Now and then he made a notation on a bit of paper lying upon his desk, and returned again to his study of the writing, each time more intent than before. The light of day was beginning to stream into the room, but the electrics over our heads still blazed on without his paying heed.

Far down below us I could hear the noises of the awakening world; the faint, faraway cries of newsboys, and the clang of the gongs of cars. But nothing disturbed in any way the concentration of the man at the desk. Presently, however, he made a last note, rose and turned off the lights, and came smiling back to his chair. "Mr. Glace, you are a most valuable assistant," he said.

"You find something of interest?" I inquired.

"Together we have found everything but the man's name," said Semi Dual.

"You mean you know his general description?" I cried.

"Precisely."

"But you can't. You say you don't know him. Then—"

"Why not?" interrupted my host, with his quiet smile.

"Well how could you—" I began.

"Mr. Glace," said Dual, "at the risk of appearing trite, I shall quote from my friend Shakespeare: 'There are more things in heaven and earth than are dreamed of in thy philosophy—Gordon.'

"My ability to describe this man without having seen him, happens to be a small part of the same. Besides, you have furnished me a very valuable aid by your clever work in getting this specimen of his handwriting, you see. I told you I had gone well forward in tracing him before you came up here. Even at that time I knew his physical characteristics.

"Now, from the writing I may say I am fairly well acquainted with his mental qualities as well. Glace, the murderer did not intend to kill until his hands were actually about the woman's throat."

"Good Lord!" I gasped. "Have you read the papers? How did you know she was choked to death?"

Semi Dual shook his head. "I am right, am I not?"

"Yes—but—"

"I have not seen the papers," said Dual. "I seldom read those records of modern violence, except for some special end. To resume:

"After he had done the deed he was horrified at his act; but he resolved to escape from the penalty of the law if possible, which was natural, as we must admit. If I am correct in my suspicions of the identity of the man, he is not a natural criminal in the sense of being without a moral sense, but one who has a certain inherent weakness of moral fiber, which makes him the plaything of temptation at certain times.

"By the way, the fact that the girl had the bits of cuticle under her nails may prove a valuable clue. Somewhere in this town there is a man with some scratches on one of his hands, presumably the left, but, of course, you have thought of that."

"I considered it as a possibly important fact," I said.

"It will prove so," said Dual. "There is some motive for the man's act which as yet I have not fully worked out. I will find it after a while, and then we shall know why he acted as he did.

"Futhermore, while the idea of making the carbon copy of the girl's uncompleted note was good, still it leaves much to be desired. A great deal of her personality is indicated, but I wish I could have a line written m her own hand, for I suspect something even from the copy, which I would like to verify. Could you get me a note of hers, do you think? Wasson might have one, might he not?"

I sat as one in a trance listening to the man speaking thus intimately of persons of whom he claimed to have no personal knowledge, discussing their manners, dissecting their characters, with the coolness of a surgeon working over a case.

A feeling almost of the uncanny crept over me, which Dual seemed to sense, for he paused.

"Mr. Glace," he resumed, addressing a personal note to me alone; "you must bear with a great deal right now, which you cannot understand until you have learned a great deal. The child does not run, it creeps; neither does the blind man leap forward—he must feel his way.

"But believe me that all I say is capable of the fullest scientific proof; that I am looking at this thing from an absolutely impersonal standpoint, and working from mathematical hypothesis to mathematical conclusion, and you will lose the sense of the mystical which is affecting you now. In reality there is nothing mystical in all the universe of worlds. Everything obeys a universal law. Do you think we might obtain that note?"

I got up and went over to a window and looked out. I had to shake myself together a bit, but presently I turned to find Dual lost in a litter of papers which he had spread on the desk.

"Mr Dual," I said; "if you'll pardon the expression, I think you've got my goat." For the first time Semi Dual laughed out loud.

"I've been in the newspaper game for some years," I went on, "and I thought I had a fairly well-developed news sense; yet, after first telling me to go to this case yesterday afternoon, and getting me into a beautiful snarl of conflicting detail, you cap the climax by sitting here and talking as though you knew practically all about the thing from beginning to end. How you do, it gets me. However, I've got to be getting along. If you'll permit it, I'd like to see you again, sometime to-night."

Dual bowed and then tapped the sheets of paper upon his desk, which I saw were covered with a mass of mathematical formula and geometrical figures.

"Much of the explanation of what puzzles you, Mr. Glace, is here before you," he said.

I nodded perfunctorily. "No doubt," I replied, "but no matter how much I'd enjoy your explanation, I must get out and go to work on this case. I've got a hard day before me, I guess, Mr. Dual."

"But not before we have broken our fast," said Semi Dual, as he reached out and struck a small bronze bell.

I stood confused for a moment. The invitation was unexpected, and I opened my mouth to protest. Without looking at me directly Dual repeated his former remark in a different way. "You will breakfast with me," he stated, and I closed my mouth and resumed my chair.

The door on the far side opened and the servant appeared, coming in silently and waiting without a word. *"Tempo maugi,"* said Dual, without raising his head from his figures, and the man disappeared. The whole thing might have been a photoplay figure save for those two spoken words.

"*'Tempo maugi'*—'Time to eat,' eh?" I said, translating. "So you add Esperanto to your other advanced ideas, Mr. Dual?"

An expression of pleasure swept over the man's face. *"Chu vi komprenas?"* he replied.

But I refused the lure. "Only a little—a half-dozen words out of every hundred I hear."

"Yet it must come," said Dual. "The world needs a universal language. It would do much to remove international differences and misunderstanding.

"But come; before we eat we have some few things to do. Draw up your chair beside the desk, Mr. Glace, while I point out certain things which shall help you on your quest for the man you desire to find."

I drew in to the desk as he requested, and Dual picked up a sheet of his notes.

"To begin with, the murderer is a large man; he will stand approximately six feet tall; he is light-complexioned, hair a very light brown and thinning, eyes a blue-gray. He is broad-shouldered and should be possessed of great strength. He is clean-shaven, with a thin-lipped mouth and a rather prominent nose, and—" He paused and referred to some sheets of his calculations: "Yes, he has a scar of some sort on his left hip well up toward the ridge of the pelvic bones."

An irrepressible spirit of flippancy took possession of me. "Hasn't he a birthmark in the form of a horseshoe, in the middle of his back, where his grandfather was kicked by a hen?" I asked.

Semi Dual stiffened and sat erect; turned and looked straight through me in a long steady boring gaze.

Under the fire of his eyes I felt myself shrivel and writhe. I was again as a boy when caught in some culpability, which I had hoped to get by with, and been detected in the act. It seemed to me that to those eyes every little secret chamber of my brain lay glaringly revealed; almost I felt the impact of his glance against the inside of the back of my skull.

I tried to sustain it and could not endure. My eyes fell against my veriest striving, and I felt a blush of shame creep into my unaccustomed cheeks.

"Mr. Glace," said Semi Dual, very quietly, without any visible sign of surprise, offense, or other emotion, "it has always been the habit of ignorance to ridicule what it doesn't understand.

"I have been endeavoring to point out some facts which should be of material assistance to you in carrying through to a conclusion a case which the police will probably muddle at first. That I have no selfish interest in this should appear from the fact that I had intended before allowing you to leave me this morning to warn you against in any way mentioning my name or letting it appear that I know of the case in any sense; making my further assistance to you obligatory upon your agreeing to that one point.

"Perhaps, however, I have erred. What is worth having is worth seeking, and I am thus made aware of the fact anew. Shall we forget what has been said?"

I had brought it upon myself, and I knew it. I think I hung my head, but I did make out to reply.

"Yes. For goodness' sake, forget what I said, if you can. I feel like I used to when mother caught me stealing jam, or tying a can to a stray dog's tail. If you say any more I'll feel like the dog."

Dual's face illumined with his smile, and he raised a hand. "I admit it must all seem strange to you, Glace, but it is true. It is my intention to help you run this man down. You should gain some credit for a piece of work like that, don't you think?"

"If I only could," I cried, with sudden enthusiasm. "I don't think Smithson thinks such an awful lot of me, just now."

Dual nodded. "Very well," he said, "suppose I go on. I have indicated the man's physical characteristics to you. Now supposing he wrote the words of the note, found on the papers—"

"But, good Lord! Dual," I broke in, "Judge Barstow wrote that."

"Did he?" replied my companion. "Perhaps. As for that I do not care. Let us see what the character of the writing indicates. Lean over here closely and watch what I point out.

"To begin with, the writing is backhand; that would indicate a person of great self-interest, one in whom personal interest takes precedence of all other emotions, utterly selfish, usually insincere.

"Secondly, the writing is heavy. This, too, indicates a selfish person. Heavy writers are apt to be shrewd, and tricky, and revengeful, and will hesitate at little to gain their ends.

"Thirdly, the writing has the appearance of tapering off at the end of the words. Where the writing tapers decidedly as it does here, the writer is usually dishonest, not through innate criminality, but because of environment—opportunity, if you like.

"It is usually a matter of circumstance and temptation. Such people are not to be trusted in financial matters and are not to be believed, as they always allow circumstances to alter cases. They will keep a promise if convenient, and only then.

"Such a person is, therefore, not a criminal *per se,* but will probably do a criminal action if given a chance to make some personal gain, with small fear of being found out. They are the men who appropriate trust funds for private speculation, meaning at first to return them if they win in their venture. If they do not win, they thus become criminal through circumstance rather than from any deliberate choice. Am I plain?"

"In your statements, yes," I admitted. "But Barstow is a man of State-wide reputation for probity. How could what you say be true if—"

"We must have another sample of Barstow's writing," said Dual. "One of your tasks will be to get that to-day. Another will be to get to see Wasson, and find out if he has a note or letter from the dead girl.

"I want to see something in her original hand. This copy you have indicates a very unusual type. Be sure and try to get me that note. Get something from Wasson also, in writing. In these things you must not fail."

I rose to my feet, and stood by the desk. On the instant all the reporter's desire to run the thing to its outcome swept over me in a wave.

What did I care who was guilty, so long as I could find out? I resolved that I would take up the trail and know no rest until I held all the ends of the skein of events in my hand. "I will not fail," I told Dual.

"Good," said he. "I shall expect you this evening with interest, and now I think Henri is bringing the breakfast in."

I had heard no sound, but as he spoke a panel of the wall slid back, and through the aperture so left a table was rolled into the room. The panel slipped once more into place, and left us with our morning's meal before us laid out with white linen, napery, and glass. There was even a great bowl of fresh roses spilling over on the damask cover. I felt like rubbing my eyes.

Again Dual smiled. "Did my dumbwaiter surprise you?" he said as he moved toward the table. "Come, Glace, don't stand on any formality, for I know none. You are a hungry mortal, and have a great deal to do to-day. Draw up your chair, man, and fortify yourself for the day."

I accepted without delay, and sat down to a most appetizing array. Crisp brown toast and poached eggs, with golden coffee, and a tempting bowl of fresh fruits, but I hesitated when I saw that all this was upon my side of the table alone.

Seeing my confusion, Dual motioned me to begin.

"I told Henri to get the eggs and coffee, last night, after I was sure you would be here to breakfast," he said. "As for myself, I never eat anything save fruit for the morning's meal."

"Do you mean to say you knew I'd be here, last night?" I fairly gasped. I began to think this man's surprises would never cease.

"I mean just that," he replied.

"How did you know?"

"I desired it," explained Dual.

"Do you always get what you desire?"

"Generally," said my queer companion; "for you see I try to desire nothing which it is not perfectly lawful that I should have."

"Then there would be some things which even you couldn't get?"

"Scarcely that. I could get anything I might desire."

"Lawful or not?"

"Lawful or not, Mr. Glace."

"But you don't?"

"Some things are too high-priced," said Dual, munching away at a peach. "You must remember one pays for everything he has; if one acquires an unlawful desire or possession, the law still remains to be atoned."

I began to see what he meant. Truly there was a lot more in his philosophy than I had ever considered before; yet I quibbled a quibble as I chewed upon the last bite of toast. "If what you say is true," I questioned, "how is it, then, some men apparently do anything with impunity and get away with it?"

"Your question answers itself," said Dual. "Their impunity is only apparent. Look up their whole life-record, and you will find that they atone. Now, by way of speeding the parting guest, permit me to suggest that in your own terms of expression, you 'get busy.'

"Report to me here at ten o'clock, and by all means bring all the specimens of handwriting you can get. Find out everything you can, and we'll sort it out to-night."

CHAPTER VI.

TWO INTERVIEWS OF IMPORTANCE.

DOWN ON the street, with a good breakfast nestling under my belt, things began to look more hopeful to me. I got a copy of the *Record* and one of the *Dispatch,* and read what Dean and myself had to say about the latest criminal mystery of the town. It made a fairly readable story, if I do say it myself.

Next I want over to the *Record* office and left a note on Smithson's desk informing him that I would be out all day on an important clue connected with the case, and left grinning at what he would probably say.

Ordinarily I would have hesitated before doing anything like that, but some of Dual's spirit of confidence seemed to have crept into me, and I never doubted that I would succeed. With his advice still fresh, in my mind, I set out and decided that I would see Wasson first.

I marched into the police station and made known my request. There I profited by the fact that in writing my story the night before I had given the arrest of Wasson a fairly prominent place.

Harrington, the desk-man, greeted me with a smile, and upon my expressing a desire for an interview with Wasson, nodded assent.

"Funny thing," he said, "an' it ain't for publication neither, Glace, me bye, but th' coroner found some little pieces of skin under the nails of the girl's hand; an' by the same token, our new boarder Wasson is shy some of the cuticle on his left mitt. Now, what do you think of that?"

I grinned. "So the coroner found it, did he?" I laughed. "Well, he was a little bit more on the job than I thought. I got next to that yesterday afternoon, but kept it under my hat, thinking it might be a good clue."

"An' that was white of ye, Glace," said Harrington. "Come on an' I'll take ye back."

I followed him to the rear, where the corridors of the city jail began, and he passed me through the heavy steel gate; told the guard to take me to Wasson's cell, and turned away. I trailed after the guard, and my brain was buzzing pretty well. If Wasson had scratches on his left hand— Well, I wondered if he had a scratch on his left hip. That was all.

The guard paused, and tapped on a cell door. The man who was sitting on the cot raised his head, and then got up and came over to the grating. This the guard unlocked, and motioned me to enter. "A newspaper man for to see you, Wasson," said he, with a grin.

The prisoner scowled. "A chap isn't safe from you fellows even behind bars, is he?" he burst out. "I've seen the papers, and they have given me a mighty rotten deal, I must say. According to them I might as well be convicted right now. As a result, I have nothing to say, Mr.—"

"Glace," I supplied. All the time I had been sizing the man up. He was above the average in height, though I fancied not six feet; he was broad of shoulder, light of complexion; his eyes were blue-gray, his hair brown and thinning, his mouth was thin-lipped; he had a rather prominent nose. I decided to look for the scar on his hip, if I had to do it by force. All this while he was berating the press.

"What do they know about me?" he cried. "Nothing at all, except that I was so unfortunate to call on a woman who was dead. Would I have been fool enough to do that if I had slain her, Glace? I wish to God I knew who did kill her, for I loved that girl. I was going to marry her, Glace. I was taking a ring to her yesterday." And he stopped. "I didn't mean to give you an interview," he said. "Now I suppose you'll print all I've said in your usual brutal way."

"Did it ever occur to you that I might be here to help you as well as to serve my paper?" I returned. I saw that I must win his confidence if I was to succeed.

"Help me?" said Wasson. "How could you do that? More likely you're only trying to get me to talk."

"There is one way I could help you," I said slowly. "If I could find the man who was guilty—"

Wasson began to pace the cell floor, finally pausing before me at my last word, and bursting into a flood of speech.

"Glace, do you mean that? You don't believe me guilty? Lord, man, it's good to hear some one say that! If you're sincere in your belief, there is nothing I could do which I wouldn't do or tell to bring the real murderer to the chair.

"It isn't only being in jail that has crushed my very soul. It's the knowledge that Madeline is dead, and that somewhere her murderer walks the streets a free man, while I am unable to raise a hand. Do you really mean that you want to help me, Glace?"

"I didn't need to interview you to find out all about you, you know," I replied. "I have reasons to believe that I am on the trail of the guilty man, and I wanted something to help me in the chase, which I fancy only you can help me to get. That's why I came to see you to-day."

Wasson threw himself back on his cot. "Then, for Heaven's sake, tell me what it is," he cried. "Ask anything you will, and I'll answer you, Glace."

I looked at his left hand. On it were some livid marks as though it had been cut or scraped raw. "How did you hurt your hand?" I asked.

Wasson raised the member and scanned it, then passed the matter off with a shrug. "When that fool of a policeman arrested me yesterday I put up a bit of a fight," he said. "I think I scratched myself on his badge. What has that to do with the case?"

"I saw the scratches and merely wondered," I replied. "Would you object to telling me what you know of Miss More's history as far as you can?"

"Is that necessary?" the man inquired.

"It might help," I said. "Still—of course—if you'd—"

"All right," said Wasson, "only don't publish all I shall say. I don't want the poor girl's life bandied about in the press. Madeline was an orphan and always made her own way. She used to work for old Judge Barstow, but left him because she couldn't stand for some of the things she had to do.

"Barstow's crooked, for all he poses as a man of very high morals. After that she began to do special work in her line, and worked up a pretty good trade. Barstow even gave her work to do at times, I guess because he didn't want to lose touch with her.

"I met her last summer, and first thing we knew we were in love. I asked her to marry me, and she said she would. Yesterday I was taking her a ring which had been my mother's, which I was going to give her for an engagement ring. Her finger just fit the thing, and I had it when I was arrested. They took it away."

"How about the watch?" I asked.

"It was hers," Wasson declared. "Last week I dropped mine and broke the spring. Madeline insisted that I take hers to wear. So you even knew about that, did you? Lord, but you fellows do nose out a lot!"

"Did you know she had been writing a note to some one just before she was killed? It was to you, I think, as it began: 'Dear Reg.'"

"Was she?" said Wasson. "Poor girl. She often wrote me, in the evenings when she was lonesome, or blue. But I didn't know, of course."

"It was found yesterday," I explained, "and taken by the police. In my scheme of procedure it is necessary for me to be sure that the note was really written in her own hand. I kept a carbon copy of the note we found. Have you anything which she has written, which I could have for a few days—say until to-morrow, at least?"

"Not here," Wasson said. "I had a note or two of hers, but they took them when I was brought in. But there's a lot at my room, if I could only get at them. I—"

"Why couldn't I get one there?" I said.

Wasson turned to face me fully and fastened his eyes upon mine. "Look here, Glace," he said. "You may be on the level. Heaven knows

I hope you are, and I want to believe in you; but I'd hate to give you leave to go poking around among Madeline's notes to me. They're personal, Glace. The poor girl put her whole heart into the things she wrote to me, and I loved her, and she's dead." He dropped his face into his hands and sat with bowed head.

I let him alone for a moment, and then I spoke. "I may be a reporter, Wasson, but aside from that, I'm a man. I'm not going to give your private notes to any curious public, if that's what you fear. Give me a line to your landlady authorizing me to enter your room and find one of those notes. It may mean your getting out of here; it may mean my success or failure in finding the guilty man."

The man on the cot raised his hand. "Give me your word not to publish the note, and I'll do it," he said.

"I've already done it, but I'll do it again," I promised. "Here, take this paper and pencil and write an order that will get me in."

I handed him my note-book and pencil, and he took them and began to write. Save for the faint-scratch of the pencil and his rather labored breathing, no sound filled the cell until he had finished, and then I rose.

"I'm going now," I said, rapping on the bars to call the guard. "I'll play fair about the note, Wasson, and as soon as I have any word for you I'll let you know."

I heard the guard approaching and turned to the cell door. "By the way," I said casually, "have you a scar of any sort on your left hip?"

Wasson whirled savagely upon me, his features writhing in a menacing scowl. "What if I have?" he cried.

"Shut up the noise," growled the guard, as he turned the key in the lock. "What's de matter with you, anyhow?"

"That man's a treacherous spy," Wasson fairly howled. "He's tricked me for his own rotten ends. Don't you let him out till I've got back what he took from me. Don't you let him out, I say!"

"Who're ye talkin' to?" demanded the official. "Say, looky here, my buck; you wanter sing small. Ready, Glace?"

I nodded and slipped through the door, which the guard promptly locked. "What d'yer get offen him?" he asked.

"A sample of his handwriting," I said, smiling, and the man with me laughed. "You reporters are sumthin' fierce," he chuckled. "I hopes yer never git nuthin' on me."

Back in the cell Wasson was yelling at the top of his voice. The words, half-choked by his rage, came faintly, but "liar and thief" was what they sounded like to me.

I lost no time in getting over into the district of "Furnished Rooms and Board," whither the address on the note Wasson had given me led me, and where I pulled a dilapidated bell and gave the note to a disheveled landlady, who read it, scowled at the signature, and told me to "Come in."

I accepted the invitation and followed her up a flight of stairs and back along the hall to the door of what was, I supposed, Wasson's room.

"You can go in and get what you want," said the woman. "Goodness knows, I don't care what you do as long as you don't write up my house. It's bad enough to have a lodger who goes and gets himself into disgrace of this sort, without having it all spread around broadcastlike. Everybody's talkin' about it to-day, an' Mr. Wasson always seemed a real nice young man, an' now to think I was harboring a murderer unawares.

"I've always tried to run a real respectable house, an' I guess this is going to do me a lot of harm, though how I was to know I really can't tell. Folks hadn't ought to blame me for it, as far as I can see. I hope, sir, you ain't going to make things worse."

I assured her I would not, and then passed into the room, leaving her still bewailing her hard fate. Wasson's note had told her to let me open his trunk, and this I now proceeded to do, and in the small side of the tray I found a bunch of letters tied with a string.

A glance sufficed to show me that the writing was similar to that of the note which had been found in the room of Madeline More. I have no excuse to offer for my next step, save that I am a reporter, and that I was on the trail of a sensational bit of news.

As a mere man, I would not have thought of doing the thing, but as a reporter the mere ethics of the situation had no place in my mind. I untied the string and let the letters fall loose in my hand, then I sat down on the edge of the trunk and proceeded to read them one by one.

The longer I read the more my interest grew, for, interspersed with the gossip of a woman to her lover, was mention after mention of the "Old Man," and again of "you know who." Always it was coupled with the mention of a sum of money running into large figures; the writer speaking as though she expected to obtain it from the problematical party to whom she referred in veiled style.

Evidently all this had not met with the full approval of Wasson, for the wording of the notes was at times an evident reply to a supposed protest of some attitude of the girl's, and at times a direct statement that she was capable of running her affairs.

I read on and on, until the landlady rapped and rather impatiently inquired if I had found what I sought I replied that I had, selected a couple of the notes, pocketed them, and returned the others to the trunk. Then I passed out, saw the woman lock the room door, and went my way, with a new bee buzzing in my bonnet, so to speak.

What had the girl been up to, from which Wasson had tried to dissuade her? I wondered; and who was the often referred to old man?

On the whole I felt elated. I had a sample of Wasson's writing, and I had an undoubted specimen of Madeline More's chirography as well. There remained Judge Barstow's note to verify, and I would have gained what I set out to get.

I pushed fate to the limit, and set out to see if I could find the judge. I decided to make the papers which I had found under the carpet in the girl's room my excuse, and when I reached his offices I sent in my card requesting a few minutes' interview.

After some delay the office-boy returned and led me down a suite of rooms to one at the farther end, where I found the judge. Again, as on the night before, I found him hatted and gloved, apparently just going out, but he waved me to a chair.

"I must ask you to be brief," he said.

"My errand will take but a moment," I explained. "Last night you spoke of leaving some papers under the door of the room in which Miss More lived in the Jason Street Hotel, I believe."

Judge Barstow was drumming with his gloved fingers on his desk.

"Well?" he inquired, as I paused.

"I found those papers, I think, judge," I went on, "and after examining them I can't see that they will probably be of any good to any one but you. To you they may be of importance, so I have brought them back." I laid them on the desk, beside which we sat.

Judge Barstow picked them up and gave them a casual glance.

"They are really of no importance," he said easily, "but thank you for your trouble, Mr. Glace, just the same. I suppose you mentioned finding them to the police."

I shook my head.

"No," I said, "I did not consider it necessary, as they could be of no possible importance in the case. Doubtless you have heard of Wasson's arrest. However, this brings me to the second part of my errand. I wish you would give me a line to state that you have received the papers, provided any questions should be asked."

"Hum!" Judge Barstow frowned. "Is that likely?" he said.

"Possibly not," I admitted. "Still, if any one else found out about it and they asked me what I had done with them, I'd like to be able to prove that I had done what I would say."

Barstow smiled.

"You're a cautious young man, Mr. Glace," he replied. "Oh, well, I suppose it can do no harm to do as you wish, since you have put yourself out to bring the things to me. Just a moment, if you please." He pressed a button, and my heart sank as a woman stenographer came in in reply.

"Miss Sutton," said Barstow, "kindly get me this at once: 'I hereby acknowledge the receipt of two legal documents'—take the titles from these papers—'from Mr. Gordon Glace, July 15th, 19—.'" He handed her the papers. "Write it at once and bring it to me," he directed. "I shall wait."

The girl withdrew, and we both sat waiting. I don't know of what the judge was thinking. As for myself, I was wondering if his mere signature was going to be enough for Dual.

"How much have they got on Wasson?" the judge inquired at length.

"Enough to send him up, I guess," I made answer. "That is, circumstantial evidence, of course. That's about all which will ever come out on this case, I think." Then I told him of the arrest, the watch and ring, and the other details of the case.

Barstow nodded at the end.

"Pretty strong. He'll have hard work breaking that, I fear," he remarked, and turned to take the typed slip which the stenographer just then laid before him on the desk. He glanced it over, picked up a pen, and wrote swiftly: "William Ferdinand Barstow," then handed it to me. "There, Mr. Glace, I hope that will prove satisfactory. And now if you will excuse me, I have an important engagement for lunch."

I bowed myself out and I went with a smile, for I had seen that the signature was in backhanded writing, and tapered toward its end.

CHAPTER VII.

THE COMMERCIAL LAND COMPANY.

MY UNUSUAL success in gaining all I had set out to obtain excited my own admiration. I walked down the street from Barstow's office mentally patting myself upon the back; and then I got an idea which seemed to me to be particularly good.

Barring his peculiar actions in bringing Dean and me down-town, alleging that he had to call upon a client, and then going directly home, he had apparently acted in good faith; but despite all that, I couldn't help feeling that he was holding out on me; that he knew more than he wanted to say.

Then, too, Wasson had said that he was not as straight, as people thought. Now it appeared to me that of the two men Wasson had talked more frankly, and surely his anger when he thought I had duped him was entirely genuine. Of course, Barstow's training in his profession would tend to make him close-mouthed, and I appreciated that fact; but despite all that I had what Dual later denominated a subconscious feeling that there was something behind his veil of suavity and apparent complaisance, which he did not intend me to ever find out.

In other words, the man didn't inspire me with a sense of either sincerity or trustworthiness. Perhaps, though, it was Dual's reading of his handwriting which impressed me so strongly; for more and more I was coming to believe in Dual's personality and the peculiar statements which he made.

All this resulted in my determining to make a visit to the courthouse for the purpose of looking up, if possible, anything of the judge's various transactions which might be on record there.

Personally I knew that from time to time various estates had been put into his hands for administration and adjustment; so in a way I knew what to look for, and acting upon the impulse, I took up my chase for facts along this new line.

A newspaperman learns to know a lot of people, and I was reasonably well acquainted around the city's legal center. So I had no difficulty in gaining access to the papers and records which I wished to examine, and plunged immediately into the task.

But there I ran up against a snag. It was easy enough to read the records, and to compile a list of the various estates in which Judge Barstow was taking or had taken an active part; but to an untrained legal mind it was next to impossible to trace the various windings of the several cases themselves.

One thing which struck me as peculiar, however, was the numerous instances where tracts of land, embodied in various estates, had been from time to time transferred by the administrator for sums patently below their actual value even at the time when the transfers were made, and later transferred again to a third party at a markedly advanced price.

This alone looked peculiar to me, novice that I was, and I wondered to myself if the several estates had profited by the advance price or not. Not only was this so, but in every instance the purchase and resale of the various parcels of land had been made in localities where its advance in value was practically a sure thing.

This set me off on a new trail. I began looking at the county records of real-estate transfers, using my memos of the tracts I had made as a clue.

In several instances I found here that the tracts after their advance sale had been assigned to the Commercial Land Company, and again sold by them at an advance of thousands of dollars. In other cases they were still the owner of choice locations in their own name; going back, I found that in these cases the land in question was all from estates which had been fully settled, and closed, so that in these instances the company's right of ownership was perfectly clear.

I shut up the books and bethought me of lunch. It was up to me to hurry, for my investigations had taken up a great deal of time, and it was nearly four o'clock. I suddenly developed a rush.

I went to a small café, and, perching upon a counter-stool, gave an imitation of the Irishman's household companion, the goat, by bolting an entire meat pie, pouring a cup of coffee over it, flinging a quarter to the cashier, and butting an incoming customer out of my way as I went out of the door. I had used up ten minutes of my time, and it was four-ten when I stood on the corner waiting for a car.

I had made up my mind to get up to the Fourth National Bank and see if Billy Baird was still working on the books. Baird was the orphan son of a former real-estate broker, who had died about two years before, and I knew him pretty well. In fact, Connie Baird was his sister, and had for some time shown a gracious interest in the newspaper world as typified by myself.

I had hopes, and Connie had intimated that I might go right on hoping, so I felt that I knew Billy pretty well. What made me want to see him particularly now was the fact that among the mass of estate matters I had been running over there was mention of the Baird name. I knew that it would be safest to approach Billy in the matter than any one else I had on the list.

I found him under a drop electric, for the day had turned cloudy, and back in the bank it was almost dusk, owing to the black clouds which were piling up in the west. He looked up and greeted me with a grin. "Hallo, Brother Glace," said he. "What brings you down this way? There's no shortage in our cash to-day."

"I just wanted to ask you what you did with your property which is now embraced in the Hyland Addition," I replied.

"I didn't do anything," said Billy. "I was a minor up to last year, you know. But if you want to know, it was sold."

"Then you haven't got it now?"

"No," said Billy. "I only wish I had. If I had I'd hold on to it, you bet."

"How'd you come to sell?" I inquired, as I lighted up.

"Well," said Billy, leaning back in his chair, "of course you know when dad died both Con and myself were 'infants,' as they call us at law. Judge Barstow administered the estate. Among other things dad left was this tract of ground which he'd got in on a trade. Barstow found a buyer for it and advised us to sell, and we did. That's about all there is to it, only I wish we'd held it. We wouldn't have to work in a bank now if we had."

"Who bought it?" I asked.

"A fellow named Jonathan Dobs Dohn. I never heard of him before or after, but he paid up all according to contract. Why?"

"Did you know that he afterward assigned the property to the Commercial Land Company, which assigned it to the Hyland Addition Company?" I asked.

Billy sat up as though thrown by a spring. "The deuce he did! Glace, is that straight?"

"Look up the county records. Who are the Hyland Addition

Company, Billy, do you know?"

"Barstow's their attorney, and he owns a big block of their stock. Oh, Lord! Do you suppose he bunked us out of that land?"

"What did you get for it?" I continued.

"One hundred an acre; one-fifth of what they're getting a lot. Say, is there anything we can do about it, Glace?"

"You'd have to prove intent to defraud," I answered. "Otherwise he'd claim to have acted upon his own judgment in good faith. After you had sold it, it was anybody's to buy. It looks shady, but you can't prove anything, I guess."

"Oh, but I'm sick," said Billy, half grinning. "Say, Glace, what are you going to do with all this?"

"Nothing, right now, Billy," I said. "I may use it, however, if I can flush the particular bird I think I'm after right now."

"I hope it's Barstow, the smug-faced old hypocrite," growled Billy. "Gee, if Con and me could have that ground now, she could keep a girl and I'd get a dress suit."

"How is Connie?" I demanded, with sudden heat as I thought of how the girl had been wronged.

"Sore on a bum reporter who don't even give her a call on the wire," said Billy. "Now, you get out of here and let me finish up, or she won't even have a brother left around the house."

I grinned and turned away.

"Say, Glace," said Billy, "why don't you marry the girl, and take Billy to live with you?"

I turned back and looked full into his grinning face. "Don't tell it to Connie, Billy, for I don't want her to know it till it's over, but that's just what I'm going to do, my dear little brother mine." Then I left before he threw the ink-well; for if there is anything Billy hates it is to be treated like a kid.

I went out and discovered that it had begun to rain, so I turned up the collar of my coat, and lit another cigarette. Then I suddenly kicked myself for a fool and looked at the clock. It was a quarter to five. I didn't hesitate, but held up a finger to a passing taxi, and told the driver to get me to the office of the Secretary of State if he had to smash all the speed ordinances in town. I had to get there by five, and time was short.

We started with a rush, and I wondered where my wits were that I hadn't waked up before. Billy's remarks had told me that Barstow had an interest in the Hyland Addition Company's affairs, and they had bought the Hyland tract from the Commercial Land Company, after Dohn had purchased it from the Baird estate, which sold it on Barstow's advice.

I must know who the Commercial Land Company was; and the Secretary's office would close at five o'clock. Well, I had to make it.

I felt that I must see the records to-night if I had to break in with an ax, and I made it, with a scant five minutes to spare.

I left my cab and rushed into the building and up the stairs, hurried to the office, and asked to inspect the records of incorporations, greatly to the annoyance of a clerk who glanced meaningly at the clock.

However, he got me the right papers, and I forgot all about him as I scanned their pages in my eagerness. The Commercial Land Company, I found, was an ordinary incorporation whose charter covered the general points of a land-holding and selling concern. This I speedily passed by.

What I wanted to know was who the incorporators were, and I cast my eye quickly over the page for what I sought. The company had been incorporated for one thousand dollars in shares of the par value, of one dollar each. Of these, John Brown, president, held one; Kitty Hicks, one; John D. Dohn, vice-president, one; Arthur Small, one; and the other nine hundred and ninety-six were held by the secretary and treasurer, Madeline More, the dead woman in the Jason Street hotel, the ex-employee of Judge Barstow, to whom he still took papers to be written up!

I almost gasped as I handed back the papers and hurried out past the scowling attendant, who was waiting to lock up.

Madeline More had practically been the Commercial Land Company herself. Undoubtedly the four other names had been dummy incorporators, holding each a share of stock which they doubtless assigned as soon as the incorporation was made.

Madeline More! I had hold of something. I had picked up another loose end of the snarl. I knew if I had any brains I could see where it led, but I was fagged. Madeline More was the Commercial Land Company, and she was dead.

Yet if she had been the company, where were the books which as secretary she should have possessed; there should be stock-books at least. Anyway, they were not in her room. We had found nothing of the sort in our search. Yet wait; there had been some small books among the mass of papers which the coroner's men had taken from the room. Perhaps there might be some sort of mention in some of them. At least I could see.

In almost a superstitious mood, I decided to try. Fate had been kind to me all day. I hurried down and got into my cab, thinking ruefully of the hole I was making in my money, and set out for the coroner's place.

All the way I kept thinking and thinking. Madeline More had been the Commercial Land Company; they had sold the Hyland Tract to the Hyland Company. Madeline More had been the employee of Barstow. Barstow was attorney for the Hyland Company. There was a connection, I felt sure of it, only I didn't have a speck of legal proof. Would I find it in the papers from the dead girl's room?

At the coroner's I found a clerk still in charge, and told him I wanted to see the papers brought in from the Jason Street case. At first he demurred, but after some little argument, I won my case. He dumped the lot before me, and went back to some papers which he was filing away.

I fell upon my spoil like a dog on a bone, but fate seemed to have deserted me at the last. I began to despair. One by one I ran through the mass of books, papers, notes, and documents to the bottom of the pile, until there remained but one little, soft, leather-bound book. Rather hopelessly I picked it up and glanced at the gilt lettering "Diary" on its back. I opened it and snorted in disgust.

It was filled with shorthand notations, interspersed with some figures and dates, and was as Greek to me. I was about to throw it down, when something else caught my eye. It was a letter-head of the Commercial Land Company, thrust between the book's leaves, and I paused and looked at the clerk. He was absorbed with his work.

I slipped the book into my pocket, picked up the rest of the pile before me, and carried them over to him. Then, with a final good night, and feeling pretty much like a thief, I got out of that room. I knew I ought not to have done it, but I was determined to have that book read to me by some one who understood shorthand. After that I'd try and slip it back some way.

I had a cup of coffee, and then hurried to the *Record* office, where I spent some considerable time writing up my story for the next day's issue, so as to turn it in before it was time to go to Dual. When I was done I carried my stuff to Smithson's desk.

Smithson looked up and greeted me with a bit of characteristic sarcasm. "Hallo!" he growled. "You working here?"

I replied that I was.

"Then why in thunder don't you come round once in a while?" he sneered.

I was tired, and his manner was offensive in the extreme, yet I tried to keep cool. "Didn't you get my note? I was out on this case," I said.

"Sure, I got your note," snarled Smithson. "Who told you to get out on the case? Since when have you been making your own assignments, I'd like to know? I sent you out yesterday because there wasn't anybody else to go. That didn't give you a mortgage on the story, did it, you cub?"

I blew up.

A seasoned writer doesn't like to be called a cub, and, as I have said, I was tired with two days' work and little sleep.

"Yes, you sent me out," I said, "and I turned in a story which even you said was good. I got onto a lot of new stuff about the case which needed chasing down. Just now I'm on the trail of one of the biggest things your little old rag ever stuck up in ink.

"That's why I went out this morning; why I worked all this day and most of last night. I'm going out again after a bit, and I'll come back when I darned please, and if I don't get you the biggest story you've had in a year, you can can me when I get back." I paused to get my breath.

And Smithson grinned. "I can can you now," he said.

I was still mad. "Go ahead and do it, then," I cried, "and I'll get the story for any one who wants to buy. I've got a big thing and I'm going to see it through. Why, right now I've got enough on a certain party to send him to jail, and I don't care what you do. I'm sick of your bullying, anyhow."

"Nice, respectful attitude you've got toward the C.E., ain't it?" said Smithson.

"Well, it goes as it stands," I asserted. I felt like a tired and cross little boy.

"All right," said the *Record's* city editor, turning back to his desk. "I guess you really mean what you say, so you're on. Go as far as you like, only if you don't make good on that bluff, Glace, it'll be the blue envelope for yours."

"I'll make good. You'll need about one page spreads for to-morrow night's story," I boasted, and set out to see Semi Dual.

CHAPTER VIII.
THE DIARY IN SHORTHAND.

ON MY way to the Urania I stopped in at the Y.M.C.A. night-school, and hunted up the professor of shorthand, who was a friend of mine.

To him I showed the little leather-bound diary, and asked him to translate some parts of it to me. He took it, smiling at what was to him my difficulty, opened it, and began to study it with an ever-increasing frown.

Presently he went so far as to give utterance to some expressions not at all suggestive of the Y.M.C.A. A moment later he handed the book back to me.

"It's shorthand, all right," he said, "but it gets me. If it's phonetic spelling, and it seems that it is, then it is written in the funniest lingo which I ever met. It's English, and it's not; it's Spanish, and it isn't; ditto as to Latin and Greek. What in the name of Sam Hill it is, I don't know. It may be a cipher; but it doesn't seem like that, either. It sounds as if it might make sense to a Chinaman with dago blood in his veins; but as for me, I pass."

"Then, you can't read it?" I asked.

"Not having an attack of *la grippe* and hay-fever at the same time, I am not fitted for the task," he assured me. "Where on earth did you get the thing?"

"I stole it," said I.

"Well, for Heaven's sake, take it back," he advised. "I should think you had troubles enough of your own. Just looking at the thing will keep me from sleeping tonight. Why, it would give even a new-spelling crank an attack of the pip."

I grinned, and put the book in my pocket.

"All the same, I'll bet there's one man in this town who can read it," I boasted, for it had suddenly occurred to me that maybe Dual himself could make the thing out. "If he can't, I'll have to give it up."

"If there is, he's a wonder. If he does, give him my regards," said my friend. "I thought the bunch of errors handed in by the class last night was going to be hard to correct; but, after that, the work will seem like play now."

"Ignorance will always find an excuse," I threw at him, and bolted for the door.

Semi Dual himself met me at the door of the tower, and we went back to his study. I threw myself into a chair, and Dual looked sharply at my face.

"You are a bit late; you have succeeded in your task beyond your expectation, and you are physically fagged out," he said. "Wait, and I will get you something which shall renew your strength."

"Never mind that," I said. "I've a lot to tell you, and we've a lot to do. The coroner's inquest is at two to-morrow, and I've got to get my man by then or lose my job."

"If you should go to pieces nervously, you'd lose your job equally, wouldn't you?" smiled Dual. "A moment spent right now will be worth a week later on, friend Glace."

I said no more, and he left the room, leaving me sprawled in the soft padding of the chair. Now that I had at last relaxed a little, I began to feel aching and sore, as though I had been beaten to a pulp. Every movement meant physical pain, and my lids drooped from the weariness I felt. I wondered idly, almost indifferently for the moment, if I could go on, and then I felt sure that Dual would find some way to keep me in the running.

Then I guess I dozed, for the next I knew Semi was shaking me gently and urging me to drink from a glass which he held in his hand.

Obediently I took it and gulped what it contained—some sort of aromatic fluid which warmed me through and seemed to build a very fire of energy in my veins. I sat up, and reached into my pockets for the various papers which I had.

"I've got a lot to tell you," I began, "only I hardly know where to begin. I've got all the notes you wanted, and a lot more facts as well. Wasson has some scratches on his hand, and corresponds to your description in a general way, only he isn't quite so tall, and his handwriting isn't like the note I brought you last night. Wait, and I'll show you."

I sorted the papers I had, and selected Wasson's order to the landlady, which I handed to Dual.

"There's something funny about the girl, too. Some of her letters indicate that she might be trying to extort money from some one;

then, too, Barstow's mixed up rather queerly in all this, and Miss More—"

"Wait," said Dual; "I have a fairly well-ordered brain, my dear Glace, but even it can only concentrate on one thing at a time. Let us first consider these bits of writing. We can then take up the other matters in turn."

He glanced at the note of Wasson's, and laid it aside.

"We can dispense with this; it is not of a criminal type. In that I cannot be mistaken. Now let me see the note or notes you found of Miss More's."

I handed him the two letters, and he opened them out upon the desk, glanced at them quickly, smiled in satisfaction, and, reaching for his magnifying glass, began to go over them word by word, line by line, while the involuntary pleasure of proven belief grew in his face.

At length he laid down the glass, folded the letters, placed them aside, and weighted them with a crystal tube. He leaned back in his chair, and turned to me.

"We are dealing with an unusual type here, Glace," he remarked— "one I have seldom been fortunate enough to find clearly defined. Under the glass the letters in the words of this letter are broken on the bottom curve. It can be seen clearly that the pen of the writer actually left the paper as it rounded the bottom of the letters, leaving a gap, well-nigh imperceptible to the naked eye, but shown clearly when magnified.

"Writers of this type are always innately criminal, though they may cleverly cover it up. Its significance is never of an ambiguous nature, and always indicates a person of monetary and financial unreliability. It shows most plainly in such letters as o, a, b, d, g, where there is a distinct loop at the bottom of the letter.

"Such writing in an employee should be absolutely damning, should he have anything to do with the handling of money or property, or any opportunity for double dealing in such affairs."

While he was speaking I leaned forward, well-nigh holding my breath. The writing he was describing was that of Madeline More, dead secretary of the Commercial Land Company, whose affairs I was positively convinced would not bear the light of day. When he finished I nodded acquiescence.

"All that only bears out my own later discoveries of the day," I said.

Dual smiled. "I am glad I gave you the reading before listening to what you know," he replied.

But I shook my head emphatically now.

"It is wonderful how you do it," I told him; "but I would have believed it, anyway. I think you have a convert in me, Mr. Dual."

More and more I marveled at the man's uncanny ability of tearing aside mere human veils and leaving men's souls bare.

I gave him the receipt I had got from Barstow, and he compared it with the note from the papers found under the carpet by Dean and me.

"They are the same," he pronounced, and laid them with the letters under the weight.

"Then," said I, "Barstow wrote the note, we found the other night, and left the papers as he said."

"So it appears," said Dual.

"And all you said of the original note applies to Judge Barstow as well?"

"Undoubtedly, Mr. Glace."

"Then, what inference do you draw?"

"I am not inferring," Dual affirmed, smiling. "I never speak unless I know. Suppose you tell me of the other things you mentioned finding out. So far, we have a dead person whose writing indicates unreliability as regards money, and a living one whose writing indicates the possibility of his being a thief with opportunity presenting. Let us see if there is any connection in the two cases. Tell me slowly, and tell me all."

"Connection?" I stammered. "Surely you can't think—"

"The story," said Dual, shaking his head at me. "When we are fully finished I shall tell you what I think."

He lay back in his chair, closing his eyes. "Go on—slowly—completely," he commanded, and I complied.

I told him every step of my day's work; of my visit to Wasson, and his words and actions; of my visit to Barstow, and of my trip to the court-house; of my interview with Baird, and my later trip to the office of the Secretary of State, and to the coroner's, and what I had found there. At the last I even told of my stopping at the Y.M.C.A., after my row with Smithson, and of my friend's failure to read the peculiar diary of Madeline More. When I had quite finished I stopped and waited for my companion to make the first remark. For some moments longer he continued to lie rather than sit in the depths of the chair, and I was wondering if he had really heard me through, when he began in a low tone.

"You did good work, Glace—very good work. I begin to see what it may lead to, this work of yours. Barstow could have organized this Commercial Land Company as a dummy holding affair, without letting his name appear at all. He could have used any of his office force, or any one on whom he had a hold, for his incorporators, giving each one a share of stock; then, with the More woman who was in his office posing as the head and main stockholder of the company, they could have incorporated; the dummy stockholders would assign their shares, and Miss More would assign hers also—in blank—and deliver the indorsed certificates to Barstow.

"Barstow could keep the books, and so far as any one knew he would have no interest in the land company, whose head would be Madeline More. With such a preliminary he could sell the lands of estates which he was administering to his phoney land company, and later through them to other persons or corporations, and, while bleeding the estates, yet remain completely covered himself."

"Wasson said Barstow was crooked when I saw him this morning."

"Did the girl tell him that?" asked Dual.

"So I fancy. He said she'd left his employ because she couldn't stand for some of the things she had to do."

Dual tapped the girl's letters. "It would appear from these that Wasson didn't approve of what she was doing," said he.

"What was she doing?" I asked.

"I would hazard the suggestion that she was trying to blackmail her former employer," replied Dual.

"For five hundred thousand?"

"Judging from her writing she was a person of large ideas," said Dual.

"But five hundred thousand—"

"Barstow is rated as worth several millions," Dual said, smiling, "and she was inviting Wasson for a tour of the Continent, you know."

"But would he give up that much, even to shut her mouth?"

"Evidently not," said Dual, "for Miss More died rather suddenly, I believe. Just how much evidence she had against him we don't know, but it must have been enough to send him to prison for a good long term. I believe you mentioned having a diary or something like that which you purloined from the coroner's office. Suppose we look at that, and see if it contains any facts."

I handed him the book. "It's written in what appears to be phonetic shorthand. Do you read shorthand?" I asked.

"Passably," said Dual.

"Well, Parker, at the Y.M.C.A., confessed himself stumped. He says it's in a language unknown to him, or else in a cipher code."

Semi Dual nodded slightly and opened the book. Presently he began to smile.

"Miss More was a lady of no small caliber, I gather from this," he said at length. "She chose a rather novel method of making her notations private by writing in a language which is but little known."

"Can you read it?" I cried in breathless eagerness, hitching my chair toward his side.

"Oh, yes," replied Dual, rather carelessly. "You see, it is written phonetically in Esperanto, which I speak rather well myself. Listen, and I will translate:

"This is a record of my daily doings as secretary and treasurer of the Commercial Land Company, into the duties of which position I have entered this day, September 1, 19—.'

"Really, Glace, you must have been working under a lucky star to-day. It looks as if we had our evidence here. Well, let's get on:

"'I shall keep careful note of all that I may do, or be asked to do, as I suspect that this company is nothing save a means to an end of the man in whose employ I now am.

"'He first mentioned the thing to me about a month ago. To-day he showed me stock-books and stationery already prepared, and at his orders I went with a certain party and filed papers of incorporation with the county clerk and Secretary of State. Nominally I am the chief stockholder, and the humor of that is that I haven't a dollar outside of my monthly check.

"'Immediately after the incorporation we dummies of the judge transferred our several shares of stock—namely John Brown, one share; Kitty Hicks, one share; J.D. Dohn, one share; A. Small, one share, and your humble servant, 996 snares—in blank to Barstow, who locked all the books and papers of the company in his safe. Me the Commercial Land Company? Oh, yes—not.

"'I fancy Barstow's up to some more of his shenannigan tricks. Well, enough of frenzied finance for one day. The old fox thinks he is covering his tracks pretty well, but he doesn't know of this record, and he couldn't read it if he did. Now, being a company, I shall close this meeting and retire to my bed. I wonder if this company will do much business. It's crooked, of course, but what's the answer, I don't just see. I will later, no doubt.'

"The next few pages are of no importance," said Dual, after looking them over briefly, "but this ought to interest us:

"'I'm wise to the real cause for my being a company, at last. To-day we bought a lot of property from the Edwards estate. Barstow is administrator for the estate, and he advised them to sell to us. Of course he did; it's a good buy at the price they got.

"'Shortly afterward he made overtures of sale—beg pardon, we did—to the Gordon Real Estate Company, and I guess the deal will go through. This little land company is merely a rake to pull the judge's chestnuts out of the fire, and keep his lily-white hands unsmudged. Great work! Honest, I'm afraid the old man is getting altogether too smooth for his own good.'

"Well, that's enough of that," said Semi. "It surely warrants our suspicions. Let's see if we can find anything bearing on any other part of the case."

Running the leaves over rapidly, so rapidly that I wondered at his remarkable ability to read the stuff, he finally began to read again, without comment of any sort:

"'July 10, 19—. I have broken with the old man at last. I may be a willing tool of his crookedness in the affairs of the Commercial Land Company, especially as he was liberal in dividing the profits at times, but that is no sign that Judge Barstow owns me, body as well as soul. I have not liked his attitude for some time, and to-day I finally told him I would leave.

"He blustered a good bit, and I told him frankly that if he went too far I'd expose his whole get-rich-quick scheme. I never saw him so angry before. He even went so far as to threaten to kill me if I ever gave him away. Of course I don't fear that, as I am perfectly able to take care of myself, but he was so rattled by the mere threat on my part that I am wondering how much it would be worth to him to keep me still. I can imagine a situation where it might possibly pay me to have been an incorporated company after all.'

"There we have it," said Dual. "Glace, you've got the whole thing here in your hand. The More woman evidently meant to use this book as evidence in case Barstow didn't pay what she asked. Maybe she'll tell us more. Wait a bit."

Once more he gave himself to a study of the leaves. Once more he paused, nodded, and started to read:

"'According to the tabulated deals in the back of this little tattle-tale book of mine, Barstow has stolen well-nigh a million on various deals in which I have helped him in one way or another. Now, if anything ever went wrong, I suppose he would have tried to make me the goat. As I have helped him to make the money, it seems to me that no one should know more about it than I, yet the judge refuses to see it that way. Well, time alone will tell.'

"So," said Dual slowly. "Let's have a look at the back. Ah, here it is. Well, well, well. Miss More surely had a logical head. Everything she did, every transaction, sale and purchase, is here set down with its dates. I guess that is all that we need to make our case. Here, Glace, take this book and hold on to it as though it were pure gold."

"She tried to blackmail Barstow, and he resisted," I said as I took the little book.

"Do you suppose he could have had anything to do with her death?"

"It was a case of two criminals of a similar bent, who fell out. One threatened to expose the other. In such a case we may look for almost anything."

"But would Barstow stoop to murder, Dual?"

"You remember, I told you he didn't mean to kill until his hands were on the woman's throat. Suppose you find out about what size hand the coroner's physician thinks made the marks on the girl's neck."

"I'll do it," I said. "Of course, then we'd want to know the size of the judge's hands."

Dual nodded. "Quite right," he said. "Also we ought to know if the judge has a scratch or so on his hands, and as a matter of interest I'd like to know if he has a scar on his left hip."

"The trouble is to find out all that," I said.

"Didn't you see the judge to-day?" questioned Dual. "Didn't you notice his hands, or was he wearing gloves?"

"As a matter of fact, he was gloved. He said he was just going out to lunch. He was gloved, when Dean and I saw him last night, too."

"Do you know any one at the Harmon baths?" Dual inquired.

"I know Joe, one of the rubbers, pretty well," I answered. "Why?"

"Because," said Dual, "that is where the judge is spending the night. I took the pains to find out before you came up tonight. If the judge has a sore hand or a mark on his hip, Joe might be able to tell us, don't you think?"

"I believe he would," I made eager answer. "I once helped him out of a rather nasty hole."

"Suppose you call up and find out," said Dual.

I reached for my hat. "I'll go to a phone and be right back," I said as I rose.

Dual shook his head, opened a door in the side of his desk, and took out a desk instrument, which he extended to me. "Use this one," said he.

I took it and looked at the man in amazement. "Do you think of everything?" I demanded. Dual only smiled.

I called up the baths, and after a bit of a wait I got Joe. I told him who I was, assured myself from his statement that the judge was actually there, and then preferred my request.

Joe listened carefully, and after a bit he laughed.

"That's funny," said he. "I've rubbed Barstow hundreds of times, and I know he's got a red sort of birthmark on his left hip all right; all we fellows here knows that. What gets me is what it is to the *Record* if he has got a sore hand. He has, all right, though, if you want to know. There's some scratches on the back of his left fin. He told me he got them tryin' to make love to his wife's long-haired cat. Don't give it out that I piped it to you, but you're in straight on the facts."

"All right, Joe," I said in a voice which trembled. "I'll see you pretty soon and make this right. For the present, thanks."

"Forget it," said Joseph, and hung up the phone.

I turned to Semi Dual and met his quizzical smile. "He has both the scratches and a scar on the hip," I said.

Dual merely nodded and continued to smile. "Tell the coroner to subpoena Judge Barstow to the inquest," he said.

"Dual, did you know all this all along?" I cried.

"What I knew was of little importance. What you needed was the legal proof. I have tried to help you get that. Knowledge such as mine does not stand at law nowadays, Glace.

"But to prove to you that it is genuine, I will make a prediction which you must never reveal; or, at least, not for a long time, and I shall put it in cryptic form:

"That which is done is done, and that which is about to be done will occur, for the law is that a man soweth what he shall reap. Like unto Jezebel shall the mighty be crushed and fallen; justice shall be done to all parties and no man shall have blood upon his hands, for only the guilty shall suffer, and they shall wreak vengeance upon themselves. Yet shall the law be upheld, and the penalty exacted, in an unexpected way. You don't understand me now, but at twenty minutes past three to-morrow afternoon, my meaning shall be plain.

"You will go to the inquest. You will tell the coroner that you have important facts to relate. You will insist upon relating them in your own way. You will tell a hypothetical tale and show this book of Madeline More's as proof of the tale. You can have the notes and papers as well. You must find out the physician's estimate of the time the girl had been dead when found, and the estimated size of the hand of the man who choked her. I think that is all."

"You are sure?" I half stammered, almost shaking with my suppressed emotion.

"I am sure," said Dual, "for the stars do not lie. To him who can read, they are an open book. You are tired, Glace; go home and get your rest. See me tomorrow night, and tell me what you feel like telling. Above all, do not doubt anything I have told you. Good night."

CHAPTER IX.

THE INQUEST.

THE CORONER'S office was on the seventh floor of the Mcintosh Building. It was here that the inquest was set for two o'clock. I was pretty busy the morning before, picking up the few remaining ends of my case, but nothing to compare with what was the afternoon of the day before.

First, I called up the coroner himself and had it arranged to subpoena Judge Barstow for the hearing. Then I got the coroner's physician and had him give me an estimate of the probable size of the hand, from the finger-marks on the throat of Madeline More. He was of the opinion that the man probably wore a number eight and a half or nine glove and I made a note of that fact.

Then, in a spirit of pure bravado, I went to the *Record* office and left a note on Smithson's desk telling him that I would have my story ready for him not later than half past three. I chuckled at what the old man would think and say when he read that note.

Afterward I found out that his remarks were not complimentary to me at all. However, when I learned of the fact, I didn't care, for the relations of Smithson and myself had completely changed, and it was he himself who told me of what he had said.

At a quarter of two I went up to the inquest room and waited while the scene of the inquest was set. The police, firm in their belief that Wasson was the man wanted, had arranged to add a touch of the dramatic, by having the body of the girl placed in the room, where he was to be confronted with the supposed evidence of his work, at the critical moment when he would be called upon to testify.

Wasson himself, handcuffed and watched by a couple of officers, was in another room, waiting the assembling of the other witnesses and the coroner and his men. The coroner's physician was sitting over by an open window.

Jepson, manager of the hotel, was there also. The chambermaid who had found the body was present in an overdressed, fussy manner. Johnson, the policeman who had arrested Wasson, was smoking a stoical cigar. Even the elevator-operator in the hotel was sitting in awed silence, apparently divided in his mind between half-frightened interest and a desire to run away.

Shortly after I had found a seat, Jimmy Dean, of the *Dispatch*, came in and dropped down beside me, grinned in friendly fashion, and lit a cigarette. The coroner and his stenographer entered sharp on the stroke of two. Everything was in readiness save the presence of Barstow.

The coroner waved his hand to a couple of attendants, and the body of the dead girl was wheeled into the center of the room, and partly undraped, so as to exhibit the marks on the throat. I was beginning to feel nervous, yet I need not, for at that moment, Barstow entered.

He took his seat quietly, and nodded to the coroner.

Now we were ready to begin. I kept my eyes fastened on Barstow. Just as he entered and saw the body, where it lay on its trestles, I fancied that he gave an involuntary start. Now, however, though I watched him closely, I could detect no evidence of nervousness in any action of the man. He had removed his hat, and was sitting apparently at ease, if one could judge from appearances, almost indifferent to what was going on.

One thing, however, I did notice, with a little swelling of my throat. Although the day was so hot that every window in the apartment was widely opened, Judge Barstow had failed to remove his gloves.

The inquest opened with the chambermaid's testimony of the finding of the body in the locked room. It was substantially what I have already given, and brought forth no new details. The coroner's jury listened to a mere repetition of what they had read in the papers, and the questioning of the witness was brief.

Yes, she had found the body, by looking over the transom. She had done so because she had rapped repeatedly and could not gain admittance, and thought it queer. Yes, the window was certainly open when she looked in first. She had immediately given the alarm to Manager Jepson himself.

The witness was excused and Manager Jepson took the stand.

He had conducted the Jason Street Hotel for two years and had never had any trouble before. The deceased first came to the hotel as a tenant one year ago. To the best of his knowledge she was a stenographer by profession. She had apparently made her living by her work. She always paid her rent promptly, and he had considered her a desirable tenant in every way.

She had few callers. One was a young man of about twenty-eight or thirty, and he described Wasson in a general way. Judge Barstow had been the other most frequent caller at her apartment. He came on business, so he understood.

Several eyes glanced at Barstow, but he sat unmoved. The chambermaid had notified him of seeing the body and he personally had seen to the entering of the room and tried to get the police department on the phone. Owing to some mistake he got the office of the *Record*, and they had then sent the police.

"Were you present at the arrest of the man Wasson?" the coroner asked.

"I was," said Manager Jepson.

"Was he the man you have described as calling frequently upon the deceased?"

"Yes, sir."

"How did he act?"

"He appeared confused, and when we attempted to make the arrest, he fought the officer until he used his stick upon him several times."

"The chambermaid's notification was the first you knew of the matter. There had been no noise or disturbance during the night or day before that time?"

"No, sir. Everything had been quiet as could be. Apparently no one had heard a sound."

"That will do," said the coroner, and Jepson moved aside.

"Billy Timmins," droned the clerk, and the elevator-boy arose, gulped once or twice, and held up his hand at the order of the clerk.

He was visibly pale, and I doubt if he heard the reading of the oath, for he stood with uplifted arm long after the clerk had ceased his jumbled formula; in fact, until the coroner put the first question to him.

"Are you Billy Timmins, my boy?"

"Yes, sir."

"Work in the Jason Street Hotel?"

"Yes, sir."

"Did you know Miss More?"

"Yes, sir. She was a nice kid, too."

"Did you ever take Mr. Wasson—the man who was arrested, up to see her?"

"Yes, sir, lots o' times."

"Did you on the night before she was found dead?"

"No, sir."

"Sure, Billy?"

"Yes, sir."

"Do you know Judge Barstow?"

"Yes, sir."

"Do you see him here?"

"Yes, sir, he's settin' over there," said Billy, pointing to the judge.

"Did he ever go to see Miss More?"

"Yes, sir."

"Did he go to see her on the evening of the day before she was found dead?"

"Yes, sir."

"Did he see her?"

"I don't know. He said he didn't, when I took him down."

"Just what did he say, Billy?"

"He said he didn't see her and had left some papers for her under the door. He asked me to tell her when she came in."

"Did you tell her?"

"No, sir, I didn't see her."

"Now, Billy, when Mr. Wasson came in on the afternoon after the girl was found, how did he act? Think carefully."

"Why," said Billy slowly, "he acted just like he always done. He got in the cage. First off I was goin' to tell him, 'cause he seemed to be feelin' good an' was whistlin', but I didn't. I kept my trap shut, an' he got off on Miss More's floor, same as always, an' I went down an' told Mr. Jepson that he had come in, an' he went back up with me, an' they pinched Wasson after a scrap."

"Did you take any one else up to Miss More's on the night she was killed?"

"No, sir, I didn't."

"All right," said the coroner, "that will do."

Johnson was next called, and described his arrest of Wasson.

He stated that his prisoner had fought hard to make his escape, and that he had found it necessary to strike him repeatedly before he had submitted to arrest. He had come down the hall to the door of room ten, and had not noticed the officer until he was quite at the door. Then he had paused, glanced quickly at Johnson, and asked if anything was wrong.

"I thought," said Johnson, "that he seemed quite nervouslike. I told him the girl was done for, an' he acted like a crazy man, so that I told him to shut up. Jes' then Mr. Jepson come outer the cage and gave me the 'office,' an' I told Wasson he was pinched. He didn't take my word for it, so I had to convince him that I knew what I was talkin' about."

The officer grinned.

Two officers from the precinct station next testified to the finding of the watch and ring on the prisoner, together with several notes from the girl, written during the last week of her life.

Wasson was next called, and was led in between his two guardians, and after being unmanacled was placed in the witness-chair. The man was pale and showed the marks of worry and anxiety.

His hands trembled and there were great circles under his eyes. As his glance fell upon the body of the girl he actually shrank and cowered in his chair, and put up his hands to cover his face.

"You are Reginald Wasson?" the coroner began.

Wasson merely bowed.

"You knew Madeline More well?"

"Very well, indeed," Wasson almost whispered his reply.

"You were engaged to marry her, I believe."

"Tacitly, yes."

"What do you mean by tacitly?"

"It was agreed between us. Nothing had been said. I was taking her an engagement ring the day she was found dead."

"Indeed?"

"Yes, sir. It had been one of my mother's rings."

"And it fitted Miss More's finger without alteration, I suppose?"

"Yes, sir, it did. I know it doesn't seem probable, but it is the truth."

"We have heard of the ring," said the coroner; "also of the watch." He fastened his eyes on Wasson closely at the words.

Wasson shifted. "Yes, sir, it was hers, she gave it to me to—"

"Wear?" cut in the coroner. "Do you expect us to believe that? It might do if she were alive, but you had it after her death."

"I'm telling you the truth," cried Wasson, visibly losing his control. The evident attitude of suspicion of those about him was plainly affecting the man's nerve.

"Mr. Wasson," said the coroner, continuing the examination; "at the time of your arrest you had several notes from the deceased upon your person. In those notes she speaks of a sum of money, and of a certain party whom she designates as the 'old man.' What was the deceased trying to do? From the tenor of the notes we are led to believe that it was something of which you did not approve. Are we correct in that view?"

"I would rather not say," Wasson replied hoarsely.

"Was it blackmail?" the coroner shot at him quickly, without giving him time to collect his faculties.

"I refuse to discuss it," said the man doggedly, moistening his lips with a nervous tongue.

"Your refusal will influence the case against you, Wasson."

"I can't help it. I can't answer." The man was apparently ready to collapse.

I moved over to the coroner's side, and leaned forward to attract his attention. "Ask him what size glove he wears," I said.

The coroner nodded. "Oh, Wasson," he said carelessly, "what size glove do you wear?"

It looked for the moment as if the question would terminate the man's ability to contain himself. He grew pale as death, his eyes darted toward the dead woman's throat, and then he dragged his gaze back to us. He trembled, opened his mouth, and failed to make any articulate sound.

Finally, he did manage to speak, and his voice was one of utter horror. "Oh, Heaven, are you trying to convict me like that? Do you think I'd kill the woman I loved? Is there no justice among any of you?"

"That will do," said the coroner. "What size glove do you wear?"

"Nine," said Wasson, and dropped his face in his hands.

The coroner motioned to the two guards, and directed them to get their prisoner out of the chair. "Take him over, and see if his fingers fit the marks," he ordered, and leaned back in his seat.

Half walking, half dragging, Wasson was taken over to the side of the body, and requested to lay his fingers on the purple marks on the girl's neck. He rebelled.

Fairly shrieking, in his now hysterical condition, he fought to evade the ordeal which the coroner had thrust upon him in this unexpected way.

"I'll not do it! I'll not do it! I'll die first!" he cried, struggling to tear away from his guards. "You brutes, you brutes! Let me out of here! I didn't do it! I swear I didn't do it! I loved her, I tell you. We were to be married. I won't fit my fingers into those marks!"

Fighting savagely now, he was literally dragged forward; and while two men held his arm, the hand was applied to the girl's throat. The coroner, who had risen and gone over, nodded his head, and the police smiled knowingly at the result, for the fingers and the marks fitted even as cause and effect may fit.

Manacled again, Wasson was half carried away by his guards. Actually, I believe that if it had not been for the sustaining hands upon him the man would have collapsed into a pitiful heap of sobbing manhood upon the floor.

The coroner's physician next took the stand, and stated that, in his opinion, the woman had been dead some twenty hours when found. Death had been due solely to strangulation.

He called attention to the finding of the bits of cuticle under the girl's nails, and to the fact that, in his opinion, the marks on the hand of Wasson might have been caused by her frantic clawing at his hand in her last few minutes of life. He was excused. Judge Barstow was called. He rose and sauntered smilingly to the chair, took the oath with dignity, seated himself, carefully arranged himself in the chair, and waited for the coroner to begin.

"Judge Barstow," said the official, "did you know Miss Madeline More?"

"Yes, Mr. Coroner," said the judge. He looked about the room and barely stifled a yawn.

"Was she employed by you?"

"At one time, something over a year ago."

"Why did she leave your employ?"

"She thought she could do better by doing special work, I believe."

"Yet she still did work for you?"

"Oh, yes, at times."

"Did you see her the night before she was found dead?"

"No; I went to see her, but could get no reply to my knock."

"Did you leave some papers in her room?"

"I thrust some under her door."

"What became of them?"

"They were found and returned to me."

"By whom?"

"A reporter on the *Record,* a Mr. Glace."

"What had been your relations with the deceased?"

"Those usual between an employer and the employed, I believe."

"There never was any trouble?"

"No."

"Why did the reporter return the papers to you rather than give them to the police?"

"They were of no importance to the police—at least, so Mr. Glace said, when he brought them to me."

"What time did you call on the particular night when you left those papers under the door?"

"Somewhere around eight," said the judge.

"I will excuse you for a moment," said the coroner. "Mr. Glace, take the stand."

Judge Barstow went back to his seat, and I rose and occupied the chair he had just left. The clerk administered the oath, and then I leaned forward and addressed the coroner direct.

"Mr. Coroner," I said, "I am going to prefer a somewhat unusual request. I desire to be allowed to tell my own story in my own way. If at the end of my testimony there shall be any points which you desire to have cleared up, I shall then gladly add anything to my narrative to make all clear."

I had given the coroner an inkling of my course before, and he nodded his acquiescence. I glanced at the clock. It was five minutes past three. Even as I began to speak I thought of Dual's prediction, and realized that a scant fifteen minutes now remained until that prediction must be fulfilled or proven false, but I never doubted that it would be verified.

I began to speak rapidly, however, as I saw how short was the time.

"I will be brief," I commenced. "I shall give my testimony in the form of a hypothetical case.

"Some two years ago a certain party—a woman, whom we will refer to as M.—was employed in this city by a man who did a large amount of work in his profession. Among the other duties of his profession, he was frequently appointed to act as administrator of various large estates. This woman M., while nominally a stenographer in his office, came to act pretty much in the part of confidential secretary to this man.

"This man formed the idea of organizing a land-holding and selling company, and, with the aid of this party M., he did organize it, and had it incorporated with her name as principal stockholder, together with four other dummy incorporators. After it was incorporated, the woman M. and the other four stockholders assigned all their stock to this man, in blank, and the man kept the certificates and all of the company's books.

"By using the make-believe company as a blind, the man was enabled to fleece the estates he was administering out of huge sums. All went well until such time as the man who had led the woman into financial turpitude presumed to endeavor to lead her into physical shame as well, when a rupture of their otherwise friendly relations occurred.

"She left his employ, and sought other means of making a living after that. But, you see, this man had trained her in business immorality, and, as a result, she conceived the idea of making herself financially independent by forcing him to give her a part of their unlawful winnings. In other words, she tried to blackmail him.

"He resisted, but finally they arranged a meeting for a certain night at which they should come to terms. They met. Instead of agreeing, they quarreled; he sprang upon her and seized her by the throat—he had once before threatened to kill her, it seems—and began to choke her to death.

"They struggled, and the woman fought desperately for her life. She reached up and dug her long nails into his strangling hands, seeking to break his grasp; but, instead, all she accomplished was to tear the skin from his hand—the left one—I think—in three places. She could not break his grasp, and she died.

"I have all this, save the last part, in black and white in a book, Mr. Coroner. May I now ask that you order the two officers from the precinct in which this dead woman here was found to remove the gloves from the hands of Judge William Barstow, so that we can see the scratches on his left hand? Also, after looking at the gloves, see if they do not fit the marks on the throat of Mad—"

A confused sound in the back of the room interrupted my further words. Judge Barstow sprang from his chair and rushed to the door. It was locked.

In frantic haste he tore at the knob, jerking and twisting it with all his power until the door creaked and groaned from his frenzied efforts; but it held fast until the officers fell upon him and dragged him backward, still fighting with all his massive strength.

For a moment it seemed that he would tear free from the hands which held him; then Johnson went to his fellows' assistance, leaping straight up and flinging his weight upon the struggling man's back.

The entire four went down in a heap, from which the officers presently crawled, still holding to their captive, upon whose wrists they had slipped a pair of handcuffs, so that he rose and stood panting and bound, like a lion, captive yet unsubdued.

The room was in a turmoil of confusion.

Even Wasson's two guards had left their prisoner and half crossed the room, when the judge was dragged erect. Now, while one of them returned to Wasson, the other crossed and, at a nod from the coroner, stripped the gloves from Barstow's bound hands.

There, in plain sight, burned the angry lines of three deep lacerations, running diagonally across the back of the left.

I lifted my voice, and spoke in the hush of surprise and consternation which followed. "What size is the glove, officer?" I cried.

The man looked at the piece of dressed kid which he was holding. "It's a No. 9, Mr. Glace," he replied.

I turned to the coroner. "Shall we try the test of the marks and the fingers?" I suggested, nodding toward the body of Madeline More.

But Barstow had suddenly regained his control. It was he himself who answered, instead of the man I addressed.

"It won't be necessary, Glace. In the words of the police, I am caught with the goods. I admit that I killed the girl, but she deserved to die. I must compliment you upon your almost devilish cleverness in running me down. The funny thing is, I didn't suspect your motive, and I felt safe, knowing our police as I did. Mr. Coroner"—he turned and addressed that official—"your inquest can come to an end, for I am ready to confess. I killed Madeline More, and I shall pay the penalty in my own way."

Even at the last no one suspected.

So quiet and calm had been the man's words that none of us dreamed of the thing seething in his brain; but on the last word, having lulled us all to a false sense of his acceptance of things, he gained his end.

Even as the last word left his lips, he tore free from all restraint. In a leap and a bound he crossed from the door near which he stood; and as his captors stared in uncomprehending inactivity, he reached an open window, seized its casing, and turned.

So, standing like a giant, he faced the room once more, and for a moment he smiled at how he had fooled us at the last; then, *"In my own way!"* he cried loudly, and plunged backward into space, to become a huddled heap of blood-oozing clothing on the pavement below.

As the others rushed to thrust heads and shoulders out of the windows and look down, I glanced at the clock over the coroner's desk.

It was three-twenty flat!

I rose from my chair and sprang to a telephone which I saw standing upon a corner of the coroner's desk, and begged wildly for Smithson on the wire.

"Smithson, Smithson!" I called. And again, as his gruff accents came to my ear: "Say, Smithson, hallo. This is Glace. Say, Smithson, go out to my table and open the drawer. In it you'll find the story I promised you for three-thirty to-day. It's all written up so as to lead up to the denouement which has just occurred. Judge William Barstow confessed to the killing of Madeline More and committed suicide by throwing himself from a window of the coroner's office at three-twenty this afternoon. Did you get that? Say, Smithson—hallo!"

For a moment I thought he had left the wire; then I got my reply. In accents unlike any which I had ever heard him use before, Smithson spoke to me.

"Great work," he said. "We'll have it on the street in half an hour, or wreck the plant. And say, when you get done down there, come right up here; I want to see you, Glace."

They took the manacles off Wasson and told him he was free. He came over to me, and put out his hand and tried to thank me, choked up, and turned away. I appreciated how he felt, shook his hand, and let him go.

Jimmy Dean felt quite cut up over my having the only real story of the affair. "You held out on me shamefully, Gordon," he said; "but I suppose, in your place, I'd have done the same." I gave him the true facts, and he left to write up the story for the *Dispatch*.

The coroner got his jury together, and it took them about a minute to return a verdict that Madeline More came to her death at the hands of one William Barstow, deceased.

I put on my hat, lit a cigarette, and prepared to depart. It was four-fifteen when I left the coroner's office, and already the newsboys were yelling the *Record's* extra on the streets. I walked up toward the *Record* office, feeling all the elation of any true reporter over a clean "beat."

I entered the local room, sat down at my typewriter, took off my hat, and began to pound out my story for the morning's edition.

Smithson stuck his head out of his door. "Glace," said he, "com'ere."

I got up and went into his office. He stuck out his hand.

For a moment I gazed at this unprecedented mark of friendliness, half comprehending; then I took the proffered hand with what I hoped was a becoming grace.

"Glace," said Smithson, "it was a great beat. We've got the whole town. I confess I didn't think you had it in you, but I hope I know when to quit; and I want to say now, that it's one of the best, if not the best, things I have seen put over in a good many years.

"I've taken it up with the management, and I'm glad to say they look at it as I do. I fancy they'll show their attitude on the matter in your envelope this week. I suppose you must have known all this yesterday when we had our little mutual love-talk, eh?"

"I was morally sure, but I didn't have the proof."

From below came the sound of the newsboy's crying the *Record's* beat.

"Uh-uh," said Smithson. "Heavens, what a beat! Well, son, you made good all right, so I'll have to keep you on." He smiled a crooked smile. "But, Glace, it has just occurred to me that I sent you on an assignment a few days ago, and you have not turned in a line on it. What about that man Semi Dual?"

For a moment I didn't know just what to say, and then I thought of what Semi had told me to do.

"Mr. Smithson," I said, "I went up there all right. He's taken the tower of the Urania, and is engaged on some scientific experiments. He forbade my printing anything about him, and after thinking it over, I don't see that there is anything for a story. I've been so busy on this later case that I forgot the other till just now." That, as it happened, was true.

"Well," said Smithson, turning back to his desk, "I'm inclined to let your judgment stand, after the way it has seen you through in this later case, as you call it; so we'll let the matter drop. Now, go out and get busy on your full story for to-morrow." I turned away.

"And, Glace—" I turned back as he addressed me. Smithson was smiling his crooked smile once more. "Go as far as you like," said he.

THE SIGNIFICANCE OF THE HIGH "D"

CHAPTER I.

UTTERING A FORGERY.

I WAS sitting in the "dog-house," as we jokingly called the reporters' room at Police Central, when they led Sheldon in. I had known him personally for some years in a casual way, because he was the paying-teller in the Fourth National Bank, and there was where Billy Baird, my prospective brother-in-law, worked over the books.

Consequently, when the motor patrol stopped and they brought him in and lined him up before Harrington, it gave me a sort of shock.

He was a clean-cut chap, with a strong, good-featured face, the latent strength of which struck one at a glance. Now he was very pale as he stood between two roundsmen, while Harrington wrote him up in the blotter, before sending him to a cell.

I edged up as close as I could, and pricked my ears to get the charge against him. It was "uttering a forgery" against the bank where he worked, and noticed that Sheldon actually flinched at the words, almost as though they had been a physical blow.

He closed his eyes for a moment, and then raised his head with a visible effort, as though deciding that after all he might as well brazen the thing out.

"Who's makin' th' charge?" asked Harrington as he finished writing it down.

"Cashier Malin, for the bank," said one of the roundsmen, and Harrington nodded his head, as he resumed work with his scratchy pen. A moment later he nodded in dismissal: "All right. Take 'im back," he said.

They were turning away when Sheldon caught my eye, and for the instant, as I nodded toward the poor devil, his expression cleared and gave way almost to one of hope. He spoke to one of his captors, who turned and looked at me.

"Oh, hallo, Glace," he said grinning. "Sheldon here wants to slip you a word or two. Come 'ere."

Rather wondering, I approached, with a nod to the officers, and waited for what the prisoner might say. It was surely brief and to the point.

"After the rest are done with me, come and see me," was all he said. Then he turned away and went back toward the cells.

I watched him walk away straight-backed, head up, then I slipped into, a phone-booth and called up Smithson, my city editor on the *Record,* and told him my little tale.

"There's something more to it than appears on the surface, and I want you to put somebody on the story of the arrest, and let me stick around Sheldon a bit."

That might have been a risky thing to say to Smithson at one time, but some time before I had won my spurs on a difficult case, and now the old man was my friend. As it was he chuckled before he yielded the point.

"All right," said he briefly, "I'll let Grant handle that end of it; get busy and dig up something good."

I left the booth and ostensibly the station, but I only went as far as the corner drug-store, where I hung about for a half-hour and then slipped back and approached Harrington with a grin.

"Did you hear what Sheldon said to me?" I inquired.

"Uh, huh," grunted Dan, smiling. "You'll be wantin' a turnkey, I suppose?"

"You're a good guesser," I countered. "Have a cigar?"

"I will, and so will me brother," said Harrington, and I handed him two, for that was our stock joke, on occasions like this. He pounded a bell, and turned me over to the officer who answered.

"Front," he cried in imitation of a hotel clerk. "Show the gentleman back. Wants to see Sheldon, Jake."

Jake and I took up our journey rearward to where the corridors of the receiving prison began their dreary rows, and he passed me through the gates with a word to the guard, while he turned his own back to light another of my cigars. A few moments after, I was at Sheldon's cell, and he rose as he saw me at the door.

"It's good of you to come, Glace," he greeted. "Excuse the appointments and take the stool." He seated himself upon the bunk at the side of the cell.

"I hardly know why I asked you to come," he continued, "unless it was that I felt the need of talking to some one, and I knew I could trust you, because young Baird has told me you were about the best in your line. Now, don't think that's said for any reason except that it is true. As for myself I don't know you personally at all, though I do by sight, of course.

"Anyway, I took the fancy to tell you all about this thing as far as I can, and first there are some parts of it which I must ask you to treat as confidences, rather than as anything for your paper; that is, if we are to talk."

"I'll try to respect your confidence, Sheldon, wherever I can," I assured him. "Here, take a cigar, and let's get down to facts."

"Thanks." He lighted the cigar at my match.

"To begin with, then. Some time ago there was a check passed through our bank for the sum of five thousand, which I believed to be good, but which later came back declared a forgery, so that our institution, which had cashed it, was naturally left with a loss on their hands.

"On the day that the check came back the assistant cashier was out and I performed his duties. The funny thing was that several similar checks, similarly indorsed, had been cashed at intervals, and as far as I could see, the signature was genuine. If it hadn't been for that, I would have been more careful than I was.

"Anyway, when I found that the check was a forgery, I did a foolish thing. Instead of reporting it at once, I began to juggle accounts so as to cover the matter up, and, in the mean time, I tried to find the man who had cashed the thing, in the hope of recovering the money or squaring the affair up somehow or other; I guess I hardly knew how.

"Then came the bank examiners, and, of course, the thing came out. In view of what I had done, I was suspected, of course, and as a result Malin had me brought down here.

"Worst of all, the writing on the blamed check resembles mine, or they say it does—yet I swear I never touched the thing save to pay out the cash."

"Is that all?" I asked as he paused for a minute and resumed puffing on his cigar.

"No; worse luck," said Sheldon. "There's more, and the confidential part. Nobody knows this but Myrtle and myself, and you've got to keep it to yourself.

"Glace, I'm engaged to be married. That's the reason I wanted to see you. I want you to go to see the girl. She's an orphan, and she's got a brother, and the brother's a poor sort. Some time ago he got into trouble, and it looked as though he was going to land where I am. Myrtle told me about it, and I agreed to help her out.

"Some time ago I sold some stocks which I held, and I got the money for them in large bills, and put them into my safe-deposit box. We bank people aren't supposed to dabble in stocks, by the way, so I didn't say anything about that.

"Well, when Myrtle's brother got into trouble, I went and got some of that money and gave it to her, and she squared things for the kid. As it happens, I did that on the day after this check was cashed, and the vault attendant remembers seeing me with the stuff in my hands after I had come from my box, and also states that they were bills of large denominations.

"Of course, I gave them to Myrtle and she paid the kid's debt, so that I can't trace them, or prove that they were other than what was paid out from our bank, and I was seen with them the day after; get that?"

"It looks bad," I remarked.

"It is bad," Sheldon replied. "Nobody knows it better than I; but what can I do? I can't drag Myrtle into this, and I won't; I'll go to the 'pen' first."

"That would be rather rough on her, too, wouldn't it?" I said.

Sheldon winced. "Don't," he said. "What a hole I'm in! Either way I look, it is bad. If I should tell this part of things, and drag Myrtle in, I'd have to expose her family secret, you see. If I keep still, I'll probably be sent up for five or ten years, be a convict at the end, and ruin all our hopes that way, too, and I swear I'm an innocent man, Glace. Man, it's tough."

"I don't doubt it," I said.

"But my story?" said Sheldon. "The one I've got to tell to the jury?"

"It's as full of holes as a Swiss cheese."

"Then what am I to do? That's really why I sent for you, Glace; it was the hope that you, a trained newspaperman, might be able to find some way out of the *impasse,* I am too upset to think of any myself."

"Do you know the man who forged the check?" I asked of a sudden and watched Sheldon's face.

He paled visibly, and finally shook his head. "Not unless I saw him," he said.

"Maybe the one who presented it didn't forge it," I suggested.

"Maybe," agreed Sheldon, with what I thought was relief.

I decided to change the subject. "About this brother of your *fiancee's*," I asked. "What do you know about him?"

"He's wild," said Sheldon. "Runs with a pretty fast set. Some years ago he ran away and went West. Now he's back and works in the office of Pearson & Co., the brokers.

"Where he went in the West he would never say, nor what he did, so I guess it was not very savory, whatever it was. Some time ago he took some of the firm's funds and speculated and lost. That's what Myrtle needed the money for—to make good his embezzlement."

"Hum— And his name?"

"Archie Parton," said Sheldon. "He lives with his sister at Number 1351 Welton Street."

"What was the amount of money you had in the safety box?" I inquired.

"Five thousand dollars." Sheldon shook a disconsolate head.

"How much did you give Miss Parton?"

"One thousand."

"How?"

"In two bills of five hundred each."

"Do you know their numbers?"

"I can get them. I have a memorandum."

"Then you have four thousand still in the box. If you know the numbers of the notes which went to cash the check, you ought to be able to prove that those are not that money, shouldn't you?"

"Yes," said Sheldon, "but how could I prove that there was no exchange made?"

"I don't know," I confessed. "Were they changed?"

Sheldon looked at me sharply. "You certainly do go right to the point, don't you?" he said. "Well, Baird told me that."

"Well, were the original bills changed?"

"Who could change them?" Sheldon laughed, and I felt sure that his laugh was forced.

"Look here," I said. "There's no use in your holding out on me, you know, if you expect my help. Who changed those bills?"

"I did," said Sheldon, and lapsed into silence, puffing gloomily on the cigar.

I looked at the man in amazement. Either he was a consummately guilty man, or he had acted in a way little more sensible than the doings of an irresponsible boy. Finally, I decided to go on with my questions and learn what I could, at least.

"Why did you do it?" I asked.

"As an accommodation," said Sheldon. "That was before I knew the check was forged," he added as an afterthought.

"As an accommodation for whom?" I snapped. The man's manner was getting on my nerves.

"That I can't tell you, Glace," said Sheldon. "To do so might make people very near to me suffer more than I care to think."

"Meaning Miss Parton and her brother, of course?" I put in.

"Perhaps," said Sheldon. "I really don't know. Anyway, I won't talk about that phase of the case. I'd rather take a sentence than go into that."

"And you're mighty apt to get the chance, unless you change your mind," I said as I rose. "By the way, I want a sample of your handwriting. You won't object to my having it, I suppose. What was the name signed to the check? Suppose you write it down for me."

"No," said Sheldon, "I don't see that that can do any harm. What do you want to do with it, anyway, Glace?"

"I want to compare it with the forgery on the check. There may be sufficient difference to give us a plausible leg to stand on, which we haven't got now."

"Have you got a bit of paper about you? They've stripped my pockets," said Sheldon, putting out his hand.

I handed him some copy stuff from my pocket, and he spread the pad on his knee and rapidly wrote a line across the top sheet, after which he returned the copy-pad to me. I thrust it into my pocket, and rapped for the guard to let me out.

Then I turned back to Sheldon where he sat.

"Ordinarily," I said, "I'd think your tale a mighty fishy one, indeed, but I know your record and I know you're a friend of Baird's, and somehow I believe there's nothing worse about it than that you've got in bad. I'll see Miss Parton and explain things to her, and I'll try to do all I can for you.

"Anyway, I'll be back and see you when I need to talk to you again, and I'll be able to tell you all the news at that time. In the mean time, keep your nerve and a close mouth. Now I'm off."

"Good-by," said Sheldon, rising. The guard unlocked the cell door and I left the prison with one of the nicest little snarls to unravel which I had ever met.

CHAPTER II.
COLONEL MACDONOHUE SHELDON.

WHEN I got outside I took the pad of copy-paper from my pocket and read what Sheldon had written and what purported to be the name signed to the forged check as written in his own hand; and for just a moment, I think I doubted my own eyes.

"Colonel MacDonohue Sheldon" was what I read or seemed to read.

For a moment I stared at the thing and then I began to see a great light. Just what were the facts about Dick Sheldon's family, I didn't know, but from his reticence I half imagined that this might explain some of that same unwillingness to talk about the check.

That the paying-teller of the Fourth National feared that Archie Parton, brother of his *fiancée,* was mixed up in the thing, was to me quite evident. Now it appeared that the forgery had been made upon some one of the same name as Sheldon; perhaps a relative of Dick's.

Anyway, I made up my mind to have a look into the thing. So the first thing I did was to get hold of a telephone and call up several of the better-class hotels, such as I fancied would be affected by a man who customarily indorsed his checks "Colonel," which was a courtesy title, I had no doubt.

After some little trouble, I managed to locate him at the Kenton, together with the further information that he had gone out immediately after lunch.

I thanked the office and made my way to the hotel as fast as I could; because I knew Jeffrys, the day clerk, and had hopes of learning something about the man I was trying to find. I approached the desk in the foyer, and told Jeffrys I wanted a word with him, and then I asked him what he knew about MacDonohue Sheldon; and he grinned in my face.

"Pretty speedy old boy, the colonel," said Jeffrys, "Looks like he might come from Kentucky, though the register says "Goldfield, so we'll let it go at that. He belongs to the champagne crowd, all right. Wears an electric search-light for a shirt-stud, and a broad-brimmed hat. Smokes nothing but maduro Havanas, and kicks because they aren't strong enough. Carries a bigger roll than is safe, and gives dollar tips to the boys. Oh, we all know the colonel, all right."

"Been here long?" I inquired.

"Long enough, but not too long," said Jeffrys. "He's a rather good sort, though pretty broad in his ways for this part of the map."

"What's his line? Do you know?"

"Do I know?" laughed my acquaintance. "Well, it's no secret. Everybody knows it five minutes after he's met Colonel Mac, as he calls himself.

"He's in the mining game both ways from the jack. He can talk for an eight-hour shift and never turn a hair or take a long breath. Carries a bunch of ore specimens in one pocket to balance the roll in the other, and recently he's been bucking the market pretty strong."

"In mining stocks?"

"That's what he says. He's been a bit worried lately, I think. Somebody played a variation or something which the colonel didn't expect, and he got run pretty close. He told me to-day that they nearly got him, but that he'd pulled through and expected to take his winnings to-day—'cash in' was what he said."

"Do you happen to know where he is right now? I'd like to get hold of him this afternoon, sure."

"What do you want with him?" Jeffrys wanted to know.

I laughed. It was evident that the colonel was standing in with the day-clerk, all right.

"I won't bite him," I assured him. "I just want to talk to him a bit about a little newspaper yarn."

"Well," said Jeffrys; "I guess you'll find him over at Pearson's office. He told me he was going over there to clean up his deal and take his profits. Asked me to have the manager hold a private banquet-room for him to celebrate in to-night, and asked me to come to the big blowout, so I guess you'll find him over there up till about four or five."

"Thanks. I think I'll look him up," I told Jeffrys, and walked out of the hotel.

I knew where Pearson & Co.'s offices were located, and I set out for the brokerage company at once. The more I heard of the redoubtable Colonel MacDonohue Sheldon the more I wanted to meet him face to face.

Another thing which caused me a momentary interest was that he had been dealing with the same firm of brokers for which Archie Parton worked.

Already I could see several threads in the case, any one of which might cross at any time, and I began to feel an interest which I believe is common to all newspaper men and detectives as well—the elusive delight of following the trail, tirelessly, persistently, until it leads to the figurative "kill."

The firm of Pearson & Co. occupied offices similar to any number of others engaged in the same business. There was the board-room, with its blackboard along one wall, the marker, his head strapped into a telephone receiving device, scampering up and down its length like a spider trailing a spun thread.

A few customers lounged in the chairs and eyed the quotations chalked up with expressions of hope, dismay, disgust, or indifference, as the case might be.

These were the petty fry. I was too old a hand to expect to find my man here. Therefore, after a glance at the gathering, I beckoned to a small, uniformed page, whispered my inquiry into his impertinent ear, and saw him disappear into the background of mahogany partitions, from which a distant buzz of voices now and then penetrated to the outer room.

As I waited and listened, there boomed out above the sound of lesser phonations, a single, blatantly confidant tone, which rose like the rumble of thunder above the diapason of a wind. Someway I felt that I had listened to the voice of Colonel MacDonohue Sheldon, and then the voice suddenly died.

Immediately one of the doors opened again, and the voice boomed forth. "What does he want, bub, anyway?"

"He's a newspaper man," came the reply, in the treble of the page.

"Well, tell 'im to sit down, an' wait," rumbled the voice in easy indifference. Then: "I tell you, Pearson—" The door was closed.

The page approached, but I shook my head and smiled. "I think I got the message, Cerebus," I told him, and I took a chair. "That was the colonel, wasn't it, that just spoke?"

"It sure was," said the boy. "An' say, he's all to the mustard. He gimme a dollar just now."

"There's another one waiting for you if you want to earn it," I suggested, and watched the light grow in his eyes.

"Want it; eh?"

"Does a Dutchman like wieners?" he replied, grinning. "I'm hep; whatjer want ter know?"

"Does Archie Parton work here now?"

"Sure he does. He's a runner," said the boy. "An' say! He uster know the colonel a long time ago. The colonel was tickled to death to find him workin' here.

"That's how he came to trade here, an' it put Arch in good, landin' the colonel's trade, cause the old boy's some sure sport when it comes to playin' a long chance. He made a winnin' to-day for fair."

There it was again. The colonel was evidently a confirmed gambler. More and more I wondered what relation he might be to Dick Sheldon of the bank.

Well, that was what I was here to find out, and I continued to sit and wait. I handed the boy a dollar, which he pocketed with a grin as "easy money"; drew out some copy-paper and appeared to be making some calculations from the figures on the board.

Ten minutes later the door in the partition was banged open and the colonel himself appeared. On the instant I felt added interest in the man.

He was about five feet ten inches tall and heavily built, wore a gray business suit and a brocaded satin vest, across which was looped the strands of a heavy gold chain; and was smoking a panatella cigar as black as a bit of tarred rope, cocked rakishly in one corner of his mouth.

His face was florid, his eyes gray, and he wore a mustache cropped to a short and aggressive length. His mouth was large and thin-lipped, and his chin that of a fighter.

Under the broad Stetson, which he had rammed upon the back of his head, his hair was flecked with gray. At the door he half paused to call back to the man inside.

"Well, so-long, Pearson; I guess they thought they had me, but I sure got their goat. See you to-night sure. It's going to be some swell feed."

Then he turned to face the front room. "Where's the gink that wanted to see me?" he inquired.

I rose, and seeing me, Sheldon approached.

"Want to see me?" he asked. "Have to excuse me for keepin' you waitin', but I been showin' these fellers how to play their own game. Cleaned up a cool fifty thousand to-day, an' a few days ago it looked as if I was sure bust. Naturally I'm feel-in' a bit good.

"When a fellow's down to his last chip an' draws an ace full he's liable to want to celebrate a bit. I don't know what you want, and I don't care. Let's go somewheres where you can shoot your load in peace.

"What yer say yer name was? Glace? All right! Come along, Mr. Glace, an' have something with Colonel Mac."

Overwhelmed by language, I allowed myself to be led off by the arm and didn't fully recover until we were seated at a small table in a near-by thirst-parlor, with the colonel still running smoothly along.

"Yes, sir, fifty thousand bucks for Colonel Mac. Pretty good, eh? An' ten days ago I was as good as broke. Well, I just kept raising the other fellow and after a while I raised him clean out. Say, I'm going to give a swell feed down to the Kenton to-night to celebrate. I think you said you was a reporter, didn't you?

"Well, you come down to the blowout. It's my party, an' I'm sure going to have one good time. I can afford it, I reckon. Fifty thousand dollars can stand that, I guess."

If the waiter hadn't appeared I imagine he would have been talking yet; but he did and it served to distract the colonel's attention. I seized my chance. "Colonel," said I, "are you any relation to Richard Sheldon of the Fourth National Bank?"

"Am I any relation?" said Sheldon, stopping with his glass half raised. "Oh, no, none at all. His mother and father just happened to be mine also, that's all. He's my brother. Why?"

"He's your brother?"

"Sure! Anything wrong with that? He's my brother, and I'm proud of Dick. He's a comer, that kid is. Worked his way up from office-boy to payin'-teller, an' I betche they make him assistant cashier after a bit. Whenever the assistant takes a day off, they put the kid on his stool now."

"You'll lose that bet about the assistant's position, Mr. Sheldon," I said.

"Hey?" said the colonel, as if doubting his ears. "Say, looky here, Mr. Man; whatjer mean by that? Nobody can't knock Dick to me an' get away with a whole skin. Why, darn it all, he's my brother, an'—"

"Now just a minute, colonel," I interrupted. "Let's understand each other." I met his belligerent glance and held his eye.

"Dick Sheldon may be your brother, and if he is, I'm glad to learn the fact; but from the way you talk I don't believe you know about his arrest."

"Hey! Hold on! What's that?" cried Sheldon, setting down his untasted glass. "His arrest? Say—are you tellin' me Dick's, been pinched?"

"He was arrested just after the bank opened this morning. I've just come from him at the city jail."

"Well—my Lord," gasped the colonel. "Did Dick tell you I was his buddy?"

"He did not."

"Then howdje find it out?"

"I'm a newspaper man," I reminded him with a smile.

"That's so," he said, frowning. "Well, blast it all; ain't that rotten? What did they grab him for?"

"They say he passed a forged check on the bank."

"The fools," sputtered Sheldon. "Don't they know the kid better'n that? Dick never done it, an' I'll gamble on that."

"Somebody did," I told him, "and it was signed with your name."

"Eh?" The colonel grew purple in the face.

"So that's it, is it? Well, that's right. Somebody did try that game a while ago, an' I said it was a forgery myself. But how in time can they get Dick on that?"

"He cashed the check."

"Well?"

"He covered up the report on the forgery."

"Well, the darned fool. What did he do that for?"

"I don't know," I replied. "I thought maybe you would. I'd like to find out."

"Well, I don't; you can bet on that, an' I thought Dick had better sense, the poor cub."

"You don't know anything about its then? I hoped you did."

"I know somebody tried to forge my name," said Sheldon, "an' that's all."

The waiter hurried up in response to a signal from Colonel Mac. "Get me one of them automobile hacks."

"A taxi, colonel?" said the man.

"I want anything that'll get me over the ground fast," howled the colonel, "and I don't give a cuss what you call it, you get it here."

"Arrest Dick, will they?" he continued as the man turned away.

"Well, I guess not. I'm goin' up to the jail and see your constable or sheriff or whatever you call him, an' fix that. I'll have the kid outen that 'fore night. Guess I can give bail.

"I suppose money talks here same as with us out West, an' I got it on me now. Say, Glace, come along with me while I bail the kid out. He don't sleep in no jag-house, while I'm in town. We'll go up an' get him right now."

I shook my head.

"I'm afraid there will be a bit more red-tape to it than that, colonel," I replied. "However, I'll be glad to go with you and introduce you at headquarters, and get you in to see Sheldon. Then you can arrange to give bail, in due form."

Sheldon pulled on his hat, threw the waiter a dollar tip, stalked toward the door and, crossing the pavement, climbed into a waiting taxicab. A few moments later we stopped at the Central Station, and I took him in and introduced him to Dan.

Harrington listened to the colonel's tirade and then shook his head.

"On Glace's say-so we'll let you see Sheldon," he said. "As for bail, he'll have to have a preliminary hearing, and after that you can arrange it with the judge. Do you want to see him now?"

"You can gamble on it, jailer," roared the colonel. "I want to see Dick in an almighty hurry, an' I don't give a darn for all your red-tape or whatever you call it. I wish this was out in Goldfield, and I'd show you how I'd get the kid out."

Harrington smiled, winked at me, and rang for a man to take the irate westerner back. Then Sheldon turned to me.

"It's been mighty kind of you, Glace, to get me in here," he said. "I'm a stranger in a strange land here, all right, an' I sure am proud to have met up with you. Now I'm goin' to try your kindness a bit more. I know you're a reporter an' crazy for news, but I want to see Dick alone. Come down an' see me at the Kenton, an' if I can do anything for you, let me know."

Well, I had hoped to be in on the brotherly interview, but I saw it wouldn't do. I couldn't afford to push things, and I must avoid exciting the colonel's suspicions in any way, so I had to make my bow as best I could and withdraw.

All the same it was with the feeling of missing something important that I saw him follow his guide back to the cell-house. Then I turned away from the station.

CHAPTER III.

SOME DISCOVERIES.

I WALKED away from the police station, turning over the facts I had gathered, and after a bit I got hold of a phone and called Smithson up. I explained all that had happened, assured him that I felt there would be big developments in the case, and got his permission to handle the thing in my own way.

Smithson seemed to agree with me that there was a good-sized nigger in the woodpile somewhere, and laughingly told me to dig him out.

"You can bet Sheldon knows more than he's saying," he said after I finished my report. "He's trying to shield some one, and for a guess I'd say it was the person who actually cashed the check. Do you know who that was?"

"Not yet; I'm trying to find out."

"Got a line?"

"I think so, but just now I'm not at liberty to mention names."

"That's a nice shape for a reporter to get himself into," jeered Smithson. "I thought we employed you to get news, not to run a confidential bureau; still, I guess you'll have to run things to suit yourself, in your usual way." And he hung up his phone.

I laughed to myself at Smithson's joshing and decided to go and see Sheldon's sweetheart, though I confess I shrank from the task.

Maybe it was because I was pretty fond of Connie Baird and imagined how the little girl would feel if it had been me instead of Sheldon and I hated to go to Miss Parton. Still, I don't think it was all that, for though I was a newspaper man, and saw a lot of the seamy side of life, yet I always tried to keep a little of the savor of romance in my life. That and ordinary human kindness; and I never have been able to see women suffer without a little grip coming in my throat.

I boarded a Welton Street car and got off at Thirteenth Street and walked up the block. No. 1351 was a small brick cottage set back a ways from the street, with some roses blooming along the walk which led up to the front door.

It looked homey and cozy, and I hated worse than ever to bring sorrow within its walls. Still I had promised Sheldon, if for no other reason, and I went up on the bit of porch and rang the bell.

A moment after the door was open and I was raising my hat to the girl herself. Then I felt still worse.

She was sweet. That is the only word I can find to describe her, and come anywhere near doing justice—just simply sweet. She had blue eyes, and real golden hair, a little straight nose, and a warm red mouth, and—oh, well, I had to admire Sheldon's taste in girls.

"Miss Parton?" I inquired.

"Yes." She smiled.

"I was asked to see you by a mutual acquaintance. May I come in?"

"Of course," said the girl, stepping back from the door, which I entered.

She took me into a pretty little front living-room and gave me a chair. Then she took another and sat easily waiting for what I might say. There was nothing of embarrassment about her attitude, rather it was one of polite attention. I began to hope she would bear the thing well.

"Miss Parton," I began, "I am Mr. Glace of the *Record*. I was asked to see you by Mr. Richard Sheldon of the Fourth National Bank. Have you seen the evening papers; may I ask?"

The girl looked a bit puzzled at my awkward introduction, then she smiled again.

"If Mr. Sheldon sent you I shall accept you on faith," she said. "Mr. Sheldon and I are very good friends. As for your question, I have not seen the papers as yet."

"Then the hardest part of my errand remains to be gone through with," I blundered along. "Miss Parton, Mr. Sheldon was arrested to-day at half after ten."

For just a moment I thought the woman before me was going to faint. She turned deadly pale and closed her eyes, and sat so while one might count ten.

Then her breast rose in a great sighing inhalation and she opened her eyes and looked me full in the face, pressing her lips close together in her effort at control. Let me tell you, I admired her a lot, right then.

After a moment more she opened her lips for a question.

"For what?" she asked.

"He is accused of forging a check," I said bluntly, because I didn't know how to put it any softer, and I had to tell.

"The check—" she began, caught her breath, and turned from white to red in an instant. "The check was really a forgery, was it?" she completed her sentence at last.

But I had caught the change of intention and I knew she hadn't meant that at first. It was almost as though some certain check had been in her mind when she started to speak.

However, I appeared not to notice and replied to her question: "So it seems."

"Where is he now?" said the girl.

"At present he is in the city jail. I believe parties are arranging to give bail."

"Have you seen him?"

"He asked me to come here."

"Of course," she said, and lapsed into silence, knitting her brows. Finally: "I must go to him," she said.

"I don't think he would wish that," I began, when she interrupted me quickly.

"Did he say that?" she asked.

"No," I admitted; "but to be frank, he told me of your relations, and told me he hoped that you would not be drawn into this thing in any way. That is quite natural, I think."

For a long minute she sat looking down, her fingers locking and unlocking in her lap.

"Poor boy," she said at last.

I saw that I had bungled things in good shape, and used the very argument best suited to take her to Sheldon's side as quick as she could go. I knew Sheldon didn't want that, and I had only one card to play to offset the error I had made.

"Miss Parton," I began again, "I guess I must tell you all the story. You see, Sheldon told me about the little matter of money which occurred recently in regard to your brother. It's as much for his sake as anything else that he wishes you both to keep completely out of this."

"Then you know about Archie?" said the girl in a low voice.

"Just what Sheldon told me—about the thousand dollars," I replied.

"Mr. Glace," said Miss Parton, "my brother is weak. I don't really believe he is vicious at heart; but he is foolish and easily led. I am sure it is nothing more than that."

"Mr. Sheldon merely told me the main facts," said I.

"Did he seem to think that Archie might be dragged into this case?"

"I think he feared it," I hastened to admit.

"And he thought it would be better for me to stay away?"

Well, I couldn't lie to the girl. "He didn't really say," I confessed, "but don't you think so yourself?"

"I don't know what to do," she said slowly. "I want to go to him. The question is, what would be best? But let me tell you Dick Sheldon never forged that check. He's the soul of honor.

"If such a thing can be, he's foolishly honorable. I've seen him do things almost quixotic, because he thought it was his duty to act as he did. That sort of a man doesn't forge checks."

"Not as a rule," I said, smiling in an endeavor to lighten the tension of the thing.

"Who could have done it, do you suppose?"

"I know little about it," I replied. "Presumably the man who issued it, or the one who cashed it—the one man may have done both."

"Then," said she, brightening, "that lets Dick out. They surely must know that he didn't write the check."

"But you see, Miss Parton, Sheldon very foolishly tried to cover the thing up."

"Yes," agreed the girl, "that was foolish, I suppose."

Again she had indicated that she had some knowledge of the matter. I wondered if Sheldon had talked it over with her, or how she knew.

"I suppose he hoped to be able to straighten it out, though I don't just see how," I threw out.

"I'm afraid he was trying to protect some one at his own risk. It would be like Dick," she said.

"The man who cashed the check?" I inquired.

She glanced at me quickly, and asked a question in turn.

"What would they do with that man, Mr. Glace, if they knew who he was?"

"They'd arrest him, I suppose." Again Myrtle Parton shivered and closed her eyes in that way of hers. It was as though she shut out all the visible world when she strove for self-control.

"And if they don't find the man who cashed the thing, they'll be almost sure to send Dick to prison—won't they, Mr. Glace?"

"It certainly looks bad for him," I had to admit.

"But if the man who cashed it were known?"

"If he were known, and could prove where he got the thing, or if he were to be proven guilty himself, it would probably let Sheldon out."

"What is the probable sentence for a thing like that?"

"Five or ten years," I answered, and was sorry the moment after that I had been so frank. Myrtle Parton swayed in her seat so that I half rose to my feet; but she waved me aside.

Then she herself rose and began to walk back and forth across the floor, back and forth, back and forth. Now and then she clenched her hands where they hung at her sides, and after a bit I became aware that she was repeating one word over and over as she walked.

"Dick—Dick—" breathed the girl, half whispering, half sobbing the words.

I didn't say a word; just sat and watched the girl fight her battle and wished I could do something to help her, yet couldn't think of anything to do or a word to say.

Back and forth, back and forth she paced across the room, and finally came back to the chair she had left and sank into it, pale and shaken, yet dry-eyed. She had not raised her voice or shed a tear. It is such grief which hurts.

But not until later did I fully realize what she had been through; what had been the question she had asked herself, and found the answer for, while she paced the floor of the little room. She sat down, and presently she looked me full in the eye.

"Dick Sheldon trusted you, Mr. Glace," she said slowly, "and I know he had a reason for that. I shall do likewise, and place the welfare of mine and myself in your hands. Come here and let me whisper to you for a moment, for if I should say the thing aloud I feel that I should scream.

"I know who cashed that check, and I am going to tell it to you, after you first promise me to divulge it only for the purpose of saving Dick Sheldon from conviction for something of which he is as innocent as myself. Will you promise me that?"

I bowed my head in assent, rose, and went over to where she sat. I put my ear down close to her lips, from which the rosy color had fled, and she whispered a few words as I bent before her, then motioned me back to my chair.

"Now you will leave me, I hope, Mr. Glace," she said. "I want to be alone, to think, to plan what to do. I may go to see Dick, and I may not. I shall decide that after a bit. If anything more happens, I hope you will let me know."

I rose and picked up my hat. Then, bidding her keep her seat, I found my way out and down to the street and caught a car.

I was full of mingled emotions, and hardly saw what I was going to do next. I had learned the name of the man who cashed the forged check, and I could understand Dick Sheldon's attitude; but I was bound by a promise which I held too sacred to break, and I couldn't see what good such information could possibly be to a reporter on the quest of news.

Then I thought of Colonel Mac, and all at once I decided that I'd stop at the Kenton and look him up. Anyway, I had a bid to his banquet, and so I'd just drop in and see what he had done toward getting Dick out of jail.

When I inquired for him at the desk, Jeffrys, who was still on duty, pulled a wry face:

"Didn't you see him to-day? If you didn't, I'd advise you to let him alone tonight. It seems that this Sheldon who was arrested to-day was a brother of his, and Colonel Mac's been raising merry blazes about it ever since. He's like an old bear whose cub's been stung by a bee. All he can do is to wish it had happened in Goldfield, so he could go out and get somebody's scalp."

"I know all that," I told him. "Is the colonel in?"

"Sure he's in," said Jeffrys. "Want to go up?"

"That's what I'm here for," I answered.

Jeffrys banged a bell. "Here, boy! Take Mr. Glace up to Suite B," he commanded and grinned as I turned away.

The boy showed me up and knocked on the door.

"Come in! Come in! And for Heaven's sake stop that darned pounding! I'm no blushing maiden of forty," bawled a voice.

I pushed open the door and passed into the room. I found the colonel in his shirtsleeves, suspenders down, a palm-leaf fan in his hand, and a long glass by his elbow; the inevitable cigar stuck into his mouth.

"Oh, hallo, Glace!" he greeted. "Come to the party? Well, it's all off. I'd be celebrating with my brother in jail now, wouldn't I? Well, now you're here, sit down. I was just thinking of chasing you up.

"I want you to do something for me. The ways of this town get on a man's nerves. Gosh, but I wish this was Goldfield, and I'd have Dick right here with us now. But here? Oh, not at all.

"'Judge,' says I, 'I'm Colonel MacDonohue Sheldon,' I tell him.

"'H-m,' says he— 'yes, yes. To-morrow at eleven, Mr. Sheldon, I think.'

"'But I want to get him out now,' I says.

"'Really, Mr. Sheldon,' says his honor, 'we must do these things in proper form.'

"'I don't give a darn for form—I want my brother,' I tells him, an' he gets as red as a tomater, an' won't say a word. Now, what do you think of that?" The "colonel" paused to drain his glass.

"Then the hearing is at eleven to-morrow?" I got in in the interval.

"That's what that pompous old billy-goat told me," said Sheldon. "Gad, but he made me mad!"

"I don't see what you can do about it," said I.

"I can't do anything—that's what makes me mad," said the colonel; "but there's another thing. To-morrow I'm going down to their little old bank and see this Malin party, and offer him his little old five thousand if he'll drop the case against Dick.

"Five thousand! What's five thousand to me if it will save Dick's hide? Not that he ever done the thing; but these folks back here will do anything for the cash, and I reckon I can get 'em to forget they lost anything if they get it back, an' I want you to go along."

"I don't hardly think they will listen to you at the bank," I told the colonel. "They might even try to make out that you were compounding a felony."

"Is that so?" howled the colonel, chewing viciously on his cigar. "Let 'em try that, an' they'll find they've got a fighter by the tail. But not them, Glace. They'll grab the coin and padlock their jaw. You'll see. Will you go along?"

"Oh, I'll go, and gladly," I assented, "and I only hope it does some good."

"How was your brother feeling this afternoon?" I asked as I resumed my chair.

"Like thunder," said the colonel very promptly. "What could you expect?"

"It's my idea he's shielding some one," I hazarded, and the colonel turned and bored me with a glance.

"That won't make no difference after tomorrow," was all he said.

"I saw his *fiancée*, Miss Parton, this afternoon," I went on.

This time I drew fire.

"His *fiancée!*" gasped Sheldon. "Say—is he engaged to that Parton girl? Heavens!"

"She's very much cut up," I vouched further, without appearing to notice his words.

"Darn it all—what did he want to get stuck on her for?" said Sheldon. "But say, I'm glad you told me. Now I know what's the matter with the fool kid."

Things were getting interesting. I had felt the end of another strand of the snarl, and decided that the colonel would be a good man to watch.

I arose.

"Meet me at quarter to ten to-morrow," said Sheldon.

So I left him, and went back down-stairs.

CHAPTER IV.

THE OCCULT DETECTOR.

I LOOKED at my watch as I was leaving the Kenton foyer, and saw that it was nine o'clock. I decided to get a bite to eat, and then go and see Semi Dual.

To those who have not heard of the man, let me here explain a little of his character, in order that they may understand why I wanted to see him of all people to-night.

Semi Dual was what he himself characterized as a "psychological physician." The world at large would call him a "mystic," I suppose.

That was how I, myself, thought of him at first, until I learned that there was nothing mystical about anything he did; that it was rather nothing more than a scientific application of universal laws which enabled him to perform some of the acts which I had witnessed myself.

In reality Semi Dual was a man who dealt in the higher mathematics of universal forces, and used them to gain certain results which he deemed good for the race of man. He was a recluse to a certain extent, and dwelt in magnificent quarters which he had fitted up on the roof of the Urania office building, and in the tower of the same.

These apartments were reached by a splendid staircase leading from the twentieth floor of the building, and at the top of these was an inlaid plate which when trod upon rang an announcing chime of sweet bells.

Here Dual could dwell apart from the rush of the every-day life, and yet keep in touch with its every event. He gave himself up to his own peculiar investigations, and seldom went down into the life of the streets, preferring rather to live apart.

Some months before I had met the man in a peculiar way, and he had helped me unravel a sensational case, by applying his occult knowledge to the same. Since then I had seen him often, and now as a matter of course, he came into my mind.

I stopped at a small café and reenforced the inner man, then I caught a car and rode up to the Urania, and took an elevator up to the top floor. I walked up the stairs to the roof, and set my foot firmly upon the inlaid plate, smiling as I did so to think of the sensations I had felt upon my first visit to Dual's abode.

Now, as then, the chime of bells broke the stillness, and I went on up the pathway, between beds of blooming flowers, until I came to the tower door. It was opened as I approached, and Dual's manservant waved me to the inner room, where I usually met Dual. I crossed and entered and Semi turned to me with a smile.

"I knew you were coming," said he, motioning me to a chair. "Caught your wave about half an hour ago. What's wrong? A new case is it not?"

I tossed my hat on his desk and took the chair at its side, and I laughed as I sat down.

"A little bit ago I would have thought you a good guesser," I answered. "Now all I have to do is to admit that, as usual, you have read my thought-currents aright."

"Incidentally, I have seen a copy of the *Record*, also," said Semi, "but, lest I depreciate my ability in your mind, let me suggest that before you tell me the story you let me see the sample of writing which you have brought."

I pulled a face. "Your ability is rated A1," I responded, as I drew out Sheldon's writing and laid it before him on the desk.

He picked it up and looked across at me with his quiet smile.

"You are learning to get these things right along, aren't you?" he quizzed, and gave his attention to the note. And then for the first time I noticed that his imperial and mustache were gone. I sat up.

"You've shaved yourself," I cried.

Dual looked up. "Rather my man did that," he said shortly, and again bent his head over the copy-pad.

"But why?" I persisted.

"My importunate friend," said Dual, laying down the paper, "I can't really see that it masters why; but if it will ease your mind, it was because I desire to be clean shaven. Will that suffice? I might add, however, that it was done within the last hour, because I suspect that I am going to become a very modern among moderns for the next few days, weeks, or months. The prevailing mode of the moment is for little hirsute adornment, I believe."

"What are you going to do?" I inquired.

"I am going to catch a scoundrel and save a man from injustice. Also, I shall help you add to your already splendid reputation as a star reporter. It is on record that Mahomet had to go to the mountain, I believe."

"Talk English, Dual," I requested, "I'm not far enough along to follow your chain of thought."

Semi laughed as he always did when he had me mystified.

"All right," he agreed; "when I read the papers this evening I decided that I wanted to see that forged document. Naturally, I couldn't do it unless I went after it myself. Therefore, I shaved as a preliminary to becoming an expert in chirography, employed by the defense."

"Good Heavens!" I gasped. "Have they been after you? For what purpose?"

"I am interested," said Dual.

"What do you get out of the signature I brought? Does it add to your interest?"

"Indeed it does," he replied.

"Do you think Sheldon forged the check?"

"What do you think?" said Dual. "You have seen the man, as witnessed by this," tapping the copy-pad.

"I think he's a romantic, high-minded fellow, who knows more than he'll say," I replied.

"And that appears to me to be a good guess," said Dual. "Well, see here."

He pushed the pad toward me and began to expound the writer's character as he read it from the written line.

"Colonel MacDonohue Sheldon, as written here by the paying-teller of the bank, shows a marked peculiarity, which is not so very common in handwriting—worse luck.

"It is contained in the size and form of the small 'd,' which, as you will notice, is extremely high, overtopping every other letter in the line. Also, it is unlooped, the upward and downward stroke following the same line, so that the finished letter appears to be formed of but one line. Now, the significance of a 'd' written in this way may be summed up thus:

"Such a 'd,' which we students of chirography designate as a 'high d,' signifies pride and great self-respect. Let me add, however, that this must not be taken to in any way mean mere vanity, egotism, or conceit, for, as a matter of fact, people who possess this peculiarity of handwriting are practically never given to vanity or conceit. They are persons who take great pride of family, of their ancestry and connections.

"On the other hand, they are neither boastful on the subject nor inclined to make any fulsome display, their pride taking rather the form of deep personal feeling, which actually forms a part of their own self-respect.

"In such persons then we may look for an inherent dignity and respect for themselves and theirs, and a great care as to their personal acts. They will not condescend to the mean or petty, lest it compromise their own standing with themselves; in fact, their sense of honor at times becomes exaggerated to an almost fanatical degree. There's no doubt that this is in the hand of Richard Sheldon, is there, Glace?"

"He wrote it for me to-day in the city jail," I replied.

"It is, then, as I thought," said Dual; "and speaking primarily, without any further definite knowledge, I would feel justified in stating that the paying-teller did not forge the check. On the other hand, it may be presumed that he knows who did."

"I suspected that myself," I agreed with him. "He exhibited a marked reticence to-day at the jail."

"Suppose," said Dual, lying back in his chair and closing his eyes, as was his custom when he desired to listen closely, "suppose you begin at the beginning and tell me all the tale. Don't overlook any detail, no matter how apparently trivial it may seem, for sometimes the least word or action may serve to point the direction along which inquiry should run."

I lit a cigarette and prepared to plunge into the account of my doings of the day. I talked for upward of an hour, and during that time Dual lay as passive as though sleeping, never interrupting me by so much as a glance or a word.

Speaking slowly, and obeying his injunction as to care about detail, I took him with me to the jail and my interview with Sheldon, to the Kenton, to the offices of Pearson & Co., to the saloon, back to the jail, to the house on Welton Street, and through the painful interview with Miss Parton. Knowing that it was safe with Dual, I even told him what Sheldon had told me of his *fiancée's* brother, Archie. Then I took him back to the Kenton, on to the café, and ended with my coming to his place.

When I had quite finished Dual opened his eyes, sat up, and nodded in satisfaction. "Quite a finished narrative," he commented, "upon which I must compliment you, Glace. On the whole, while adding a lot of interesting and useful detail, it does not however change my first opinion of Sheldon in the least.

"It does, however, confirm my belief that he knows, or thinks he knows, who forged the check, and I would venture the opinion that he thinks Archie Parton the guilty man.

"That would explain why he is keeping still about it, and hoping to escape in some other way. Your description of this Western brother of Sheldon's interests me very much. He may bear a little investigation himself.

"There is a chance that getting caught short in a stock deal, he actually issued a check against funds he did not have in such a manner as to have it declared a forgery, hoping to put his deal through in time to replace the money before the thing was found out. I believe you said that the bank-examiners came a little before they were expected, did you not?"

I acquiesced.

"There you are," said Dual; "though that is all theory as yet. Sheldon, however, I feel sure, thinks Parton forged the check. His having stolen from his present employers would support that in his mind.

"Now I want to meet this 'Colonel Mac,' and I have an idea that I can kill a couple of birds with the proverbial single stone. I intended going to the bank to-morrow and asking to see the check, posing as an expert in handwriting, who was acting in Sheldon's behalf.

"However, in view of what you have told me, I shall change my plans a bit. Tomorrow morning you will come here not later than half past nine. You and I will go to the Kenton, and you will there introduce me to this Western stock gambler as a friend of yours who is a professional writing expert.

"I shall accompany you both to the bank and find a way to see the check; also I shall have a good opportunity to see this older Sheldon in such circumstances that the real character of the man will probably be revealed. Now you had better go home and get some sleep and leave me to my work."

"Aren't you going to sleep, too?" I laughed.

"Not on as clear a night as this, with as interesting a case on my hands," said Dual. "I may catch an hour before dawn, but I want to ask a few questions of the stars before then and, on such a night, their answer should be clear."

"Astrology?" I asked.

"Mean planetary magnetism as affecting earth, man," laughed Dual.

"I suppose you're going to look for Sheldon in the stars?" I guessed.

"He'll be there, all right, if I do," said Semi. "Also I shall look for a number of things. If all goes well I shall tell you tomorrow whether he will be convicted or not, in order that you may ease the mind of a certain little woman at 1381 Welton Street."

"That will be a godsend to her," I said with fervor; I was going to add that it would be kind of him, when I remembered that Dual was uniformly kind, and meant to be.

"Exactly," he answered with a smile. "I am glad to see that you appreciate that the rest of your remark would have been fulsome. I told you once that my mission was to help."

I laughed and picked up my hat. "I'm going home before you tell me what I'll dream about," I said. "A man's very thoughts aren't safe with you, Dual."

"You think with a strong amperage," said my friend.

"All the same," I replied, smiling, "I sometimes feel as though I must have a head of glass when I'm with you. If I didn't know you so well, you'd get on my nerves."

"And that from a star reporter," said Dual, smiling. "Well, see you to-morrow. Shall I ring, or will you let yourself out?"

"I'll get out," I told him and, as I turned away, he was making for the curtains at the end of the room, which I knew concealed the stairs which led to his observatory in the tower's top.

CHAPTER V.
"COMPOUNDING A FELONY."

HALF PAST nine of the following morning found me again on the Urania's roof. As my foot struck the plate of inlaid glass at the head of the stairs, I became conscious of Dual. He was lounging on a bench beneath some vines which grew up over the parapet of the building, and when he saw me he rose and met me half-way.

It was the first time I had ever seen him dressed for the street, and the man's appearance struck me with fresh strength. He was clothed in a modish morning suit of gray-black worsted, in the lapel of which he had fastened a fresh little rosebud, and was wearing a soft hat which blended with his suit.

His feet were thrust into shoes of a dull black finish. He had a pair of light-weight gray gloves on his hands, was carrying a small swagger cane, and smoking a cigarette.

"Good morning," he greeted, laying his hand on my shoulder and turning me around. "You are punctual, which gives me pleasure; suppose we set out at once. Will you have a cigarette?"

"I didn't know you used them," I said in mild surprise, as he offered me his case.

"Gordon," said Semi, with his hand still on my arm, "I use anything I wish, when I so desire. To-day I am no longer Semi Dual the recluse; I am an expert in chirography, my friend. I am going down into the life of your streets, and I prefer to live as well as act the part. As for the cigarette, you will find it good. My friend, the present Khedive of Egypt, gave me something like a million of the things some time ago."

"Mine are made by the Sultan of Sulu," I countered, as I lit the cigarette.

Dual closed his case. "You should have learned by this time, Mr. Glace of the *Record,* that I do not misstate facts," he said with his dry smile. "Suppose, my doubting Thomas, that you look at that cigarette again."

I did so, and opened my eyes. On the paper in front of the mouthpiece, was a tiny armorial crest.

"The arms of my friend, the Khedive," Dual told me. "Suppose we get down to the street."

After that I followed in silence. We passed down the stairs, took an elevator, and soon dropped to the ground floor. Outside, Dual held up his stick to a taxi. We got in and were whirled away to the Kenton, where we arrived at a quarter to ten.

On the way I had kept my mouth shut, and not until we stopped in front of the hotel itself, did Dual utter a word.

"Suppose you produce the 'colonel,'" he suggested, as he settled himself back in his seat.

I found the colonel pacing the lobby and opening and shutting the case of his watch. When he saw me enter he came forward at once.

"Oh, there you are!" he cried in an evident relief. "I been waiting for you for a half hour. Of course you weren't due till now, but I'm all of a sweat over this thing of Dick's. I called up your paper, and some fellow told me if I knew where you were I had one on him.

"Said if I found you to put a tag on you an' deliver you by express. Well come on! Let's get goin'. I want to see that Malin person mighty quick, 'fore he gets to chinnin' with anybody else. Hey boy!" to a passing page. "Get me one of them taxi things quick."

I held up my hand to the boy. "I've got one at the door, colonel," I informed him. "Also I've got a friend of mine with me too. He's Professor Dual, who is a professional writing expert, and I thought it might be well to let him have a look at the forged check. Do you mind? It might help Dick."

For just a moment it seemed to me that Colonel Sheldon was not so well pleased as might have been expected by my zeal in his brother's behalf; then he nodded shortly, and strode toward the doors.

"All right! Come on!" he threw back with the trail of his cigar's smoke. "If you think your writin' sharp can help the kid any, why I'll take a chance."

I followed him out and we got into the cab. Then I introduced Semi Dual. Colonel Sheldon eyed him closely, as he put out his hand.

"I've heard about you fellers," he said as Dual took the tendered palm and shook it. "They say you can do some funny things. Well, my brother's in bad, as I reckon Glace has told you; so if you can do anything for him, go as far as you like; I've got enough coin to see the kid through, an' if I ain't, I can get more."

Dual smiled and shook his head.

"You don't just understand, Colonel Sheldon," he replied. "I'm in this as a matter of professional interest pure and simple. I asked Glace to bring me along. If I can help your brother free himself from the circumstances by which he is involved at present, I shall be only too glad. As for remuneration, I neither ask nor expect anything more than that."

I could see that his remarks took Sheldon aback. For maybe a minute he sat silent, before he made any reply at all.

"That's a good sporting proposition," he said after the interval. "I've sure been lucky in meetin' Glace and his pals. But see here, professor; us Sheldons always figger on payin' fer what we get."

"Let us discuss it later then," said Dual with indifference. "There is no time now, for we are about at the bank."

The taxi stopped in front of the Fourth National, and Dual told the driver to wait. Then we all turned and entered the doors, the blinds of which a porter was just rolling up.

Cashier Malin was already at his desk, and the porter took us back and knocked on his door. A moment later we were in the man's presence, and, acting as spokesman, I presented Sheldon and Dual.

George Malin was the human incarnation of the hog. He was large and short and stout. His head was round with heavy jowls, and his neck rose straight up from his shoulders until it was lost in the close-cropped hair of his scalp.

His eyes were small and set deeply between fat pouched eyelids. His nose was broad, his lips loose, and a series of double chins dropped downward until constricted by a low, roll collar. His hands were pudgy and ornamented by a couple of diamond rings.

He fastened his small eyes sharply upon the coloned, who was puffing furiously upon his long cigar, giving Dual and myself scarcely a glance.

"Sit down Mr. Sheldon," he said after an interval of scrutiny. "What can I do for you?"

"You can drop this here case against Dick Sheldon," said Colonel MacDonohue, coming directly to the point. "He's my brother, and he never forged no check in all his life. That kid's straight. But he's in bad and I know it, an' that's why I come to you.

"I tell you Malin, money ain't no object to me alongside of Dick's goin' to the pen, so I'm going to give you folks your little old five thou and you can drop this thing about Dick. How does that strike you; eh? Sounds pretty good, hey? Get your money back, and never have no bother at all. Pretty soft, Malin; don't you think?"

Malin narrowed his pig eyes to slits. "It looks like a confession of guilt to me," he replied, pursing his lips. "From your method of expression, Mr. Sheldon, I presume you are from the region commonly known as the West. I am not familiar with your methods of justice in that section, but here, we are not in the habit of compounding felonies, my dear sir."

Colonel MacDonohue Sheldon dropped into a chair, and leaned forward toward Malin, across his desk; stretched, forth a long bony hand and shook a finger in the cashier's face.

"Compoundin' nuthin'!" he roared. "I told you Dick didn't do it, didn't I? Well if I say he didn't he didn't, an' that settles that. Now can you compound somethin' what wasn't done? You tell me that. I know somethin' about your methods here, if you ain't wise to us out in the West, an' all I got to say, is that if this was in Goldfield, we'd get this fixed up in about two minutes, and there wouldn't be no trouble at all."

"That may be so," remarked Malin, leaning back in his seat, "but you must admit that to me you are personally unknown. Your mere assertion that your brother is innocent has no weight at all—"

"Are you tryin' to tell me that I'm lyin'?" said Sheldon in very mild accents.

"I am merely pointing out the futility of your present course," the cashier replied.

"Because if you are," the colonel continued as though not interrupted, "it will give me great pleasure to make you eat them words."

Malin held up a hand. "This is all useless," he said. "In the first place, I could not do what you ask, without consulting the rest of the directors of the bank. Secondly, the hearing is at eleven and there is no time to do that.

"Thirdly, the case against Mr. Sheldon is clear. The forgery was concealed from this bank by him. He had the exact amount in his safety deposit-box. He claims it was private funds, but if so why did he not deposit them in the bank instead of concealing them in the box?

"Further, the day after the forged check was cashed, he used a thousand dollars. The vault attendant saw him take two five-hundred-dollar bills from the vault. The forged check was paid from a new issue of currency we had just got in. We have been able to trace, at least partially, the two five hundred dollar bills which our paying-teller took from his vault that night.

"They are deposited in another bank by a young woman, who placed them to the credit of a certain firm, which banks there as well as with us. The numbers on those bills happen to correspond to some of the currency used in paying the forged check.

"Now," he leaned forward and fixed the colonel with his eyes, "don't you think you've gone a little far in asking me to accept hush money to allow a proven forger to escape?"

For a minute or more Sheldon sat staring at the other's face as though but half comprehending. Under the tan of his skin he grew a pasty sort of white.

Then he rolled his cigar to the other side of his mouth, set his jaw squarely, and opened his lips. "D'ye mean that them two five-hundred bills clinches this thing on to Dick?" was what he said.

"Any jury will convict on such evidence, I assure you," replied the cashier.

Sheldon nodded, slowly. "But if it could be proved that he didn't have them in his box at first; that he didn't know nuthin' about it, to begin with?" he asked.

I sat up; so did Dual. Malin leaned back and shook his head. "It would have to be pretty strong evidence to shake our case."

"And you won't consider my proposition?" said Sheldon. "Look here, Malin, I'll double that bet. Make it ten thousand, and call the thing off. Why—"

"Are you offering me a bribe?" Malin's flabby features grew a purplish red. "No!" he cried, pounding the desk with his jeweled hand. "Sheldon, your brother's guilty, and we both know it. Now, then, this is my last word, and after I've said it, you can get out: I shall appear against him at eleven o'clock, and before I am done with him he'll be wearing stripes."

Sheldon sprang to his feet with something very near a howl. With both hands on the desk, he leaned across toward the opposite man.

"My Lord," he cried, "but I wish this was Goldfield! I'd show you what I'd do if it was. I'd get you—yes, sir, I'd get you. Why, I've a mind to do it, anyhow, you— you—"

Dual pulled the irate man down, and Malin turned to me with a slow, cruel smile.

"I would suggest that you get your friend out quietly, Mr. Glace, as I have no desire to make another arrest of the Sheldon tribe. I have no family feud against them, you know."

Dual spoke on the instant, however, having got the colonel into a seat, where he sat chewing upon his cigar and gazing moodily at the floor.

"Before we go, Mr. Malin, I desire to examine the forged check for a moment. Mr. Glace told you, I believe, that I am a writing expert. It was for that that I came along."

"The check is not on exhibit," said the cashier.

"Of course not," agreed Semi; "but equally, of course, I will get to see it sooner or later in due process of law, and I felt assured that it would make little difference to you what that time might be."

"What good would it do you?" queried Malin.

"I hope to be able to find certain things about it which will be of use to the defense."

"And naturally you would find them, wouldn't you?" Malin indulged in a grin.

Dual rose, went over and sat down upon an end of the desk. Then he looked the cashier full in the eye.

Slowly the grin faded from the flabby face, and he became evidently uncomfortable under that silent stare.

Then Dual replied.

"Mr. Malin," he said very quietly, yet clearly, "there was not the slightest excuse for your gratuitous insult. Therefore, I am not minded to overlook it in any degree. It was caused by the impulse of a bully, and decent men sometimes have to call the bullies down. Mr. Malin,

I desire to see the forged document in this case, and you are going to let me see it. That is so, is it not?"

Malin nodded his head. "I've got it with me," said he, reaching into an inner pocket. "Look at it all you want, but be careful of the thing."

"You shall have it back in a moment," said Semi. "Glace, come here. Take this check, straighten it out, and go over and hold it in the sunlight. Steady—so!"

He rose and, taking a small pocket camera from one of his pockets, approached me, focused carefully, and a moment after was in possession of a copy of the check.

When he was done he took the paper-slip from my fingers and returned it to Malin, who sat as we had left him. Malin took it and replaced it in a bill-fold without a word

"And now," said Semi Dual, "suppose we be going. I shall not have to trouble you again, Mr. Malin. That is mutually acceptable, I presume? Allow me to add, however, in parting, that should I desire to consult the cashier of the Fourth National at any time, after, say about thirty days, I shall find a more courteous man in the chair."

Malin still sat at his desk. He made no sign as we filed out of the room. When we were out in the general banking-room, however, Dual turned to me and slowly winked one eye.

We left the bank and went out to our cab. Dual motioned the colonel to enter, and, as I would have followed, placed a hand on my arm.

"One moment, Glace," said he; "I'm not going with you, because I am not needed, and I have work to do. When you see Miss Parton this morning, as you doubtless will at court, tell her that I said she should stop all worry as far as necessary; that I promise her Sheldon's release within thirty days."

In turn, I seized him by the arm. "Dual," I cried, speaking shrilly in my excitement, "do you really mean that?"

"S-s-sh!" said Semi. "You remember that I told you that I would ask a question last night? The answer was plain, I have given you the salient part. You may rest assured of the outcome, for the stars do not lie. See me to-night without fail."

He turned away. I entered the cab, and the colonel and I set out for the court. As the taxi swung out into the street I looked back and saw my strange friend lifting his cane to another cab which was passing, and then I lost him in the crowd.

The hearing was pretty tame, after all. True to his word, Malin appeared against Sheldon, and on his evidence the prisoner was held for trial. Thereupon the colonel's attorneys made application for bail, and the court fixed the sum of ten thousand, which Colonel Mac immediately put up.

While the details were being arranged Dick Sheldon was allowed to go into a private room, and as he disappeared through its door I rose and went back to the rear where I had noticed Myrtle Parton sitting as I came in.

I spoke to her, gave her Dual's message, and saw her grasp at it, as though it might have been a sort of spiritual straw to her drowning soul. Then I suggested that we go to see Dick.

She sprang to her feet and I led her back to the waiting-room, and took her in. Sheldon was sitting with bowed head as we entered, but got up quickly and came to meet her with outstretched hands. I turned away, but not before they had met and he had drawn her into his arms. Then as I was closing the door I heard Dick Sheldon speak quickly.

"Where is Archie?" he asked.

"At his work as us—" The door came shut and cut the girl's answer in two. But I had heard Archie's name again in connection with the case.

I hung around until Sheldon was released; then I left Colonel Mac, Dick, and the girl and went up to the office of the *Record* to try and put my story in shape as far as I could.

Smithson listened to my report and shook his head.

"I was beginning to fancy you'd fallen down, and were afraid to come back," he said, grinning; "but I guess we can look for some funny developments. Well, if Sheldon didn't forge the check, this 'Colonel Mac' knows something about it for a safe bet. Take a tip from me and stick to his trail."

"Thanks," I told him, rising and getting my hat. "When I get the answer I'll tell you all about it, rest assured of that."

"And report once in a while," grinned Smithson, "or I'll run you in the 'Lost— Reward.'"

CHAPTER VI.

THE TRAIL LEADS WEST.

I DIDN'T forget my appointment with Dual that evening, for I was very anxious to learn what he had discovered. Consequently, as soon as I had had a bite of dinner, I went up to the Urania with a mind primed for startling things.

I got what I expected, for as soon as I was seated Dual turned to me actually grinning, and fairly took my breath away.

"I've engaged a Pullman section for you on the midnight train for Chicago. You leave for Goldfield to-night," said he.

I dropped my cigarette. "I do what?" I gasped in my surprise.

"Take the midnight train for Chicago. Get a train there for Goldfield, Nevada. I believe the Union Pacific to Ogden, and the Salt Lake route from there southwest will about fill the bill."

"But see here," I cried, "I'm a newspaper man, and I can't run away like that without notice. Besides, I haven't the money to do it. The *Record* won't send me, and I haven't got time to get my things ready by twelve o'clock."

"All but the first objection are already removed," said Dual. "Your passage is taken to Chicago. I shall give you whatever else you need for expenses. Also, I took the liberty of sending my man to your rooms to-day, and, as he is a good judge, all your best belongings are now reposing in a couple of suit-cases in the outer room. There remains, therefore, but one thing for you to do, and that—make your farewell to Smithson as soon as you like."

I looked at the man, and again he grinned.

"I was looking for some new developments when I came up here to-night," I said after a moment, "but this surpasses anything I ever dreamed. If I can get away from Smithson, hanged if I don't go."

"You will go in any event," said Dual.

"But my job, Semi? I've got to live when I get back."

"Suggest to Smithson that you go as a special writer for the *Record* at your own expense," said my friend. "He'll let you off."

"It's the limit," I said in feeble protest, "but I'll do it if I break my neck. I'll go see him now."

"Why see him at all?" said Semi Dual. "Use my phone."

I nodded. "After a bit," I said slowly. "Wait till I get it myself. I am going to Goldfield, but why Goldfield of all places in the world?"

"Because," said Semi Dual, "I need a man at the other end of the line."

"All right—where's the lamp?" I said.

Semi smiled. "The lamp?" he repeated.

"Sure! I begin to feel like the slave of one. Go on and rub it and I'll be in Goldfield. Why bother with trains?"

"Your arrival on the limited will cause less comment," said Dual. "Now, if you'll listen closely I'll tell you why you are going and what you are to do. You can then break the news to Smithson, and go down and get your train.

"After I came back from the bank I developed my plate of the forged check. I admit I had seen some of its details at the bank, but I wanted to study the thing, so I took the photograph.

"I had been fortunate in getting a very clear negative, and I was able to follow the writing's characteristics closely, thereby learning some interesting things. To begin with, there is a difference in the writing of the body of the check and the signature. It is contained in one letter alone; but that is, I think, enough.

"Now, let's take up the signature itself. It shows a marked difference from the same name written for you by the paying-teller, and rather oddly the most marked difference is found again in the letter 'd,' which in the signature on the forged check is written with a large loop.

"The primary significance of such a 'd' is sensitiveness. The pride of this writer is worn on the sleeve and is very easily wounded; he is touchy, and liable to anger over trivial causes. He takes offense hastily, and frequently over the merest trifle. He is apt to continually feel that he has been wronged or insulted, and may at times violently resent the same.

"If the loop is greatly exaggerated, it shows extreme morbidness on the subject of one's pride and rights. It often occurs in the writings of persons who are mentally deranged, and always denotes some morbid quality of the mind along the lines I have indicated.

"This signature is presumably a clever imitation of the colonel's, and, while he pronounces it a forgery, still we must remember that it was sufficiently like the real thing to fool his own brother, who presumably should know his writing quite well.

"Therefore, we may assume that it is a very close copy of the elder Sheldon's signature. It remains, therefore, to find out if the writing in the body of the check is similar to his, and a study of it will show a peculiarity of the shape of the small 'i' in the word 'five.'

"In all other respects it resembles the signature, but that 'i' does not harmonize. It is bent over at the end, almost like a half 'c,' so that unless dotted it might pass for that letter instead of an 'i.'

"While my man was getting your wardrobe together this afternoon I had him stop at the Kenton and examine the register, to see how Sheldon had written Goldfield, which contains an 'i.' He reports that it in no way varies from the usual form of the letter, and does not resemble the 'i' which appears in this check."

"Who then could have written the thing?" I inquired.

"That is what we have to find out within the next four weeks," said Dual. "After I found out the peculiarities of the check I sent a message to Goldfield. I have a friend there, whom I once helped to locate a mine some few years ago. I wired him to see what he knew about this elder Sheldon, and he replied at once:

"'It seems that the colonel lives in Goldfield, all right. He has a house there, and a daughter and a maiden sister. The women are at home right now.'

"When I heard that I decided to send you out there. You can pass yourself off for an Eastern writer, who is after material for special articles, and it will be your duty to find out all you can about Colonel Sheldon and his family, or anybody connected with them, and write me a daily report of anything you find out.

"You can stop with my friend, John Curzon. I shall wire him that you are coming, and he'll put you up. I would advise that you carry out your character of writer, even to him, for though he would be willing to do anything to help me, he can serve us best by believing you what you claim to be. He is not much of a talker, but you'll have a good excuse on your part for asking questions, and in wiring I'll suggest that he help you out on local facts.

"He knows everybody in that section almost. Find a way to meet Miss Sheldon, and get on intimate terms if you can. Time spent in her society is likely to yield big results. I have packed a camera among your cases, and I want you to try and send me likenesses of any interesting characters you meet.

"Also keep up your habit of collecting handwritings, and forward them to me. You say the paying-teller told you that Archie Parton spent some time out West; you also mentioned that the page in Pearson & Co.'s offices said Parton knew the colonel at some previous time.

"Try and find out whether Parton ever spent any time in Goldfield by any chance. I have prepared a letter to my friend which will serve to introduce you in your capacity of special correspondent. Also he is in possession of a special code cipher, which he and I sometimes use in telegraphing concerning important business.

"Should you need to communicate with me upon anything urgent, ask him for it, and he will let you use it, I am sure."

He handed me the letter he had mentioned, and I stored it in my coat.

"And now," said Semi Dual, glancing at his watch; "I would suggest that you call up your friend Smithson, and break the news that you are going away." He opened a door in one end of his desk and drew out a telephone equipment, which he placed before me.

I took up the instrument and gave the Central Exchange the *Record's* number. After a bit a voice came to me over the wire.

"Give me Smithson," I directed.

"Hello, Smithson?"

"Yep."

"This is Glace."

"Hello, you candied prune," growled the city editor facetiously. "What's the news?"

"I'm going to Goldfield to-night," said I.

"You're going to get fired if you do. What's the matter in Goldfield that they need you?"

"The Sheldon trail leads that far."

"Then let it lead," said Smithson. "You don't have to follow, do you, hey?"

"But I want to put this through."

"Goin' to walk?" said Smithson. "I sha'n't pay your way."

"I'll pay my own way, and I'll send you back a lot of feature stories," I told him, and waited to see what he would say.

"Yes you will," he jeered at me, and I could seem to see him grinning. "Who's the angel, Gordon? Say, honest, is this thing on the level, now, Glace?"

"I'm going, if that's what you mean," I informed him, "only I don't want to cut loose from the paper. Let me be your special correspondent, without salary, till I get back, and I'll pay all my own expenses on the trip."

For a few seconds Smithson didn't reply. Then he grunted in evident disgust. "You sure are a nice one," said he, "running around the country, when I may need you any day. Still, if you want a vacation as darned bad as that, why beat it, but don't you fall down on the stories, or I'll fire you whenever you do get back."

"I'll not forget," I assured him.

"Say, Glace." Smithson dropped his jeering tone and grew serious, as he sometimes did. "Is this straight about the Sheldon case? Are you really on the trail of a sensation?"

"I am giving it to you straight," I told him, "and I'll give you a good story when I get back. I am going to Goldfield in Sheldon's behalf. Now you know who the angel is."

"All right," my editor answered. "Go to it, and good luck, old man." He hung up the phone.

I put the receiver back on the hook and turned again to Semi Dual. "That is all fixed, and the last tear of parting is shed. From now on till the end of this case, I am in your hands, O maker of destinies, and ruler of fate."

Dual smiled. "Here is an envelope. It contains one thousand dollars," he remarked, flipping a sealed package across the desk to me. "If you need more, tell John Curzon to give it to you, and charge it to me."

"Look here, Dual," I said, as I picked it up; "why send me to Goldfield? Why don't you use your powers to work things out, without all this bother and fuss? I'll bet you know the outcome right now."

"You're getting quite clairvoyant yourself," laughed Semi, "but you want to remember that modern courts of law do not recognize the evidence of trance mediums or astrologers as being of value, my friend. Personally I have worked the case out to its end, and I might venture to tell you what you will discover in Goldfield.

"I prefer to let you work it out yourself, and get such substantiating facts as we may use in the case in Sheldon's behalf. And now I would suggest that you get down to your train. When you return to New York the final scenes will be played out right here. When I telegraph for your return, come at once. Good-by, and good luck to you, Glace."

He rang for his man to bring out my grips. I took my hat and extended my hand.

"You're the most practical mystic I ever met," I told him, "and I'm yours to command. Behold me on my way to Goldfield. I shall write you every day."

CHAPTER VII.

FATE AT SALT LAKE.

NOTHING OF any interest happened on my trip westward. I had never been west of Chicago, however, and after leaving that busy city I found plenty to amuse me during the time spent on the train.

I cultivated the acquaintance of several men, and picked up all the stray information concerning my destination which they were able to give me, and, on the whole, enjoyed myself pretty well. At Salt Lake City fate stepped into the game and gave me a pat on the back. I had varied Dual's plan a bit at Chicago, and taken the through flyer on the Salt Lake route, so that I did not have to change at Ogden.

In that way I avoided all trouble over berth reservations, and the other annoyances which go with changing cars. When we pulled into the Salt Lake depot I was sitting on the rear observation-platform, taking a good look around. It was there the porter found me, and suggested that I take a ride up-town, as they stopped for an hour before going on.

I naturally availed myself of the privilege to stretch my legs, after being cooped up for days, and leaving the car I went out to a trolley, and rode up through the business section, got off and purchased some books and papers, and took a car back to the train. Then occurred one of those freaks of electricity which are always bobbing up. The power failed and we were stalled.

I looked at my watch. We had fifteen minutes left to make my train. I glanced about the car, and noticed a number of other persons taking the same anxious interest in the matter as was I myself. Five minutes passed, and at last the car started.

When we reached the station everybody tried to get off at once. Just ahead of me was a girl, who, even in my anxiety not to miss my train, had caught my eye. She was what I would call brilliantly dark. That is, she had dark hair and eyes, black eyebrows, and vividly red lips. While small, she was in no wise calculated to give an impression of delicacy, for she was as smooth and trim in her movements as a well-built machine.

As is always the case at such a time, somebody shoved, as they tried to get out of the car in some one else's turn, and the little girl was thrown from her feet, just as she reached the steps.

Chance or something put me where I could catch her as she fell. I supported her to one side and set her firmly on her feet, where she smiled and thanked me, endeavored to take a step forward, and stopped with an involuntary cry.

"I'm afraid I've hurt my ankle," she gasped.

I glanced at the station clock. We had two minutes left. "What train were you taking?" I made bold to ask.

"The Salt Lake, west," said the girl briefly, "and I just must make it if I can."

It was no time for ceremony.

"Pardon me," I said quickly, and before she could protest I had gathered her up in my arms and was running toward our train. I just skimmed through the barriers as they were closing, hopped and jumped over the tracks, and ran alongside the already moving train.

My porter saw me, and lent a willing hand. Together we got the girl onto the platform, and I climbed up myself and hung on to a hand-hold while I regained a bit of breath. Then, rather inanely, perhaps, I gasped:

"Well, we made it!"

I climbed on up the steps, and together the porter and I helped the now blushing girl inside. Then I gave the darky the high sign that a tip was coming, and ordered him to take the girl to a stateroom and hunt up some woman to assist her.

"She's sprained her ankle, I think," I made an end.

"Oh, but you mustn't do that?" said the girl. "I'll be all right."

But I overruled her protests. We helped her to a seat, and the porter hunted up the conductor, and he unlocked a stateroom, and we got the girl onto the divan.

Then the porter hunted up a motherly old lady, and she soon had him running around with pitchers of hot water, while I made him grin at the tip I put into his hand.

"Golly," said that dusky son of Ham, "dis yere is sure mighty romantic; yes, sir, it certainly is."

Some time later the porter hunted me up.

"Say, boss," he remarked, grinning, "the young lady in de stateroom wants to know kin you come in for a minute?"

I got up and answered the summons with alacrity.

I found my chance acquaintance reclining in a seat with the injured ankle supported upon a pillow.

"How is the foot now?" I inquired.

"As well as possible," she replied smiling, and extended her hand. "I sent for you to express my appreciation of your kindness. I am Miss Sheldon, and I live in Goldfield. Won't you sit down?"

Here was news indeed. I took the girl's proffered hand and dropped upon a seat.

"I am George Gordon," I told her—that was the name Dual and I had agreed upon—"and I am a special writer for the Eastern papers. As for what little I have done, pray forget it. We were literally thrown together, you know."

Miss Sheldon laughed at my rather poor joke. "You are very kind to treat my mishap in that light," she replied.

"It was fate," I stated. "The funny thing about it all is that I intended hunting up a man whom I now suspect is your father, when I arrived in Goldfield—'Colonel MacDonohue Sheldon.'"

"Are you going to Goldfield?" Miss Sheldon cried in evident delight.

"If the train stays on the track," I replied.

"Oh, I'm so glad," said the girl. "You know we have to change at Las Vegas, and I've been wondering how I was ever to manage it. Now perhaps I can impose upon you still farther. I've no one else I can depend upon, you see."

"I am doubly glad I'm going to Goldfield," said I. "It really was a providential meeting, I suspect."

"And you meant to look up father?" said Miss Sheldon. "I'm sorry, but he's in the East right now, though I expect him home very soon. I can't say just when, because for the last week I've been in Salt Lake with a girl friend who is in a hospital, and am just getting back."

"If it won't be too long I think I must wait," I suggested. "You see, I was told that he is an authority on your local mining situation, and as I am writing up that subject for my paper, I am naturally very anxious to have a talk with him."

"I'm sorry he's away," said the girl; "but, of course, you will call, and as soon as I get home I will find out when father is expected back. Let me give you my address. I hope you will come soon, and let me show you that I really do appreciate all you have done."

I had an idea.

"You are very good," I accepted. "I'll be glad to come up and mark the progress of the foot." Then I made a pretense of feeling in my pockets.

"I'm afraid I've left my note-book in my section," I confessed. "If you'll excuse me I'll go get it and write the address down."

"No matter," said Miss Sheldon. "I ought to have my hand-bag here somewhere with my cards. Look about if you will and see if you can find it, Mr. Gordon."

I complied, but there was no hand-bag in sight. I admitted my inability to find it, and Miss Sheldon made a little wry face.

"I probably dropped it when I fell from the car, and we neither one of us noticed. Well, then it's gone. Lucky I had my ticket in my suit-case." She began to laugh.

"We must have been a funny spectacle, Mr. Gordon, when you so cavalierly bore me to my train, with my suit-case bumping against your knees."

"I thought they felt sore," I admitted, entering into her spirit. "I was wondering if I was developing rheumatism or what."

"If you'll hand me the case I'll get something to write on," said Miss Sheldon. And I got the bag up, opened it for her, and laid it at her side.

She fumbled about among some letters and papers, and finally removing a letter from the envelope, wrote her name and address on the back, and handed it to me.

"That isn't any more formal than all the rest of our intercourse," said she smiling, "but it will suffice till you can get to your section and copy it in your book."

I read the address and folded up the envelope to put it away. I had got what I wanted, which was a copy of her writing; but, as it happened, I had obtained something more, for, as I folded the paper together, there appeared a return notice in the upper corner, and I caught the name of Archie Parton on the thing.

I was so surprised that I started, and I saw Miss Sheldon noticed the act. There was but one way to cover my action, and that the natural one, of course. Therefore I turned to her and pointed to the written name. "Do you know Parton?" I asked.

"Why, yes," said Miss Sheldon. "Do you?"

I shook my head. "Not personally, but I do know his sister. She is a very sweet girl. I know of her brother, who is working for a brokerage company in my home, and when I saw his name on this envelope I naturally was surprised."

"I see," said Miss Sheldon. "Really, Mr. Gordon, this meeting is a funny thing. Here you are coming way out here to meet papa, and he was actually in your own town when you started, I think. He will laugh when I tell him about that.

"As for Archie, he was out here two years ago, and worked for papa until he went back East. We correspond occasionally. I received that letter while I was in Salt Lake. He is a very nice boy, though a little inclined to be wild, and we used to have him up at the house a good deal when he was out here. How is he getting along?"

There was a heightened color in the girl's face, and I felt that I had probably opened a personal affair.

"I believe he is doing all right," I hastened to assure her. "I have been told that Pearson & Co. think quite well of him."

"I am glad of that," she said quickly. "Sometimes I have thought papa didn't seem very well pleased at my getting letters from Archie, but I know the boy is all right at heart. He has a very sensitive nature, and I don't think most people understand him very well." Then she changed the subject to other things.

The afternoon passed very pleasantly. As the dinner hour drew on I had the porter get us a little table, and we had a cozy supper sent in from the dining-car. We ate and drank and talked and laughed.

After a bit I excused myself and went out for a smoke. When I was alone in a seat in the buffet I drew out the envelope and gazed at it in admiration. I had surely accomplished a lot of my task already, and felt highly pleased at the turn of events. I had clearly proven that Miss Sheldon knew Archie Parton, and that he had been in Goldfield, and in Sheldon's employ.

Better than all else, I had a sample of his handwriting, and as I examined it under the light of an overhanging reading-lamp screwed to the window-frame, I suddenly felt shaken at a discovery which I made. The address was clearly written, in a small, running hand.

"Miss Alice Sheldon, Hotel Utah, Salt Lake City, Utah." In the upper corner was a five-day return order to Archie Parton. And every "i" in the entire superscription had that strange half-curved form which Dual had mentioned to me.

My hand shook as I put the envelope carefully away in my bill-fold. I wondered if I had found the man, even before reaching my destination. The curved "i's" of the letter and the curved "i's" of the forged check swam and intermingled before my mental vision, and I confess I felt actually faint.

I got up and went back, and mechanically inquired for my fair protégé's condition. Even as I did so the old lady came again to assist her to bed, and I was glad of the fact. I felt that I could not bear a good part in small talk to-night.

I went back to my section and had my berth made up. Then I climbed in and spent an hour writing up my report to Semi Dual, after which I turned off the light and lay looking out of the window at the speeding landscape, my head full of a veritable jumble of things, mixed up with which were the faces of two women, one blond and valiant, one brunette and smiling. I knew that my being right, would bring heartache and tears to both of them.

CHAPTER VIII.
"COLONEL MAC'S" REPUTATION.

MORNING FOUND us still speeding across the barren country, and we made Las Vegas without further incident, got the train for Goldfield, and in due time arrived at that place. I assisted Miss Sheldon in the change at Las Vegas, and we chatted together until we reached her home town.

A bluff and ruddy Englishman met me at the steps of the coach as I alighted, and introduced himself to me as John Curzon, Dual's friend. To him I mentioned Miss Sheldon's accident, and we saw her safely to a cab. She shook my hand at parting and urged me once more to call, and I promised to do so on the subsequent evening, after which Curzon and I returned to his waiting motor. He spun the crank and the engine exploded with a roar. We climbed in and were soon whirling away for his town house.

"I got Abdul's message," said Curzon, after we were running on the third speed. "He wired me to meet you on this train."

"Whose message?" I inquired.

"Abdul's— Oh, Dual's," said my acquaintance. He smiled at me in quizzical fashion. "Just how well do you know that chap?"

I explained that I had met Dual while working for my paper, and Curzon nodded his head. "He's a funny old chap," he remarked. "Not everybody knows his real name. You see his father was a high-caste Persian, and his mother a Russian princess, or something like that, I believe, but Abdul didn't like his name. Said it attracted too much attention to his oriental blood, so he dropped the 'b,' shuffled the 'a' about a bit, and got Dual as a result.

"His first name, Semi, he took because, as he explained, he was only half Abdul anyway, his mother being of a different race, and there you've got the whole thing. I believe you have a letter for me? He mentioned that you would."

I handed over Dual's letter of introduction, and Curzon put it in his pocket without a glance.

"Any friend of Abdul's is a friend of mine," he declared. "Some years ago he made me rich. It was on his advice that I bought up the abandoned prospect, which is now our mine, and which has made us both independently well off. He insisted that it was a mine, and it was.

"He certainly has a wonderful brain, and he does a lot of things which I don't pretend to understand. Still, I always feel that I owe him all I have. If it hadn't been for him I suppose I'd still be wandering round with a burro and a bag of beans, as I was when he took me up. Now, Mr. Gordon, that we are introduced, I want you to consider yourself my guest. As Semi himself would say: 'My house and all that is in it are yours.'"

I was expressing my thanks for such hospitality when we arrived at the Curzon place, and my host turned me over to a sort of Jap butler, who escorted me to my rooms. After I had bathed and freshened myself up a bit I went down and joined Curzon, and shortly after dinner was announced.

Conversation at the meal was limited to small talk mostly, and it was not until we had gone out on the porch for an after-dinner smoke, and the cigars were going well, that it reached any connected state. It was a beautiful, warm night, in early September, and there was a full moon which made the whole world look like silver, and softened the outlines of the surrounding hills.

Curzon took his cigar from his lips and blew a little spiral of smoke.

"Abdul used to like these nights," he said in a reminiscent tone. "He used to say they reminded him of Persia. He's a peculiar fellow, that friend of mine, and he's been all over the world, more or less."

"He has never told me anything about himself," I admitted. "I have often wished he would do so. Thus far he has not."

"He's done it to two people in his life, he tells me," said Curzon, "and I was the second one. The first, it seems, rather disappointed the chap. Woman, of course."

I laughed, and continued to smoke.

"To-morrow we must go up to the mine." Curzon abruptly changed the subject. "From your letter to me I expect you will be wanting to see our workings here, and get a lot of notes.

"If you'd like, I'll call up Schiff, my superintendent, and arrange to go through our properties, say to-morrow afternoon."

"I would like nothing better," said I. I had a part to play, and I was resolved to make good.

"Right," said Curzon. "I'll call Schiff up to-night."

"Mr. Curzon," I said, resolving at least to throw out a feeler, "I believe you know most of the folks around here, do you not?"

"Rather well," said my host. "Any particular ones?"

I thought he chuckled, where he sat in the shadow of some vines, and I had an idea I could make a guess at his thoughts.

"I may as well admit that I like a pretty face," I confessed with what I hoped was a slight embarrassment. "The young lady whom I met on the train said her name was Sheldon. What sort of folks are they?"

"That, Mr. Gordon, is a very bald question," Curzon replied. "I would certainly be no gallant if I admitted anything wrong with Alice Sheldon. As a matter of fact, the girl is all right. Equally as a matter of fact, her father, Colonel Sheldon, and I, are not exactly bosom friends."

"I was referred to Sheldon as an authority on mines by a mutual acquaintance," I explained. "I was speaking of that rather than with any other idea in mind. I am old enough myself to know that the girl is a lady, I hope."

"There, there," said Curzon, "maybe I spoke hastily myself. I confess I'm a bit touchy on the Sheldons. The colonel's methods are not mine, Gordon, but the girl's all right; she's her mother over again."

"The colonel's something of a character, I take it," I said.

"He's pretty smooth," replied Curzon. "None of us can say more than that."

"Has he always been in mines?"

"He's been into nearly everything except the 'pen,'" replied Curzon with some heat.

"That sounds interesting," I laughed.

Curzon smoked in silence, and after a bit he chuckled again.

"Although I don't like the chap, there are times when I almost have to admire him for his cool *sang-froid*," he said. "Some men in the position he has been in at times would have gone to pieces and got caught, but the colonel always had an eye out for what the criminal calls his 'getaway.'

"Maybe I ought not to tell you this, and mind you, it's not for publication, though everybody around here knows the tale."

He threw away the stub of his cigar and lighted a fresh one before he went on.

"Some time ago there were a lot of forged certificates of the stock of a certain mine hereabouts turned into the company offices for transfer. To all appearances they were genuine. Sheldon had a lot of them himself, and he had sold a lot to his friends. Well, when the things were brought in for transfer it was discovered that there had already been a transfer made of that stock, so that the certificates brought in were worthless, and then a howl went up.

"Of course, Sheldon claimed that he had been duped as badly as any one, and he was actually able to show where he had drawn a check on his personal account in the bank to pay for the shares he held, as well as what he had sold to his friends. However, the upshot was that some of the buyers sued the colonel for fraud. It then developed that the certificates which the colonel held and those held by the mining company were such exact duplicates that they could not be told apart.

"All that the company officers could do was to swear that one of the two was a false issue, but when pinned down by Sheldon's lawyers, they admitted that they couldn't tell which was which. That let the colonel out; the court holding that the plaintiff had no redress except a writ of mandamus against the company to make them issue stock to cover the number of shares held.

"After it was all done with, Sheldon actually reimbursed some of his more intimate friends, but there were a lot of people who had to pocket their loss. To this day nobody knows whether the first or last certificates presented for transfer were the true ones, though naturally a lot of people believe it was a shrewd bit of work on the colonel's part.

"Still, nobody can say, for the simple reason that nobody knows; and at the very least, the colonel was dismissed by the courts and has the law on his side."

"Couldn't they find any clue as to who actually might have forged the certificates in the first place?" I asked.

"The only clue was that they were sold by a man with a black beard and mustache. A very suave, smooth, ingratiating sort of chap, who got out of town before the bomb burst and was never heard of since."

"So that the colonel might actually have been victimized as well as the rest?"

"That's the beauty of the scheme," said Curzon, "if scheme it was. Equally to prove himself a man of honor, the only ones the colonel reimbursed were persons he had himself advised to buy the stock."

"Which would indicate that he desired to make good where he felt a sense of responsibility."

"Quite right. The joker was that a lot of folks bought the stuff after they heard that the colonel's friends were in."

"Either way you look at it, it may have been straight or a frame-up?"

"Exactly," said Curzon. "That's why I said the colonel was pretty smooth. If he is crooked, he always has been able to get the law to assist him. It takes a shrewd crook to do that."

"If he had been so crooked as that, though, one would hardly expect him to continue to live on here."

"Oh, the colonel doesn't care," said Curzon. "He is one of the sort who will brazen the thing out. He's a gambler in spirit, and the kind of man who will stake everything on the turn of a card, win or lose. The man's an anomaly.

"Nobody, who was ever in actual partnership with him, will say that they didn't get a fair deal, or that Sheldon ever tried in any way to escape from a promise or an agreement once made. He is almost morbidly sensitive on the subject of the 'gentleman's agreement,' and his word, if given, is said to be easily as valuable as his bond. He is, of my knowledge, kind of heart.

"There are a lot of poor folks in this burg who swear by Colonel Mac. Sometimes I fancy he's been born out of his time, and is really a sort of tender-hearted buccaneer, like the romantic highwaymen of some centuries ago, who stole from the rich and gave to the poor. Now mind you, with all this he's never been proven crooked, yet among the moneyed classes here he is regarded as a weasel which has not been caught as yet."

"Anyway, I should like to meet him," I said, laughing, as I tossed my cigar away. "I'll wager he would make good material for a Western story; what we writers call a bit of 'local color,' you know."

"He would that," agreed Curzon, rising. "Well, suppose we turn in. You are doubtless more or less weary from your journey, and I've a job to do befone we go to the mine to-morrow. If you've got any old clothes, put 'em on before you start up to the workings. It isn't exactly a clean place."

"Will there be any objections to my taking photographs?" I wanted to know.

Curzon smiled and shook his head. "Snap anything on or under the ground," he gave his permission; "we have absolutely nothing to conceal."

I wrote Dual my report on Sheldon and then went to bed and slept like a top. It was the Jap who woke me after he had prepared my bath.

CHAPTER IX.

THE MINE AND SCHIFF.

OBEDIENT TO orders, Curzon's Jap, who seemed to be a sort of general factotum about the place, brought his master's auto to the door shortly after luncheon, and Curzon and I prepared to set off.

I had put on the oldest things which Dual's man had been kind enough to pack for me; though I confess I looked rather ruefully at the perfectly good suit which I seemed fated to spoil. Curzon sized it up with a grin.

"Best you can do?" he inquired. "Well, never mind, we'll get you some overalls and a jumper when we get to the mine. Come along."

I picked up my camera and we climbed into the roadster. The Jap cranked up, and we were off in a cloud of dust. It was a good machine, and Curzon was a good driver. There seemed to be a sort of sympathy between man and machine, so that he eased it where necessary and drove it to the full where he could do so to advantage.

We fled through the town and out into the foot-hills and began to climb. I said little on the way, contenting myself with watching the topography of the region and glorying in the performance of the stanch little machine.

After some time Curzon pointed ahead.

"There's our bonanza," he directed, and as I followed his directing hand, I saw a scar on the face of the hill, where clustered some buildings, and then they were shut off by a turn in the road.

"Five years ago that was pronounced a hopeless proposition by some of the best men of the region," said Curzon, "and was given up by the people who had been holding it. Then Abdul, or Dual, dropped into Goldfield, and I met him, and we took to each other. The upshot was that we went out to look at this claim.

"Dual said it was a good thing and I laughed at him. He came back at me by offering to buy it and give me half of it if I'd stay and work it. Well, it's made us both rich. Funny chap, Dual, but a most wonderful brain."

"How did he know it was a good mine?" I inquired.

"That's the funniest thing," Curzon replied. "He hardly looked at the thing, but he insisted on working out its exact latitude and longitude, went back to his hotel, and told me the next day that he was going to buy the mine. He also made me acquire a claim on the other side of the gulch, a little higher up, and hanged if we didn't cut the same vein there that we were working on this side. That's why I say he's a wonder. A man who can find gold by a geographical calculation, hadn't ever ought to be poor."

I laughed. I imagined Dual had used his astrological knowledge in determining the facts about the mine.

"Did he take the time when you were out at the mine that day?" I asked.

"Did he?" said Curzon. "He made an awful fuss about getting it right. Say, do you know how the thing was done?"

"I suspect, at least, though I am not certain, but my idea would at least be like Dual's."

"Well, it sure got me," said my host, as he slowed down near the clump of buildings.

"However, in view of the results, I don't care if he had help from the Old Nick himself. Well, here we are, Gordon. Come into the office and talk to Schiff, while I hunt you up some clothes."

I climbed down from the seat and followed Curzon into the small frame building which they used as an office. It was perhaps twenty feet square and strongly constructed. In front was a vacant space before a railing.

Back of this were some desks and a stenographer's table, at which sat a young man industriously pounding the keys. At the desks two other youngsters pored over some ledgers. They all glanced up as we came in.

Curzon swept his eyes over the room. "Where's Schiff?" he inquired.

"Mr. Schiff went over to No. 2," said the stenographer. "He tried to get you on the phone, but you'd just left. He left a note for you."

He produced a sheet of paper and extended it to Curzon as he spoke.

Curzon read it, grunted, and handed it to me.

"Read that," he said. "There's some more 'local color.' It will give you an idea of what running a mine is like. It's like sitting on a volcano without any tips as to when the blowout will occur."

I glanced over the lines the superintendent had left:

> Dear Curzon:
> They have just phoned me that there is a slip in No. 2. This will require my presence, as you will agree. Sorry not to be here, but they insist that I come over at once.   Schiff.

I folded the thing up and carelessly stuffed it into my pocket.

"Anybody hurt?" inquired Curzon of the stenographer.

"I think not," said the man. "Mr. Schiff didn't mention it if there was."

"All right," said Curzon, "that's good. Well, Gordon, I guess I'll have to act as your guide, so sit down and I'll get you some old rags and we'll go through right away."

I dropped into a chair and busied myself getting my camera and flash-light gun in order, while Curzon disappeared. Presently he returned with a set of heavy overalls and a canvas jumper and told me to put them on. He crowned the bizarre outfit with an old, stained, and battered hat, equipped himself likewise, and we went out to the hoisting-house.

On the way I took some plates of the buildings, and I also snapped a couple of pictures of the upper part of the hoist. It was the first time

I had ever been down a mine, and it was a rather eery sensation when the cage began to drop us into the earth. Down and down we went past the various levels. It was something like going down the shaft of an immense skyscraper in the dark.

The cage settled smoothly into darkness; the daylight faded. After a bit there was a light, and a long string of incandescents dwindling away into the dark; then darkness again; then another row of lights; and so on, down and down.

After a while we stopped and Curzon led me off the platform.

"Thousand foot working. Mind your footing," he said.

We spent a couple of hours in the mine and I took a lot of flashlights of everything that it was safe to take. Then we climbed back onto the cage and went back to the sunlight and the fresh air.

We walked out of the shaft-house and Curzon waved his hand up into the air.

"There's how we bring the ore from No. 2," he said.

I looked up and saw a couple of steel cables stretching out into space across the gulch, supported at intervals upon steel towers. To and fro, across this aerial bridge, great buckets were swinging, which my host explained contained the rich ore from the other shaft.

"See!" he said. "There's one just starting out. It contains at least a ton of ore, worth not less than fifty dollars. No, I'm hanged if it does! That particular bucket contains a man."

"A man!" I gasped.

Curzon smiled. "Quite right," he replied. "Lots of times when we're in a hurry we ride across in the buckets. It saves a lot of time, for it's a long road round."

"Well, I'd rather you'd do it than I," said I, smiling. "I'd get air-sick or something if I tried that stunt."

"It's all in being used to a thing," Curzon said, watching the man, who now swung high over the drop of the cañon.

"After you've done it a time or two you never give it a thought. I'll bet that's Schiff coming back now," he added, after a moment's longer scrutiny of the approaching bucket, as it swung up toward where we stood.

"By the way, Gordon, better get a photograph of that. Show 'em back East how we ride around out here."

The suggestion was a good one, and I was doubly anxious to take it when I remembered Dual's directions to get snaps of any new characters whom I met.

I got out my camera and focused on a part of the aerial tramway, which was quite near at hand; then I waited as the bucket with its passenger drew up the slope. Nearer and nearer it came, until I could mark the man's features quite clearly.

He was leaning over the edge of the bucket and waving a hand to Curzon as he saw us standing, looking up. He was dark, with a warm olive skin and close-cropped black hair, and he wore a small mustache, curled up at the ends. So much I saw before the bucket swung into my range, and just then the man straightened and half turned so that his profile came full into my lens.

I pressed the button, and as I heard the shutter click I heaved a sigh of relief over a task well done, for at that range and with that pose I knew that I could not have failed.

"Get him?" asked Curzon, smiling. "That's Schiff, and you're lucky to catch him at all. He's foolishly averse to having his picture taken. Some of the girls downtown have tried to get him to give them a photograph, but they've never got one out of Schiff yet. Well, if you're done, let's go over to the office. I'm sort of anxious to learn how much damage was done."

We went over to the small frame, and met Schiff as he was getting out of the bucket. Curzon presented me, and we shook hands. Then Curzon led him away to talk over the occurrence at No. 2, telling me to make myself at home while he was engaged.

I strolled about and took a couple more pictures. I really thought I might send them to Smithson with the story I was going to write.

Then I sat down in the sun on the hillside and proceeded to dream. I thought of a lot of things, among them Connie Baird, and from that to Myrtle Parton and Dick Sheldon, and all the rest. Of course, I thought of my strange friend Semi Dual—half of Abdul. It was an odd conceit, strangely in keeping with the rest I knew of the man.

I got out a cigarette and went to smoking and looking over the rolling hills, and after a bit I got up and walked back to Curzon's machine and sat down in the left-hand seat and waited until he came out.

"Sorry to keep you waiting," he apologized, as he put up the spark and gas and went round to crank up; "but there were several things which needed my attention. However, we'll get you home in a jiffy, and you'll have plenty of time to eat and go see the girl."

He climbed in, and we were soon falling swiftly into the valley. I asked about the accident in the other tunnel, and Curzon replied that fortunately it had not been of any great importance. It was not until we got into the town itself that I noticed that I was still wearing the mine clothes. I mentioned the fact to Curzon, and he laughed.

"I thought maybe you wanted them for a souvenir," he said. It was thus that I came to have them still on when I went to my room, and it was in taking off the jacket that the bit of paper fell out of a pocket of the thing. I picked it up and unfolded it into a telegraph-form, and naturally I looked at it; and the longer I looked the less I knew. It was a queer telegram and no mistake, when one considered that it came out of a workman's jacket in a Goldfield mine.

JESS:
Send me insole, usual brand, number five.
CAM.

For the life of me I couldn't find any meaning to it, unless it was a code, so on the off-chance I decided to send it with my snap of the superintendent and the note to Semi Dual.

CHAPTER X.

"RETURN."

I CALLED upon Miss Sheldon that evening and spent a very pleasant hour. Rather long for a first call; but we got to talking about things of mutual interest, and neither one of us noticed how the time went. As I was leaving I mentioned that I had been up at the mine during the afternoon, and spoke of my having snapped the superintendent in the aerial bucket as he came back from the other shaft.

Miss Sheldon laughed.

"The redoubtable J.E.S.," she said. "I reckon he'd have a fit if he knew you'd taken his photograph."

"Curzon said he was gun-shy," I said as I rose to depart.

"He's funny in a lot of ways," said Alice Sheldon. "He fancies he's a lady's-man. He used to work for papa before he went away, and since he's come back he's been working for Mr. Curzon. He makes me tired. He actually has the nerve to come up here at times and act as if he was fond of me."

"I don't see anything funny in that," I told her, and she laughed.

"Really, Mr. Gordon, I don't like him," she said; then, in a more serious manner: "He's too—too—oily, I guess."

I said good night, after promising to call again, and went back to Curzon's place.

The next day I hunted up a photographer and had my films developed, and I stayed with him as he worked. When he came to the picture of Schiff in the bucket he, too, expressed surprise.

"Masher Schiff takin' a ride, eh?" he said, grinning. "Now, if he knew you got that, I wonder what he'd say? He won't never have a picter took. You got this swell, Mr. Gordon, for kodak work."

We bent over the negative, and I confess I felt proud of my work. It was a perfect profile of the mine-superintendent, and against the background of the sky his features came out with the distinctness of a cameo.

I told the photographer to print it at once, and take his time with the others; and an hour later I left his studio with a copy of the negative, which I at once sent off to Dual.

Then, having nothing to do, I went about the town a bit, had some lunch, and went back to Curzon's and wrote a story for Smithson, giving my impressions of the town and the situation there as it appeared to me.

I posted the thing, and then I borrowed Curzon's car and drove out to Sheldon's, where I found Miss Alice, trying to read a book on the front veranda, and dared her to come for a ride.

"Will I?" she cried, jumping up in a swirl of cool skirts. "Just wait till I get my hat."

"How is the foot?" I called; "shall I carry you down?"

"It's strapped and I can hobble," she answered. "Wait, I'll be right out."

I throttled the engine and sat and waited until she came slowly down to the street. Then I assisted her in, and we were soon out of the town and sweeping off toward the hills.

"This is simply glorious," said the girl, with heightened color in her cheeks. "I always wanted a machine, but papa said I would get to be a speed-crank and break my neck. I do like to go fast, don't you?"

I replied with a burst of speed.

"Archie always used to say he'd get me one of the things after we were—" began Miss Sheldon, and stopped and began to blush. Then she laughed and tossed her head.

"Oh, well, I suppose I might as well tell it all now," she said defiantly. "Arch and I are engaged, though we haven't told papa yet. That's why I am so interested in Arch. I want him to get ahead, so he can take care of me."

I looked at the girl's radiant face and shining eyes, and for the moment I felt that I could rather sympathize with Archie Parton in his losing speculation.

The girl, while not my style of beauty, was certainly worth winning for any man who could love her, and to-day she looked as though she would not be hard to love.

"Archie writes that he's in a little trouble," she went on after a bit.

"It seems somebody forged papa's name to a check, and Archie got the thing cashed at the bank. There's been a man arrested for forging the thing, and Archie is afraid papa and he may get drawn into the case. He said he thought he ought to tell me about it. But I can't see that it can hurt Archie any, can you?"

For a moment I hesitated how to answer; then I decided that generalities were best.

"It should be easy for Archie to prove where he got the check," I told her, "and that ought to let him out, I should think."

"Oh, I hope so," said Miss Sheldon. "Archie seemed quite worried, I thought; but I shall write him what you say this very night. Suppose we go home now?"

I turned around and we went back to the town. Miss Sheldon said little on the backward track, and when we drew up in front of the house she climbed out, and beyond thanking me for the ride in preoccupied fashion, said nothing as I drove away.

I felt sorry for the girl from the bottom of my heart as I thought of the envelope I had sent to Semi, with its queer slanting and curved "i's."

That was the beginning of the dullest two weeks I ever spent before or since. There was little or nothing to do, and beyond calling on Miss Sheldon, a trip with her to a mine of her father's, and an occasional automobile-ride, I found time hang heavy indeed.

I got so that my report to Dual amounted to the words "nothing doing" scrawled on a piece of paper and signed with my name. Finally in desperation I turned to the Jap, Hashimoto, and began to study Japanese and the customs of his land. He was a smart little beggar, and taught me a lot of wrestling tricks, among other things, as the days went by.

It was just two weeks from the day I had first driven out with Alice Sheldon that Curzon stormed into breakfast with his usually ruddy face changed to a purple hue.

"Hello, Gordon!" he greeted. "I'm in the deuce of a fix. They've just telephoned from the mine that a couple of plain-clothes men from your town came up to the mine after dark last evening, dragged Schiff out of the quarters, and placed him under arrest.

"What do you know about it, anyway, if I may ask so plain a question? It sure looks to me like your work. If you hadn't come from Abdul and brought his letter, damme if I wouldn't think you a detective yourself."

Worst of all, Curzon meant it, as I could see at a glance; yet I was as much surprised as himself. Schiff's arrest was the very last thing in the world I had been expecting, and I know Curzon saw the genuine bewilderment in my face.

I opened my lips to deny any conscious complicity in depriving him of his mine-boss, when he cut me short.

"I beg your pardon, old chap!" he said. "I'm a good bit upset. But when I look at your face I have to admit it gets you in the wind yourself. I'm mighty glad to know that, too. I'd hate to think any friend of Dual's was a snake. Anyway, this thing leaves me in a hole. I guess I'll have to go up there for a few days. So I'll have to ask you to get along with 'Hash' as best you can. Hang it all, Schiff was the best 'super' I ever had!"

It being the psychological moment, Hashimoto at this instant appeared. He carried a telegraph envelope, which he handed to me. Asking Curzon's permission, I opened it and read what it contained:

> Mr. George Gordon,
> Care John Curzon, Goldfield, Nevada: Return.

There was no signature at all, but it gave me a sense of escaping from bondage; and I was doubly glad that it came when it did, because it cleared the domestic atmosphere for Curzon as well. I had been going to suggest that I find a hotel.

I tossed the message across to him, and smiled as he picked it up.

"My boss is evidently of the opinion that I am better at home than abroad," I remarked, tossing down my napkin. "I am called home, as you see. When can I get a train out?"

"Some time this afternoon," said Curzon; "I'll have Hash look it up for you if you like. Hang it, Gordon, I'm not going to say that I'm sorry you got it, if you have to go, anyway, just at this time, though I am sorry you have to go at all."

"Well, the special correspondent, like the soldier, goes when ordered," I said, rising; "so all I can do is to express my greatest thanks for your hospitality, and hope to reciprocate some day."

"I'll be leaving for the mine almost immediately," said Curzon; "so I'll say good-by now. I'm jolly glad to have met you, Gordon, and if ever this way again, be sure you drop in."

We parted with a clasp of the hands, and I went up-stairs to pack. All the time I was wondering if anything I had done could have made trouble for my host. After a bit I heard the snort of his roadster as he rushed off for the mine. Then I called Hashimoto, and told him to look up my train.

When I had finished packing I put on my coat and hat and walked over to the Sheldon place. I told Miss Sheldon that I was recalled, and expressed my disappointment in not meeting her father.

Also, I offered to take any messages to Parton which she might wish to send. Of course, that was not all gallantry. I had never met the boy, and I wanted to do so. Therefore a message from Miss Sheldon would offer a very fair excuse.

Of course, Alice Sheldon could not know this, and she thanked me so prettily that I felt like a hypocrite. "You are awfully kind and thoughtful, Mr. Gordon," she said.

"Some day I'm going to tell Archie how nice you have been to me, and he will thank you, too. If you see him, tell him I am well, and said not to worry about anything, but to just keep his promise to me, and that I am sure everything will come out all right."

"Keep his promise to her." Now, I wondered what she meant by that, but I didn't know, and I was sure she didn't mean that I should, so all I could do was to promise and say good-by.

I went back to Curzon's. Hashimoto served me some luncheon and called a cab to take me to the train. I got off with little bother, and sat smoking and thinking until I made Las Vegas, where I caught the train for Salt Lake and the East.

To me my trip seemed almost like a waste of time and money. For the life of me I couldn't see what I had accomplished, or why Dual had kept me waiting in idleness for over two weeks before sending me that single word: "Return."

The car-wheels drummed and pounded beneath me that night, and all through my sleep their dull rumble seemed to frame the words "Semi Dual" in my brain.

CHAPTER XI.

DUAL'S CALLER.

I WENT directly to Dual's from my train, only stopping to leave my cases at my room. Semi met me with a smile on his face and an outstretched hand.

"On time to the minute; I was expecting you to-night," he said.

"Does nothing ever surprise you, Dual?" I asked. I had hoped to catch him for once without that stock phrase on his lips.

"Why should one be surprised at what one expects?" said Semi. "Well, sit down and tell me what you have to report."

"I wrote you the whole thing from Goldfield," I answered half sulkily. "Of all the wild goose chases, that was the worst."

"Think so?" said Semi absently. "You surprise me."

He turned away and went on fussing with something which he was doing to one wall of the room. I lighted a cigarette which I took from a case on his desk, and lay back and watched him as he worked. Now and then he would touch a switch, and there would be a sudden flash of light in the room. Presently he turned toward me again.

"Would you mind taking that padded chair?" he inquired.

I got up and occupied the designated seat, and Semi turned his switch. Instantly. I felt a beam of light strike me in the eyes, and a few seconds later it was repeated. I blinked at the unwarranted brilliance.

"Get it?" said Dual.

"I got it or it got me," I answered. "What are you trying to do?"

"It's a trifling invention of my own," Dual explained. "There's a small electric light back of this prism of glass here, you see. The light is automatically turned on and off every so many seconds by a circular revolving switch which is operated by a concealed motor. Every time the circuit is made the light flashes through the plate and focuses on the chair. How does it feel? It should prove rather tiring to the eye."

"It does," I assured him. "Is there any particular reason why I should occupy this chair for very long?"

"Not at all," said Dual. "You can leave it as soon as you choose. I just wanted to be sure of the effect, and that I had the distance judged right."

He came back, and sat down and picked up a cigarette. Then he rang for his man, and directed him to remove all but three chairs from the room.

I looked on with a total lack of understanding. Finally his smug silence got on my nerves.

"What *are* you trying to do?" I burst out.

"A little stage-setting," said Semi, with a wave of the hand.

"For what?"

Dual grinned. "I am expecting Archie Parton up here after a bit," he said in his matter-of-fact tone. "I sent for him to come. I could have got him before, but I wanted to wait until you were here, so I made it to-night. I want to ask him about several things."

"Do you think he will answer?" I asked in some doubt.

"He will answer me," Dual replied easily. "I told him to be here about eight. He ought to be coming soon."

"By the way," I said, taking another cigarette, "I met the girl Archie is engaged to, and she told me a bit about the fellow. In one way I'm sort of sorry for the kid. She gave me a message for him."

"You can deliver it in a moment," said Semi, as the chime of the annunciator broke the silence of the room.

"Sit still," he went on. "I want Archie to take the padded chair." He crossed the room swiftly and turned on his little switch. A moment later Dual's man showed Parton into the room.

The boy came in rather nervously. I noticed that he looked worn and pale, and had circles under his eyes, as though he might have lost a deal of sleep. He stood looking about him a moment, then approached Dual.

"I am here, Mr. Dual," he said in a low tone. Semi waved him to the padded chair.

"Sit down, Mr. Parton," he said, "and don't be disturbed. Believe me, I have asked you here for your own good. Suppose we first have a little coffee and cognac, and then we will get down to business, so that you can get away? You know Mr. Glace?" indicating me.

Parton half rose. "I have heard of Mr. Glace from my sister," he acknowledged, "and I wish to thank him for the interest he has taken in her behalf." It was well said, and I felt a sort of liking for the boy. Semi crossed and ordered coffee and cognac from his man, and while he was about it I addressed Parton myself.

"I've just got back from Goldfield, Parton," I said. "While out there I met a young lady who is a friend of yours. Miss Sheldon asked to be remembered to you, and asked me to tell you to keep your promise to her."

Parton flinched at the words, and grew, if anything, paler than before. After an interval, in which he sat staring directly at me, he made shift to utter the one phrase: "Thank you," and lapsed into silence again.

I noticed that at times he passed his hand before his eyes, and I knew that Dual's little lamp was doing its work.

Dual now brought the coffee, placed the sugar in the spoons, poured on the brandy and ignited it, and handed us each a cup. As soon as we had disposed of the beverage he turned to Parton and began his attack.

"Mr. Parton," he began speaking, "I have reason to believe that you know about the passing of a forged check at the Fourth National Bank some time ago. Also, I am aware that it was you who cashed the check. I have found that out in the simplest way, although neither Mr. Dick Sheldon nor any other friend has told it to me. Now I want to show you a photograph of that check, and then I want to show you a letter addressed in your own hand."

He drew out his copy of the forgery and the envelope I had sent him from Goldfield; and while my heart ached for the lad, he laid them before him, spread out on a sheet of stiff cardboard, which he held in his hand.

"You will notice," said Semi, "that the small 'i' in the word 'five' on the check, and the small 'i's' on the letter are each curved quite a little. I want you to explain this to me."

The lad began to tremble. His fingers gripped into the arms of the chair, and before he spoke he moistened his lips with his tongue.

"You mean to show that I forged the check, don't you?" he said. "I can see it now. And yet I'll swear to God I never touched the thing till I took it to the bank. It was given to me just as it was when Dick Sheldon cashed it for me. But you won't believe me, I guess."

"On the contrary, Archie, I do believe you," said Semi Dual, and I think I heaved a sigh of relief. "Now I want you to tell me who gave you the check."

"Mr. Dual," said the boy slowly, "I can't do that; really I can't."

"These two documents and my testimony would convict you, Archie," Dual reminded, tapping the cardboard he held.

"And if I told you I'd probably go to the pen all the same," said the boy hopelessly. "At least, he's always said he'd send, me if I ever snitched."

"Sheldon?" Dual shot the word forth so suddenly that the boy actually jumped. "See here, Parton," he continued, "what hold has 'Colonel Mac' got on you?"

"Why, none at all, that I know of," said Parton, trying to look his inquisitor in the eye from between heavy lids.

Semi Dual rose and laid down the piece of cardboard, went around back of the boy's chair, and laid his hands on each of his temples, slowly drawing his long fingers up and back into the lad's hair.

"Archie," he said, "you look sleepy. Are you a little bit sleepy, perhaps?"

"I feel funny; sort of—drowsy—I guess I am sleepy," admitted the boy. "I haven't—slept much—of late."

"Suppose," said Dual, still sweeping the boy's temples, "that you take a little nap—eh? Just a little nap—it will do you good. Let yourself go to sleep Archie— See, you are getting more and more drowsy. Your eyes are closing; go to sleep, Archie." Then, in the compelling voice he had once used to me: "Sleep."

Parton's head dropped upon his chest, and he breathed slow and deep. Dual looked at me and smiled.

"The eye strain, and a small hypnotic in the coffee, and a little suggestion," he said.

"Now, Parton"—he addressed the lad who sat wrapped in slumber—"I am your friend. You have wanted a friend for a long time, my boy; some one to whom you could talk as to a father. I am that friend.

"For a long time you have had something preying on your conscience which you wanted to tell. This is your chance. Tell it to me. Go way back to the beginning, Archie, and tell me all about it from the time you first met Colonel Sheldon until to-night, my boy. Go on."

The sleeping figure opened its lips and spoke, while we sat and listened to the poor entangled spirit's tale.

"When I went West," said Parton, or Parton's spirit, "I went to Goldfield, and got a job in Colonel Mac's office. After a bit I met Alice, and I got to think a great deal of her.

"Lots of the boys in the office gambled, and I got to gambling, too. But I didn't win; I lost. I needed money to pay what I lost, and I took it from Colonel Mac. He found me out, and I thought he was going to send me to jail; but he told me he'd let me off, and not tell Alice, if I'd do anything he told me; only if I ever told about any of the things, he'd send me up.

"Well, after a while I wanted to come home, and I came back here and went to work for Pearson & Co.; and every day, if there was something that looked good, I had to put the colonel next. Then, when he came here, I had to give him inside tips.

"I was crazy to get some money so's I could marry Alice; and when I thought I saw a good thing I took some money from the company and speculated, only I didn't have sense enough to let go at the right time and I lost, and I couldn't pay the money back.

"Well, I told Alice about it, and she got Dick Sheldon to get me some money, and I paid it all up, so no one ever found out. But all I got for trying to make money for Alice was to go a thousand into the hole. I guess I deserved it, for I'd promised her to cut out gambling and fast company. But it looked like a sure thing, and I wanted the girl.

"Then, on the day this check was forged, or cashed, I mean, Pearson telephoned to Colonel Mac for more margin. Colonel Mac said to send me over and he'd give me the money.

"When I got there he gave me the check, told me to get it cashed, and bring the money to him. Well, I did it, and he kept a thousand dollars in bills and gave me four thousand, and I took them to Pearson, and the colonel's deal went through."

"Just a minute, Archie," Dual interrupted. "Do you remember what form the thousand he kept was in? What sized bills?"

"Dick gave me ten five-hundred-dollar bills," said Parton, "and the colonel kept two of them."

"All right," said Dual. "Go on."

"Well, then, they arrested Sheldon, and I guess he was afraid I'd done the whole thing; and I can't blame him, when he knew what Myrtle had told him I'd done at Pearson's, so he wouldn't say a word for fear of getting me into it. Myrtle's been awfully worried, and so have I. I'd have told all I knew only I didn't dare, 'cause Colonel Mac would have sent me up for what I did in Goldfield, and I haven't known what to do." He paused, and two tears rolled down over his cheeks.

"Now, just a moment, Archie," said Dual. "Who do you think forged the check?"

"I don't know for sure," said the lad; "but I've got a suspicion. There used to be a fellow working for Colonel Mac who was mighty handy with a pen. He used to always make his 'i's' like that one in the check. That was how I got to doing it. I'd never seen any one else do it, and it looked sort of nifty, I thought."

Dual looked over and smiled at me with a very glad expression.

"A weak soul, easily led, not inherently vicious," he said. "I saw that when you sent me the envelope from Goldfield the day you arrived."

He rose, picked the boy up in his arms, and laid him down gently on the couch. Then he went over and turned off his switch which flashed the light. He turned back to the boy.

"Archie, Archie. Forget that you have told me anything. Wake up, my boy."

Parton dug his knuckles into his eyes, yawned, and started to a sitting position.

"Good Lord! Did I go to sleep?" he cried.

"Coffee and cognac seemed too much for you, Parton," Dual reassured him, "so I laid you down to finish your nap."

"I'm awfully sorry, Mr. Dual," Parton apologized.

Dual waved him aside. "Perhaps you had better be going home," he suggested. "I will ring for my man to show you out. And Parton; stop worrying. Everything will come out all right. Tell your sister that. Good night."

When the boy was gone, Dual lit another cigarette, and suggested that I tell him about my last days in Goldfield. I plunged into the tale and ended with the arrest of Schiff.

"It was totally unexpected," I made an end. "Neither Curzon nor I could imagine who was back of the arrest."

"I was," said Dual, with a smile.

"You were? What did you have him arrested for?"

"Let me see; what was it?" said Semi. "Bigamy, I think."

"Why bigamy?" I gasped.

"Because he's a bigamist," my friend replied.

"You see," he continued, chuckling at my amazement, "Mr. J.E.S. Schiff, as he calls himself, is a very interesting man.

"When you so kindly sent me his profile, I recognized him as a man who some years ago escaped from the State prison, where he was serving a sentence for having more than the legal number of wives. The first thing I did was to show the picture to headquarters, and they did all the rest, toward bringing him East for me."

"But what did you want with Schiff?" I began, and then I, too, remembered.

"You don't mean—" I began again.

Semi laughed. "Have you remembered the curved 'i' in the note Mr. Schiff, nee Silvio, wrote to Curzon?" he asked.

"Then he is—"

"Wait," said Dual. "When you left, I told you that the final scenes of this drama would be played out here. I am waiting for our friend Colonel Mac, right now. You can be a witness if you like. I also have another one, but it is merely a dictograph, with a wire connecting me with a private detective agency, so you may as well stay."

I gasped and subsided into a surprised and admiring silence, as I looked at my friend.

Ten o'clock sounded from Dual's monster clock as I sat, and hard on the stroke, came again the annunciator chimes. Dual smiled slightly as he caught my questioning eye, but said nothing.

A moment later the door opened, and Colonel MacDonohue Sheldon entered the room.

CHAPTER XII.

A SECOND CALLER.

DUAL MADE no move toward rising to his feet, but merely waved Sheldon to a chair.

"Good evening, Colonel Sheldon," he said, smiling. "I am glad to find you punctual. Take a chair. I have ordered my man to prepare you a highball, as soon as he showed you in. He's rather good at the thing, and I believe you'll have no need to wish you were in Goldfield when you put your lips to the glass."

"Thank you, sir," said the colonel, as he took the proffered chair, and laid his hat beside him on the floor.

"Colonel Sheldon," Dual resumed speaking, "some years ago I happened to be in Goldfield. It may interest you to know that I am John Curzon's silent partner in the Rediscovery group of claims."

"Is that so!" cried the colonel. "Well, now, I've often wondered about that. I tell you that was a lucky strike. What always got me was that I had a chance to buy them there claims and passed it up. So you're the fellow who bought in with Curzon, eh? Well, sir, I congratulate you."

It was an attempt at the colonel's old style of bluster, but as I looked at the man I saw that he looked strangely worn and fagged out; quite unlike the man of success I had met in Pearson's place that August afternoon. Try as he would he could not keep the harassment out of face and voice.

"The fact that I am Curzon's partner has nothing to do, however, with my asking you to call here, save to explain my being in Goldfield some years ago. As a matter of fact, I have a little story which I have made up from various fragments, and I want to tell it to you. I want you to listen closely and if I make any mistakes, I want you to correct me at once," said Dual.

"My story starts in Goldfield as it happens and has to do with my picking up a stray envelope in the street one day. You see, I am a student of chirography—or handwriting—and wherever I find an interesting sample of anything like that, I add it to my collection, which is quite extensive, by the way.

"This particular letter, which I found in the streets of Goldfield, had a very unusual characteristic, which made me very careful to preserve it. I brought it home and filed it away, and have kept it ever since. The envelope which I picked up was addressed to— Ah! Here is my man with the highball, colonel. Allow me to suggest that you take a drink before I tell any more."

Sheldon shot Dual a glance of suspicion, then lifted the glass from the tray in Dual's man's hands and half drained it at a gulp.

"How do you find it, colonel?" Dual inquired with solicitation. "Is it up to the Goldfield mark?" To me he seemed playing with the man.

Sheldon finished the mixture and set down the glass. "It is very excellent, Mr. Dual," he said shortly. "Suppose you get on with the tale."

"Right!" said Dual. "Where was I? Oh, yes—the envelope, was addressed to Colonel MacDonohue Sheldon, Goldfield, Nevada. In the upper corner was a return address to J.E.S., Box 55.

"As I said, I picked it up and kept it, but I have never seen another like it until recently, when I discovered the same peculiar character in the writing on the check forged at the Fourth National Bank. The peculiarity which I refer to is in the shape of the letter 'i' in the word 'Five' on the check. It is the same as the 'i' in the word Goldfield, on the envelope I picked up.

"When I saw the check, I immediately remembered the specimen in my collection, and came immediately home to examine the thing. Still more recently I have come into possession of a note written by this J.E.S.—this Schiff, as he calls himself— Sit still, Sheldon! A movement of my finger will strike you dead!"

Colonel MacDonohue Sheldon sank back into the chair from which he had been about to leap toward Dual, and for the first time I noticed Semi's hand hovering above a button on his desk. It was a new button, and I wondered what it was.

"If I press this small switch," Dual explained to the now pallid-faced colonel, "you would get something like a lethal dose of a high-frequency current. Furthermore, I could press it, my dear colonel, before you could draw on me.

"The 'i's' in this note of Schiff's are the same as appear on the envelope I found in Goldfield, and the 'i' on the forged check. Now, Colonel Sheldon, I shall leave facts and tell you my composite tale.

"Some years ago you employed a young boy in your offices in Goldfield. This lad got in with wrong companions, and stole from you to pay a gambling debt. Instead of trying to put him back on the right course, when you discovered his misdemeanor, you took advantage of his position to still further corrupt him, and make him your tool. His name was—Archie Parton, wasn't it, Glace?"

I nodded my head, with an eye on Colonel Mac, who was again shifting in his chair.

"The boy loved your daughter, and you could have made him run straight, Colonel Sheldon," Dual went on, "but you needed a scapegoat, maybe, and a tool to do your dirty work. After a bit, the boy came

East and you still made him play into your hands by stealing information for you from the men for whom he worked.

"Then you came East, and entered upon a stock speculation. As margins were called for, you put up the money, from time to time. In order to get the cash quickly you had your brother, who was paying-teller for a bank, cash them and send them for collection to your own bank.

"After a bit your account was exhausted, and you saw bankruptcy staring you in the face. You had to have money and you prepared to get it any way you could. You sent Schiff, who had been a former associate of yours, a telegram for 'an insole'—I have the telegram—and he forged the check for five thousand in your name, and sent it to you.

"Thus you could, if need be, swear that it was a forgery, and by having Parton, over whom you held a threat of the penitentiary, cash it, you felt safe from having him tell anything he knew. Parton cashed the thing at your orders, and the four thousand additional margin carried your deal through.

"Your brother never hesitated to honor the check, for he never suspected that his own brother would do such a thing as utter false paper against the bank where he worked. I shall give you the benefit of the doubt here, Sheldon, for it may be possible that you actually hoped that the deal would go through in time for you to get the five thousand back in time to prevent trouble. But the deal dragged and you had to hold on, and as a result the bank examiners found the shortage which your brother was concealing, because he thought his *fiancée's* brother was the forger, before he could raise the money he was trying to get, to replace the amount.

"The first thing which made me suspicious of this was your own remark to Malin, that day in the bank, when you asked if it would help your brother if it were shown that the numbers of the notes in his box, in the first place, had not corresponded to those on the new issue of currency used in cashing the forged check. That was a slip.

"Further, we discovered that up to the day of your brother's arrest you had been hard run, and the day after you were certainly in funds. You see how it all fits in. Now, if I am in any way wrong, suppose you show me where."

Sheldon now sat with head sunk upon his chest, breathing in the nervous manner of a man greatly overwrought.

"You are devilish clever, Dual," he said, as Semi ceased talking; "and I guess I know when I'm licked. I've fancied I was a pretty smooth cuss, but I might have known I'd get caught up with some of these days. I suppose you've got a bunch of policemen concealed somewhere around here. Well, call 'em in. At least it will let Dick out. I'm glad of that."

"I should have told you that I had Schiff, whose real name is Silvio, arrested," said Dual. "He is now in the State prison, from which he escaped over six years ago, while serving a charge of bigamy. He is pretty likely to stay there this time, and will be a good witness for the defense of your brother Dick. As for the policemen, I haven't any of them here, so you need not fear instant arrest. Whether you are arrested or not seems to me to depend wholly upon you."

"What do you mean?" gasped the colonel. "Why, Lord, man, you've got every card in the deck. I can't take a trick."

"Just so," said Dual. "Therefore I should be in a position to dictate terms; don't you think?"

"Terms?" said the colonel. "Say, I don't get you at all."

"Then I shall explain," Semi replied. "When the bank is shown the evidence which we possess, they will see that they cannot convict Dick Sheldon of the charge. Failing that, they will still be their five thousand out. Now if you, who were the cause of all this course of events, were to reimburse the bank, in view of the circumstances, they would be glad to drop the case. Furthermore, I give you credit for not meaning to get your brother into jail."

"You're dead right there," said the colonel. Forgetting Dual's warning, he sprang from his chair, and began to pace the room. "God, when I saw where I was, and what I'd done, I was groggy, I tell you, Dual. Honest, if it hadn't been for my girl Alice, I'd have blowed the whole game, to get Dick out, but I hated to give my kiddie a jailbird for a dad."

He brushed a hand across his eyes, and sat down again in the chair, turning his face, which was working with emotion, away from Dual and myself.

"That being the case," resumed Semi, "if you, who can best afford it, were to reimburse the bank, and pay all other costs, and stand what suffering you have, for myself, I fancy justice would be sufficiently satisfied.

"The real forger is now under bolt and bar, and pretty likely to stay there for the next three years. He himself agreed to turn State's evidence in this case, if I'd assure him against prosecution, so I've held him as a sort of joker in the game. But, as what I suggest will exonerate Dick, and protect the bank from loss, and spare the feelings of your daughter, I fancy it is better than fitting you to a prison suit, Colonel Mac."

"Do you mean to let me off if I'll square the loss to the bank? Is that what you mean?" Sheldon cried.

"That is what I mean, if it can be arranged," replied Semi. "I have good reasons to think it can. I have, in fact, talked with the prosecuting attorney about the entire thing."

Again Sheldon rose and began to pace the room. Finally he crossed and stood towering over Dual.

"I'm not going to offer to shake hands with you, Mr. Dual," he began, "but I want to tell you that I've met a lot of men in my lifetime, and you're the whitest one of the lot. Well, we've got a way of binding a bargain in my circle. When we take a a man, we say: 'You're on,' and that's what I'm saying to you: 'You're on.'

"Man, you don't know what you've done for me, and to think I was tryin' for the drop on you a half-hour ago. Say, I feel like a yaller dog, and I never said that to no one before. You bet I'll pay the bank. I always meant to, only you was right when you said they shut down on me too quick. As for them two five-hundred bills, I did that without ever meanin' nuthin' at all. They was too big to use handy, so I went to the bank to get some 'chicken feed.' The bank was shut, and Dick said he couldn't get into the vaults, so he gave me some smaller bills out of his own safety-box, and put the two fives in their place. I never once thought how it was goin' to look, for I was somewhat worried over my stock deal, or I guess I'd not have overlooked that bet."

"I rather imagined something like that, though I had no proof," said Semi Dual.

Sheldon drew out a check-book, and sat down in his chair.

"Let's get this thing settled right now," he said, and began to fill in a check. "Shall I make this payable to—"

"Bearer," said Semi Dual.

The colonel filled the blank, tore it out, and passed it across. Then he began to fill in another blank. "You said you didn't want nuthin' outen this," he said, as he wrote, "so I'm going to make a check to any sort of charity you suggest, an' for any amount you want. How shall I make it out?"

Semi Dual smiled. "Suppose that you make it payable to Archie Parton, and give your consent to his marriage to your daughter," he said.

"Alice Sheldon is the best thing which ever came into the boy's life, as you were the worst. Make the check for five thousand to Parton, and I'll see that he gets it, with the proviso that the day he marries your daughter, he turns it over to her as evidence that from now he intends to run straight. I might mention, also, that there is a matter of fifteen hundred expenses which I have incurred in carrying the case thus far."

Sheldon nodded. "Does my girl love Parton?" he asked.

"Glace says they are engaged," replied Dual.

Sheldon looked at me. I nodded my head. "Miss Alice told me herself," I said. Sheldon filled in the checks, and when they were done and blotted, tore them out and added them to the other which Semi still held. Then he put his check-book away, picked up his hat, rose, and faced Dual with a smile.

"I reckon," he said, "that you win on every turn. But I've always said it wasn't no disgrace to be licked by a real man, and I ain't changin' my mind now. I reckon I'd better go back to Goldfield and get out of the game. I've got a good mine and a good home, and a good girl. I guess I'll go out there and settle down. When do you think they will let Dick out?"

"As soon as I can adjust things," said Semi Dual. "I believe I may say you can all spend Sunday together, at least."

Sheldon nodded again. "When I come East, I reckoned myself as some wise guy," he said, "but I guess there was a lot I didn't know. When I first met you, I didn't think a lot of you, Mf. Dual, and all the time you was gettin' ready to drop on me like a ton of ore. I reckon I don't belong back here. I can get along better out in the West, *an' I wish I was in Goldfield right now.*"

He turned and went out without another word.

CHAPTER XIII.
THE END OF THE CASE.

"AND SO ends the Sheldon case," said Semi, when we were alone again, and the chimes had sounded the passing of Colonel Mac. "There were a few little things which I held out on Sheldon, for reasons of my own. First, I have already taken the thing up with the bank. After proving to them by the prosecuting attorney that they could not get a conviction of Sheldon over the evidences I would introduce, I got them to listen to a compromise. They will take their money and agree to stop all action whatever in the case.

"You will remember my little prediction to our acquaintance, Malin of the pig eyes? Well, when it appeared that he had never mentioned Sheldon's proposition to the directorate, they didn't seem to approve at all. When they saw that he had let his personal grudge against young Sheldon outweigh the interests of the bank, they suggested to him that he hand in his resignation. As a result, the assistant cashier will occupy the cashier's desk after the first of the month.

"Further, as a mark of their restored faith in their recent paying-teller, they are going to move him up to the position left vacant by the promotion of the assistant cashier; so that Colonel Mac's prediction for his brother seems in a fair way to be fulfilled after all. That will smooth things for Sheldon and the Parton girl. Oh, things might have ended worse," he smiled.

"To-morrow," he went on after a moment's thought, "I shall send the bank their money. Upon that being received the prosecutor will ask the judge for a dismissal of the charges against Sheldon, and his immediate release.

"And now I fancy you can go and see Smithson, and tell him all about the thing. By the way, when Schiff was extradited back here from Goldfield, I tipped your editor off, and gave you the credit for the tip. They made what I believe you call a 'scoop.' They ought to make another one on the story you can give him to-night. Well, run along. I confess after it is all over I feel a bit fatigued. I think I'll have another cup of coffee, and try to get a little rest."

"So that my trip to Goldfield did some good after all?" I said as I picked up my hat.

"It helped to make everybody happy," said Semi Dual; "for after the sting of the first shock is over, even Colonel MacDonohue Sheldon will be a far more contented man."

I went to see Smithson and told him all of the tale. When I had ended he sat and looked at his desk-blotter for quite a long time. Finally he looked me in the eye.

"Glace," said the city editor, "you are a wonder. But I fancy you're wasted in the newspaper game. Why, man, you ought to be running a detective department. You've got a lot of these dubs skinned a mile."

"Do you wonder I wanted to go to Goldfield," I laughed.

Smithson shook his head, and picked up some papers from his desk.

"The paper's got to come out," he said slowly, "and I can't talk any more now. Some day I want you to tell me about the whole thing again. Go along and write your story, and make a good thing out of it, Glace. Play up the exoneration of Dick Sheldon mighty strong. We owe it to him to give him a clean bill of moral health, I think."

THE
WISTARIA
SCARF

CHAPTER I.
A "KARMIC VIBRATION."

I THINK I once described Alice Sheldon as a "brilliant brunette." That was when she was a girl living in Goldfield at the time I was out there on the trail of a man who forged her father's name to a check. She was at that time engaged to a young fellow named Archibald Parton, who lived in my home town, and circumstances made me see quite a little of the girl.

She was a beauty of the type, and Archie was fairly wild about her. He proved it by marrying her a short time after I had returned to my paper from Goldfield. The first thing I heard about it, was that they were going for a belated honeymoon on the Continent.

Although they had been married for some six months, they had waited to take the trip in order that Colonel MacDonohue Sheldon, the girl's father, might wind up his affairs and accompany them as a sort of rough and blustering fairy godfather. As "Colonel Mac" said, the honeymoon was on "dad."

I was cooling my heels one day in late March by elevating them on my typewriter-table in the local room, when I was called to the phone. Though it had a familiar ring, I didn't recognize the voice, until the man at the other end informed me that he was at the Kenton and for once wasn't wishing he were in Goldfield. Then I woke up and asked him what it was all about.

"We want you to come up if you can," said the colonel. "Archie and Alice and I are takin' our honeymoon an' we want to say howdy to one of the men that made it possible. You come on up here, Glace, an' see the kids. They were married sort of quiet like last October, just after I got back home, an' they've been waitin' so's I could come along. We're goin' to do Europe 'fore we get back. I'm stakin' the kids to a good blowout, you bet."

"I'll be right up," I told him, and reached for my hat.

"Where you goin'?" said Smithson, my city editor, as I turned away.

"I'm going to interview three of the principals in the Sheldon forgery case," I responded. He scowled.

"If you get dragged into any more trans-continental trips," he threatened, "I won't stand for it; you understand?"

"Since I am going to see a bride and groom taking papa on their honeymoon, I don't believe I'm in much danger," I assured him, and left the office of the *Record* for the hotel.

Alice Sheldon-Parton met me as one welcomes an old friend. The girl had ripened since her marriage. She seemed to have taken on an even greater, more womanly beauty, and her figure had rounded out into fuller and more gracious lines.

They insisted upon my sitting down and Colonel Mac was at the phone ordering refreshments before I had fairly done shaking Mrs. Parton's hand.

"Make 'em a man's size now, for the sake of kindness," I heard him exhorting, and I smiled at him as he turned toward where I sat.

"Well, here we are!" said Sheldon. "When we decided to start East, Allie here wouldn't have it any way but we must stop here and see you and look up Dick and his wife, Archie's sister, and the meat of the whole nut I suspect is that more'n all else she wanted to see if she couldn't meet that funny Dual chap that put it all over her dad."

It was the first time I had seen Sheldon since the night Dual and he had had the strange meeting in Dual's apartments, and it did me good to see that he was a good loser and bore no resentment against the man who had beaten him in fair fight. It takes a considerable degree of thoroughbredness to take a defeat like that, and I was glad to find the old Westerner in that class.

"I will see what can be done," I promised. "Dual is a queer sort of person and receives but few people, usually only at his own behest."

"Who asked him to receive us?" said Sheldon. "He can come down here, can't he, Glace? I sure owe that fellow a lot more'n I can ever pay, and so do Alice and Archie here."

This time I shook my head.

"He wouldn't come, colonel," I was forced to say. "But I shall try to arrange for Mrs. Parton to meet him while she is here."

"Tell him," said Alice Parton, "that I wish to express my heartfelt thanks for all he did for me and mine. He can hardly refuse me that privilege, I think."

I agreed, promised to dine with them that evening, and left the hotel. Then I made up my mind that I might as well see Dual right away.

I took a car up to the Urania, where he lived and carried on his peculiar investigations of nature's higher forces, as he described the strange powers which he invoked at times to produce results beyond the ken of the average man. Few persons, as I had said, had the *entrée* of Dual's place. I was so fortunate as to be one of them.

It all started by my going to interview him and getting both myself and him mixed up in a murder case. Since then I had been glad of his aid in another case, in which, but for Dual, an innocent man probably would have gone to jail. The man was Sheldon's own brother, and be it said with regret, the colonel's own act was largely responsible for his brother's predicament. Everything ended, happily, thanks to Dual.

Dual was an odd genius and dwelt in a tower on the roof of the Urania, one of our largest office structures. He had fitted up the roof as a regular garden and constructed a magnificent approach from the building's upper floor. Being one of the elect, I might approach him at any time of the day or night, and I did so now.

I found him lying on a couch covered by an immense lion skin and wheeled full into the rays of the afternoon sun. He was utterly divested of clothing, save for a towel about the loins, and was lying relaxed as I came in.

It was the first time I had seen the man's body, and I marveled at its superb lines. He was the athlete without any of the overdevelopment which one so often finds in the strong man. But this man might have been a beautiful, olive-tinted Apollo as he lay at ease on the tawny hide of the dead king of beasts.

He rolled lazily on one side and greeted me with a smile as I dropped into a chair.

"Letting my body breathe," he explained easily. "One trouble with our modern methods of clothing ourselves, Glace, is that the pores don't get half a chance to functionate. Furthermore, we constrict our arterial and venous trunks with bands and garters and wonder why poor circulation overtakes us after a time. Even a school-boy knows that water won't run through a plugged hose; but we older children expect the heart to pump the blood through clogged and compressed channels and remain strong."

I rolled a cigarette and nodded. "Keep right on," I said. Dual laughed.

"I like to lie in the sun and blink my eyes and let its rays warm me through and through. One can feel the kinetic energy almost absorb through the skin. In that respect I am like the brute on whose skin I am lying. Who knows, maybe I was a lion once myself, and it is an inherited trait, this dreaming in the sun."

I looked at his splendid limbs.

"I'll warrant you were a very magnificent beast," I drawled, humoring his mood. For some time he lay silent; then: "How would you like to go to Persia?" he asked, apropos of nothing at all.

"Getting homesick?" I inquired.

"Eh?" said Dual, narrowing his eyes.

"Or are there lions in Persia?" I inquired.

Dual rolled completely over and swung to a sitting position.

"Glace," said he, "for once you have surprised me. I suppose John Curzon told you I was half Persian, my friend."

As usual he was right. Curzon was a friend of his and had, in fact, given me the information. I nodded my head.

"Because," said Dual, "he is the only person in this country who is aware of the fact, excepting yourself. However, it was not homesickness which made me ask you the question I did. While lying here, before you came in, I had what some people who do not understand would call an intuition; what is really a karmic vibration. I believe that I am soon going to find it necessary to go to Persia. In other words, friend Gordon, I had what you would call a 'hunch.' If my hunch is correct, do you want to go along?"

"Are you serious?" I asked.

"Perfectly," said Semi Dual. "Now, what brings you here?"

I preferred Mrs. Parton's (*née* Sheldon) request and waited for what Dual might say. After a moment he smiled.

"You are dining with them this evening," he remarked after a few minutes' silence. "Suppose after dinner you bring them on up here."

I expressed my surprise. Dual continued to smile.

"I have a reason for my action," he told me. "Besides, you must admit that the young woman's request is a natural one under the circumstances."

I grinned. "If I went on the principle that you would do the natural thing, I'd make a great showing, wouldn't I?" I said.

Dual laughed out loud. He seemed very human, very likable, very happy and buoyant to-day.

"I'd really enjoy meeting her," he said. "These young American women interest me every day. They are such splendid examples of what evolution will do; with their high heads, their brave eyes, their strong, elastic swing of limb. I glory in their exhibition of what the race of man may become, with education and freedom to expand mentally and physically to its best. They are the fit mates for fit men; none of your languorous voluptuaries, good only to drag men down and clog their souls and bodies with the anesthetic of their narcotic perfumes. They have the perfume of health and clean living. Such women are the gift of God."

"Bravo!" I cried as he finished and faced me with shining eyes. "And all the time I have half suspected that you were a woman-hater, Dual."

"You?" said Semi, almost as I imagine Caesar cried out to Brutus, and I was sorry that I had said what I had.

The glow faded from Dual's face. "Gordon," he said sadly, "when a man knows much, he only increases his capacity for suffering. The higher one climbs, the greater the fall, should he be cast down. I hate women? Does a true man hate any of the Creator's children? Why, I hate nothing of which I can think. There is beauty even in the lowly earthworm, if one will but look, and it was made by the same law as was man."

He began to pace the room in nervous strides.

"Hate woman! No! I love her—the whole wondrous complement of man. I have none of her, because—and, Gordon, I have told this to none save you yourself—because I am seeking for one I lost and will some day find again. That is why I am—a lion without a mate."

He flung himself into a chair and after a moment he smiled his old smile, only, perhaps, there was an added touch of sadness in it now.

"Bring your friends up after the dinner," he said, changing his tone abruptly. "I shall be very glad to meet the little woman from Goldfield, and accept the thanks she really means."

"Semi," I said, rising and looking at him where he sat, "I'm sorry. I didn't mean to wound or rub old sores. Don't be angry at the blunder

I made."

"The offer for Persia is still open," said my friend.

I put out my hand. He took it.

"You're a wonderful man," I began.

"Don't," Dual interrupted sharply. "Wonderful, never; I try at least to be a—man."

CHAPTER II.
SEMI DUAL AT HOME.

I TOOK Dual's invitation with me when I kept my engagement with the Sheldons at the Kenton that evening. Alice Parton clapped her hands in undisguised delight.

"Good!" she cried. "I am so glad. Papa has told me a lot about Mr. Dual and how he cleared up all that dreadful case without any publicity or anything at all. After Dick married Myrtle he came out West to see us and he, too, had nothing but good to say of the man. I am sure, Mr. Glace, that you must value the friendship of that wonderful man a great deal. How does he get his results?"

"He gets them in ways I myself only dimly understand," I replied. "Some day I hope that he will consider it possible to explain his methods more fully to me. As for his friendship, I value it above that of all other men."

"Papa says his apartments are the most remarkable things he has ever seen. Is that right?"

"They are certainly unusual enough for an occidental city," I answered, smiling. "The first time I saw them I half fancied I was having a dream of the Orient, and felt like rubbing my eyes to make sure I was really awake." Then I went on and described Dual's quarters as best I could.

"I'll never forget the night I went there," said young Parton. "Say, Glace, what did he do to me?"

I laughed. "I rather fancy he used a little hypnotic suggestion that time, Archie," I said.

"I half suspected that," said Parton. "He's the very devil of a fellow, Alice; a sort of combination of an East Indian fakir and a *Sherlock Holmes*."

His wife smiled and shook her head.

"He is a man to whom we owe a great deal," she said.

The dinner ran its course and we took a taxi up to the Urania. Alice wanted to walk, but the colonel swore he was going to do things in "shape"; and when we were deposited at the great building's entrance, I became guide and soon had my friends shot up to the twentieth floor.

We turned toward the great marble stair case which led to the roof and Dual's domain; and Alice Parton cried out with the pleasure of a child as she saw its magnificent sweep.

"They told me," she cried, her eyes shining, "but this is better than I dreamed; it is fairy-land."

"Wait," I told her, "until we get to the top."

We mounted the flight of steps and even I was surprised at the way in which my prophecy was fulfilled. As we mounted I became aware of a subdued harmony which grew as we went up, and when we stepped out at the top into the garden, I caught my breath in surprise.

Fairy lights in parti-colored miniature globes dotted the shrubbery throughout the entire place, winking and flashing like a myriad of fireflies in the dusk of the night, for Dual had had his garden protected as winter crept on by building a glass canopy over it from the building's parapets.

We stood in a veritable conservatory full of the perfume of flowers and filled with a low sweet sound of music from no visible source.

"Beautiful!" cried Alice. "Oh, Mr. Glace, I never dreamed of any place like this."

"Neither did I," I admitted. "Semi must have fixed it in your honor, I think; the lights and the music, I mean."

I stepped on the inlaid annunciator-plate at the head of the stairs, and a chime of bells rang out in soft, fairy tones, at which Alice Parton again cried out in pleasure. Then I led them all up the broad passageway between the twinkling lights to the tower's door.

It opened as we approached, and Semi's man stood bowing as we entered. He led us silently across to the inner room where Dual always received his visitors, and stood aside for us to pass.

Semi Dual, in all the regalia of the man of fashion, rose as we entered the door, and bowed over Alice Parton's hand.

"Welcome, Mrs. Parton," he said in his rich soft tones; "I am doubly glad to see you and make you free of my abode."

He made a splendid appearance in evening dress, and I noted a look of bewildered surprise light up Alice Parton's eyes as she surveyed the man. Like me she had at first no doubt formed some strange idea of this man, not in accord with the polished gentleman who relinquished her hand and bowed her to a seat.

"Thank you," she murmured as she sank into the proffered chair; "I feel like Alice in wonderland, I think."

Dual smiled.

"A pretty conceit," he replied, and turned to Parton and Colonel Sheldon in turn. "Take the padded chair, colonel," he suggested, indicating the chair Sheldon had occupied six months before.

"No danger of electrocution, is there?" grinned the colonel, as he took to his seat.

Dual laughed quietly.

"No more than then, colonel," he replied. "The button on my desk that night was a button, nothing more. It was gummed to the desk and there were no wires."

For a moment Colonel MacDonohue Sheldon looked fixedly at the man. Then, as Dual continued to smile in quizzical fashion, he slapped his knee and went off into a howl of deep laughter.

"Bluffed, by Jingo!" cried the colonel. "Bluffed. And I thought I could play poker, too."

"Sometimes, however, it is a wise man who does not call a bluff, Colonel Sheldon," Dual said, still smiling. "Had I wished, the mere absence of wires would not have prevented my protecting myself. But enough of past unpleasantness; we are here to enjoy ourselves to-night." He pressed a button and threw himself into a chair.

Meanwhile Alice Parton had caught sight of Dual's odd light. I once described this as a life-sized bronze of Venus, holding an apple in her hand. It stood beside Dual's desk, and from the apple poured a soft, golden light.

Dual followed the direction of her eyes.

"You notice my light-bearer?" said he.

"It is beautiful," said Mrs. Parton; "so beautifully modeled. I have never seen anything like it, Mr. Dual."

"It is a fine specimen of bronze," said Dual. "You enjoy *objets de vertu,* perhaps, Mrs. Parton?"

"I love them!" cried Alice Parton. "Oh, Mr. Dual, I've been admiring everything about this splendid place of yours ever since I came in! I actually do feel as though I were in fairy-land. All my life I have read about such things and longed to see them. I never miss a chance to go anywhere where I can feast myself on the beautiful things of art, and I love good literature as well."

"When my servant comes in within the next few moments, I shall have him bring in some of my Eastern embroideries," Dual promised. "No doubt they will appeal to you, too."

A few minutes later Semi's man appeared with a tray of the wonderful fruit juices, such as he had served me on our first meeting, and a plate of cakes, and handed them around. Then Dual despatched him for the promised art-treasures, and we all sat sipping our drink and nibbling cakes.

Dual actually lapsed into silence, though I saw that his eyes never quite left his fair guest's face. He seemed actually absorbed in his contemplation, and I wondered at the man.

Presently, however, when his servant returned with the silks, he rose, cleared his desk, and spread them before Alice in a shimmering mass.

"They are good examples of the work of the Persian needlewomen," he said, smiling; and after seeing her engrossed in her examination, turned to Archie and Sheldon, apparently leaving me to attend to Mrs. Parton as best I might.

It was little I had to do, however, for she was lost in her contemplation of the fabrics and only raised her eyes to smile as I approached. It was thus that I managed to give an ear to the conversation running between the other three men.

Dual sauntered over and stopped beside the colonel's chair.

"I believe you said your itinerary was London, then Paris, did you not, Colonel Sheldon?" he said.

"That's right, unless Allie changes her mind," Sheldon replied.

"I also believe that it is on record that Julius Caesar was warned to be careful on the day he was assassinated, is it not?"

Sheldon looked puzzled.

"I don't know," he admitted. "Ask Allie, she's the history shark of this bunch."

Dual smiled. "It will not be necessary," he said. "History records that a soothsayer told Caesar to beware of a certain date. He failed to heed the warning, and disaster overtook him by the way."

"I don't get you, Dual," said Sheldon. "Suppose you wise me up a bit."

"You will be in Paris in April," said Semi. "Let me give you a warning, Colonel Sheldon. Be very careful about meeting any unusual strangers while there."

Colonel Mac laughed.

"Ha, ha!" said he. "It's a joke, isn't it, Dual? Well, don't you worry at all. I'm a fairly old bird, and nobody's sold me a gold brick yet. I know those foreigners have an idea that all we Americans are gold-plated at least, but I'll bet you no confidence man gets next to Colonel Mac."

Dual half frowned.

"I see you don't understand me," he replied. "I meant that you should be careful on Mrs. Parton's account. I can scarcely tell myself as yet what it is I fear, though I can fix a provisional date. Colonel Sheldon, and you, too, Mr. Parton, let me warn you to be careful of the ides of April. Suppose you say these words to Mrs. Parton after you leave here; she will probably be able to get more out of them than will you."

"Allie?" said the colonel, while Parton sat forward. "Why, what could happen to Allie? Pshaw, Mr. Dual, that little girl's pretty able to take care of herself. She's a Western woman, she is, an' anybody that tries to get gay with her is going to find trouble without hunting very far."

"Just what do you mean, Mr. Dual?" Parton put in here.

"More than I have said I cannot tell you," said Semi. "Only let me repeat as a sincerely meant warning—guard you wife closely between the nineteenth and twenty-second of April. That is all I know myself at this time; that and that a danger will threaten her at about that time."

"You talk like a fortune-teller, Dual," laughed Sheldon. "Why, good Lord, Allie's goin' to be right with us all the time, an' I'd like to see any frog-eatin' Frencher start anything with us around. I kin still use a gun, mister, an' so kin the girl herself."

Dual turned away, and I thought he sighed. He returned to the desk where Alice was still fingering the silks, and turned to her with a smile.

"Do you find them interesting?" he inquired.

"Do I?" she laughed in nervous pleasure. "They are beautiful, beyond anything like them I ever saw. This one is simply a dream."

She held up a long scarf of sheer yellow tissue, embroidered with the mauve and purple of wistaria.

"It is something to drive a woman to tears of delight, Mr. Dual."

"It is yours," said Semi Dual.

"Mr. Dual!" Alice Parton seemed scarcely able to believe her ears.

Then fearing lest her enthusiastic praise may have been the cause of the man's act, she began an attempt to explain. Dual cut her short with an uplifted hand.

"That you should admire and wear it is more than sufficient recompense to me," he said. "Such things are for those who can truly appreciate. The fact that you have shown your appreciation makes it your own for the mere saying. I hope you may be as happy in its possession as I am in passing it on to you."

In another man it would have sounded as a stilted, fulsome compliment. But such was Dual's character that the words actually seemed natural.

"Lay it over your hair and let us step into the garden," Dual suggested. With a little gasp of pleasure Alice complied.

We all went out of the tower into the soft dusk of the roof, where the little lights still twinkled and shone; and as we strolled along the pathways laid out among the beds of flowers the soft harmony again filled the air. I was walking with Parton and Sheldon, behind Semi and Alice, and my curiosity at length got the better of me.

"Where do you get the music, Semi?" I made bold to ask.

Semi straightened from where he was smelling the bud of a crimson rose, and slowly nodded his head.

"That, friend Gordon, is the 'Music of the Spheres,'" he replied.

Alice clapped her hands.

"Surprise upon surprise!" she cried. "First the wonderful garden, then my beautiful scarf, and now the 'Music of the Spheres.' Mr. Dual, is it really that?"

Dual smiled upon her eager face, faint in the roof's twilight.

"It is really that, Mrs. Parton," he replied.

"But how—" I began, when Semi interrupted.

"It is produced by a machine of my own contrivance. A machine so constructed that it receives and condenses the ethereal waves of universal vibration and releases them as waves of sound. One may get the exact harmony of the actual vibration, or by another bit of apparatus, vary it so that any melody may be produced. For myself I like best the simple, grand harmony of life; such as rises and falls about us to-night. When men shall learn to vibrate in soul sympathy with that music they will become as gods."

He ceased speaking and we all heard a sob. Alice Parton stood leaning upon the arm of a bench, her hand at her throat. "Take me back! I want to go back!" she said in a voice which was stifled. "I am almost afraid." For a moment she swayed.

Archie sprang to her side.

"Afraid of what, Alice?" he said, putting an arm about her waist. "Surely there is nothing of which to be afraid."

"Dog-gone it, Allie, I'll admit the whole thing's sort of creepy," affirmed the colonel, "but if I was you I wouldn't go to gittin' scared."

That broke the spell.

Dual led the way back to the tower, after a smiling glance at me, and we were soon fully restored to ease in the lighted room.

Later still his man served tiny cups of real coffee, and soon afterward we took our leave, with the good wishes of our host for a pleasant journey still ringing in our ears as we went down over the dusky roof, where the lights twinkled and died.

CHAPTER III.

OFF FOR PARIS.

LOOKING BACK over the affair now, I can see how from the first everything led in unbroken sequence to the final denouement of the remarkable experience which took Dual and I half across the world, and which seems more like the weird imaginings of some drug-clogged brain than sane happenings in this epoch of the world.

At that time, however, I went about my business all unsuspecting that I was soon to be drawn into the very vortex of events. I shall try and set down the things as nearly as possible as they happened, and if I overlook anything it will be because at times I can scarcely believe them myself, even though they are a part of my own life, and of that strangest of men, Semi Dual.

The Partons and Colonel Sheldon departed for their trip abroad and I went back to my duties for the *Record*, and, it must be confessed, soon forgot all about the travelers. I was busy and didn't even find time to go up to see Dual after the night which we five had spent together, just before the young people and their elder companion set sail. Then, one day when I was pounding out copy at the fastest rate of which I was capable, he called me to the phone. I could hardly believe my ears, for Semi rarely resorted to the telephone.

Usually he sent me one of his odd telepathic commands to appear. For instance, I would be sitting at my desk, or running about the town, and the impulse to see him would overtake me, no matter where I might be. It appeared to be born in my own brain, but usually when I followed it and reached Dual's apartments, I would find that he had wished to see me, and was expecting me when I came.

Therefore when I heard his voice over the wire I was surprised. His message surprised me still more.

"Get ready to start for Paris to-night," he commanded.

I say "commanded" because his words were not a question or a request, but a simple statement of what I was to do. I started to protest, but he cut me short.

"Tell Smithson you are going, then come up here."

"Dual," I cried, as he finished, "I simply can't get away now!"

Dual didn't say anything for a minute, then spoke quietly.

"If I tell you that this concerns Alice Parton, her welfare, perhaps her life, I think you will perhaps find a way."

The words thrilled me. My mind went back to the night we had spent at Semi's and the odd warning he had given to Sheldon and young Parton, and even as all that flashed through my brain I decided upon my course.

"Look for me on the jump," I cried into the instrument, and then I hung up the receiver.

I left the telephone and went into Smithson's office. As I entered he looked up, and what he no doubt saw in my face made him lay down the papers he was inspecting and wait for my first word.

"Smithson," I said, "I am leaving for Paris to-night."

"Are you going to elope?" questioned the "old man."

"I am going to help some friends of mine," I explained.

"Very commendable," grunted Smithson. "If not impertinent, may I ask what you think we will be doing while you are away?"

"Look here, Smithson," I burst out, "don't try to be funny. This is deadly serious. I just got a telephone call to get ready to start to-night. I can't refuse, for it may be the story of a lifetime. Anyway, I'm going to give you a tip on the thing." Then I rapidly sketched in all that I knew, ending with the statement that the Partons must be in trouble.

Smithson sat quiet while I talked, while in his face grew the intent alert expression of the news-hunter when he finds a trail. When I had finished he turned sharply upon me and asked one of his incisive questions:

"Is this Semi Dual the same man I once sent you to interview?"

I confessed that it was.

"You've been holding out on me, eh?" said the city editor, "upon that."

"He helped me to run down a couple of good scoops for the *Record* and only asked to be let alone by us."

Smithson nodded. "I guess that's right, too," he admitted. "Now he wants you to go chasing off to Europe. Well, Glace, I don't know. We need you here."

"There is nothing to prevent my resigning, is there?" I asked, though I hated to do it like sin. A chap grows to love the sheet for which he works.

"Eh?" said Smithson. "Quitting, you mean? Say, would you gamble that much on this affair?"

"If Dual advised it, yes," I said slowly, and got up.

"Sit down!" roared Smithson. "I'm still your boss yet. Supposing you could get us wires from over there, keepin' us in touch with the whole thing." His manner was tentative, but I saw he meant to yield.

"I'll do better," I said. "I'll find out the real state of things and give you the story before we start, and I'll keep you in touch from day to day."

"Good day, Mr. Special Correspondent," said Smithson, and I knew that I had won the point. "If you ever get back, come in and tell me what to let you do next," Smithson continued, grinning, and then put out his hand.

I took it and returned the sincere clasp which he gave, and turned away.

"And, Glace," said Smithson, as I was passing the door; "we'll pay you the regular rate for telegraphic stuff."

I laughed and waved my hand. Then I went out and down the

stairs. After that day it was a long time before I saw the *Record* office again.

I found Semi Dual in his study surrounded by a mass of papers covered with cabalistic signs and mathematical computations, with a Western Union messenger waiting at his elbow, while he covered some cable blanks with a lot of words.

He nodded to me, finished his messages, and sent the boy away. Then he turned to me.

"Alice Parton disappeared from the 'Champs Elysées Palace,' where they were stopping, yesterday afternoon," he said sharply. "Sheldon cabled me this morning. Those messages were my reply. If we leave to-night we can get a boat sailing to-morrow morning, and make Havre in a matter of five days. Go on down to your rooms and pack up. Pack for the purpose of traveling far and fast. If you forget anything we can get it in Paris. I have telegraphed to Sheldon to reserve us rooms at his hotel. My man is out now arranging for our transportation. He will remain here while I am away."

"You say Mrs. Parton disappeared—" I began, but Semi cut me short.

"Sheldon says so," he said quickly. "Here's his message; you can read it yourself." He tossed a sheet of the telegraph company across to me, and went back to the papers spread out on his desk.

I picked up the typewritten paper and glanced along its lines. It was not such as to give me much light, but I could see reason for Semi Dual's decision to go at once. After the name and address Sheldon had written:

> Alice disappeared yesterday while visiting suite of Hafiz Ibrahim, our hotel. No clue. Police seem mystified. You fought me once, help me now.

There followed the name of Colonel MacDonohue Sheldon, and that was all. It was dated at the "Champs Elysées Palace," Paris, April 22. That was to-day.

I laid the yellow sheet down on Dual's desk and he glanced up.

"I cabled that you and I would start to-night," he said. "Then I informed you. Later I called the boy who just left and sent some further messages, which I fancied might help us along with the case. I am trying to make some calculations which I hope will give me some light on the matter; so now that you know all about it that is necessary, suppose you go along and get packed up. If you want to give Smithson a sort of advance story, why it will do no harm that I can see. Meet me at the station to-night at eight. That is all, I think."

"But this message says Mrs. Parton disappeared from her hotel; how could she do that and leave no trace?"

"That is for us to find out," said Dual, smiling slightly. "At least we know she loved her husband, so we may assume that she did not go of her own free will."

"Evidently they didn't heed your warning," I said.

"They seldom do; that is the trouble with warnings," said Dual, without surprise that I knew of the thing. "Humanity makes a great deal of its own troubles in just that way. That, however, is now aside from any phase of the case. We have to undo what has been done."

He turned back to his papers and I left him deep in his calculations and went down to my boarding-house to put my things into such shape as I could for the trip. Even then, as I worked over my choosing of coats and vests and collars and ties, I began to have a faint perception of what Semi must have meant when he warned Sheldon that night.

The man had had one of his peculiar impressions of some impending danger, which might be avoided with care. He had given his warnings, which had been unheeded, and, true to his fears, the danger had appeared.

"Guard your wife between the nineteenth and twenty-second of April," he had said. Sheldon had cabled the morning of the twenty-second, so that the danger had struck them on the twenty-first. I tossed the things I was going to take on the bed and started to pack. I could hardly believe it. It seemed impossible that a grown woman could disappear from a crowded modern hotel, in the midst of a modern city, and do it so secretly that there should be no clue left for the police; yet if we were to believe Sheldon's message, just that thing had occurred.

I felt almost like a hero of some modern tale of mystery as I put my things into the cases, and added a little black automatic revolver and some cartridge-clips. I wondered if I would really need the thing, but decided to take it on the off chance. When everything was done, I strapped the cases and went down and told the landlady that I was going to Europe for my paper and asked her to hold my room. Then I got a car and went out to see Connie Baird.

The little girl was naturally surprised and not too well pleased at the turn of events; but on the whole we spent a very pleasant afternoon, and at the end I took her in my arms and kissed her and promised to write just as often as I could. She clung to me a little bit at the last and I confess I felt sort of sorry for the going, and yet I couldn't see what else to do. I often thought of her standing there in their home, during the days and nights which followed that afternoon, and more than once I wished that I were back and vowed that if I ever did get back I'd not leave in a hurry again.

I stopped at the *Record* office and saw Smithson and told him all I knew about what had happened to the Partons, and he whistled softly as I made an end.

"For two bits I'd stop being city editor and go along," he said half wistfully, and then sighed and smiled slowly. "But some of us have got to stay here, and you seem to be the only foot-loose one among us. It's a good thing, too, because the paper has got to come out."

At ten minutes to eight Dual appeared at the station with his man. He walked leisurely out to the gate; which was just being opened, and as I fell into step beside him he greeted me with a smile.

"What did Smithson say to the latest?" he inquired.

"He said he'd like to come along," I replied.

"Poor Smithson," said Semi. "These newspaper men really have my sympathy, Glace. They toil day and night to get out their papers; they may not rest or relax for fear something escapes them; no wonder they wear out soon. It is exciting, no doubt, and the excitement keeps them up and wears out their nerves until, like old horses, they break and are turned out to die. It is all wrong, of course, but it will go on equally, of course, for years, as long as people demand artificial excitement and amusement with which to waste their time.

"And now we are off for Paris," he added, as the train trembled into motion and then slid smoothly off into the night. "You hardly thought, even this morning, that you would be undertaking the journey to-night, friend Glace?"

"It was the last thing I would ever have thought of," I replied with a grin.

"Which," said Dual, "is a little synopsis of all life, as lived by the average man. Do you get seasick, Glace?"

"I don't know, never having tried," I said, laughing at the sudden change of subject. "I suppose I am in a fair way to find out."

"I thought of that, and had Henri pack a hammock for you," Dual went on. "As for myself, I am ocean-proof. If they would build their liner berths so that they could swing less people would be affected. Later, however, the gyroscope may help that."

"It was very thoughtful of you," I said humbly as I realized that in the midst of all his other arrangements he had thought of my comfort as well.

"It isn't so much a hammock as a light folding mattress or canvas stretcher, which fits into the berth," Dual explained. "It is so arranged that its swing compensates the steamer's roll, but you will see. I had it fixed for Henri, poor fellow, and he packed it in the steamer-trunk to-day. Now as we are to be up early to-morrow, I suggest that we retire. We shall go directly to the boat when we get in to-morrow. Henri engaged our berths by wire to-day."

I left him and went forward to smoke a cigar. When I returned, the curtains of his berth were drawn, and I slipped into my own section and stretched out between the sheets.

CHAPTER IV.

IN THE FOG.

MORNING FOUND us at the pier, and a few minutes later we went aboard the liner and one of the stewards showed us to our staterooms, I dropped onto a seat and looked at Dual.

"I suppose I am awake, but I can't believe it even yet," I gasped. "This looks like the stateroom of a steamship, but maybe I am dreaming after all. What do you think?"

Dual smiled and went on arranging his luggage.

"You are wide enough awake," he responded. "I would suggest that you remain that way on the trip we are going to make."

"Where are we going anyway?" I inquired.

"To Paris," said Semi Dual.

"And then?"

"I will tell you that after we get to Paris," my companion replied.

I kicked a suit-case to one side and stretched out my legs, and yawned.

"Just what do you fancy happened to Mrs. Parton?" I wanted to know.

"Abduction," Dual answered me in the word.

I sat up and looked at him closely to make sure that he was serious. "Well—good lord, Semi, who's going to abduct another man's wife?"

"I believe it has been done, even in these United States," said Semi with a grin. "Suppose we go on deck. If you've never seen it the sailing of a liner is a rather interesting study in the ways of man." He handed me a light cap. "That is better than a hat," he suggested, and I put the thing on.

We went up and took a position beside the rail. I looked down. Far below me, as it seemed, swarmed the deck, full of an orderly confusion as the sailing hour approached. Passengers and their friends were coming aboard. The air was full of cries of greeting and farewell. Women with their arms full of flowers passed us or leaned over the rail waving to friends and acquaintances on the pier. There was laughter, and smiles, and tears, a waving of kerchiefs and hands.

Above all lesser sounds boomed a hoarse yellow as the leviathan gave voice before waking to her long race. The voices of stewards came through the crowd warning all persons not sailing, to go ashore. There was a clutching of hands, a clasping of arms, more smiles, some kisses, more tears. The rail of the liner blossomed into a waving of bouquets and the flutter of white linen, waved at the last; then the vessel trembled slightly.

The pier began to slip away from our sides as the busy little tugs began to warp us out of our berth. Further and further out we swung. There was clear water between us and the shore. The rail began to clear as the passengers turned away to their staterooms. More and more we swung in the stream. Like water-beetles about a chip, the tugs pulled and hauled, dragged us out, turned and straightened us. The voyage had begun.

I stood and watched, with Semi silent by my side. We slipped down and out into the bay. The great statue of Bartholdi towered above us and fell astern. "A great country," said Semi Dual. "The day is fast coming, Gordon, when the West shall enlighten the East."

The purser was making his rounds, and Dual selected a couple of deck-chairs and saw our tickets affixed to the same. Then he threw his long figure into one of them, motioned me to the other, and lapsed into a silent watching of the shipping in the lower bay. We dropped down the harbor, the tugs cast off. The last shore-going mail was sent over the side. Sandy Hook faded away to the right.

Everything was of interest to me, and I enjoyed a keen delight in sitting and watching with both eyes as the life of the ship developed around me. Semi might have been a graven image for any sound which came out of him. Our places at the tables were together, and at night he rigged Henri's stretcher for me in my berth and I passed a pleasant night. True, I felt some few qualms of discomfort as we got out and caught the full swell of the ocean, but beyond that I was happy enough.

As for our plans, I found out little beyond the fact that we were going directly to Paris. Semi seemed loath to say much about the case, though he spent many hours over his charts and calculations, and at times remained on deck for half the night, wrapped in silent thought. At such times I used to lean against the rail and smoke and watch the slow swing of the stars, until chilled through I would creep below, leaving him still there wrapped up in his steamer rug.

As luck would have it, when we approached the French shore we ran into a fine specimen of channel fog, through which we felt our way with hoarse bellowings of the siren, as we plowed along at reduced speed.

It was like the crying of a lost soul in the night of perdition, as Semi whimsically remarked, but our captain seemed to know where he was going, and the rest of us could do nothing but pass the time as best we might.

We were still playing blind-man's buff with the fog, when a messenger from the wireless came for Dual. Motioning me to come along, Semi rose with a smile and made his way to the door of the wireless station, and paused. The liner's captain was there, bending over the table beside which the operator sat. He straightened at our approach. "Are you M. Semi Dual?" he asked of Dual.

Semi bowed.

"*Oui*, M. le Capitaine," he replied.

"There's a police boat out there calling for us, and asking if you are aboard," said the captain; "what does *monsieur* think I had better reply?" He fixed Dual shrewdly and looked him through with a glance from a very black eye.

Semi smiled slightly. "If M. le Capitaine will be so kind, I desire that the police boat be informed that I am on board." For a few moments the operator worked rapidly at his sending, then cut out, and awaited a reply. It came on the instant:

"Stand by; we want to board you."

The operator showed his transcription to the captain, who scowled ferociously and left the office at once.

Dual turned away and we walked slowly back to the smoking-room, before he said a word to keep my curiosity from bursting all bounds.

"I was expecting that," he finally volunteered.

"A visit from the police?"

"The arrival of Parton and Sheldon," he corrected with a smile.

"But how—and why?"

"To answer the last first," said Semi, his eyes twinkling slightly; "because I wanted to see them as soon as I could. It will save time to hear their story before we get to Paris. Also I want to see how the land lies before I go there, friend Glace. As for the first part of your question; I sent a cable to Grimaud, chief of the Paris Detective Bureau, the day we left home, asking him to find Sheldon and Parton and send them out to meet us, as he has evidently done. Hark! Isn't that another whistle? That should be the police vessel now. Suppose we go above and meet our friends."

Once more I followed him above. Looking back now, it seems that during the thing from first to last, my main part was following the man around. I was a sort of shadow which he took or left behind at will, and surely what little service I rendered was as a direct result of his wonderful handling of the matter and the commands of his remarkable brain.

Already a group of officers were standing at the vessel's side and through the fog we could dimly perceive a low-lying vessel swinging in toward the liner, which had almost halted, and was under steerage way only. Closer and closer came the other vessel, until she lay seemingly under our side. Then a voice hailed us out of the fog.

"*Oui!*" came from the bridge.

"Prepare to take two persons aboard," was the command, which caused no little surprise among the liner's officials.

Evidently they had expected to lose rather than receive. However, they sprang to instant action, and after an interval there crawled up to the liner's deck, first Archie Parton, and after him Colonel Mac-Donohue Sheldon himself.

As Parton came over, Dual went forward and had him by the hand.

"Mr. Dual," cried the boy in relief and pleasure; and then Sheldon seized Semi's other hand.

"Well, now I sure am glad to see you, Dual," cried the colonel. "This here has been the longest five days I ever waited in my life. When it all happened I says to Archie, if there's anybody livin' what can help us, I know his name, and it's Semi Dual. I got busy and sent you that cable, an' we been just holdin' on till you could arrive. Now you're here, I reckon we can get action at last. If we don't do somethin' soon, I'm goin' bughouse, I reckon. I told you Allie was gone, but I couldn't wise you up to that. I reckon that's why you sent for us to meet you out here, Mr. Dual. Allie was stole; I'll bet on that. Allie—my little girl was—" He choked up and turned away. "Say," he burst forth in a minute, "kin a man get a drink on this here boat?"

The police boat was already sheering off, and the steamship was again forging forward through the fog. Dual turned away toward our cabin, with Sheldon. I followed with Parton. When we were seated and a steward had departed for the colonel's drink, Dual turned to the two men.

"You didn't heed the soothsayer's warning," he said.

"Heed nuthin'," cried the colonel. "Why Dual, Allie just simply vanished while Archie here was lookin' on. We never let her go nowhere alone. Arch or me was with her all the time. It's enough to give a fellow the creeps."

Dual dropped down on the edge of a berth. "Suppose you tell me all about it," he said.

Colonel Sheldon put up a hand and brushed his eyes.

"I reckon Arch had better tell you," he said slowly. "I've got the colly woggles so bad I can't talk about the thing."

Dual turned to Parton, who sat humped on a suit-case.

"Suppose you go back to the beginning of your stay in Paris, Mr. Parton," he directed, "and tell me all that happened from the time you stopped at your hotel, or before if you think advisable, up to the time when your wife disappeared. Try and give me everything which happened, for sometimes the least thing serves to connect the major incidents so as to make them make sense. Take your time and try to omit nothing. First, however, have you reserved the Hafiz suite in your hotel?"

"We sure did," broke in Sheldon. "I've got it locked up, an' there hain't even been a chambermaid in there since that feller left."

"That is good," said Semi. "I cabled you to do that in order that the apartment might not be disturbed. I wanted to be the first person to enter after Hafiz left. Did I understand you to say he was gone? When did he leave?"

"He left last evenin'," said Sheldon, "an' I took the rooms for you. The manager wanted to clean 'em up, but I said no. He thought I was crazy, I guess, by the way he waved his hands, and got off something about the 'mad Americans.' You see I told him you was funny an' wanted things left just as they were."

Dual smiled slightly.

"That was the spirit of my instructions, colonel," he said lightly, and turned back to Parton again. "Now, Mr. Parton, we are ready for your narrative, if you please."

"Of course you know we went to London first," said Parton. "We first saw this Hafiz Ibrahim at the St. Cecil there, though we didn't meet him until we got to Paris, as a matter of fact. He is some sort of an Eastern prince, they tell me; Persian, I believe. Anyway, it seems he comes over to Europe every so often. The manager of the Champs Elysées Palace tells me he often stops there, and seemed to think he was all right. He has a regular retinue of servants with him and he surely does put on a lot of style.

"The first time I ever noticed him was one night in the restaurant of the St. Cecil. He was sitting at a table near ours, and after a bit Alice noticed that he was watching us closely, and called my attention to the fact. I have sometimes thought that it was the scarf which you gave to Alice which made the fellow eye us so closely. She was wearing it over her shoulders that night in the café, and I know I saw this Hafiz point to it, and say something to the man who was with him, and sort of laugh.

"The other man scowled and said something in reply, and Hafiz smiled and apparently changed the subject. He continued to keep an eye on Alice, however, till I felt like getting up and telling him to look the other way. When he left the restaurant, which was before we did, he made a point of passing near our table, and he fairly stared into Alice's face as he went by.

"The next day, however, we were leaving for Paris, and so I never thought anything more about it, until I saw him on the boat, as we were crossings to Calais. Even then beyond thinking that he was pretty much lacking in manners, I never thought anything about it, except that he was crossing on the same boat. Anybody might do that.

I never once even dreamed that he might be following us, though now, after what has happened I sometimes think that is how it was."

He paused as a rap sounded on the door, and the steward returned with the colonel's refreshment. After he had departed, and while the colonel was sipping from a tall glass, Parton went on with his tale.

CHAPTER V.

ARCHIE'S STORY.

"AFTER WE got to Paris we went at once to the Champs Elysées Palace," Archie continued, "and engaged a suite of rooms on the third floor. They were pretty good rooms, though well back along the hall. The whole front part of the building was taken up on that floor by a *suite de luxe,* generally rented to special personages or millionaires, or somebody who could stand the tariff, which is pretty high. We found that out when we rented the thing, after you cabled that we should."

"That's all right," broke in Sheldon; "I don't give a cuss for the money if I kin get my little girl back again."

Parton's face began to work at the other's words, and he rose and paced the stateroom for a moment, before he went on. It was evident to us all that the boy was making a hard fight to remain cool and collected while all the time his heart was aching for the young wife who had left him in such a strange way.

"Well," he resumed after a few moments, "on the day after we stopped at the hotel I saw this Hafiz fellow in the corridor of our floor, and from time to time during the day I saw some one or the other of his attendants running around on errands. Even then I didn't feel anything but a mild interest. Any one could stop at the hotel, which was a prominent one. I did, however, ask one of the hall-men about him, and managed to understand that he was a Prince Hafiz, and quite well known around the hotel, as he had occasionally stopped there before.

"That evening as we were going down to attend a theater, Alice and I met him in the hall. He drew aside and made us a very marked bow. I spoke to Alice about it at the time, and she laughed and said she had always heard about the marked politeness of those fellows, which was rated at pretty nearly skin-deep.

"We went to the theater, and along during the second act of the play I noticed that the fellow was in a box quite close to us. Alice looked up when I mentioned it, and the fellow actually had the nerve to bow again. I felt a bit sore, but know I tried to treat the thing lightly, and told Alice that it looked to me as if she had made a mash. She wore the scarf you gave her again that night, and all through the play I saw that the chap kept his eyes upon her rather than on the stage.

"The next afternoon one of Hafiz's servants brought us a note. It asked her very courteously if she would not allow him to examine the scarf. He said that he believed it to be a rarely fine example of embroidery, and expressed the hope that she would allow his servant who brought the note to take the scarf to Hafiz, so that he might look it over and return it to us.

"I wanted Alice to send the servant back and tell Hafiz to mind his own business, but she said that wouldn't be polite; that after all it was only natural that he should admire the scarf and be surprised to see her wearing it, and that she couldn't see any harm in allowing the man to examine it if he really wanted to do so as badly as his note would indicate.

"Anyway, she ended by sending the scarf to him. Then we all went over to the Louvre, and Alice got so excited about the pictures in the galleries there that the colonel and I couldn't get her away until quite late. When we got back to the hotel we found a black servant of Hafiz standing at our door. He was a funny fellow, and in his big turban and baggy breeches, he looked as if he might have come out of a picture-book.

"When he saw Alice, he bowed low, and went down upon one knee, offering her the scarf and a note. Allie took the note and the scarf, and after the colonel had given the fellow a franc for his trouble, he went away. We went into the rooms and Alice let out a yell—that's just what she did. The place was full of flowers, roses, and lilies, and orange-blossoms—the blamedest lot of flowers I ever saw together at once outside of a florist's shop."

"Smelled like six weddings and a funeral," said Colonel Sheldon; "and if I ever catch that saffron-tinted slob I'll furnish the makings for another funeral, too."

"When Alice saw all the flowers," continued Parton, "she remembered the note, which she had rolled up in the scarf as we were coming in, and she opened it.

"It was a most remarkable missive, I assure you, Mr. Dual. It began by addressing Alice as the 'Beauteous Flower of the Western World'; gave a full catalogue of her various charms; assured her she was fit to wear the scarf, which was a gem of its kind; stated that the flowers had been placed in her room by the orders of Hafiz, and ended by asking permission to call.

"The thing made me mad, but Alice sat down and laughed. Then I wanted her to dump the flowers out, but she refused. She said they were beautiful, and that she thought Hafiz was very considerate to repay her so beautifully for letting him see the scarf. I told her if she wanted flowers I'd go out and buy her a wagon-load, but she only laughed and said that would be a waste, when she had all she needed already; and that night she told me she was going to let Hafiz come to call. She thought it would be a great experience to talk about when we got home, I guess.

"The next day she sent him a note saying she would be glad to receive him, and sure enough that afternoon he came to our suite. I must admit that his manners at that time were charming. He spoke fairly good English, and conversed impartially with us all. He had evidently traveled widely and seen a great many parts of the world, and the first thing we knew he was telling us all about his various experiences in a way to hold us interested in spite of ourselves.

"After a time he mentioned the scarf. He fairly raved over that. He said it was one of the finest pieces of work of his native country-women that he had ever beheld. He apologized for his former apparent interest in us, by asserting that he had been so surprised to see a Western woman, plainly an American— he didn't say how he knew that—wearing a native scarf over her shoulders in an English hotel.

"He laughed and said he was, frankly, a crank on the subject, and that whenever he saw anything like the wistaria scarf his fingers itched until he had had a chance to examine it for himself. He explained that he had known he had acted rudely, and had desired to call in order that we might understand the reason for his acts.

"When a fellow comes at you like that, Mr. Dual, you can hardly hold a resentment, and after a bit I fancy his manner and evident sincerity had its effect, so that we all came to like him better than at first. Anyway, I know, when he asked us to drop in that evening for a cup of coffee, and a bit of oriental entertainment, I accepted with a real pleasure in anticipating the event.

"'I shall be please to give you one leetle peep into ze mannaire in which we of ze East pleasure ourselves,' he told us in giving the invitation, just as he was leaving; and we promised and went.

"There wasn't anything special happened that night. Hafiz gave us just what he had promised. There was some oriental music, and a dance by some of the men servants, and a lot of incense floating around. He had some coffee brewed for us, and it was certainly strong enough when it was finished. He even got Colonel Mac to try and smoke a water-pipe, and we all had a laugh at the figure he cut.

"On the whole it was a novel experience, and we enjoyed ourselves, and at the end Hafiz bowed us out, after asking Alice to come in the next day to look over a lot of silks and other embroideries which he said he had. Alice promised, and we arranged for me to take her to Hafiz's suite on the next afternoon, so that she could see the things.

"There was nothing at any time to arouse our suspicions that everything wasn't just as it ought to be. If I had but suspected, Mr. Dual, I'd have taken a gun with me the next day and filled that beggar full of holes."

For a moment he ceased speaking, and sat clenching and opening his fingers, as though he imagined they might grip the man he described. Then, seeing Semi's look of interest, he went on.

"Well, my acting like a kid won't help any now, though I would like to have Hafiz right here now. The next day about three o'clock I took Alice and we went to Hafiz's suite. We went in, and I remember that I noticed that there seemed to be a lot of his servants about. Still I never thought, for those chaps have their people lying around like a lot of house-dogs, and I fancied it was nothing out of the ordinary run of things.

"Hafiz came put bowing and smiling like a floor-walker, and when we were seated he clapped his hands and ordered some of his men to bring out the silks, and satins, and brocades, and all the rest. Then he and Alice fell to rummaging the things over, and talking about them while I sat and looked on. I guess they must have been most half an hour before they reached the last piece, and then Hafiz pulled the conversation around to art and literature. He said he had some very fine manuscripts and sketches, and what not, and asked me if I would step into another room with him and help him carry them out.

"Like a fool I went with him. I might have known something was wrong, because he could have had his servants bring the things out just as well; or have taken Alice and me to where they were. But as I tell you I had stopped suspecting the fellow of any wrong intentions, and so I got up and followed him into another room, and then on into still another one. Hafiz seemed to have some trouble finding the things he was after, and I guess maybe we were ten minutes in getting the stuff together.

"I say that now, but then he kept up such a running line of talk that it didn't seem long to me. After a bit though a black fellow stuck his head into the room, and Hafiz jabbered to him a minute, and then explained to me that the man had just heard us talking and looked in to see who it might be, as he thought Hafiz was out with us. All that seems strange to me now, but then I swallowed it innocently like all the rest.

"Hafiz gave me a bundle of things to carry, and took up one himself, and we went back to where we had left Alice. She wasn't there. Hafiz put down his bundle, and raised his eyebrows at me. 'I haf fancy zat *madame* was to wait, was it not?' he inquired as if he thought I knew where she was.

"'I thought so, too,' I said like a softhead. 'I wonder where she can be.'

"'Perhaps it is zat she haf stepped out for a moment,' suggested Hafiz. '*Voilà!* Is it zat we shall sit us down and await her return?'

"Well, I didn't think anything could have happened, and his explanation seemed reasonable. I sat down and he offered me a cigarette. I accepted it and sat smoking and talking to him, and not worrying for a while, but Alice didn't come back. When my cigarette was pretty nearly smoked I began to wonder what could be keeping her, and I told Hafiz I believed that I would go and see where she was. He assented, and urged me to bring her back to finish looking at the things. Even then I never suspected that he could know anything of what had happened to her.

"I went back to our suite. Colonel Mac was asleep in his chair. I asked him about Alice, and he said she hadn't been back since she and I went to Hafiz's rooms. I began to feel funny and ran back to the Persian's quarters. I told him that my wife was not at our suite and had not been.

"'Where then can *madame* be?' he inquired.

"'I don't know,' I told him, 'but I'm going to find out.'

"'Perhaps it is zat *madame* haf gone on ze streets,' said Hafiz.

"'She wouldn't do that without telling me, and she didn't have on a hat,' I reminded the beggar. 'I left her here and I want to know where she is now.'

"'Is it zat *monsieur* suspects zat she is in my apartments?' said Hafiz with a fine show of anger.

"'I don't know. All I know is where I saw her last,' I yelled at him and started to push by him toward another room.

"'*Monsieur* does not need to become wat you call violent,' he had the nerve to remind me. '*Monsieur* is at perfect liberty to entaire an' make ze search.'

"I took him at his word and just about tore that flat to pieces, and I never found a trace of a single thing. When I got done I was just about scared to death about Alice, and I ran out of Hafiz's place and went back to our suite and told Colonel Mac all that had occurred.

"We sent for the house-detectives and they went up and questioned Hafiz, but you could see that they felt that he was a well-known person and we strangers, so it didn't amount to much.

"Then we got in the police, gendarmes, or whatever they call 'em, and they got in some other detectives and they all jabbered to Hafiz, and finally one of them thought to ask Hafiz's men if any of them had seen Alice go away. One of them swore he had seen her leave Hafiz's suite and go down the corridor. Hafiz expressed great sorrow over the affair, and offered to do anything in his power, and the police seemed satisfied that he was acting in good faith. They searched his rooms, of course, but nothing was found.

"Hafiz insisted on remaining for several days longer than he said he had intended, to see if we would be able to find any trace of Alice; but finally he went away yesterday. He actually had the nerve to call and offer us his best wishes for luck in our search. I wanted the police to hold him till you came, but they said they had nothing to hold him for, and as his servant swore Alice left the suite of her own accord, they'd have to let him go.

"And that's all, Mr. Dual. What can we do? I must find Alice—I can't give her up—I just—can't."

Suddenly his voice broke utterly and he dropped his face in his hands.

"You—don't know—what this means—to me," he sobbed. "I've loved her—for years—and to lose her now—with me right there—oh, Mr. Dual—for God's sake, try and find Alice for me."

Dual rose and laid a hand on the boy's head, and his voice was sad and low when he spoke, yet it had confidence and encouragement in its tones.

"I will find her, Archie Parton," he said slowly. "Get control of yourself, my boy, and answer a question or two for me."

With an effort Parton ceased his sobbing and raised his head.

Semi resumed his seat. "Just how was your wife dressed the day she disappeared?" he asked.

"She was wearing a sort of light cloth gown," replied Parton, "and she had the scarf with her, when we went to Hafiz's rooms. She looked beautiful."

"Any jewelry or ornaments?" continued Dual.

"She had on a string of pink coral beads and her wedding and engagement rings."

"Nothing else?"

"Not that I remember, Mr. Dual."

"You heard nothing—no sounds—no cry—no struggle?" said Dual.

"No."

"When you and Hafiz returned to the room where she had waited for you, there was nothing to indicate that there had been a struggle?"

"Not a thing. I'm sure I would have noticed that."

Dual nodded his head. "Parton," he said, "I know this Ibrahim more or less well. In fact we know each other by sight. If I should admit such a thing, I would say that he is an enemy of mine, at least, of my house. Few know it, but I, too, am part Persian. This man is one of the sort who make me ashamed of my race. He is a polished rogue. He will stop at nothing to gratify a whim of his selfish nature. Do you know where he went when he left the hotel yesterday?"

"He said he was going home," said Archie. "He said he was going to stop in Constantinople for a while on the way."

Dual smiled grimly.

"He probably lied," he remarked. "However, I fancy I will find a way to run the scoundrel to earth when I begin to try."

This practically ended the conversation. We berthed at Havre, and went ashore. At the customs we were detained but a few moments, and caught the first train out for Paris, where we went directly to the Champs Elysées Palace.

Things began to happen shortly after Sheldon handed Dual the key to the Hafiz apartments.

CHAPTER VI.

IN HAFIZ'S APARTMENTS.

SEMI DUAL paused before the door of Hafiz's suite in the Champs Elysees Palace, and spoke to me.

"I am going to take you in with me," he said, "because I know you can hold your tongue. I left Parton and Sheldon in their rooms for fear they would not. After we get inside I do not want you to say a word until I speak to you. I want nothing to disturb the vibration of the room's atmosphere until I shall have had a chance to read it, and understand what it may have for me. That is why I had the rooms locked up as soon as Hafiz had left; I wanted his thoughts to be the last things thrown into the place. Thoughts are really things, Gordon, and live until they are received by some other brain. One who knows how can read them long after they are born. Now, if you understand me, suppose we go in."

He turned the key in the lock and we entered the suite.

Dual crossed to a low divan and laid himself at full length upon it. I slid softly into a chair. Semi raised a hand in caution, and seeing that I caught the motion, closed his eyes.

Such was his beginning at ferreting out the mystery of how Alice Parton had disappeared. For minutes I sat and watched him as he lay passive. Not a line of his features moved, not a muscle of his body quivered. The only sign of life was the slow rise and fall of his chest, in a measured breathing. A sense of wonder, of almost superstitious awe, crept over me as I sat.

A vision of other detectives whom I had seen at work came over me. I could see them as they would be now, running all over the place, peeking under tables, chairs and couches, examining floors and window-sills, making a great show of activity; then talking in words of veiled meaning, while inwardly wondering what to do next. My eyes came back to Dual stretched in apparent slumber, and after a bit I found that I was trembling with a species of nervousness.

Was he really reading some subtle message, which was totally unperceived, totally unperceivable, to me?

Almost as if in answer to the thought Dual moved, lifted himself up, and reached into the pocket of his coat. He produced a small electric flash-light, and leaving the divan got down upon the floor, and peered beneath the divan itself, throwing the ray of the light far back into the dusky corners, as if he sought for something he expected to find.

I made no movement, uttered no sound; just sat and watched the man as he swept the pencil of light back and forth over the shadowed floor. Presently he changed the search-light to his other hand; stooped still farther until he well-nigh lay upon the floor, and reaching back under the divan, brought out something in his hand.

He rose and held what he had discovered in his hand as he got up, and I saw that it was a strand of some ten or twelve coral beads, threaded upon a broken string.

Semi eyed the thing closely; then put his torch away, and clasped the strand of beads tightly between both palms. Holding them so he stood and gazed at his clasped hands for a long minute. Then he raised them and pressed them to his forehead, and turning, threw the beads to me.

"Keep them, Gordon," he told me, and walked out through a door which opened into the room.

I rose and followed him through the door which gave access to another room, and across that into still another apartment. I now found myself in a room which opened upon a balcony, projecting from the side of the building, and overhanging a sort of small court.

Here Dual paused, while his eyes swept the entire room. Close by the long windows which gave upon the balcony was another couch of Spanish leather, tufted and padded to an exquisite softness of appearance. After a moment, Dual, apparently oblivious of my presence, crossed to this and began to pull back the individual tufts of the leather peering intently into the folds.

A few minutes passed, as he pulled and tugged at the leather; then he was rewarded, for his fingers darted downward quickly and came back, holding still another coral bead. He nodded in satisfaction, and turned again to me.

"The trail begins here," he said.

"You think she was in this room after she was kidnaped or abducted, or whatever it was?"

"Abducted is the better word," said Dual. "Yes, she was here. She was overpowered in the other room. She struggled, but it was a silent struggle. Believe me, Gordon, these countrymen of mine know how to do things without noise, and Mrs. Parton was small. However, she struggled, and in the moment it took to overpower her, her string of beads was broken, and no doubt the few I found rolled under the divan, and were not found. You remember Parton said Hafiz had a good many men here that day. They were here for a purpose. No doubt they picked up the beads and straightened the room before Hafiz and Parton returned and found Mrs. Parton gone. The black who looked into the room where Hafiz and Parton were, probably told Hafiz that the coast was clear. Meanwhile they had carried her in here and probably laid her down on this couch, while arranging to get her out. I suspect she was actually lying here while Hafiz and Parton sat smoking and waiting for her return."

"Good Heavens, Dual!"

Semi smiled. "In fact I am sure she was laid here, for you saw me find the bead, and if you will look at the wall back of the couch, you will notice the impression of the heel of a boot, such as Western women wear. It is, furthermore, a fresh mark smudged into the slight soil of the paper, as if the person in her struggles might have struck the wall forcibly with her heel. If you look still more closely you can even see the imprint of the nails of the heel, so that the shoes which made it must have been worn for some little time. Also, it was never made by any footwear such as Oriental house-servants affect, and it is too small for anything other than that of a woman or a child."

"Granting that what you say is true, how did they ever get her out? Parton says he came back here immediately and made search, and failing to find her had the detectives connected with the hotel up at once."

"You overlook the fact that between searching himself, in an overwrought condition, which would prevent his being thorough, he went back and told Sheldon all about it before calling the detectives in," said Dual. "Also, I do not see that they necessarily took her out of the apartment at once."

"You mean that she may have been here all this time? Then what about the search made by the officers? I'm willing to admit that Parton might have been fooled."

"To look for a thing and to find it, are separate actions," said Semi Dual concisely. "To find the thing, one must look where it is."

"Well then?"

"The searchers failed to look in the right place."

"And you think she was here at that time?"

"She must have been. That much is clear, surely," said Dual. "It was daylight when she disappeared, and they had no opportunity to get her out without being seen by any number of persons, you must admit."

He rose and passed out of the windows and stood on the balcony, wrapped in thought. Once or twice he raised his fingers and pressed them to his temples, and after a few moments he knelt down on the balcony floor, and began going over it, bit by bit. Now and then he nodded to himself, and, as if sure of what he were doing, redoubled the care of his search. Presently he raised his head, and beckoned me to approach. I went out and bent down beside him. Semi Dual pointed to the balcony's floor.

I looked and saw that it was fashioned of several strips of metal, soldered together and painted. At the outer edge, near the rail, one of these strips had sprung loose from the soldering, and curled upward slightly, presenting a ragged edge. It was to this that Dual was pointing. I know at the time I thought whimsically that he was like a bird-dog, on a dead point, and even as I followed his directing finger, I wondered what I was going to see about that bit of ragged metal, which could have any bearing on the whereabouts of the woman we sought.

But as my eyes followed the serrated edge of the loosened plate, I caught my breath in a sort of gasp. *There, held by the jagged points of the upending edge, was a tiny thread of yellow silk. That was all.*

Dual smiled at the question in my eyes, and picked the yellow thread away. Then he got up and sauntered back into the room.

"That looks like Mrs. Parton's hiding-place to me," he said in his way of easy smoothness. "Suppose you ask our friends to come on in here now."

I went for Sheldon and Archie, and told them Dual wanted them at once. They came on the instant, Archie pale and silent, Sheldon bubbling over with questions which I didn't either have a chance or the inclination to answer just then. Dual bade them sit down and plunged at once into an interrogation of Archie.

"When you searched these rooms on the day your wife was abducted, Mr. Parton," he began, "did you look on the balcony which opens into the second room beyond this?"

"Of course," said Parton. "I looked out there, but there was no sign of her at all."

"Did you, perhaps, go out on to the balcony?"

"Why, no," responded Archie. "I could see the whole thing from the windows, and Alice wasn't there."

Semi Dual smiled at me.

"My countrymen have a sort of habit of draping balconies and alcove windows and such, with rugs and such things, Mr. Parton. Did you by any chance notice if there were any rugs hanging over the railing of that balcony that afternoon?"

I saw it in a moment, and waited almost breathless for Parton's reply.

"Yes," he answered slowly, like one trying to be sure of a half-remembered thing; "I think so. I am sure when I think of it that there was a large brownish—no—between a brown and a tan colored rug thrown over the rail when I looked out there. Why?"

"Because," said Dual rising, "your wife was lying behind that rug, Mr. Parton. I have a reason for what I say."

"My God!" cried the boy hoarsely. "I was within touch of her then and never knew."

"Exactly," said Semi. "It was a well-thought out place of concealment. Probably Hafiz had had the balcony draped like. that all during his stay here. The hotel authorities and the gendarmes of this section would think nothing of the rug hanging there, and the shape of the balcony railing lent itself to the scheme. Hafiz was shrewd. He hid your wife well-nigh in full sight, and you all missed the spot. Even the color of the rug lent itself to the deception of your eyes. It was like Hafiz to do that. Come with me and I will show you how it was done."

We went out to the balcony and Semi Dual pointed to the rail. It was of a scroll pattern.

"See," he said, calling our attention to the shape; "each bar of the rail is of the shape almost of an 'S.' That leaves quite a little space at the floor, as you will notice, and it would be easy to roll a bound body into such a space, and drop the rug over it, and yet have the rug fall in natural folds to the floor. Parton says it was a large rug. The other end would fall below the floor on the outside and hide the body from the street. Beside the possibility, however, I found a bit of the scarf I gave your wife, Mr. Parton, stuck fast to a jagged bit of the flooring right here."

He indicated the spot where he had found the yellow thread.

He turned back into the room. "Our Hafiz is a fox," said he; "a nice little thieving Persian fox. Presumably, having done his stealing, he will go home for his burrow to feed at his will. It remains, therefore, to get passports for Germany and Russia for the four of us and arrange for transportation—that is," turning to Parton and Sheldon, "if you intend coming along?"

"You can bet your last chip we're going along," shouted Colonel Sheldon, fidgeting in his excitement. "Hafiz may be a fox, but I'm a fox-hunter from this minute to the finish, Dual, you bet."

"Suppose, then," said Dual, "that you ask the management to arrange for us to leave as soon as possible, and take passage for us as far as Baku. I shall allow you to go that far toward the scene of trouble. From there Glace and I will go on alone."

"You will like thunder!" bellowed the colonel. "D'you think I'm goin' to be sittin' around waitin' for somebody else to see this through, Dual?"

"You are going to get those tickets, and do anything else I direct you to do," said Dual slowly. "You and Mr. Parton are going to Baku. After that you would only be in the way. From Baku we must move with the greatest secrecy. We can't hunt Hafiz with a brass band."

For fully a minute Sheldon said nothing, while a slow flush crept into his face. Then he cleared his throat.

"All right, perfesser," he said, with an attempt to turn the matter off, "I'll do what you say. Baku, you said, wasn't it? though the Lord knows where that may be! But I want to tell you this, Mr. Dual: You're not a father, an' you ain't lost no girl, so I reckon you can't appreciate how an old man like me feels right about now."

"But I can sympathize," said Dual quickly. "That, Colonel Sheldon, is why I am here."

"An' I guess you're right," acquiesced the colonel. "Go on and tell me what to do, Dual. Shouldn't we tell the police what you've found out?"

"Tell them by all means," said Semi; "but if Hafiz is Hafiz, he will not be caught."

"Well they might find out what train he took, don't you think?"

"Of what use would that be?" Semi questioned. "We know where his burrow is. He will take to earth at last. However, I shall see to it that Paris is ransacked while we are away. Archie," to Parton, "telephone for a taxicab."

While Parton was complying, Semi asked Sheldon and Parton to meet him in the morning at the American consulate to attend to the passports. Then he dismissed them and, taking me with him, went down to the taxi and set out for the office of Grimaud, head of the detective bureau, where he was soon closeted with the chief.

When he came out he met me with a smile.

"I have learned two things of interest," he said, as we went back to the cab. "First, on the evening of the day Mrs. Parton disappeared, the gendarme on duty near, the hotel reports that he saw two men carrying a rolled-up rug. He questioned them, and they told him in broken French that it had fallen from Hafiz's balcony and they were taking it back. Secondly, that same night Hafiz's special car was attached to the train which went east, yet we know Hafiz remained at the hotel till yesterday. Though I cannot prove it, I surmise that the rolled up rug went along, and that it was rolled about the figure of the girl. In view of all which I think I shall go to the hotel and get our traveling companions, rout up your counsel, and try to catch the same train ourselves." He leaned forward and urged the driver to greater speed.

From that time on my recollection of the night is of short frenzied rushes hither and yon about the night streets of the city; of sleepy and half-angry officials scowling over papers; of an arguing and gabbling of polyglot tongues.

We routed Archie and Sheldon out of the palace, and went to the American consulate. Together with our yawning countrymen and the police authorities, whom Dual had already enlisted, we got our passports arranged for somehow, after heartbreaking endeavor, while the clock ticked the minutes away. Through it all Dual dominated the situation, urging his point at every turn, hurrying official routine into unaccustomed channels of speed, arguing, protesting, commanding, until at length he had his way, while I marveled at the man.

Then again a frantic clash back to our hotel, and a frenzied flinging of apparel into traveling cases, a procuring of our tickets from the management, another swift dash for a depot, a frantic argumentation and gesticulation over a change of transportation to an earlier train than our billets called for; a dash, down a platform to a string of coaches; a ringing of bells and a tooting of horns and a bawling of orders; then the slow tremble of motion and a gliding away of the lights of the depot.

Even Dual heaved a sigh of relief and laughed as he threw himself on a seat.

"Yoiks! Gone away!" he said, as he stretched out his limbs. "We are on the trail of the fox at last."

CHAPTER VII.
AT THE PERSIAN GATE.

FROM THAT time on the journey seems to me, at this time, like a sort of weird nightmare of haste, of swaying, dimly lighted wagon-lits, a pounding of wheels, and the occasional shriek of a whistle, mixed and blended with a jumble of different languages, which ever changed and varied as we fled east, and farther east.

The sibilant whispering French gave way to the grumbling gutturals of the German. Bearded or fiercely mustached faces peered into our compartments, inquiring for our passports. Then the swift rush forward again.

Morning came and brought the checkerboard farms of Germany, its hamlets and towns, where the platforms of the stations swarmed with a ruddy-faced population, totally unlike the people whom we had just left. From time to time Dual left us and it seemed to me that he was trying to learn something of the man we pursued by a discreet questioning of the guards.

Now and then I saw money change hands. Once, when we were in eastern Germany, he came back smiling and told me he had definite information that Hafiz's private car and some of his servants had passed that way.

So we fled onward, each of us thinking his own thoughts; the colonel volubly enthusiastic about running Hafiz down; Parton white-faced and silent; Dual cheerful, confident, smiling, and working to pick up information; I waiting for orders and wondering where it was all going to end, and if we should ever pass this way again.

Russia came with a gruff demand for our papers, a close scrutiny, and a final viseing. We crossed the frontier and rushed on toward Moscow, where we would make a change of trains. Dual smiled as he gazed from the window at the flat sweep of the landscape.

"Here," said he, "Europe's Man of Destiny saw his star begin to wane. Russia began for Napoleon what England and Germany finished, and winter and these broad plains fought for Russia as nothing else could."

Moscow! Dual did not tarry, but rushed us along. We left our train and took passage over the South Russian railway. Moscow fell away behind. Down and down the map we fled southward across the broad steppes of southern Russia, where the verst-posts whirled by and reeled backward each with its carefully piled and whitewashed cairn of stones about its base.

One heard nothing now save the guttural cough and sneeze of the Russian language. The coaches filled with bearded men, who smoked incessantly their little long, thin cigarettes. At several stations Cossacks, in their queer caps and coats, boarded the train.

So fled the days and nights and brought us finally to Rostov and the broad flood of the Don, across which we crawled; then up and up around the shoulder of the Caucasus Mountains, while the valley of the Don fell lower and lower and the clouds came closer; and the long, coasting slide back into the stretches of the Transcaucasus to Jorat, with its blending of the Occident and the Orient, where Western coats rub shoulders with the flowing garments of the mysterious East; with its blending of tongues and faces; its quaint, old-world glamour, and its smells. Then on and on over the Central Asian Railway, south and east toward the Caspian Sea, on and on by long, clanking trains of oil-cars, on and on to Baku; where the black oil pours unceasingly from the earth, and at last the end of the railway.

As we stopped in the station at Baku, Dual gathered up his cases and turned to Parton and Sheldon before leaving the train.

"I would advise you to hunt up some good, quiet hotel and take quarters indefinitely there," he remarked. "From now on Glace and I shall not appear to be connected with you in any way. Furthermore, I would not go about any more than I could help. There are, to the best of my present knowledge, several American families living here whom you might look up. Report yourself to the Russian police as soon as you can find a stopping place, and leave your address at headquarters for me. Now I think we had better say good-by. When we leave the train go your way as if you had never seen me before."

He put out his hand and shook hands with each of the men in turn.

"Letting you go off this way on a risky business, which don't concern nobody but me an' mine, sure don't make a hit with me, Mr. Dual," said Colonel Mac. "Hain't there no way in which you could fix it so I could go along anyway? I'm a tough old cock an' I've roughed it all my life, so you don't need to worry none about my not bein' able to stand the gaff. When I think of Allie alone with that smoked herring I feel as if I want to sit up and yell. Gad, sir, if I have to sit around this oil-camp and cool my heels I'll go bughouse in a week. I want action the worst way, Mr. Dual."

Dual shook his head.

"Colonel Sheldon," he said slowly and firmly, "while I realize that I am assigning you to a difficult part, I am doing it for the best. Sometimes I have doubted the wisdom of bringing you even this far. But for my respect for a father's feelings I would have left you in Paris some days ago. We are now in the country of the man we seek. Criminal though he is, he has people like himself, who will warn him of anything which appears like a pursuit to them. We have to hunt from a blind from, now on. Should you meet me to-morrow you, yourself, would not recognize me, my friend. You say this case concerns you alone. You are wrong; it concerns every true man who desires to benefit the race, who frowns down on the degradation of woman by such men as Hafiz Ibrahim and his ilk. Primarily, I am acting as your friend; but over and aside from that, I am acting as an agent of justice, and a protector of innocent womanhood."

Sheldon seized his hand and wrung it. "You're one white man, Mr. Dual," he cried. "You can bet your last sou marquee that there won't be a minute of the day or the night when me and Arch won't be thinkin' of you two. Well, I suppose we better be gettin' along."

"And," said Dual, "when you think of us, think of us as succeeding in our mission. The instinctive thought and wish of a brave heart is one of the strongest things in all God's universe."

A guard came up and opened the door of our carriage and peered in. Dual turned and told him shortly that he had dropped something and had been searching for it, and the man passed on, but Semi shook his head.

"They keep a close watch on you around here," he remarked in a pointed manner. "Let that serve to show you, colonel, and you, too, Mr. Parton, that the Great Bear is never asleep. Be careful of what you do until I return."

We left the train and passed out of the station. Semi Dual never glanced in the direction of our two friends after leaving the railway coach. He called a porter, several of whom were lounging about the depot, and gave him our bags, which he shouldered and set off with at a swinging, shuffling gait, that took him over the ground at a surprising rate of speed.

Dual and I followed, and here I met my first surprise. Instead of making for the European part of the city, our bearer led us quickly toward what was, to even my uninitiated eye, the native quarter. We finally turned in at the gate of a sort of courtyard, where donkeys, horses, men, women, and children mingled in a gesticulating, jabbering, jostling crowd, through which slunk and crawled uncountable dogs.

Semi Dual laughed lightly, as he pushed through the mob with myself upon his heels.

"I sometimes wonder what makes the Eastern peoples prefer incense to water," he flung to me over his shoulder. "How does it seem to your Occidental nose?"

"Beyond description," I replied, grinning, and Semi Dual laughed yet again.

Our porter took us to a near-by doorway, where squatted an old man. He was brown and wrinkled and had a white beard. Two bright, beady eyes shone out of his skull, predicating anything but an old mind, if I was any judge.

Him Dual addressed in a few words of what I took to be Persian, for after a first glance of surprise, the old fellow replied in the same language, to judge by sound, rose, and guided us down a dark passage to the door of a room, which he threw open that we might enter. At a word from Dual he followed us in.

Again Dual spoke to him, and suddenly the man bent his back in a most profound bow, his hands spread wide. He came close to Dual and gazed full into his face, while a dry smile creased his cheeks. Then he laid his palm upon his forehead, and salaamed again.

Dual beckoned him closer, laid a hand upon his shoulder, and spoke low words into his ear. The man nodded in comprehension, and, turning, left the room, after closing the door carefully as he went out.

I looked about the room. It was practically bare. There was a sort of pallet of straw in one corner, and a couple of peculiar stools. That was all. Semi Dual dropped upon one of the stools. I started to seat myself upon the pallet, by preference, but Dual waved me away with one of his whimsical smiles.

"From my knowledge of Eastern caravansaries, friend Gordon," he said lightly, "I would suggest the stool. That bed may not be as unoccupied as it appears."

I grinned appreciatively and took the tip, also the stool, and sat down. Dual continued speaking, as I seated myself, and I began to get an idea of what would be our position in the days to come.

"As soon as Ali returns," said my companion, "I shall become again a native Persian, which after all I really am. You, Glace, will become an actor in the role of my personal attendant. Ali has gone to get us our make-up and when he returns you will enter immediately upon your part. In view of the fact that you do not speak the language, I suggest that you assume the role of a dumb man. You may maintain your hearing if you wish, but do not try to speak when others are around.

"As we travel southward from here I shall endeavor to teach you such simple phrases as will enable you to understand my spoken commands and directions, and I will ask you to remember at all times that anything I may do or say to you in the future will be things dictated by necessity. No matter what may happen, keep that in mind and act from that hypothesis.

"We are going directly to Teheran, where Hafiz has a palace, and where I may as well tell you now my ancestral home is located, and is still kept up by an old servant whom I left in charge a good many years ago. If he has been true to his trust we should be able to slip into the house and work from its cover, without Hafiz even being aware that I am in the East at all. Now, with this explanation, suppose I give you some instruction in the Persian tongue."

For upward of an hour I listened and parroted Persian. Dual seemed pleased at the progress which I made, and presently gave over his teaching, saying that I had enough to remember for the time.

Shortly afterward the old innkeeper returned with several bundles, which he deposited on the floor. Then, after salaaming deeply once more, he took some money from Dual and withdrew from the room.

Dual opened the bundles and spread their contents out. From one of his cases he drew a large bottle and sponge, and, turning to me, ordered me briefly to remove all my clothes. I complied in silence, and when I was stripped to the skin, Dual set to work sponging a dark fluid which he took from the bottle over my face, body, and limbs.

Under his rapid working, my skin quickly took on a light brownish hue, which he deepened on face and hands by applying a second coat of the stain.

My hair was naturally brown and straight. Dual made it black by recourse to the contents of a second bottle, which he took from his case. When he had finished, I am sure if I hadn't known what had been done I wouldn't have recognized myself.

Dual laughed softly and put his bottles away. "It will last for three weeks if not sooner removed by a reagent," he assured me. "Now, suppose we put some clothes on you, and make you into an attendant."

He selected several of the garments from the pile on the floor, and assisted me in getting into the same, finally rolling me a turban, with a few deft turns, and handing me a small traveling mirror. As he finished tricking me out, I looked into the glass and beheld a dark-skinned, turban-crowned face, which grinned at me in half consternation, half amused derision. I gave Dual the mirror, and awkwardly attempted a salaam, nearly losing my turban in the act.

"Fair for a novice," grinned Semi, and set to work donning his own new attire. "When you have added some few days' dirt and grime to your newly-varnished features, and get your raiment smudged and travel-stained and have forgotten to wash your hands for a week, you'll quite look the part," he affirmed.

I grunted. "May one smoke?" I wanted to know.

"By all means," said Semi. "And while you are getting your tobacco you might as well put that automatic gun of yours into your sash. We shall soon be in a country where every man is still pretty much his own law."

I did as he suggested, then made a cigarette and sat puffing while Dual finished his dressing. At the last he surprised me by fastening his turban with a magnificent jewel, the filigree setting of which held an egret plume; whirling upon me and standing with folded arms and a scowl upon his face.

"Shades of Xerxes!" I cried, taking my cigarette out of my mouth. "What picture-book did you crawl out of? Say, Semi, can the fierce looks and tell me where you got that ruby; it's a peach."

Dual stamped a foot in seeming anger, subsided upon the stool, and grinned.

"As a body-servant, you are slightly too occidental," he said, smiling. "The jewel is a family heirloom, and would cause much veneration among certain people whom I know. I have put it on because it marks me for what I desire to seem—a Persian of the blood royal."

"You look the part," I muttered, with a shake of my head. "Are you going to scowl and stamp your tootsie at me as we go south?"

"If you don't act your part better I may cut off your head," said Semi Dual.

I patted my sash.

"Not while I've got the little gun," I reminded, and Dual laughed.

"Well, suppose you accompany your master into the busy marts of trade."

He rose and pushed the door open.

Hard on his heels I followed into the crowded courtyard, past the salaaming Selim, and saw the immediate sensation which his appearance created among the swarming life of the place. A hush fell where we walked, a pathway opened before us, and passing out into the narrow street, turned off toward what I later saw was the Caspian water-front.

Dogging Dual's heels, I found him presently in earnest bickering with the captain of an oil steamer, during which conversation from time to time I heard the word "Resht," and presently some money changed hands. I imagined that Dual had engaged passage for us on the outgoing vessel, and my surmise proved to be correct, for, after turning away from the docks, Semi spoke to me over his shoulder, while keeping his head turned straight to the front.

"We go south on that boat to Resht this evening," he informed me. "Now I am going to the headquarters of the local police."

For this purpose he hailed a public conveyance and had us driven to the station, where he entered into a long conversation in Russian with the official in charge. Meanwhile I sat, kicking my legs and twiddling my toes. Presently Dual called me to where he and the police officer were talking, and introduced me to the man. The officer turned toward me and surprised me by speaking in English.

"Are you Mistaire Glace?" he demanded, with an official frown.

Semi nodded.

"I am," I answered, on the nod.

"You are really seeking a kidnaped gurl?"

"That is correct."

"Mr. Dual is correct in stating that this woman's parent and husband are now in Baku, Mr. Glace?"

"He is."

"Their names?"

"Colonel Sheldon and Mr. Archibald Parton, officer."

"So," said the man. "This Mistaire Sheldon haf called upon me. I haf recommend them to one hotel. They can be reach at any time, through me. So, that is well."

"That is all right," said Dual. "Now we leave for Teheran to-night, going by boat to Resht, then overland from there. Probably you would know if Prince Hafiz Ibrahim has passed through here recently? He would most likely be in disguise."

"Is it then that Hafiz has the gurl?" questioned the man.

"That is what I believe," Dual replied.

"He has already stolen at one time a woman of my country," said the official. "You may well have right. Wait, I shall write you a line to Colonel Kahrloff, at Teheran, in case you should need help. Also you will, of course, see your own consul there."

"Of course," said Dual. "However, I should appreciate the note to the colonel. Rumor states that our consul has little influence at that place."

Some moments later we left the station, and set out for the caravansary again.

"Luck is with us," said Dual, when we were again in our room. "Our friend at the station didn't reply in words to my question about Hafiz, but I looked in his eyes and I saw. He started to answer, said more about the Russian woman than any Russian policeman is ever expected to say and froze up. But he knew, and I read it from him, that Hafiz has passed this way. As I suspected, his alleged stopping at Constantinople was merely a clumsy lie. Suppose we eat." He went to the door and opened it.

"Go to the end of the passage, clap your hands to Selim, and point to your mouth, as though eating. You may as well begin your part now," said he.

I passed out and found Selim, and carried out the pantomime. He nodded, and I went back to the room. Some time afterward Selim himself brought in a sort of platter of stewed goat, a loaf of hard bread, and a bottle of some light wine. We sat down on the stools with the food between us and ate. I confess I didn't eat much, and Dual noticed it.

"I could have spared you this a day longer," he said half in apology, "but it is what we will get on the trip to Teheran, and you had better get used to it, Glace."

I nodded, and choken down the mouthful I had been trying to chew, in the hope that my stomach would dispose of it in some manner and derive good of it in the process. All the time my mind was back home, and I was wishing it were time to go home and I was stopping at Shinn's place for a sandwich and a cup of coffee.

Night found us on the boat. The next day we made Resht. Semi Dual engaged horses for our journey to Teheran, some hundred and fifty miles further south and east. It was while we were arranging for the horses that Semi again found the trail of the fox. He told me about it afterward, with his grim smile.

"Our friend the horse dealer tells me," he said, "that a man answering the general description of our friend Hafiz bought some horses from him yesterday. We are running the fox to earth."

CHAPTER VIII.

DUAL'S ANCESTRAL PALACE.

I AM not going to try to describe that ride of one hundred and fifty odd miles from Resht. To me it is still indescribable. A Persian saddle resembles nothing so much as a packing case with the sides knocked off and the ends left on—and I had not been on a horse for years. Tricked out in gaudy garments I imagine I looked like a monkey in a circus. I felt even worse than that.

With Dual it was different. The man was a constant source of amazed lack of understanding to me. To my personal knowledge he had been leading the life of a recluse and scholar for years; yet now, back in the land of his fathers, he would eat a handful of dates, slip a couple of the seeds under his tongue to promote the flow of saliva, get on his horse, and ride all day at a killing gait, apparently not turning a hair.

Our horses were good ones, and the first day out of Resht we made fifty miles. I am sure we could have gone farther had not Dual held back out of pity for me.

Dual insisted upon my taking the first sleep that night. I protested against his sitting up to keep a watch, but he waved me away with a smile.

"In Persia one watches at night, Gordon," he said with finality, and sat down near the horses, while I stretched out on the warm earth and dropped to sleep as though shot.

Hours after he aroused me from my deep sleep, and lay down in his turn, while I kept the vigil he had maintained. Nothing happened as the night dragged away. I ached in every bone arid muscle, and walked about a bit to try and shake off the cramp. Aside from the champ of the horses, there was no sound.

I looked up at the stars, very clear and bright, and wondered if they were looking down on home as they were here, and realized that they probably were not. I thought of Connie Baird and wondered what she would think if she could see me now, and then I wondered if she were thinking of me. Then my thoughts went to Alice Parton, and wondered what she was doing, and where she really might be, and if the fox Hafiz had reached Teheran as yet. With that thought came an inward urge to go on despite the physical discomfort. A woman's happiness and welfare depended upon our speed—a good woman's, too. I turned toward Dual to urge him to get up and go on; then I turned back and looked at the east. Would daylight never come? Would the east never grow gray?

But it came at last, and I roused Dual. We ate some bread and dates, had a drink of water, and rode on to the south and east. Late that day we came upon the trail of another party going in the same direction, and camped for the night some forty miles out of Teheran, according to Semi Dual.

The next day was a repetition of the others, save that we went forward more slowly, and that I was growing more used to riding, and so did not find the work so hard. Dual told me that we were going to enter the city at nightfall, however, and so held back our pace.

Late in the afternoon he pointed before us from a little rise in the road, and I beheld the white walls, squat buildings, and pointed minarets of a town.

"Teheran!" said Semi Dual.

Dusk fell, and Dual pressed onward at a good speed now, but when quite near to the city he turned off to the side and began skirting around the town.

"Where are we going?" I asked.

"To mine ancestral mansion," said Dual lightly. "It lies outside the older portion of the town."

I followed his lead, as he swung in circuitous fashion about the more thickly settled districts, threading his way always in one general direction, and finally he paused before a gate, let into a vine-grown wall.

From the top of the arch of the gate there hung a bell, or gong, of what, in the dark, I took to be bronze. Sitting on his horse, Semi Dual drew a jeweled dagger, which he wore at his waist, and with the hilt struck three times upon the gong.

The mellow echoes took up the sound and quivered and died on the night. Once more Dual struck three times in measured cadence upon the gong, and when again the tones had died, he struck again, a single blow.

Then he put away the dagger, and sat waiting the answer to the summons he had struck.

Rising in my stirrups, I could see over the top of the wall the dim outline of trees, and the odor of vegetation and the coolness of their life, and of wet earth, came to my nostrils where I sat. By and by I caught the twinkle of a moving light through the grating of the gateway, and saw that it was coming slowly our way.

Semi Dual saw it, too, as evidenced by the fact that he gave no more alarms, yet he said no word to me. Afterward he told me all that was said at the first meeting with his old retainer, which at the time, I could not understand. For the sake of the reader's understanding I shall give the translation of what was actually said, as nearly as possible as Dual told it to me.

The light came nearer and nearer, and was finally deposited upon the ground just inside the gate. Next a bearded face of a very old man was thrust against the bars, as the man peered out at us from under bushy white eyebrows, striving to recognize whom we might be.

Then came his quavering voice, asking who rang at his master's gate at night, striking seven times. Dual replied:

"It is I, O Musab Ben Musik. It is I, Abdul, the son of Abdul, who seeks admission to his father's house, of whom thou art the appointed guardian. Who else should know of the seven rings, fool that thou art? Open, then, and admit thy master, and stand no longer gaping as though thou hadst seen a spirit. Hasten, I say!"

"Is it really thou, O Abdul, son of Abdul?" quavered the old man, beginning to tremble.

"And thou openest not the gate, I shall of a surety show thee that I have not forgotten how to command obedience," cried Dual. "Open, then, dog, and keep me no longer waiting here."

The old retainer evidently was satisfied that it was really his master, for after a period of fumbling he unfastened the gate. We rode through and up a path under the trees until we came out into an open paved space before a flight of stairs leading up to the house itself.

Here Dual swung from his horse and I followed suit. Then Semi turned the animals over to the man.

"See that they have water and food, Musab Ben," he commanded; "and when thou hast finished, come to me. See that thou tellest no one that I have returned. Go."

The old man led away the horses, and Semi Dual turned and began to climb the stairs. I followed, and at the top he produced the little electric torch he had used in Paris, and pushing open a door, led me into the house, where all was dark.

Using the tiny flare of the torch, Semi guided me down what was palpably a passage, paved with tiling, to judge by the feel of the floor under my feet, and finally turned off into a side room. Though it had been years since he trod that way, he seemed perfectly at home, for, telling me to wait, he crossed to the nearest wall. A match sputtered, and a moment after a candle flared from a sconce, giving a dim illumination to the room. One after another Dual lighted the candles about the apartment, and presently came back to me.

"Welcome to the palace of Abdul," he said, smiling. "Here, if you wish, you may gain the power of speech."

But the place itself had well-nigh rendered me speechless, and asking Dual's forbearance, I continued to gaze about the room. It was a large apartment, the floor of which was tiled in a most intricate pattern. Its walls were high and pillared and raftered, covered with rich frescoes and hung with priceless tapestries.

The rafters of the ceiling were gilded and covered with what I supposed were Persian inscriptions. Rugs of fur and beautiful work of the looms were scattered about the floor. Teakwood chairs, tabourets, and couches furnished the apartment. I dropped upon a chair and gazed and gazed. Presently I sighed and looked at Dual to see him smiling at my evident delight.

"Now," said I, "I know you are a veritable jinnee, and this is a magic palace which you have conjured up."

"It is my ancestral home," said Dual. "You shall look it over at your pleasure during the days we shall remain here. You will enjoy it, I think."

The old man came back, and bowed before Semi Dual.

"Thy horses are attended to, O master," he said.

"Then," said Dual, "suppose you attend to the master as well. I would have food."

"Master," said Musab, "I hear and obey."

He turned and shuffled out of the room, to return presently with an immense silver ewer, a pitcher of water, and a towel of damask. With these he approached Dual and knelt, poured water into the ewer, and held it up, with averted head.

Dual washed and dried his hands, then motioned the old man to me.

"Musab," said he, "this man is my friend and companion. In semblance he is a servant; in this house he's as my equal. Serve thou him, even as me, under my displeasure. Remember this, Musab Ben."

Musab made no reply, but approached me with the ewer, and I in turn performed my ablutions. Then he rose and withdrew once more.

When he returned he brought in a low teakwood table, placed it before Semi Dual and myself, and laid a beautifully drawn piece of damask upon its top. Departing again, he returned with some cakes, a cold fowl, and some sweetmeats, which he set before us, together with some silver cups containing a light wine.

When he had finished he salaamed and turned to leave the room. Dual halted him by a clap of the hands.

"O Musab Ben Musik, thou hast a daughter. This it seemeth to me were formerly her duty. Why is it that Mousin no longer renders attendance to her master? Speak."

For a moment Musab seemed undecided just what to do, and shifted uneasily upon his feet without making any reply. He was as one caught in an indiscretion, without any excuse thought up. Dual watched him out of narrowed eyes.

"Well," he said at length. "Well, Musab, why dost thou stand like a rooster on a hot stone? Speak!"

"Mousin is at present in the city, O Abdul, son of Abdul; therefore she is not here to serve her master, which will no doubt give her great grief."

"And what does Mousin in the city?" said Dual. "Speak truly, O

Musab, and remember that I see thy thoughts as a man sees the pebbles in a clear pool."

The old man began to tremble, and licked his bearded lips with his tongue before he made reply.

"Mousin, my daughter, is at service in the city, O my master," he said at length.

"And wert the moneys I gave thee for service not enough, O miserly Musab, that thou shouldst send thy daughter out to service? Didst think to draw two wages for Mousin? Fool! Tell me where doth this daughter of a greedy father work?"

At this question I thought the old servitor was going to collapse. He trembled violently and looked about him as if seeking some escape. Dual half rose, then sat back and fixed the man with his eyes.

"Enough of this mystery," he shouted. "Speak, and truly, or be the consequences on thine own head."

Musab sank to his knees and his head to the floor.

"Thy pardon, O Abdul, for I have done wrong, and I fear, but though thou shouldst kill me, yet will I speak true. Mousin has service at the palace of Hafiz Ibrahim."

For a moment I thought Semi Dual was going to laugh. It was as well that Musab was groveling at his feet, else he would have had less fear of his master's attitude toward himself. For an instant triumph and exultation burned in Dual's eyes, then he controlled his features and spoke to the man on the floor.

"Thou dog!" he cried, pushing him with his foot. "Hast dared to send a daughter of thine into the house of mine ancestral enemy. In the time of my father thou wouldst have died for less. Rise and leave my face. To-morrow I shall find what to do with thee. Now go before I shall act without thinking, in my just rage."

Musab scrambled up with surprising agility for one of his years, and started swiftly from the room, his footsteps aided by his evident fears. As he reached the door Dual halted him by a word.

"Hold!" he cried. "O Musab, thou hast served me well, and long, and I do not desire to forget that, nor to be harsh with thee. Wouldst atone thy fault to me?"

"Gladly, O my master," quavered Musab, as he turned and advanced trembling into the room.

"So be it," said Semi Dual. "From now on, while I shall remain, thou and thy daughter must do as I say in everything. My life shall depend upon it, O Musab. Wilt hold my life as thy own?"

"Aye master." The old man knelt and kissed the edge of the robe Dual wore.

"Good," said Dual. "Go thou and prepare a place for me to sleep, and for my friend. To-morrow find thou a cook for us, and when thou hast accomplished that I shall give thee other missions to perform. Now go and leave me to refresh myself. Depart."

When the old man had shuffled out, and Dual had satisfied himself that we were alone, he came back and attacked the food, after seeing that I was served.

"The stars surely work for us, Gordon," he said with a smile of pleasure. "There was need that I make Musab fancy me greatly displeased. In reality I felt like shouting for joy when he told me we had a spy already to hand in Hafiz's household in the person of his daughter. I made him think me very angry in order to make him bend his daughter to my will, for his own skin's good. The old rascal really needs it in a manner of speaking, though what he has done will be worth much to us. I know my people; they will do much for their parents; much for gold. If they can help their parents and earn gold as well, there is little they won't do.

"Mousin will find out for us whether Hafiz has taken Alice Parton to his palace seraglio. Mayhap Mousin can also help us to get her out. In fact, Mousin looks like a Heaven-sent means of deliverance to me. Now I know what the other woman, who appeared as an instrument in my astrological figures meant. That woman was Mousin, and she will enable us to do much. Truly, my friend, the stars do not lie. Let this again prove it to you."

He ceased speaking and raised his drink to his lips, and his eyes shone.

"Glace," he resumed as he set down the cup, "I feel morally certain now that we shall succeed in rescuing Alice Parton before she shall have come to any harm. Kismet! It is fate."

"Do you mean that you foresaw the assistance of another woman in the case, days ago, before we left for Paris at all?"

"The stars foretold it," said Semi Dual.

I shook my head. "It's all beyond me, but it gets results," I admitted, and drained my cup of wine.

"To-morrow Musab will show you to the American consulate," Dual advised me, after a moment's thinking. "He will also take you to see Colonel Kahrloff, and you will deliver my note from the official at Baku. I shall write a letter to go with it, in case we need to appeal to him. Personally I shall remain in the house and try to work unseen. And now, if you have finished, I fancy that bed would appeal to you. Musab will show you. I have a bit of work to do."

He crossed the room and struck a gong. A few moments later Musab conducted me to a far room, where he assisted me to disrobe and stretch out between sheets of snowy linen, on a couch of literally downy ease. My head had hardly touched the pillow before I was fast asleep.

CHAPTER IX.

WORD FROM ALICE.

DUAL HIMSELF awoke me in the morning by coming into my room and shaking me.

"Wake up, friend Glace," he smiled, as I opened still sleepy eyes. "How would you like to take a swim?"

"A swim in Persia? Where did you get all the water? Well, if it isn't a joke, lead me to it," I agreed eagerly, and swung my legs out of bed.

Dual laughed. He was clad in a light robe which fell to his heels.

"I can give you a swim such as you never had," he boasted. "That is one thing which I have here which I have never been able to equal anywhere else. Never mind dressing; there are no women about. This is truly a bachelor's hall. In fact the bath I mention is in the women's wing of the palace, and used to be their private bath."

I rose and followed him out into the corridor, where I again marveled at the beauty of fresco, tiling, and gilding. The place reminded me more and more of some of the scenes depicted in an old edition of the "Arabian Nights" which I had cherished for years. It was a veritable palace of Oriental splendor, somewhat toned down by years of disuse and partial neglect.

Presently Dual turned off to the left and led me through a grilled and fretted barrier into another broad salon, then down a passage again, between doors, opening into empty rooms, full of dust-covered rare bits of rare furniture, and so on at last into a great room, or half-open court, surrounded by walls of marble and soft yellow stucco, left open to the sky.

A flock of doves rose up and swirled out of the open roof as we approached, settled along the cornice, and strutted and cooed. Then as we entered fully I saw the pool and stopped short to admire.

It was fashioned with walls of pink marble, in a floor of green tile. At one end a bronze elephant threw water into it from his uplifted trunk. At the other the water overflowed through what was built to look like a natural grotto of moss and plant-covered rocks.

Semi Dual smiled, as he turned and saw me standing in silent amazement. Then, dropping the robe from his shoulders, he sprang into the pool. Through the clear water every line of his superb body glistened and shone, while little bubbles of the water's imprisoned gases clung to his skin. He swung down his feet and rose dripping and laughing.

"Come on in," he chuckled; "the water's fine. Welcome to Aphrodite's bath. That's what it used to be, even if this is an Eveless Eden right now. Abdul, my father, had it entirely remodeled for my mother, after he brought her home. It was after that that this wing ceased to be the women's portion of the palace and became the abode of the Goddess of love, as I am told Abdul, my father, used to call the woman who bore him a son—myself. She was his one wife. He was an oddity among Persian nobility in those days. But then," he added slowly, "I fancy my father met the one woman who could satisfy every need of his soul. Men sometimes do that, Glace. Happy he who takes her to his heart."

He turned and dived precipitately down under the water, gliding easily down the pool.

I leaped into the pool, and a thousand needles of delight kissed my skin, as the cool waters closed around me, and woke every cell into acute life. I swam over to Dual and rose to my feet.

"Do you mean," I asked, "that your mother and father were what is called twin souls?"

Dual shot me a glance, then sat down on a jutting ledge of marble, and clasped a knee in his hands.

"Glace," he said, after an interval apparently spent in making up his mind, "I think I shall tell you something about myself. To you I am a man of mystery, when in reality there is no mystery at all. I frankly like you. I want you for a friend, and Semi Dual says that to few, very few souls. Yes, friend, my father met his twin soul. He put away all other women, married my mother by the rites of the Russian church, and brought her here to live. He built this bath for her. This was their bower of love. Here they dwelt in simple harmony, and, by and by, she gave him a son.

"I was that son. They lived and loved on. To them there was no night or day, no mine or thine, no question of man and woman—they were one, and they lived as one, and died two days apart. I remained, and after some years I met one whom I now believe was my own mate, as my mother was my father's, only I did not know the law in those days. I was a child of love, and surrounded by dissolute society. The gentle soul I finally found would have none of me, while I was what I was. An arrogant fool, I did as I pleased. She died. I have lived—a long time—hundreds of years."

"Hundreds!" I cried.

"Hundreds," said Semi Dual. "I learned how to do that. That woman who died left me a note telling me that though she died she was mine in spirit; asking me to so live that when she came again to this life, as she would, we might be as one. It was then that I resolved to live until she came again, lest should I die I might forget when I came back." He smiled.

"Of course, now, I know that was foolish, but I have lived so long that I think I might as well continue to wait, now. It will only be a few years probably, and I know how to keep myself young."

I looked him full in the face. "Dual," I said, "are you mad?"

He smiled sadly and returned my glance. "Am I mad, my friend?" he replied.

"You are not mad; you are wise beyond the wisdom of one life," I answered, strangely shaken, and to conceal my emotion, slipped off into the pool.

Dual left the ledge and swam easily after me.

"I have sent Musab to call upon his daughter," he said as he approached. "No doubt he will return before long. I have offered him pardon, five thousand rubles, and protection for Mousin, in return for her help. Judging from the gleam in my old servitor's eyes, he will get results."

"I hope so with all my heart," I responded, and I meant every word.

"And now for breakfast," said Dual, as he climbed out of the pool and threw his robe over his shoulders. "Come down as soon as you are clothed. There should be much to do to-day."

I climbed out and sought my room, where I dressed speedily and then joined Dual below. He took me into a room where the morning sunlight flooded the floor and motioned me to a seat before a table where stood a great bowl of fruit, a pitcher of milk, and some oddly flavored cakes, which Dual explained were made from the ground seed of the millet, sweetened with honey, and of which I ate heartily. While we broke our fast, Semi continued to talk of our quest for the girl.

"I told Musab to tell his daughter that I held his life forfeit for his misconduct, and that it depended upon her to win his pardon, as well as my favor, and a purse of gold. I told him to tell her all that had occurred and gave him a note to be given to Alice Parton, if she should really chance to be in Hafiz's seraglio. I wrote her in English, and impressed upon Musab that she, and she alone, was to have the note. Also, I made a provisional suggestion for her rescue. It would not do to have Musab making too many trips to Hafiz's palace, so it was necessary to cover the ground, as far as possible, in one trip. Everything now depends upon what he finds out and tells us upon his return."

"But what of Mousin if Hafiz finds out?" I inquired.

"We must take the chance," said Dual. "Afterward I shall find means to render the girl safe."

Footsteps shuffled up the corridor and Musab entered the room. "Hail, Abdul, son of Abdul, to whom is the secret of life," he mumbled, falling upon one knee. "Behold I, Musab, thy servant, have returned from the errand upon which I went."

"It is well," said Dual. "Arise, Musab, and deliver thy message to me."

The old man rose and began speaking rapidly, and under evident excitement, his words pouring forth in an unbroken stream, while Dual sat silent, not once interrupting

At the end he fumbled within his dingy sash and produced a note, which he laid before Dual. Again his hands fumbled with the folds of the cloth, and before my almost unbelieving eyes, he withdrew a corner cut from the wistaria scarf.

Dual caught it from his hand, gazed at it a moment, then handed it to me.

"As I said, the stars work for us, Gordon," he said in a voice which trembled slightly, and gave his attention to the note. After he had read it, he passed it over to me. I read it in turn, and my eyes grew damp.

MR. DUAL:

Surely God is good to me to give me such friends. I am here a prisoner of that dreadful man. Can it be possible that I may escape? Hope grows in my heart. Try, my friend, ah, try—even though it mean my death, try. How are my dear husband and my father? Are they with you? Give them my love. Every hour I pray for release or death, but I want to live more than ever now, for a reason which only I know. In haste,

ALICE PARTON.

P.S. I hate to do it, but I have cut the beautiful scarf to prove it is really I.

ALICE.

Meanwhile Dual was questioning Musab, asking him of every detail, and nodding now and then, as though satisfied. Presently he dismissed the old man and turned to me.

"He saw Mousin without any trouble," he said in satisfaction. "He has often gone to see her, so his visit excited no comment to-day. He easily discovered from her that a woman answering Alice Parton's description had been brought here some six days ago. They made good time. Hafiz himself arrived only yesterday.

"After explaining everything to Mousin, she agreed to help. She took the note to Alice Parton. The answer you have read. To-night Mousin will find a means to leave a wicket open in the wall about the seraglio garden and will leave a door open in the wing of the seraglio building itself. She will meet us in the garden and guide us to the women's apartments.

"After that we must do things for ourselves. It is our best chance. Now I am going to send you to see your consul. Explain the entire incident to him, and arrange for him to take Mrs. Parton under his protection some time to-night. After you have seen him, go to Colonel Kahrloff and tell him our story and give him the note from the official at Baku and one which I shall write. Ask his aid in case we should need it.

"That, I think, is all. Now, while I write the note to Kahrloff, suppose you get ready to go. Take your automatic for use in case of need. Try to avoid all observation, and get back here before night."

He left me, and I went up to my room, got the gun and saw that it was loaded. Then I came down, and, under Musab's guidance, set out on foot for the American consulate.

I had some trouble getting in when I got there, and had left Musab loafing on a corner, to await my return. The man at the door evidently didn't see any reason why a servant, who looked like a Persian, should seek admission to the American official, but I drew out Dual's note and made signs that I must deliver it in person, and as he didn't see the address, it did as well as any other would.

I found our national representative sitting with his feet on a desk and a cigar between his lips. When he saw me he took his feet down and withdrew the cigar, in evident astonishment.

"Well, what the devil are you doin' in here?" he wanted to know.

I added to his surprise by replying in English as crisp as his own.

"I am seeking your aid in protecting an American citizen, my friend."

"Eh?" said the man. "Good Lord, where did you learn to sling United States, my boy?"

"In my home town. I was born there," I replied.

"Then why the masquerade?"

"For a purpose which I want to explain when I get a chance," I answered, rather testily I guess.

"Eh? Oh, yes, yes," said the consul. "Take a seat."

I dropped into a chair and plunged into my narrative, ending finally with the assertion that Alice Parton was in Hafiz's palace, and that Dual and I were going to get her out.

"I wouldn't try that," said the man. "Now, let me take this up in the regular way. The United States will see that this Hafiz fellow gives her up, I'll be bound."

"And in the mean time, while you cable to the government, and they cable back, and you send diplomatic notes to the palace, and the palace denies all knowledge, and the wheels of the official gods go round, what will happen to the girl?" I asked.

"But what you suggest is practically entering and seizure," the man protested.

"I hope it will be," I agreed.

"No one may tell what may come of it."

"I hope the liberty and physical welfare of a countrywoman will come of it," I said, getting up. "Now, Mr. Consul, answer me this: Will you give this woman the protection of the consulate, after we get her here?"

"Why, of course," he replied in surprise. "I hope I'd not fail to do that, Mr. Glace. Only it's mighty irregular, mighty irregular indeed."

"Hang the irregularity, Mr. Consul," I cried. "What we want is results. Will you take care of the girl, after we deliver her? That's all you have to do."

"And I told you I'd do it," said the man. "I've got to do it, haven't I? You bring her here to-night, an' she'll be safe. I'll see to that."

"Thank you," I made answer, and turned to the door. "We'll be here some time before midnight, I think."

"I'll have a room fixed for her for tonight," he informed me. "Going? Well, so long. Wish you could stay and chin a bit. A fellow gets a bit seedy in this hole. Where you going now?"

I told him I was off to see Kahrloff, and at once he wanted to go along.

"I know that fellow," he said. "He's a pretty decent sort for an 'offsky,' as I call these Russians. He's one of the few who can speak English. I'll take you up there and introduce you to him."

For a moment I was tempted to accept, then I thought of Dual's advice to act quietly, and I fancied that riding around with the American consul would not be living up to that; especially when I was clothed as I was.

I explained all this to the consul and he nodded his head.

"Uh-uh," he agreed. "Well, I'll go up there and you come along. How's that?"

I could see no harm in that, and agreed. I went out and picked up Musab, and we set off for the Cossack barracks to find Kahrloff, and give him Dual's note.

Kahrloff listened while I told him my story, then nodded his head. He also read Dual's communication, and the letter from the Baku officer. Then he turned to the consul, who had come up in the mean time, and addressed us both.

"Of course, I have no real official knowledge of all this," he said. "Linvitch merely writes that you are seeking a girl believed to have been kidnaped, and tells me you will call on me. You say, Mr. Glace, that you have located her. Of course, if you desire you can lay the information with the proper authorities, and we will do what we can, but it will take time."

"That is the one thing we can't afford," I broke in.

"Nor can Mrs. Parton, I fancy," said Kahrloff. "Now, I would suggest that what you have told me be for me alone. Officially I know nothing. Act as you think best, and if you get into trouble, get word to me and I will do what I can to get you out. Of course, if you get the girl and have trouble, I can then interfere in the interests of public peace."

"That is all we would expect," I said, and thanked him. Then I left him with the consul and went back to Semi Dual.

CHAPTER X.

THE MASTER COUP.

I RETURNED and told Dual of my errand, and he expressed himself as well pleased.

"Everything is going smoothly," he said with marked satisfaction. "Now all we have to do is to wait for night. If you wish, we will go over the house and I shall show you some of its treasures while we wait."

I assented eagerly and the rest of the afternoon was spent in a tour of the palace, where I felt like a child again, in my enjoyment of the beautiful gems of furniture and art which Dual presented for my inspection, and whose history he told me in his quiet way.

Night came, and we had a frugal supper.

"Enough to sustain strength, and not dull action," as Semi Dual explained. After that Semi took me with him and proceeded to dress me in a complete outfit of dark material, arraying himself similarly, and throwing a cloak of black velvet over his shoulders at the last.

"Have you your gun? Be sure and take it," he cautioned. "While I do not wish to shed blood, I do not intend to fail in my undertaking, and if we are detected, Hafiz will certainly show fight."

I displayed my little automatic.

"Personally," I responded, "I don't share your antipathy toward shedding blood to-night. I'd rather like one shot at the fox."

"Young blood and the natural man," said Semi lightly. "Well, let's get Musab and set out."

We found the old man, and Dual sent him ahead as a sort of vedette, to see that the coast was clear. After him we went down into the garden and passed through the arched gateway into the road. Then we turned toward the city and walked rapidly along in the night.

Save for the sound of his feet, I could scarcely distinguish Dual. His black cloak made him nothing but a shadow in the night. I suspected that I was equally elusive in the suit I wore.

"It will be lighter after a bit, when the moon rises," said Semi once as I stumbled over some roughness in the way.

We passed on into the denser populated parts of the town, and here Dual sauntered forward with the easy familiarity of a denizen, throwing off all attitude of being upon anything but pleasure bent. I trailed him closely, playing up to my part of attendant. We both followed the shuffling figure of Musab, who walked always some way in advance, and would presently show us the unlocked door in the wall of the Hafiz place.

By and by we turned down a dark alley and as we crept along I saw that we were skirting the sides of a blind wall, over which hung the trailing ends of vines, swaying ghostlike in the dusk. Somewhere ahead old Musab had disappeared and I could no longer hear the scraping sound of his shuffling feet. A chill breeze swept up the throat of the narrow passage, and I shivered as I walked, half from cold, half from nervousness.

Now that the enterprise was close at hand I confess I felt as I have been told raw recruits sometimes feel before going under fire. I wasn't exactly afraid. Nothing I could think of then would have induced me to turn back. Yet as I walked after my silent companion, I shivered again, and I confess to wondering somewhat anxiously as to what lay for us on the other side of the vine-clad wall.

Dual never faltered in his stride, while I trailed along, and presently a sibilant hiss came out of the darkness. Semi paused so quickly that I nearly trod upon his heels. There in the dark mass of the wall was a darker blotch of a rectangular shape, and out of it crept the figure of Musab, whispering a low word to Dual.

"The gate is indeed unlocked, O my master. Behold, Mousin has kept her word."

"'Tis well," said Dual in low accents. "Retire thou to the outer end of the passage and await my commands." He turned and stepped into the dark oblong. With a deep breath I followed where he led.

I found him fumbling with the latch of the gate, and he swung it inward as I joined him. Together we slipped through and stood in the garden, and Dual swung the door back into place. We slunk up the path toward the dim light walls of the house, where they showed through the trees and shrubbery, Dual still leading, I following close in his wake. No sound broke the stillness save the light scuff of our feet, and the tinkle of water falling into some fountain basin. That and the whisper of the wind in the trees.

We approached the wall of the house by degrees. Suddenly another shadow detached itself from the shrubbery and slipped to Dual's side.

"It is I, master—Mousin," breathed a woman's voice.

Dual paused and for a few moments held the girl in whispered conversation. Then he drew me close to him in the darkness and spoke close to my ear.

"Mousin says that Hafiz is entertaining this evening. There is only one guard in the women's section of the palace—a eunuch by the name of Hasan. We must find a means of entering the women's quarters and holding this man until we can get Mrs. Parton out. Mousin says he is stationed by the door through which we must enter. When we go in, have your gun ready, Glace, and get the drop on him at once. Under no circumstances let him get away, but don't shoot if you can possibly help it. Mousin has but just come out. She says Mrs. Parton is in the main salon of the women's quarters now. We are going in at once. Come quietly and keep cool."

He turned to Mousin and spoke to her.

"When you have shown us the door, go out and leave the garden and go up the passage quickly. Your father Musab is waiting at the end. Tell him I said he should take you home at once and admit no one to the palace until I come. Now, girl, lead the way."

Mousin turned and slid away before us. We followed, passed a door let into the side of the building, and found ourselves in a darkened hall. Drawing his flash-light, Dual showed a tiny ray of brilliance, and at the end the figure of the Persian girl, creeping stealthily along.

As though drawn onward by the pencil of radiance we followed down the passage, around a bend, again down a passage, and came upon Mousin, standing silent before a barred and brass-studded door, from beyond which came the muffled sound of voices and a woman's laugh.

She silently pointed to this door and nodded. Dual motioned her to leave, and she bent in a salutation and fled softly back the way she had come.

"Get your gun ready," Dual whispered softly, and laid his hand to the door.

It yielded readily enough and swung inward, showing us a vast room, pillared and groined with pointed arches, its filed floor covered with rugs, cushions, and divans, with palms and other potted vegetation set about it; lighted by swinging lamps dependent from the ceiling, its air redolent of sandalwood and musk.

All this I saw in a glance as I pressed upon Dual's steps and then my eyes searched for and found the guardian of the place.

He was a gigantic negro, black as the pits of hell, and he stood with his back to the door, surveying the room, as we came in. He whirled on the instant and his great hand flashed toward his belt where he wore a long and curved dagger, or dirk, suspended in a jeweled sheath.

Even as he moved Dual cried out to him an order to halt, and remembering my part, I slipped forward and pointed my short little gun full at the fellow's bulging paunch. He never flinched nor batted an eyelid, but merely dropped his hands and gazed into my eyes with an ugly leer.

So we stood, each apparently awaiting the other's next motion, while one might count ten. Then Dual spoke slowly to the black.

"Thou art Hasan, head eunuch, and should know what women Hafiz has here present. I seek one—an American—who arrived six days ago. Speak, dog, and show me where she is."

The leer on the negro's face increased to a grin.

"Thou mayest seek in the foulest pits of perdition, O Abdul," he said in defiance. "Hasan serves Hafiz, not thee, thou eater of unclean meats and wanderer in far lands. Search, and it please thee, for I may not prevent, while thy jackal holds the fire toy to my stomach; and may thy search lead thee to the regions of the damned."

"It is well, dog," said Dual in Persian, then to me in English: "Hold him tight, Glace."

That sentence was a sort of bomb, which exploded the situation. At the far end of the room the women of the palace had been huddled in a voiceless, frightened group ever since we had entered the door, but as Dual addressed me, bidding me watch the negro, there came a shriek of joy and amazement from the group.

A figure, clad in a short red jacket, baggy yellow trousers, and a full undershirt of white silk, detached itself from the other clustering women, and fled toward us, crying aloud to Dual.

In that moment, as my eyes turned for an instant at the sudden commotion, Hasan hurled himself upon me. His giant fist crashed into my jaw so that my head snapped backward, until I thought that my neck would surely break. His other hand seized me and flung me aside, and he sprang for the door.

Sick and dizzy I staggered for just the necessary instant he needed for his purpose. The door jerked inward, framed his flying figure, then even as I raised my hand to chance a hasty shot, it was pulled shut, and the eunuch fled down the passage in full cry.

CHAPTER XI.

THE FOUND IS LOST.

DUAL GLANCED toward me, then turned to meet the woman who rushed forward, seizing his arms, peering into his face.

"Mr. Dual! Mr. Dual! Is it you? Oh, is it you? Oh, thank God!"

Dual caught her hands and pulled them from their clutch on his sleeves; jerked the cloak from his shoulders and flung it about her form, then passed her on to me.

"Quick, Glace, get her out of here before you are cut off!" he cried in short, crisp words, pushing us both toward the door. "Quick, man! Hasan will rouse the entire palace. Get to the consulate and wait for me."

Even then I hung back, necessary as I knew haste to be. But for my clumsiness we could have left as quietly as we came. Cursing my rank incompetence, I waited a moment to protest.

"You go, Semi," I pleaded. "Let me be the rear guard. Man, I am all to blame. If any one stays behind let it be me. I am armed and I can fight."

"Yes," said Dual very calmly; "you are to blame, Glace. Are you going to stand here and throw away our last chance of success? I have ordered you to take Mrs. Parton to the consulate. Unless you really wish us all to perish, go and leave the rest to me."

I felt the hot blood of shame rise in my cheeks. I knew Dual was right.

I turned again toward the door, and sought to leave the room. Then, and only then, did I discover that the door was locked. I turned back toward Dual, and he met my glance. Even as he did so he made a gesture of impatience.

"Your gun, man, your gun, to the lock," he cried sharply, and turned his face the other way.

Cries and shouts were coming from some distant part of the palace, and as I drew my automatic and pressed it to the lock of the door through which Hasan had fled, I could dimly hear the beat of footsteps coming from some passage on the other side of the apartment where we stood. I placed the muzzle of the gun to the lock and fired. There was the snap of the high powered powder, a crack of metal, and I wrenched the shattered door wide. Dual looked on, and the man was actually smiling.

"Good work," he said shortly, and turned away just as Hafiz Ibrahim burst through a door from the other side.

Hafiz Ibrahim was no coward, no matter how big a scoundrel he may have been. For one instant he stood confronting Dual across the room, the door at his back full of the excited faces of his followers. Then he came boldly toward Dual.

As once before, I picked up the form of Alice Parton and turned toward the door, and as I did so I glanced again at my friend, whose plan my clumsiness had well nigh spoiled. There was something of farewell in the look I cast him, for I never expected to see him again.

But for the woman in my arms, I would have stood shoulder to shoulder with him and let his fate be my own. The soft throb of the girl's heart told me my first duty was to our mutual trust. Yet even then, as I felt her panting breath on my throat, her slight arms about my neck, I vowed that I would come back to Dual when I had once got her out of the house and seen her safe.

As my glance turned toward him and I leaped through the door, Semi Dual was standing awaiting the approach of Hafiz, still with the smile upon his face.

His arms were folded and he had not moved from his position in the slightest since Hafiz entered the room. But as I drew the girl to my breast and turned through the door, Hafiz's hand darted downward toward his broad belt, and Dual's hand came out from under his armpit, holding a short black gun. His voice came to me clearly as I passed the door.

"Stop! Up with your hands, Hafiz! It is I, Abdul, who commands you. Obey!"

So I left him standing, still smiling, with Hafiz the fox glaring unexpressed hate into his face.

Back down the passage where Mousin had led us, I carried the girl in my arms. Back down its dark length until I pushed open the garden door and we slipped into the cool outer air. Not once were we challenged on the way.

No doubt Hasan had told about locking the door, and they fancied our escape impossible from that side. Then when we blew the lock, Hafiz was already in Dual's power for the moment and might not order our flight cut off, however much he may have wished. But I was afraid of the garden. It did not seem possible to me that it would be left unpatrolled.

Not once during our flight down the dark passage to the garden had the woman in my arms spoken or moved, except to shift her weight a little by lifting herself up by her arms; but when we were without the building she awoke to instant speech.

"Put me down, Mr. Glace," she cried quickly. "Put me down and go back to Mr. Dual. Quick! Oh, quick! Otherwise it may be too late!"

"And have you picked up and dragged back? No!" I cried. "Once to-night I failed Dual, but this time I'll do as I'm told."

"But I tell you to go back," said the girl, struggling in my arms. "Mr. Glace, I shall never forgive you, no, nor myself, if you leave that splendid man to fight that mob alone."

I held her tighter, so that I fear I hurt her, for she cried out, and, despite her struggles, I fled on down toward where the gate in the wall ought to be.

"Mr. Glace," she began pleading, "please put me down. I'll hide in the bushes while you go back. No matter if I am retaken. If I escape like this I shall feel that I murdered Mr. Dual."

"For Heaven's sake, Mrs. Parton, don't argue," I gasped, as I ran forward. "I'll get you safe, and then I swear I'll go back. I feel as much a coward as a man can, but Dual is trusting you to me, and I'll fulfil the trust. If you'll only keep still and not struggle, and help me to get you away, I can get back that much quicker. Please!"

"Put me down and let me run," panted the girl. "I am tiring you this way, needlessly. I promise to hurry. Put me down, Mr. Glace."

I complied with what I confess was relief. Under other circumstances Alice Parton was surely a sweet load; still, after a man has dashed down dark halls and through a dusky garden, with the fear of instant attack goading him on, he is no mere human unless he feels at least a physical relief when the person he has been carrying, be she ever so darling a woman, elects to use her own feet.

I put her down and took her hand, which was cold, as I noticed even then, and we ran on. And as we ran, the moon, which Dual had promised for later that night, broke out from behind some clouds and filled all the garden with a yellow-red light, throwing the shrubs and bushes into black relief, yet showing us better where to go.

With the girl's hand held fast in mine we ran on, and reached the wall of the garden and began to creep along it, seeking for the gate where Dual and I had entered earlier in the night. At last I saw it yawning blackly in the face of the wall and quickened my pace again, that we might the sooner escape from the imprisoning walls.

But even as we fled toward it, relief and hope mounting in our panting hearts, that which I had feared came to pass. A figure detached itself from the black shadow of a bush and flung itself upon me.

So sudden was the man's appearance and attack that I had barely time to throw myself in front of the girl before he was upon me in his mad assault. Then, as his body hurtled against mine, by one of those strange vagaries of the mental processes, my thoughts flew back to Goldfield and the days I had spent under John Curzon's roof, and to the little Hashimoto, Curzon's servant, and his odd wrestling tricks.

The little Jap had taught me some of the more common of the holds and methods of defense as used by his countrymen, and into my mind, dazed by my assailant's rush, there came a wild thought of possible quick relief. As he fell upon me, reaching for a sure hold, my right hand shot out and seized him by the baggy fulness of his shirt, and at the instant I fell back before his attack; yet as I fell, dragging him with me, my right foot rose and planted its heel full in the middle of his abdomen, so that he grunted in surprise and pain. My arm flexed and dragged him up over the fulcrum of my uplifted foot; then, still falling from him, I suddenly arrested my fall, kicked out and upward with my foot, and threw the fellow clear over my shoulder so that for an instant he sprawled pawing in the red-yellow moonlight, then fell face downward into a tangle of bushes, and lay still.

I turned to the gate. Again my path was barred by a lock. The gate was fast. I waited only for one long breath, then hurled myself against it in a short, desperate rush.

Again and again, gritting my teeth at the pain of my throbbing shoulder, I flung myself against it, until, with a splintering of wooden bars, it yielded and sprawled me on all fours into the dark alley beside the wall.

I scrambled up, turned and helped Alice Barton over the wreck of the gate, seized her hand, and set out up the dark passage, urging her into a run. And as we ran I became conscious that the woman was sobbing—not loudly, but softly like a frightened child.

"Don't cry, don't cry," I panted. "Save your breath. Everything—will come out—all right. Don't cry—please."

I slipped my hand up under her arm, and we ran on. By and by we came to the mouth of the impasse and turned out of it into a wider street, where we could see better from an occasional light which burned dimly here and there on a corner. We turned from this street into a still wider thoroughfare. The girl was stumbling now in her stride, and I halted her for a moment under one of the lights in order to see how badly she was winded and give her a chance for a breath or two at her ease.

It was then that a carriage, flanked by a couple of outriders, came toward us down the street. I heard the sound of the horses and the rumble of wheels, and glanced up, watching them as they approached. There was no use trying to run away, for I made sure they had seen us under the light, and beside, I saw that the riders wore the Cossack cap. They dashed on as if to drive by, and I was glad, but on the instant a voice spoke in command, the carriage stopped, and one of the outriders whirled and rode over to us, halted, and motioned that we should approach the carriage at once. I obeyed. There was no use in resistance, and these were Russians. At least, I thought, they were better than some of Hafiz's desperadoes whom we might have met.

The man in the carriage descended as we drew near, and removed his cap.

"This is Mrs. Parton, I presume," he said, bowing before her. "Will you not enter my carriage and permit me to see you to a safe place? So the venture went to success, M. Glace? I am glad. I congratulate you most sincerely." He turned and assisted Alice Parton to step to a seat.

"How did you know me, Colonel Kahrloff?" I questioned as I climbed in after Alice. "Your powers of perception and remembrance for faces must be very acute."

"They have to be," said Kahrloff as he sprang in. "Where to? The

American consulate, I think you said to-day? Right?"

I bowed, and he shouted the address to the driver. In a clatter of hoofs we were off.

"I must really congratulate you, Mrs. Parton, upon a most fortunate and remarkable escape; and upon the friends who brought it about. I recognized M. Glace as you stood under the lamp, and as he had told me of to-night's adventure, I was delighted to be able to lend a hand. You will soon be safe from any further cause for alarm."

For a moment Alice Parton made no reply, so that I wondered if she had not heard or understood. Then in a voice of choked emotion:

"I am fortunate above all women in my friends. I thank you, Colonel Kahrloff," she said.

"By the way," said the colonel, turning to me, "I thought Abdul was to be with you. Did anything happen to him?"

I hastened to tell him of the rescue, not omitting my unlucky blunder, and ending with my leaving Dual still in the palace of Hafiz, with its angry master held under his weapon's point.

"*Peste!*" cried Kahrloff when I finished; "why didn't you tell me this before?"

He cried out to one of the Cossacks to ride in close, as I judged from his doing so. Then he gave some order in Russian, at which the man saluted, whirled his mount, and set off on the back trail, with a shower of sparks as his horse's hoofs struck fire from the stones in the road.

"I have sent for a squad of men to go at once to Hafiz's palace. They may be in time or too late. Anyway, Abdul is half Russian, as he told me in his note, and I shall make that an excuse to search Hafiz's place if we don't find him living or dead, without."

The carriage drew up in front of the consulate, and stopped, and I sprang out and ran up the steps.

"I want to see that everything is all right," I called back to the two in the carriage.

Stevens—which was the consul's name—was seated very much as I had seen him earlier in the day, but sprang to his feet.

"The deuce; you look as if you'd been in a free for all," he exclaimed as he saw me. "Well, where's the girl? I've been sitting up waiting for beauty in distress."

"Mrs. Parton is outside in Colonel Kahrloff's carriage," I informed him. "Is everything ready here?"

"Sure," said Stevens. "I fixed my own room up for her. It's right back along the hall, and all the rear doors are locked. I shall stay here to-night, and there nobody will get in, except over me."

"Good," I exclaimed, and dashed back to the carriage, where I assisted Alice Parton to alight, and led her up the steps. She came quickly, and as soon as I had presented her to Stevens, she turned and urged me to go.

"Go quickly, Mr. Glace. Don't wait. I am safe now; return to Mr. Dual as quickly as you can. I am sure you can get there before the soldiers can do it. Oh, please go! Every moment you stand here is time wasted from him."

"You're sure you'll be all right?" I remembered Dual had said to stay with her, but that was immediately after my fluke with Hasan, and before he knew we would escape surely and every impulse of my own being urged me to go to the aid of my friend; and certainly Mrs. Parton didn't need me now.

"Of course, I'm all right," cried Alice Parton. "Oh, go, go," she half sobbed.

I turned and ran back down the stairs and turned down the street up which we had come.

"Hold on," cried a voice. Kahrloff was leaning out of his carriage where he had waited: "Where are you off to now?"

"I'm going back to Dual—Abdul," I shouted, and turned to run again.

"Well, don't be a fool," Kahrloff said with almost official roughness. "Get in here, man. Good Lord, did you think I wasn't going along now?"

I climbed into the carriage with a thankful heart.

"Hasan's jolt to the jaw must have unsettled your brain pan," said Kahrloff, "for you to be running off to Hafiz like that. What chance would you stand with them all on the watchout for you? With me along it is different. Hafiz may growl, but he won't dare to bite. If Abdul is alive we'll have him out. I know that chap by reputation and he's about the best Persian that ever occurred, from all I can hear."

"You're right, Kahrloff," I assented, breathing deeply, and getting a grip on myself. "I guess I am a bit rattled, as we say in America. Things have happened pretty fast."

"Sit back and get a bit rested," advised Kahrloff, and we drove on after I had asked him if he knew the way to the dark alley beside

Hafiz's palace, and he had assured me that he did.

We rattled along and finally turned down the narrow street which led to the *impasse,* while I fumed at even our rapid pace; and just as we reached the mouth of the passage, I cried out in amazement, for clearly visible in the light of the now unclouded moon, Semi Dual sauntered leisurely out of the black entrance to the place.

"Dual!" I cried, springing to my feet in the carriage, which had been drawing to a halt. "Semi! It's Glace. I am here with Colonel Kahrloff. Gad, but I'm glad to see you, man."

In one spring as it seemed, Dual reached our side, and peered into my face.

"You here," he cried in tones of reproach. "Where is Mrs. Parton, Glace?"

"I left her at the consulate," I said rather shortly. Of course I had bungled earlier, but I had proved my loyalty by coming back.

"You left her—after I told you to stay with her?" said Dual slowly. "Will you never learn to obey?"

He sprang into the carriage and turned to where Kahrloff had sat throughout our first speech.

"Colonel, may I impose upon you still further and ask you to return with us to the American consulate at once?" he asked. "Believe me, there is no time to lose. I fancied that Glace would at least carry out my orders to remain there an guard, but you see he has not."

Kahrloff assented, and gave the necessary directions, and Dual dropped to a seat. As for myself I sat silent, scarce knowing what to say or expect.

Dual's words had excited a wild sense of fear in my brain, and I leaned forward, mentally urging the flying horses as we rushed over the rough street.

What had I done? What did Dual fear? Why should Alice Parton not be safe under the protection of her own countryman and her flag? It was all becoming a nightmare of my own inability to do the right thing at the right time. I fretted inwardly and curbed myself for an incompetent ass.

"We were expecting to find you at least a prisoner," said Kahrloff as we swayed along. "Glace seamed to think your escape at least beyond possibility. How, if I may ask, did you get out?"

Dual smiled slightly. "Glace let his own understanding of the situation blind him to several things," he replied. "I got out by the simple expedient of walking up to our friend Hafiz, taking away his revolver, placing my own against his left side, and suggesting that we take a walk in the garden. Hafiz agreed to the stroll, and I left him just outside his palace wall. I think he was glad to see me go."

Kahrloff lay back on the cushions and roared.

"You're the devil of a fellow," he cried between chuckles. "Well, there's no harm done and I must congratulate you."

"Wait until we reach the consulate," Dual replied, and Kahrloff eyed him in still more surprise.

Everything was quiet when we drew up in front of the home of the American Charge d'Affaires. We all climbed out and walked up the steps and entered the room where Stevens sat nodding over a book. He looked up and greeted me with a grin.

"The lady's in bed by now," he advanced. "She was clear done up, the poor thing." Then he saw Kahrloff. "Hello, Alexius!" he said.

Dual advanced and faced the man. "Are you sure the lady is safe?" he asked.

Stevens looked at me for enlightenment, and I hastened to give it. "This is Mr. Dual, of whom I told you," I explained.

Stevens bowed. "Pleased to meet you," he said in acknowledgment of the introduction. "As for the lady, she's in my own room, and at her request I locked the door from this side. I reckon she's still there as nobody has asked me for the key." He paused and grinned at his own humor; but Dual remained unsatisfied.

"At the risk of seeming unreasonably hard to convince," he said seriously, "I wish you would accompany us to Mrs. Parton's room, that we may satisfy ourselves that she is perfectly safe. Would that be asking too much?"

"Sure not," Stevens acquiesced, as he got out of his chair and produced a key from his pocket. "Come along, if it will make you feel any better. She'll be glad to know you're safe too, Mr. Dual. She was scared to death about you, and before she would agree to retire she made me promise to let her know about you as soon as I heard." He turned and led us into the hall and down that to the door of the room where he had placed Alice Parton some time before. He lifted his hand and rapped softly upon the panels. There was no answer, and after a bit he repeated his rap.

"I bet she's dead to the world," he said as the silence still continued.

"Your pardon," said Semi Dual, as he pushed in beside him, lifted his hand, and struck loudly upon the door.

"Mrs. Parton," he cried through the woodwork. "It is I—Semi Dual."

Silence was his reward.

Dual turned and shot one glance at me, and my heart sank at the fear I saw in his face. He put out his hand and silently took the key from Stevens, out of whose face some of the ruddy assurance had fled. Silently he turned the lock; then pushed open the door.

A dim light burned upon a table in the center of the room; a curtain fluttered before an open window. On the floor, mid-way between the table and the bed lay Semi Dual's cloak, which he had cast about Alice Parton's shoulders as she came to him in Hafiz's palace. Beyond that there was nothing.

Of the girl herself there was absolutely no sign.

CHAPTER XII.
THE TRAIL OF THE SCARF.

SEMI DUAL turned to Stevens and pointed to the open window.

"Was that open when you left Mrs. Parton here," he demanded sharply.

"It was not," said the consul. "I know it was shut. Whether I locked it or not I really can't say."

Dual turned and left the apartment without another word and walked quickly toward the front, motioning to me that I should follow. He passed out of the doors and went down the street, and then Kahrloff caught us up.

"If the carriage will be of service—" he tendered, and Dual took him up at once.

"Thanks," he said frankly; "if you will be so kind as to allow the imposition." He turned and climbed into the equipage.

"Where to?" inquired Kahrloff as we followed Dual.

"My own palace, if not too much trouble," replied Semi. "I must make some investigation, see something about the lay of the land, before I go any further in this case. At present it is hard to say just where we stand."

"If I can be of assistance in any way, command me," said Kahrloff as we rattled away down the street.

Dual bowed his head in acknowledgment, beyond which he made no sign, nor spoke a word as we were driven toward his palace, but sat wrapped in what was apparently gloomy thought.

As we neared his dwelling he finally raised his head.

"To me it appears quite clear that Glace was followed by some one from Hafiz, and was trailed to the consulate. Personally I don't know what became of Hasan after he bowled Glace over and made his escape from the seraglio. He may even have trailed Glace after he left the palace and followed him all the way, and have been prevented from attacking, by your interference, Colonel Kahrloff.

"Then, after you had left the consulate, and after Stevens had left Mrs. Parton in the room, he entered and stole her away. The next question for us to find out is where she may be now."

When we arrived at the entrance to his residence he left the carriage, and after shaking hands with Kahrloff, and thanking him for his assistance, and accepting his offers of further possible aid, he turned into the garden, with me at his heels.

Not a word did he say as we threaded the garden pathway, and I followed in silence, dreading to interrupt the man's mood. We had almost reached the steps of the palace when Hafiz, the fox, again showed his teeth. As silently as the mists of the night, a figure rose at our approach and hurled itself toward Dual.

I cried aloud; and even as the cry of warning left my lips, and I sprang forward to come between, some sixth sense seemed to warn Dual of the danger, for he whirled quickly. His hand shot out toward the other and gripped the uplifted hand of the man, where glittered a long-bladed dirk, raised for the downward plunge.

Without apparent effort Dual gave the arm he held a swift wrench and twist, and I heard the bone snap with an audible crack. The man groaned in agony, and the knife rattled and lay shining upon the ground.

With a grim smile Semi Dual flung the man from him so that he staggered and fell. Then as he lay writhing upon the path Dual spoke to him sharply, yet with a half chuckle as I thought.

"Get thee gone, to thy master, and tell Hafiz the fox, not to trifle with the lion."

The man crawled clumsily up and slunk into the shrubbery, cursing under his breath. Dual turned to me.

"Thou wouldst have taken the blow, my friend," he said softly. "Such acts as that prove the true friend. Come on into the house for we have much to do."

But I stood in my place and put out my hand to him.

"We have everything to do—to do over; and it is all my fault," I cried in the deepest humiliation I have ever felt. "Everything I have done has been wrong, Dual."

"To err is human," said Semi slowly, laying a hand on my shoulder. "To err in seeking to aid others is surely deserving of excuse. Forget all that has happened, yet profit by the lesson it may teach you. Such is the path of advancement. Now, come with me—my friend."

Side by side we went up the steps to the doors of the palace, and on into its depths, until Musab stood bowing before his lord.

On the instant Dual was again all action.

"Go. Fetch me Mousin," he cried. Then as the old man turned to obey, he flung himself upon a carved divan and sank into deep thought.

Mousin came and bowed before him. He rushed into a rapid flow of questions, pausing now and then for the girl to make reply. It was all incomprehensible to me, though now and then I caught the words Hafiz, and some other, which appeared to be a surname of some sort, and again as I listened, Alice Parton's name came to my ears.

At first Dual's manner was stern and unbending. Gradually it relaxed and became more mild, though no less eager. Watching the man, I fancied I saw renewed hope and purpose grow and kindle in his face. Then of a sudden he clapped his hands, calling Musab, and at the same time ordered Mousin away.

Musab appeared and he gabbled a string of orders to the old man, who departed even as had done his daughter, with a look of wonder upon his ancient face.

Then, and only then, Dual turned back to me.

"There is still a chance to retrieve all we have lost," he announced.

I leaned forward in my eagerness and drank in every word.

"It seems," said Dual, "that our Musab's daughter has developed a love affair with one Younus, a sort of secretary and trusted lieutenant of Hafiz. As usual, Younus has told more of his master's business to his mistress than it was proper that he should. I now know for a certainty what I have long been morally sure of. Hafiz is in reality the head of a regular band of slavers, the individual members of which organization are in the habit of traveling all over Europe and picking up any white girls upon whom they can lay hands.

"Customarily they bring them to their own places, and after the hue and cry has died down, provided always that any arises, they dispose of them at high prices to any of my noble countrymen who desire to buy. However, on the chance that at some time they might need a special place of concealment, one has been prepared.

"Mousin tells me that there is a secret cave, somewhere up in the Elburz Mountains, which lie some sixty odd miles to the north and east of Teheran, where Hafiz and his gang have once or twice kept white women for a time. Just where it is she does not know, except that it is near Mount Demavend; and is reached by a trail up a gulch or cañon, which leads to what she describes as a well-nigh impassable defile in the rocks, where one or two men could easily stand off a much larger band.

"Hafiz knows now that I am after the girl, and there is small doubt in my mind that he will have her taken to this cave, trusting to my ignorance of it, or else relying upon his ability to drive me off if I should find him out. Come. We will prepare for riding. From now on masquerade or concealment is impossible. We will fight in the open. Go, put on your own clothing, and I shall hunt up a suit of English riding togs, which I once possessed. I have already sent Mousin to prepare us some food for our journey, and Musab is saddling the horses. Dress as quickly as possible and meet me here as soon as you can."

Fifteen minutes later I returned to find Dual booted and spurred, and wearing a belt, in which two service revolvers were thrust. He was examining another weapon as I entered and thrust it into a pocket as he turned to me. The man was smiling again, and waved his hand toward a steaming cup of chocolate on a silver tray.

"Drink that and we will be riding," he commanded; picked up a pith helmet and placed it on his head, and threw its mate across to me.

I drained my cup in a few swallows, and followed Dual out into the night. Here Musab was holding three horses. Mousin met us and gave us each a canvas-covered canteen and a packet of food.

Without further delay Dual and I swung to the saddle and Musab slipped the bridle of the led horse into Deal's hand. Dual handed the old man a sealed note, and I heard the name of Kahrloff mentioned.

"I have sent Musab to the Russian to ask him to start a troop of

Cossacks after us at daylight," Dual told me as we rode under the arch in the palace wall.

Dual turned north and east and set spurs to his horse. I followed. Dual laughed as we swung into our stride.

"It is good to feel a horse between one's thighs again," he said gladly, "and these are good animals we have." Then, with a whimsical mood he laughed yet once again. "Take to the earth, O fox Hafiz," he chuckled; "the lion is hunting to-night."

The red-yellow moon was far down the western sky as we left the city behind and galloped out into the plain. I thought of what Dual had said before we reached Teheran, and looked about me as we swept on with the horses running freely.

My trip to the Persian capital had hardened me to the saddle, and I felt no discomfort as I rode. In fact, as Dual had said, there was a pleasurable thrill to the surge and fall of the animal's body, as we dashed through the cool night.

All about us was a red-yellow world lined and blotched with the black shadows of night. A sort of land mist dimmed the farther reaches of the plain, and the moon cast our flying shadows behind us like the remembrances of sins lived out and flung into the past. Little by little the moon sank and disappeared.

Slowly the east began to grow gray, then pink, then red. At last the ball of the sun leaped clear of the line of distant mountains and made the whole plain clear in its light. Through the entire ride Dual and I had spoken but seldom. We had just sat down and rode. As the day dawned fully, I retrieved in part some of my blunders of the night. We were running freely, our horses seemingly still fresh, and I was sitting well up in my saddle and glancing around, when under the level arrows of the sun a fleck of fluttering yellow caught my eye. I reined so suddenly that for a moment I well-nigh dismounted over my horse's head; then I turned and rode slowly toward the little yellow strand, my heart beating high with the hope wild as it seemed that I knew what it was.

While Dual waited, I swung from my horse and plucked the bit of cloth from a tuft of hardy grass, remounted, and rode back to Dual, with a smile upon my face. He took the frayed bit of cloth in his hand, glanced at it, then back to me, and nodded his head.

"She is laying a trail for us, wise little woman. You did well to observe it, my friend," he said.

We stopped for a breathing spell right there, watered the horses from a water-skin on the back of the led horse, and had a bite to eat. While we munched our cakes and dates and squares of chocolate, Dual examined the ground, near which I had found the bit of yellow silk, and on to the front.

"There is no doubt that four horses have passed this way recently," he announced, as he rose from inspecting the trail. "That should mean three men and the woman we seek. If you are ready, let us push on."

We remounted and swung back into our gallop, Dual saying we must make our best time while the day was cool. There is nothing to say of that day. It was a steady push forward, with now and then a pause to rest the horses or give them a sip from the water-skin.

Late in the afternoon we first noticed the cloud of dust. Dual pointed toward it as it moved steadily forward close under the foot of the mountains, which were now drawing near.

"Our friends the enemy, I fancy," was all he said.

From time to time as we rode we had picked up other bits of silken fabric torn from the wistaria scarf and dropped by the way, so we knew that we were pressing them close. Now, however, Dual set spurs to his animal, and together we charged down upon the fleeing dust-cloud, rapidly closing up the gap. Dual took the weapon from his pocket and held it up.

"Ammonia pistol," he grinned. "If I can get close enough, it is as good in its temporary effects as any bullet, and it gives time for repentance to a man." He dropped it back into his pocket and we rode on.

"If you're going to use that, why the service artillery?" I said laughing, and pointing to his belt.

"I may need artillery, at the worst," he said somewhat ruefully. "A wise general tries to provide for all contingencies."

As we reared the entrance to a great gash in the hills, the cloud of dust fled out of sight. Dual reined in and we went forward at a slower pace.

We swung about a corner of the jutting cliff, and on the instant the sound of a rifle split the air. A bullet flattened upon the rocks beside Dual. From farther up the gorge a faint veil of smoke drifted up and faded into mist. I pulled my revolver and sent a couple of shots up the cañon. Dual shook his head.

"No use," he said shortly; "if we were stronger, I would rush them.

As it is, we must be careful for Mrs. Parton's sake."

Though it galled me, I saw the force of his reasoning. We drew back a little out of range, and presently saw two men, with a third figure between them, go slowly up the trail. Again Dual nodded.

"They have left the third man, to hold us," he said.

He slipped from his horse, threw its reins to me, and crawled into some low-growing bushes, and was lost to sight. It was not until some fifteen minutes afterward that I heard from him, then a commotion up the trail made me ride out where I could see, and I beheld a third horseman scampering madly up the trail. An instant afterward Dual came running toward me and swung on to the horse I led up for him. His face was an odd mixture of boyish mischief and chagrin.

"Maybe I am foolish to hate to shed some blood," he remarked, "but the fact remains. Anyway, our friend Hasan has some very sore eyes. I got quite close to where he sat on his horse and took a shot at him with the ammonia gun. I hoped he'd fall from his horse. Instead, the beggar stuck on like a burr and rode off up the cañon, yelling like seven devils. Well, the way is clear for a little distance, anyhow. Let us go on."

That was a great ride. We didn't see anything more of our foemen until we reached the defile in the rocks, which Mousin's lover had told her about. There, as we expected, we met resistance again. As soon as we approached the robbers opened fire from some very serviceable rifles, and I grinned over at Dual.

"Evidently they don't share your antipathy to bloodshed," I told him, as a bullet clipped a hole in his hat.

He nodded coolly and slid from the saddle.

"We've got them treed, at any rate," he remarked, smiling. "They can't come out, even if we can't go in. We may as well sit down and wait. Better get off your horse."

I started to comply, when the animal beneath me flinched violently, staggered, and fell, almost rolling me under as he went down. That was a sufficient lesson, and we quickly drew back out of range, yet within sight of the pass in the rocks.

By and by a flutter of white showed at the mouth of the pass, and the negro, Hasan, stepped out and came toward us down the trail, waving a white cloth tied fast to a stick.

"A parley," said Semi Dual, and started to walk toward him. With my revolver gripped tightly in my hand, I followed his steps.

When Hasan was within fifteen paces, Dual motioned to him and then spoke, asking him what he sought. The black replied in what seemed to me threatening language, running on and on, and finally pausing as if awaiting a reply.

Dual had made no sign while he talked, but now he turned to me, after signing Hasan to wait a moment for his answer, and rapidly translated what the eunuch had said.

"He tells me that our continued presence here can result only in Mrs. Parton's death. Hafiz, it seems, has resolved to sacrifice her rather than give her up. Hafiz has commanded Hasan that if he should be followed and pressed to a degree where escape should be impossible, he was to kill her out of hand. Now Hasan threatens that unless we withdraw at once, he will carry out his master's decree."

A great wave of sick despondency settled upon my soul. I did not try to answer or argue, but turned away to conceal all I felt. Dual evidently perceived my hopelessness, for he turned back to Hasan and spoke a few brief words. The black bowed and replied in what was apparently an affirmative.

Dual nodded and, turning upon his heel, walked back to the horses and swung up to the saddle. Then as I followed, in heartsick silence, he urged his mount forward down the trail. I dropped in beside him, and we went down into the gloom of the cañon. Behind us rang Hasan's mocking laugh.

CHAPTER XIII.

THE RESCUE.

"DUAL," I cried out in desperation of spirit, as we went slowly down the rock-strewn trail, "are you really giving up? Is there nothing, not anything, we can do? Are we going to quit?"

"I never quit," said my companion. "As for your own actions, they depend entirely upon yourself."

I glanced sharply at him in the dusk, not quite understanding.

"Dual," I cried again, "tell me—tell me, Semi Dual, just what you mean."

Dual rode in still closer to me as we picked our way downward, yet for a moment he was silent. Presently, after appearing to weigh the matter carefully, he began to speak.

"Up to now, Glace, I have not told you everything which Mousin's lover told her and she related to me. This cave where Hafiz has frequently kept his victims in the past is, it seems, not really so much a cave as a sort of tunnel though a shoulder of the mountain.

"The gulch up which we have ridden today continues on the other side of the pass; not only that, but it turns about the shoulder of the mountain and doubles back in the form of an immense 'U.' The farther side of this curve runs back so as to almost parallel our present course, and the cave runs through this shoulder of the mountain, between the two sides of the loop, opening by another aperture in the sheer face of the other leg of the cañon, under an overhanging ledge. Thus, while the opening is in the far side of the loop, it is on the other side of the gulch as reached from here.

"A far easier trail than this we are on leads up to the near side of the chasm, across from the opening of the cave, and in former times the Hafiz band have taken advantage of this to send provisions to the cave. In order to do this they have stretched a rope from the cave's opening to the cliff on this side, and by means of a block and hook and a drawing line they can slide bundles across the gorge and pull them into the cave.

"If we can find the trail and get up there and swing across, we might take Hafiz's assassins in the rear and still succeed in our task. I know nothing more than what Mousin told. I do not know that the rope is still there. I do not know whether it is still strong enough to bear our weight. It might break and hurl us on to the rocks a thousand feet below. It is only something which we can try."

He paused, and for a moment we rode in silence; then he spoke again.

"It is the only hope, but I want you to look at the thing from all sides. I tell you that I do not think you morally called upon to undertake the venture unless of your own free will. It is something from which most men would shrink. Therefore I have told you all at this time. It is for you to decide."

"And you?" I asked in reply.

"I told you I never quit. I shall attempt it in any event," said Dual.

I put out my hand and gripped his in the dark.

"Then count me in," I told him. "I thought you knew me better than to think I would quit as long as you were in the game. If you

can't save Alice Parton she might as well commend her soul to God."
I fancied Dual smiled as he returned the pressure of my hand.

"To tell you the truth, I suspected you would make the venture," he responded. "Well, let us look for the other trail."

We rode on down into the gloom of the gorge, seeking now on the left hand wall for any break or other evidences of a passage leading off in the way we must go.

After a long time we came to what seemed to be a side gully cutting into the main one, and Dual stopped his horse and got down.

"There's a path leading up this way," he said presently. "Better get off and tie your horse; we'll leave them here and go on on foot."

I dismounted, and Dual and I led our mounts into the bushes and fastened them securely by the bridle-reins, taking the tether-ropes with us in case of need, when we set out. As Dual said, they would be handy to bind up our foes with, if nothing more.

With the ropes coiled about our middles we set off up the side path, clambering forward in the darkness along a constantly ascending way. Even on foot, however, I could sense that it was an easier ascent than the one we had ridden along in the after noon. Up and up we scrambled, and as we climbed there began to come a lightening of the gloom.

A sort of soft twilight filled the wild region through which we hastened, and presently I became aware that it was due to the rising moon. How long it was that we toiled upward I do not rightly know, but at length we came out at the top, and as we stopped to catch our panting breach Dual pointed off to the left.

There I beheld a ragged gash in the plateau upon which we stood, and understood that it was the gorge. After a moment Dual turned off toward it, and I trailed along.

Even yet, at times, I dream of that awful place as I first saw it under the red moon. Sometimes at night I seem to be back there, and imagine that I am falling, falling, falling into a bottomless abyss, and wake with a cry of mortal terror, to find myself in bed, and give thanks.

Then Semi Dual gave me but little time to dwell upon the horrors of the place. Yet, even in the time I had, the brief interval while he prepared for our hazard, I saw enough to haunt me the rest of my life. We stood on the lip of a chasm which fell away into depths of utter darkness as yet unillumined by the risen moon, and filled with a dull reverberation as of waters dashing themselves upon unseen stones.

Where we stood the lip jutted out so that we stood sheer above the drop of the abyss, with nothing on either side of us or in front, save night-shrouded space.

Off to the right hung the ball of the moon, red and sullen, throwing our shadows across the narrow ledge until they ended in decapitated trunks, the heads cut off by the darkness of the empty air beyond.

I woke from a sort of nervous enchantment of wonder and awe to find that Dual was speaking to me. I saw him kneeling on the outer tip of the ledge, fumbling outward over that dizzying space, feeling, I knew, for the rope. It was his announcement that he had found it which brought me back to time and place.

"The rope is here," he was saying. "I have found it, and it seems to be firm. Also, here is the draw-rope for their pulley. Let us see if we can get the block across."

Tentatively, as I watched, he drew in on the smaller rope. It gave, and Semi heaved a sigh of relief. Hand over hand I watched him haul in on the line until a wooden pulley-block, with a swaying dependent hook, came out of the farther shadows and swung into view. Dual drew it across and made it fast.

Then he rose to his feet and stood peering into the distance as if puzzling something out. At length he drew a long breath and turned to me.

"I see how it is," he said slowly. "I was trying to get it quite right in my head. This greater rope which crosses to the other side is hung with enough slack so that when anything is swung on the hook it will be carried across mainly by its own weight, the shorter end of the rope swinging more and more to a perpendicular as the momentum of the weight on the pulley forces the load across and takes up the slack by crowding the lower end of the rope down.

"When the weight's momentum is overcome, however, unless it is pulled in by the draw-rope; the spring of the supporting rope would slide it back, so that it would hang over the chasm. Why they fastened the upper rope above the ledge which juts over the cave's mouth I can't see to-night. Perhaps there was some natural reason why they couldn't fasten it in the cave itself. Anyway, it makes it difficult for us; for, failing the aid of some one to draw us in at the other end, I'm afraid we'll have to jump when we get there—or at least—I will.

"Well, I think I shall go first. I will leave you here in case I should not swing far enough the first time to make the leap. If I fall short you can pull me back. If I get across all right you will pull the block back, and I will steady you so that you won't have to jump."

He turned to the block, pushed it a little way out from the lip of the wall, lay flat upon his stomach, and seized the hook in both hands.

"If you should not feel the rope grow slack in a moment or two after I swing off, pull me back," he commanded. "If I get across I'll twitch the draw-rope, and you can come ahead. You had better fasten a loop of the rope around your body and slip it over the hook."

All this time I had stood speechless, full of the horror of the idea of the swing out over that chasm of darkness. Now I woke to speech.

"Semi," I cried, "the rope may break when you swing off. Isn't there some way to test it first? Man, you may be going to certain death."

"Very true," the man responded without a quaver. "However, we shall soon know. Now watch the rope."

With a wriggling motion of his body he was gone. I saw him shoot out into space and swing rapidly downward, then as I looked he disappeared into the shadow, and I stood alone on the narrow ledge, wondering if I was going to turn coward or be man enough to follow the way Dual had gone.

I cursed myself as I found myself trembling, while I knelt with my fingers feeling for the twitch of the rope, which would show that Dual was safe. I know I sobbed dryly when it came.

Gritting my teeth to still their chattering, I began hauling in on the block. After a time I saw it coming to me along the slender way of the rope, swaying slightly from side to side.

Forcing myself to the action, I pulled it in, got down on my stomach, and slipped a loop of the rope about my waist over the hook, and grasped the hook itself with both hands. Then I lay for a moment, trying to gather myself for the attempt.

As I lay my head was over the edge of the chasm, and I looked down info the dark where there was no light. I thought of a little girl far away in the United States, whom I had held in my arms on that afternoon before I started off with Semi Dual to trail half-way around the world. I looked over my shoulder and gazed at the red moon. Then I wriggled yet farther forward, clutching desperately at the hook. I thought rather than uttered a swift prayer, my feet slipped from the ledge, and I plunged into space.

Over and over again I have lived the moments of that swift flight out and down, over the gorge. With a wrench and jerk I swung downward until I hung perpendicular below the shrieking block. A wind born of my passage beat into my face. The iron of the hook cut into my hands and hurt.

A swift sensation of falling started in my innermost being and mounted and made me dizzy and faint. My brain reeled and swam. From far below the unseen waters rose in a sullen roar.

Onward and downward I plunged until the rise of the rope began to check my momentum, and I stopped in mid air and began to slide slowly down the rope back the way I had come.

A strangled cry rose in my throat and died unuttered. I hung struggling on the hook much like a fish hooked and swung into the air. Then, when I had all but despaired, I began to move slowly inward toward the rocky face of the cliff again, and knew that Dual was pulling upon the draw-rope.

In another moment I felt his hands as he seized and held me fast, and as he released me from the rope which held me I staggered and sank down on the ledge in front of the cave.

Dual seized my shoulders and pulled me up. "Come on," he said sharply. "You've got no time to faint."

Still staggering in my stride, I followed him into the hole in the rocks. We were in the cave.

Slowly, step by step, we made our progress inward and upward, following the slant of the rising floor. The passage turned and twisted, and was dark as the grave. We could go but slowly, guided only by the sense of touch.

We had to tread softly, lest we dislodge some loose stone and betray our approach. Yet we did advance, and after a seemingly long time, which was in reality but a few minutes as I now know, there began to be a faint radiance reflected from the overhanging walls.

Back of a jutting angle Dual paused, and, feeling for my hand, drew me close to his side. Together we peered around the face of the rock, and saw what lay before. Huddled against one wall of the cave was a woman's figure. Near by it stood the negro Hasan.

Farther to the front crouched two other men, apparently guarding the mouth of the cave, for their backs were turned toward Hasan and the girl, A flare stuck into a crevice of the wall showed us all this plainly, and as we gazed in silence Dual slowly nodded his head.

He drew himself slowly forward, sliding his ammonia pistol into one hand and crouching like a racer set for the start. Another instant and I stood alone. Dual was rushing in upon Hasan, who whirled at his approach, gave him one look, and threw both hands before his eyes.

The negro evidently remembered the cañon episode that afternoon. Hard on Dual's heels I followed, carrying a loop of the rope I had brought coiled about my waist.

Dual discharged his pistol full against the spreading fingers of the eunuch, and the strangling fumes of the burning liquid filled the air of the cave. I flung myself forward, and, dropping the loop of the rope over the negro's head and shoulders, pulled it tight, binding his arms.

He offered little or no resistance at all, seemingly overcome by the pain of his eyes and face, and I quickly slipped a noose about his legs and laid him flat with a savage jerk, into which I put all the rage against the fellow which I felt.

Meanwhile Dual had not waited to see the outcome, but had flung himself upon the other two guardians of the cave, and now I ran to his assistance, leaving Hasan groaning on the floor.

One of the two men at the front was writhing upon the earth as I approached, while Dual was holding the other down by sitting astride his form. I ran up and quickly had the uncaptured rascal neatly trussed. Then, with a piece of Semi's rope, we secured the individual upon whom he sat. As I pulled the last knot tight Semi Dual rose and faced me with a smile.

"A bloodless victory, after all, friend Glace," he cried. "Still if I'd had to take another shot at these chaps, I fancy I'd have strangled myself."

His absolute coolness struck some bizarre streak of humor in my overwrought brain, and I leaned against the side of the cave and began to laugh, until Dual caught me firmly by the arm and gave me a reminding shake.

I calmed down, and together we walked back toward the spot where Alice Parton had sat. We found her standing, gazing at us, as we approached, in unbelieving wonder. I don't think Semi Dual said a single word to her then—just walked up and took both her little hands, as he might those of a child, and began to lead her out of the cave. I gave a last look to Hasan's bonds, and followed them out into the mountain defile.

We found the horses of Hafiz's followers tied a little way from the cave mouth, and while I untied them Dual assisted Alice Parton to a seat. Then we men mounted, and together we threaded the narrow pass in the rocks and began to descend the trail.

I only remember one time when Dual spoke to the woman we had rescued as we went slowly down the rocky path, and that was when we both heard her sobbing as she rode.

"Did they harm you in any way, Mrs. Parton?" said Semi Dual, very low.

The woman ceased her sobbing, and, after riding forward in silence for a moment, said quietly:

"No."

I thought I heard Dual draw a quick, deep sigh.

Later we found our own mounts where we had left them, and took them with us, Dual and I each leading a horse.

Just at daylight we reached the mouth of the gorge, halted, and had a bite to eat; then we mounted and pressed forward again.

"Now, if Kahrloff sends out his Cossacks, and Hafiz doesn't get into the game again before we meet him, everything should end well," said Dual.

We rode forward, chatting easily, and just before noon, while Alice was telling us how she had torn up her scarf and dropped the pieces in the hope that we would find them, a cloud of dust appeared far to the front.

Presently there came out of it a body of horsemen, moving swiftly forward, which in turn developed into Kahrloff himself at the head of a detachment from the Cossacks under his command.

Kahrloff listened to our story with numerous interruptions of admiring congratulation. Then, after sending some half-dozen men on to bring in Hasan and his fellow bandits, he turned and escorted us back to the city with the remainder of his men.

We arrived at Teheran late that afternoon, Alice riding the last leg of the journey in Kahrloff's own carriage, which he had had follow along, and we went at once to the American consulate.

For the second time I led Alice up the steps and presented her to Stevens, who met her with actual tears in his eyes, and again showed her to his room. But we took no chances, and so by an odd course of circumstances, and at Kahrloff's own suggestion, the troopers of the Czar guarded the American consulate that night.

CHAPTER XIV.

ALICE'S STORY.

BAKU. KAHRLOFF sent us under escort to Resht. We came by boat to the end of the Asian railway, and we came unannounced, for Dual decided not to excite Parton's or Sheldon's anticipations until we had really arrived.

Of Hafiz there was no longer any fear. Kahrloff had netted the crafty fox that night when Dual and I rode into the mountains. He had sent to Hafiz's palace and intercepted him just setting out for some place he refused to name. With Hasan and his two men he was now under close guard in his own home, awaiting the result of Kahrloff's report on the affair.

We left the boat at Baku, and, entering a carriage, were driven first to police headquarters, where Dual got our friends' address, and went on to the International Hotel. There inquiry elicited the information that our parties were in their room, and we went up at once.

Dual rapped on the door, and a voice, plainly that of Sheldon, bade us come in. Semi pushed the door before him, and we entered the room.

As we entered and were recognized, both Parton and Sheldon sprang to their feet, and an instant later Alice Parton was sobbing in her husband's arms, which crushed her close, while his lips sought and found hers.

After a long moment he released her and held her at arm's length, as though to devour her with his eyes, then clasped her close again to his heart and held her so.

Presently she freed herself from his clasp as she remembered the other man, who stood with his haggard face working strangely, his quivering arms held outstretched, and with a glad little cry she fled in between those arms.

Colonel Mac gathered her in like a child, and held her, petting her cheek.

"My little girl—my little—my little girlie—" he mumbled, and broke utterly down into a sob-shaken old man. Dual and I turned away together, to be brought back presently by the colonel's voice.

"Say, Glace, go down and get me a quart of champagne; I gotter have a drink on this."

I laughed outright and departed, to return after a time with the liquor, and to find Alice Parton sitting openly upon her husband's knee, chattering to the three men like a magpie.

We had our drink, and then we all together cried out that we wanted to go home. Dual despatched a messenger for information as to the earliest time of departure possible, and when he returned we sent down to have our bill made up for morning. We slept that night in the hotel.

The next day we started, westward now, but with what different feelings only we knew.

As we rushed homeward Alice Parton told us the story which Dual would not permit her to speak of that first day in the Baku hotel. We all listened eagerly as the girl ran along in her description. It was indeed a queer tale which she told, between interruptions from Parton and Colonel Mac.

"When Archie left me that day to go with Hafiz—ugh, how I hate the brute!—I never dreamed that anything could go wrong. There had been nothing in the man's manner to excite suspicion, since we had really met, and before that nothing except that he seemed a little bit rude in staring at me so I guess Archie and he hadn't been gone over a couple of minutes, though, when a black man, whom I now know was one of his eunuchs, approached me and spoke to me, so that I raised my head. As I did so he threw a scarf or cloth of some sort around my neck and pulled it so tight that I could neither breathe nor cry out.

"I was terribly frightened, and I tried to struggle as well as I could. I remember that my string of coral beads broke while I was resisting the men, and the beads were scattered all over the floor; but I was powerless and fast strangling, and couldn't do much against three of them, for two others had picked me up as soon as the black man had twisted the cloth about my neck. They picked me up and carried me into another room, and through that into still another one, where they laid me down on a couch near some windows which opened on to a sort of balcony. I began to struggle again and kick my heels against the wall, thinking some one might hear and come. Then they tied my feet together so that I couldn't do that any more.

"After a bit the black who had first seized me, and who had left as soon as they got me into the far room, came back. He had a cup in his hand, and he motioned that I was to drink the stuff in it. I shook my head, but he only grinned and made a sign to the two men who had carried me into the room.

"One of them came over and took me by the throat back of the angle of the jaws, and the other untwisted the scarf from my neck. I tried to cry out then, and he shoved the scarf into my mouth, while the other fellow pressed his fingers into my throat until I would have screamed if I could, and I simply had to open my mouth.

"When I had my mouth open they took the scarf out and poured what was in the cup between my lips, and, after holding me till I was nearly suffocated, the man holding my throat suddenly let go and clapped his hand over my lips so that I could not cry out. Even then I tried to spit the stuff out; but he was too strong, so after a bit I swallowed it just because I had to have air. After that they gagged me again and watched me closely, and after a time I began to feel that I didn't care what they did with me.

"Of course I wanted to see Archie and dad, but I felt so tired that I really wanted to sleep more than anything else. The room began to look funny, like it had grown into a hall. The walls seemed ever so far apart, and the man beside me seemed a long way off. I know I wondered once if I couldn't get up and run away before he could catch me, but my legs felt like lead, and then I know they picked me up and carried me a long way out a door or window. After a long time they laid me down and covered me over with something. Then I guess I went to sleep.

"After that I can't seem to remember anything until I woke up on the train. I don't know how I got there, and when I did wake up we were in motion. It seemed to be some sort of a private car which I was in, for my meals were served to me regularly by the same black eunuch who had thrown the cloth around my neck in the hotel, and there were some other men there, too, and a couple of women who took my own clothes away and insisted upon dressing me in things similar to those they themselves wore.

"On the whole they did not treaty me badly, leaving me have the freedom of the entire car except when we were in stations along the line, when they guarded me very carefully, so that I did not have any chance to give any sort of an alarm.

"Of course I know now that Hafiz had had me kidnaped, and I was fearfully anxious, still I tried to keep as good control of myself as

I could and not break down. I ate what they gave me, to keep strong so that if an opportunity to escape presented I might have the physical strength necessary to make the attempt. But I didn't have a chance from the time we left Paris until we got to Baku.

"When we were leaving Baku I thought I saw an opportunity, and tried to throw myself over the rail of the boat, trusting to my being a good swimmer to enable me to get to land, but one of the other women grabbed me and started to screaming, and they made me go below.

"Then once on the way down from Resht, as you say it is called, I tried to steal a horse one night when I fancied the guard was asleep, but all I accomplished was to be thrown down and bound hand and foot, and after that they guarded me every night.

"When we got to Teheran they took me to the palace of Hafiz, and I stayed there until Mr. Dual and Mr. Glace got me away. I didn't see anything of Hafiz until the night before I was rescued from the palace. Then he came in for a moment or two and informed me that he had selected me for his favorite, and hoped that after a time I would learn to make the best of it. I told him I'd die before I yielded, and he laughed and said that I'd die unless I did. Then he went away.

"That is practically all I have to tell, though it seemed terrible to me during the time it was happening, and but for the hope that somehow you would find a way to follow and come for me, I sometimes think I would have gone utterly mad."

After she had finished Dual and I told what we had to tell, and having all unbosomed ourselves we returned to a basis of general friendship, and passed the time very pleasantly as we sped on across Russia, Germany, and France.

Paris came at last.

We left the railway station and hailed a passing fiacre, leaving our luggage to come after us on another cab. Then we went up through the spring-greened streets of the city, where the early lights were beginning to twinkle, and the early amusement seekers were already coming forth, and were soon at the hotel.

When we had entered and faced the gaping employees, who knew of the strange disappearance, and were again up at the Parton suite, Dual turned to us all with a smile.

"Here the trail ends," he said lightly; "even where it began."

At Dual's request we tarried a few days in the French capital. I hunted up a cable office that first night and sent Smithson a story which made him sit up and howl the first time he saw me after I did get back. Then, as Dual's guest, I spent some days poking into the various phases of Parisian life, from Montmartre to the Rue St. Germain.

On the night before we finally left for home Dual and I called upon our friends to say *au revoir*. They were going south into Italy and from there, on Alice Parton's expressed desire, they would take a boat for New York.

We spent a very pleasant hour in their suite, and just before we left Alice asked us to wait a minute longer, rose and ran into her room.

In a moment she was back and, dropping into her chair, she spread out upon her lap one end of the now sadly abbreviated wistaria scarf.

"See," she said half wistfully, "I have still so much to remind me of what true friendship means. Badly as I needed to use it in various ways, I managed to keep so much, not only because I love it, but because of a plan which I have formed. I wonder," looking at Semi Dual, "if you can guess what it can be."

"I could try," laughed my friend, and lay back in his chair, looking full into the woman's eyes, which sparkled and shone with a glad light.

For a long moment he sat so, then leaned slightly toward her.

"It would make a very dainty little cap, I should think," said he.